A TRUE
ACCOUNT

A TRUE ACCOUNT

*Hannah Masury's
Sojourn Amongst the Pyrates,
Written by Herself*

KATHERINE HOWE

HENRY HOLT AND COMPANY

NEW YORK

Henry Holt and Company
Publishers since 1866
120 Broadway
New York, New York 10271
www.henryholt.com

Henry Holt® and Ⓗ® are registered trademarks of
Macmillan Publishing Group, LLC.

Library of Congress Cataloging-in-Publication Data

Names: Howe, Katherine, 1977– author.
Title: A true account : Hannah Masury's sojourn amongst the pyrates,
    written by herself / Katherine Howe.
Description: First edition. | New York : Henry Holt and Company, 2023.
Identifiers: LCCN 2023024656 (print) | LCCN 2023024657 (ebook) |
    ISBN 9781250304889 (hardcover) | ISBN 9781250304896 (ebook)
Subjects: LCSH: Pirates—Fiction. | Self-realization in women—Fiction. |
    LCGFT: Action and adventure fiction. | Novels.
Classification: LCC PS3608.O947 T78 2023 (print) | LCC PS3608.O947 (ebook) |
    DDC 813/.6—dc23/eng/20230526
LC record available at https://lccn.loc.gov/2023024656
LC ebook record available at https://lccn.loc.gov/2023024657

Our books may be purchased in bulk for promotional, educational, or business use. Please
contact your local bookseller or the Macmillan Corporate and Premium Sales Department at
(800) 221-7945, extension 5442, or by e-mail at MacmillanSpecialMarkets@macmillan.com.

First Edition 2023

Ornamental flourishes: © Maryfleur / Shuttersock.com

Designed by Kelly S. Too

Printed in the United States of America

1 3 5 7 9 10 8 6 4 2

For Hannah and Edward
And of course, for Charles

In an honest Service, there is thin Commons, low Wages, and hard Labour; in this, Plenty and Satiety, Pleasure and Ease, Liberty and Power . . . when all the Hazard that is run for it, at worst, is only a sower Look or two at choking. No, a merry Life and a short one, shall be my motto.

—Captain Bartholomew Roberts

A TRUE
ACCOUNT

Chapter 1

~

I don't know what made me determined to go to the hanging.

I'd always made a point of avoiding them. I resisted the entreaties of my friends who wanted to be in amongst the throngs of onlookers, ears pricked for the last words and the pious advice of the soon-to-be-damned.

Of course, I'd always been curious. You cannot help but wonder about the face of one condemned. To see his carriage toward the crowd, and himself. To feel the swelling cheers and cries of all the townsfolk, to hear the crack of the felon's neck snapped like a chicken's.

I wondered if their eyes were open or closed when their moment came. What happens, in the instant in between being a living, breathing creature, trembling with needs and wants and fears, and being an empty sack of flesh and bone? Is it the same for an old woman alone in her bed with the covers pulled up tight as it is for a man mounting the scaffold before God and everyone? Does an unearthly light of heaven attained shine upon the greasy strings of their hair if they have confessed and repented? Everyone repents at the end. Or so I've been told.

I'd heard the moment of public death described often enough, usually by someone with a hand around a glass. But I had always been of too delicate a nature to see for myself. I didn't like to drown kittens or stomp tremble-whiskered mice and, as often as not, found a way to avoid such grim chores on the occasion Mrs. Tomlinson chose to impose them on me. I even crossed the street from dogs lying dead in the gutter.

But something about William Fly was different. I made up my mind that I would go.

Summer wears long on the Boston wharves, with early sunrise and late nightfall dragging its feet to deliver our relief. And so, the afternoon was stifling in Ship Tavern when I first heard the name of William Fly. The ordinary was generally tolerably cool in summer, being a dim cavern of rooms built of ancient brick, squatting like a naiad's grotto for almost a hundred years at the foot of Clark's Wharf. Ship Tavern stands close enough to the harbor waters that a brig can moor nearly at the lip of our door. Well situated to swallow up the passing seamen as they stumble ashore, land-sick and looking for all the things sailors look for when they have been long at sea. But that June day the sun shone especially heavy, bleaching the color out of the air and leaving us all wilted and damp. Inside, the usually cool hollow of the larger dining room had warmed by degrees until it felt like the inside of a beehive oven. The sand on the floor was hot underfoot. The front door stood propped open to catch any whisper of a passing breeze, but the water in Boston Harbor was as flat and slick as molten glass.

I was sitting on an old apple barrel outside, leaning on the brick wall of my home and place of employ, my skirts knotted up to my shins to get some air on my bare and aching feet. I should have been getting back inside to stoke something, or serve something, or carve something, or scour something. Inside the tavern a few men lazed indolently about, looking into their cups, waiting for the day to end. No one was calling my name. Mrs. Tomlinson was I knew not where. As I gazed up the narrow length of Fish Street, I spied not a living soul, save the odd gull perched on a piling or tabby cat slithering amongst coils of rope in search of rats. My heels bumped on the hollow barrel.

I packed a small wad of tobacco and hemp into the slender clay pipe someone had left behind in one of the rooms, sparked it with a few sucks of my cheeks, and settled back to stare over the water, smoke coiling from my lower lip up into my nostrils. Clark's Wharf is nearly as long as Long Wharf, but older. Half a dozen snows and brigs and a couple of little schooners and sloops rubbed their hulls against the pilings, their lines and rigging creaking. Sails all furled and put away. No one was about. No bent-over boys scrubbing any decks or barefoot figures climbing rigging silhouetted by the sun. Even the gulls were quiet. The water shimmered away to the horizon, low ridges of the harbor islands rising through the orange and yellow summer haze.

I closed my eyes and wished for a ripe apple.

"Cut his hand off," I heard someone say softly. So softly, it might have been spoken in my mind.

I opened my eyes but saw no one.

"Off! With what?" another voice said, in an accent that hinted at time in Jamaica. So, not inside my head after all.

I got off the apple barrel, ears straining to listen. The voices hadn't come from inside the tavern. Fish Street was as abandoned as it would be after the Rapture.

"Broadaxe," said the first voice, who was from somewhere that wasn't Boston. "As he clung to the mainsheet hanging over the side."

Someone laughed merrily.

I could hear them clear as a church bell. But where were they?

Presently I discerned the shape of a small rowboat emerging from the haze, its oars dipping and rising in circles. The rowboat contained two boys about my own age, seventeen or so, not more than twenty, in sun-whitened shirts and breeches. The one pulling on the oars wore a checked kerchief over his head to keep the sweat from his eyes. His companion, the Jamaican, wore his knotted around his neck, his hair in tidy twists all over his head. They edged close to the nearest moored brig, and the boy with his back to me leaned on an oar to clear the stern.

I could have gone to help them tie up, but it was too hot. Instead, I sat back on the barrel and drew on my new pipe.

"That's one way to discharge your sailing master," the Jamaican said with gravity. "Handless into the deep. One o'clock in the morning."

"I knew that John Green," his mate, the not-Bostonian, continued. "Their captain. At Port Royal."

The rowboat bumped up to the piling almost exactly below my idle feet, grating against the barnacles. The not-Bostonian sprang ashore with a line in his hand and made it fast. I tried to make a ring with my smoke to watch them through, but it came out a cloud.

"And?" the Jamaican said as he lifted himself out of the rowboat, landing on his hands and feet on the wharf like a cat.

"And if I could, I'd have handed William Fly the axe myself," said the not-Bostonian. "Can we get something to eat?"

This last remark was apparently directed at myself. I decided that if I wasn't actually addressed, I needn't respond. This boy was pale and reddish, his cheeks spotted pink with the heat, and he mopped his streaming face with his kerchief and rerolled a sleeve while I ignored him.

"He beg?" the Jamaican asked, paying me no heed. Sweat beaded on his whiskerless upper lip. They were both standing close enough to smell.

"They'd let him choose, they said. Would he leap like a brave fellow, or would he be tossed overboard like the sneaking rascal he was? And he cried, 'For the Lord's sake, boatswain, don't throw me overboard!'" the not-Bostonian mimicked, clasping his hands beneath his chin, eyes beseeching imaginary tormentors. "'For if you do, you throw me into hell immediately!'"

The two boys dissolved in laughter and through gasps and tears the not-Bostonian added, "And Fly, Fly said, 'D—n you! Since he's so devilish Godly, we'll give him time to say his prayers and I'll be parson. Now say after me, Lord have mercy on my soul!' And then the people chucked him over!"

"Ah! That would've been a sight to see!" his mate clapped his hands in delight. Turning to me he added, "Here, now, the boy asked you a question. We want to eat!"

I swiveled my eyes over to the two of them, letting my gaze rest upon their faces long enough for them to feel that they were interrupting my idle afternoon. If they felt any remorse at troubling me, they surely didn't show it.

I unfolded myself from my sentry post, knocked the ashes out of my pipe, and slid it into my pocket.

"Oh certainly, your Lordships," I said, joking as was my wont with the cabin boys who came my way. "Right this way, your Grace."

I stepped through the open front door not bothering to see if they were following. It never ceases to amaze me that hungry sailors will willingly stop at the first ordinary they see, no matter how many rats might be fattening themselves in the cellar.

"But what of the mate?" the Jamaican boy continued to his friend as they followed me into the largest dining room. He moved with a sailor's bowlegged gait. Inside the tavern smelled of boiled lemons in rum and roasted chicken grease and burnt wood and tired men.

"Thomas Jenkins?" the other boy said. He was taller but thinner. "Cut at the shoulder with the broadaxe, then flung overboard by the main shrouds."

"No!" cried the Jamaican, loudly enough that a pickled gentleman in a ripped greatcoat stirred in his sleep across a table.

"He cried like a girl. 'For the Lord's sake, fling me a rope!'" mocked the pink-cheeked not-Bostonian. "'Doctor, doctor! A rope! A rope!'"

I stopped abruptly near the settle by the fireplace and said, "What color's your money?"

The boys looked surprised to discover that I could speak, as if the fireplace poker or a Windsor chair had offered to knit them up a muffler.

"What's it to you?" said the not-Bostonian. "You own the tavern now?"

I weighed the risk that these rascals might cut and run with the pleasure such a prank would give me when presented to Mrs. Tomlinson alongside their licked-dry chicken bones and empty cups and decided the rewards were many and the risks were few. It wasn't especially Christian of me to make a sport of vexing Mrs. Tomlinson. But I was powerless to help myself. Also, I had a running wager with some of the other girls about which of our masters could be cheated worst by our customers before next meeting day. These two rogues would win me a peach and a half.

"Fine," I said, waving my hand at a table not too far from the door, on which a lone maggot twisted in the streaming afternoon sunlight.

They sat down together to continue their feast of stories. "That William Fly. Turned pyrate," said the sturdy Jamaican with evident admiration. "Out on his own account and caught just as fast. Poor b—d. But why'd they do it?"

"What do you think?" said his skinny friend. "Bad usage." They shared a moment of silent mutual understanding.

I was on the point of asking for more details, no doubt shocking them with my ability to not only speak but inquire, when a rum-thickened voice in the other room called, "Hannah! Hannah Misery!" I left them at the table with some bitterness. But as my hands moved thoughtlessly through their labors the rest of that day, cleaning and scrubbing and wiping and pouring, my thoughts lingered on this William Fly and his broadaxe. I started to wonder what it might be like to look upon his face and read it in the dare of freedom.

My name isn't Hannah Misery. It's Hannah Masury. I was born a bit before 1710 in Beverly, I've been told, an easy day's sail or so from Boston, and though I suppose I had brothers and sisters and a mother and father, I couldn't tell you a thing about them, because I was bound out when I still had milk teeth. I remember a mean little house with a smoking chimney, sleeping in a trundle crowded with hands and feet, and the smell of the ocean in the fog. That's all. Since then, it's been Mrs. Tomlinson, her baker's dozen children, and the bustle and ebb and flow of Ship Tavern. I have friends around the wharves, miscellaneous pups like me, lent and bossed and sometimes fed and clothed, tucked into attics and doorways and kitchens at night and dragged out and scrubbed clean when it's time to go to meeting. Mrs. Tomlinson might be my dead mother's cousin. Or perhaps she was her aunt? I don't remember.

Though I never had any schooling, and cannot read the Bible, Mrs. Tomlinson insists that I go to church on the Sabbath and hear the Word. She says it's never too late to be redeemed. I know she means to help me. I do. But indolence is my greatest sin. Sabbath day is supposed to be a day of rest, and church drags on for hours and the beadle whacks us on the head if we fall asleep. And I always fall asleep.

She likes to go to the North meetinghouse, where she can bask in the fame of Reverend Cotton Mather. He drove the witches out of Salem before I was born, a feat as impossible-seeming to me as a man driving fairies out of holes in the ground. But for all Reverend Mather's good works, Satan's power still hangs heavy in Boston, and maybe it hangs heaviest on the wharves. I've glimpsed the Devil myself, a time or two, in his cups at Ship Tavern.

Sabbath day is the ripest chance for gossip and rumor to be confirmed or denied in Boston. So the Sunday after I met the two boys from the rowboat I thought to learn more of this William Fly. The whispering classes had told me he'd been brought ashore in irons and thrown into jail the very day the boys arrived. After tossing their master and mate overboard and claiming the ship *Elizabeth* as their own, they'd rechristened her the *Fame's Revenge*, hoisted the black flag, and gone pyrating off Cape Hatteras. They'd been betrayed by a fisherman they entrusted as their pilot after taking a rich prize off Carolina, who instead of leading them safe to Martha's Vineyard for water took them all the way to Boston and fooled them into surrender. They were all sure to hang. Reverend Mather sought to bring them back to the Lord first. They might even be in church that day, their wrists all bound together, their ashamed heads hanging, heavy under the curious stares and barely concealed whispers of all of us. For once, I was actually excited to go to meeting. I even prettied myself up a bit. Scrubbed my face and arms and made up a cleanish tucker.

You probably want to know what I look like. But what does it matter? I look hungry, is what I look like. Skin and bones. Sunburnt. Rough-footed. I have hair on my head, and it's long, and I wear it in a pigtail down my back, or a braid wound at the nape of my neck, under a kerchief, usually, or sometimes one of Mrs. Tomlinson's discarded linen caps. My face is freckle-stained, like I've been sprinkled with gingerbread batter. My age is hard to tell. I could tell you I was anything from fifteen to twenty-five, and you might believe me. I have eyes that can see better than passing well. No one has ever called me especially pretty, but then again, I have boys whenever I want them. And I still have all my teeth.

That Sabbath day we were all on alert for the pyrates as we gathered on the steps of the North meetinghouse, under the clanging of the church bells. Old North sits only a block away from Ship Tavern, a shabby wooden edifice as dark and stuffy as the houses crowded round about it. There's a new brick North Church, a block farther on, just finished a couple of years ago. Its proud white steeple lords over the entire town, visible as far away as Charles Town and the marshlands, and it has bright arched windows and fresh-painted pews, its fineness befitting a celebrated cleric followed by fame and fortune.

"Here, they're coming!" one of the girls said next to me, and excited fingers clamped onto my elbow.

It was hard to see through all the shoulders and backs and heads, because I am skinny and not tall. I spotted first the profile of a well-fed gentleman in black broadcloth with a fresh white kerchief at his neck and a plain black hat, his lips pressed together in the manner of one who speaks for the Lord. The people parted before him like the Red Sea, pushing back against me, my slight body moving in the current of the crowd. There is something exciting about being within a fingertip's length from such fame. Mrs. Tomlinson always returned from Sabbath meeting with a high color to her cheeks that had little to do, I thought, with whatever hymns might have been sung that day.

The crowd knitted back together and for a time I saw nothing but the hairy inside of an old man's ear, before everyone shifted again and in the gap between two women's necks, I spied a beaten man limping up the church steps. This would be Samuel Cole, William Fly's quartermaster. Neither old nor young, Samuel Cole had creases around his careworn eyes. I'd heard he had a wife somewhere and seven children to feed. The whisperers told me that William Fly had suspected him of mutiny and delivered a hundred lashes to his back, and so Cole hobbled with the grimaces of a man in terrible pain.

The crowd blurred and parted again, affording me a fleet glimpse of a man hangdogging in Cole's footsteps. This rogue was about forty, with hard blue eyes. He sported the long pigtail of a man who has spent his life at sea, weedy like kelp, with bristly red whiskers. Someone standing behind me informed someone else that this was Henry Greenville. Married too, they said. I couldn't imagine being married to a man like him. Any wife of his would spend her days making sure not to turn her back to the door.

Just behind Henry Greenville staggered a boy about twenty, so stewed in strong drink that even after so many days in Boston jail I could smell him as he passed me by. This would be George Condick, so blind drunk that he hadn't even been able to hold a gun when they took the *Elizabeth*. He served as cook for the pyrate company. His nose was a starburst of busted blood vessels, and his eyes were rimmed in red as if he had been crying.

I was borne along in the crush of bodies streaming toward the doors of the meetinghouse, the donging of the steeple bell in my ears. The girls I came with were carried off in the crush, and I couldn't even find Mrs. Tomlinson in the tangle of arms and legs, skirts and chins, and sweating temples touched with gray.

"But where is William Fly?" I asked.

No one bothered to answer me.

"Where's the captain?" I raised my voice. "I would look upon William Fly!"

"Not coming," a pinched-nose matron with a bonneted baby in her arms said to me.

"Not coming!" I exclaimed.

"He refused," she said, as a sweet rope of drool dripped from her baby's lower lip onto my shoulder.

I marveled at this novel idea. He had *refused*.

"But why?" I asked the matron's shoulder as it pressed up against my cheek.

"Said he wouldn't have the mob gaze upon him," she replied.

I was funneled with some other youths of obscure parentage and no prospects along the back wall of the meetinghouse while the quality elbowed their way to the tidy pews that they paid for. Cole, Greenville, and Condick were maneuvered to a pew near the front, that we might all gaze upon their hanging heads while Reverend Mather read his text and took the measure of their souls.

We were the mob, sitting in judgment upon these hard-used men. I saw the staring, curious faces of men and women I had known to some degree or other for most of my life. At Sabbath meeting, in Ship Tavern, on the wharf, at the market, on the street. The whispering classes know everything that happens in small towns like Boston, and I knew all of these people. Adulterers and liars, some of them. Full of wrathful thoughts they hid under their tidy lace-tipped bonnets and felted hats. Eyes glaring covetously at one another's healthy children, or unburned houses, or bustling businesses, or gold rings. Sabbath-breakers like me, lazy as dogs and loving our sleep. Mouths full of oaths when they thought God wasn't listening. Shirkers of work. Players at dice or cards for money. Secret hearts aflame with lust at the curve of a cheek or the bend of a wrist. In their sober New England eyes, I read all the stolen kisses, pocketed apples, long-nursed resentments, weaknesses, sorrows, and shame that ribboned through their lives, livened on occasion with transient candle flames of joy and pleasure and passion and maybe even grace.

We all stood, we mob, and sang, and then we all sat down—those of us with pews to sit in—and Reverend Mather mounted the pulpit and gazed down with the authority of God upon the lowered heads of the embittered pyrates. George Condick loudly sniffling and wiping his wet nose on a sleeve.

"They die," intoned the famous cleric, beginning the sermon that would entertain us all that Sunday afternoon, and which would echo in our heads for days afterward, "even without wisdom."

But William Fly wasn't there.

William Fly refused.

Chapter 2

$\mathcal{T}$hen it was July, and the time had come for them to die.

Mrs. Tomlinson wanted to go see the hangings as badly as I did, which is why she made such a point of refusing me.

"You can't possibly," she said with her back turned. "Not with every bed full twice over."

It was true that the cots in the warren of rooms upstairs were stacked with sailors two and three deep, sleeping head to toe or sometimes in shifts. Shifty-eyed creatures haunted our hallways, pinching me when I passed. Some of them had arms that were stained blue with tattoos—ghostly anchor rode wound around their wrists, heavy-breasted women garlanded in flowers winking from their shoulders.

"They'll all be going too," I pointed out. "I'll wager the whole place will be empty all afternoon."

Mrs. Tomlinson gave me her don't-talk-back glare and returned to her work. "No," she said.

I sulked with my lip out, but she affected not to notice. I was on the point of arguing that such a performance of abject repentance could only do good things for my immortal soul. How could I not go? Would she have me miss such a display of God's goodness? Would she have me stay a sinner? Mrs. Tomlinson once said I could argue a beggar out of a penny, before wishing she could have a penny for every gray hair I'd given her.

"Hannah!" a grizzled voice shouted from the smaller dining room, curtailing my case. "Hannah Misery! God d—n ye, girl. Hannah!"

"Go and see what he wants," Mrs. Tomlinson told me. "And then see to the piss pots upstairs."

I stalked from the kitchen down the back hall to the dining rooms muttering, "I'll see to your piss pots," and pushed open the door into the low-raftered room where men sat scattered about, bent over cards and cups or laboring over letters home.

"Hannah!" the sot was still shouting. Not one of the new arrivals, most of whom weren't drunk enough to be rude until after the noonday meal, this was a pickled regular so firmly installed in the Windsor chair in the corner that he might have grown into it like a vine. "Hannah!" he yelled as loudly with me standing before him as he would if I were in the stable out back.

"Ephraim, what," I said to the drunkard.

"I'm dry!" he said through a rheumy cough, waving his mug at me.

"Oh, you're dry," I cried, pulling the dented pewter mug from his fist. "Here in the sight of Christ and all that's holy, dry? Everyone, you hear that? Ephraim's dry! Did you ever hear of such a thing!" I raised my voice so that everyone in the dining room could hear and chuckle.

It was Ephraim's favorite mug, the one chased with a bunch of grapes. I clutched it to my chest and stalked away muttering. One of my hands yanked at my snarled apron strings while I strode to the front door of Ship Tavern. I shouldered open the door and burst out onto Fish Street, shoving past knots of boys lounging on the barrels outside. I flung my tangled apron aside and went to the edge of Clark's Wharf and pitched the mug into the water, shouting, "Now see how dry you are!"

Some boys laughed and hooted, because there is nothing funnier to them than a girl who is enraged. But as soon as the mug disappeared into the water, I felt ashamed of myself. My cheeks burned. My temper was second only to my laziness for making me such a good-for-nothing, Mrs. Tomlinson always reminded me.

A small boy, even skinnier than me, dove off a piling in his breeches to see if he could pluck the cup from the silty bottom.

It would be at least an hour before I was missed in a way that would get me lashed, for shirking my duties and disobeying my mistress and stealing the mug from the old rummy. If I was going to be punished, I determined to make the most of it. I hustled down Ship Street and past the North Battery, dodging red-coated soldiers and sunburnt sailors and carts stacked high with silvery codfish. Women leaned out of windows, gulls wheeled in low hunting for scraps, and here and there boxes of slick black lobsters stacked three deep rustled as their claws scrabbled for escape. The naked wooden ribs of a ship stood sentinel in Thornton's shipyard, silhouetted in the sun like the carcass of a whale. The heat had broken, and Boston once again crawled with life, and much of that life was stirring to make its way through the streets to watch the hangings.

They were building the scaffolding in the tidal flats near the Charles Town ferry landing. I could reach the spot either by worming through the narrow streets of town or by going the longer route along the waterfront. I chose the longer path, thinking I could end by climbing atop the mill-dam to get a fine view of the spectacle and still be in hearing distance of the speechifying. In Lynn Street by a lemon cart I met two of the other girls I knew, absconders like myself, one in a ribboned straw hat plainly stolen from her mistress.

"I heard he's very handsome," Mary Brown said, because she was the sort of person who was always wondering aloud whether someone was very handsome or not. She tied her hair in rags every night to make corkscrew curls and pinched her cheeks in the morning just in case.

"I heard he hasn't been eating," said Sarah Wildes with proprietary authority from under the straw hat.

"Bet he's been drinking his grog, though," I said with some sympathy, and the other girls laughed. "What!" I exclaimed. "I would!"

"Oh, we know you would, Hannah," Sarah said with her long arm around my neck.

By the time we came to Hudson's Point, the streets were jammed as tightly with people as the lobsters were in their traps, slick with sweat and shining with fear and excitement. A chestnut horse with a rope bridle stood in the street hemmed in by people around him, unable to turn or back up, lifting his tail and disgorging the contents of his bowels with an anxious nicker. The eager faces crowding around us all belonged to strangers. A lot of them were men and boys discharged from the ships in the harbor. Any sailing master worth his salt would have wanted his crew ashore that day, to see how authority dealt with mutineers. William Fly would be forced to kneel before the feet of the magistrates and reverends and tell all of us that the only right way of living was to obey. Go to Sabbath meeting. Don't drink. Don't swear. Don't talk back. Don't take what isn't yours. Obey the Lord thy God. Obey thy reverends and masters. Obey thy parents and thy husband and thy Mrs. Tomlinson and thy whoever else should happen to come along and demand that thou obey.

There were plenty of women and girls too. And old men, and withered women, and servants and slaves given liberty for the day, and a few Wampanoag with babies on their backs. Many of the people carried baskets over their arms packed with bread and cheese as if on their way to a festival, or a church day of thanksgiving, or a country wedding. People who had come to make a day of it. People who had traveled in from the outlying villages and farms, setting out in the pale gray of not-yet-dawn, just so they could hear the subjugation of the pyrates and watch the bending neck of William Fly.

"We'll never get through this way," I said. Already the bodies pressing in around us were making it hard to move.

"Let's cut," Sarah suggested. She steered us out of the street, along a narrow alley stinking of urine, over a low stone wall, and into the old burying ground. We dodged through thin slate headstones carved with grinning skulls and crossed long bones. Relict of this and son of that and Bible quotes none of us could read but which we were all somehow expected to know. Here and there blooming dandelions and berry brambles. Not a hanged man amongst them.

I tripped on a footstone and skinned my knee.

"Hurry," Mary said, lifting me by an armpit. I hobbled after her, sucking my teeth to dull the pain.

Over another wall slippery with loose stones and into Prince Street in the shadow of a slowly rotating windmill, and here the crowds were thinner, maybe because most of the inns and ordinaries were closer to the wharves. We were approaching the millpond. The millpond was a greasy shimmer in the afternoon sun, dotted with napping ducks tucked amongst the cattails. Its banks were lined with wooden wharves and tenders small enough to navigate the creek, leaning wood-frame houses and the Baptist meetinghouse. The air smelled of grinding corn and boiling molasses and leather. But the millpond dam was high enough for our purpose, overlooking Gee's shipyard with its spars draped in rigging like spiderwebs and masts pointing into the cloudless sky. Beyond the shipyard stretched the tidal flats where the Charles River crept its lazy way to the sea. Usually a naked expanse of mud dotted with gasping freshwater clam holes, today the flats teemed with humanity, crowding together at the foot of a hastily assembled wooden stage and scaffold. On the crossbeam over the stage, from which dangled three knotted hemp ropes, hung a black flag expertly stitched with a white sailcloth skull and crossbones, like the grinning hollow faces of the burying ground headstones we had just fled past.

We balanced along the milldam wall, arms extended, toe to heel to toe, to the commingled sound of lapping water and buzzing gossip amongst the people below.

"I was worried we'd miss it," Sarah said.

"Mrs. Tomlinson was all set to stop my coming," I said.

"Hah," said Mary. "D—n her eyes and her Bible too."

Mary was better at oaths than you would think, to look at her.

A few schooners up on jacks in Gee's yard in various states of disrepair blocked our view until we were well out to the center of the dam. The far side of the pond was sparser, hillier, with the copper works out by Roxbury Flats and then the fine houses tucked up on Beacon Hill. Beyond Beacon we could see the gently rolling rise of the Common, dotted with cattle and grazing sheep. We found our spot, together with a few boys from the mills, apprentices and workers and cabin boys and a few girls from the street. Mary and Sarah and I sat down, our feet hanging, our chins in our hands. It wouldn't be long now. Not if the nooses were already up.

For a time, the crowd watched and speculated and tried not to grow bored. Then around noon a rill of excitement rippled through the people with a roar and a cheer. We couldn't see at first around the ships in the yard, and I got to my feet to see if that would help my aspect any, but it didn't. The roars grew louder, and presently a three-sided wooden cart, like a hay wain, dragged by a tired mare, lurched into view, drawing ruts behind it in the mud. The crowds parted but slowly to allow the wagon to pass and dotted in amongst the people, walking before the mare, we spied three eminences in black with books tucked under their arms. One of them bore the unmistakable bearing of Reverend Mather. Hands from the crowd reached out to touch him, and he touched hands and heads in a manner as Christlike as anybody.

Behind these divines whose sacred duty it was to usher some impoverished unfortunates into hell, the cart carried three men standing, swaying with each lurch of the mare. I thought I knew the bent-over hobble of Samuel Cole, still seeping and raw, and next to him the reedy drink that was Henry Greenville, his shoulders rounded as though he were finally broken. I saw no sign of young George Condick, who I heard had been reprieved, and a good thing too. At least pity was available to some of us sinners.

The third man was swathed in shadow. Then a rock of the cart caused the shadows within to move, and at last my eyes could feast upon the face of William Fly.

Mary was right. He was handsome.

Handsome in a hard-used way, at any rate. Perhaps ten years older than myself, slim and wiry, sea-hardened, he stood with his head high, his dark locks pulled back from a seemingly unconcerned brow. He had a well-formed nose and like all men of his trade was tanned almost nut-brown. He seemed to be smiling. No, smirking. He nodded here and there, his mouth moving as though greeting friends and well-wishers, making his compliments.

"What's that he's got in his hand?" Sarah said, now on her feet next to me.

I squinted with my hand over my eyes to shade away the sun and perceived that under the ruffled cuffs of his shirt, where his hands were manacled together at the wrists, William Fly was holding a nosegay of violets. No sooner had I made this incredible determination than he brought the posy to his nose with a delicate sniff. As he did so, I thought his eyes might have settled on mine and held them. I smiled out of one side of my mouth, feeling as though his flamboyant nosegay were a joke meant only for me.

Of course, he couldn't see me. I was but one face in the mob, as unknown to him as if I had stayed at my labors in the tavern. I like to imagine that he did, though. *This is all ridiculous*, his sniff seemed to say. *No one truly understands how ridiculous it is but you and me.*

I have thought of our joke often since.

It is ridiculous, Will, I agreed silently from the safety of the dam.

The cart drew up to the scaffold and creaked to a stop. The three ministers had already mounted the stage, staring down at the wagon with its chained cargo. They had been joined by the hangman in his black hood and hat. A wave of silence pooled at the foot of the stage and swelled slowly over the assembly, cresting and breaking over those of us perched atop the dam. A lone gull cried as it drifted on an unseen wave of air, seemingly hanging motionless above us.

"Bring them up," one of the men on stage said.

One by one, Fly, Cole, and Greenville were led down from the back of the cart, through the crowd, and up the ladder to stand where we all could feast on them in their misery and despair. Cole and Greenville looked pale and drawn under their tanned skin, their eyes on their feet, but Fly gazed haughtily out over the silently watching crowd. A breath of wind sparkled across the surface of the river and stirred the black flag hanging over their heads. The three nooses swayed gently.

William Fly stepped up behind one of the nooses and took the measure of it with one look.

"Oh, come now," Fly said to the hangman, taking the noose in his hands. "Don't you know your trade?"

Quick as a wink, he untied the noose and retied it expertly, as a sailor would. The mob exclaimed in delighted shock, but the ministers weren't having it. They shushed and demanded our silence.

"William Fly," Reverend Mather intoned when we had settled down. "Will you speak what you should judge proper to be spoken on this sad occasion? At the very least will you make the warning of survivors, that they might escape the fate which now stands before you?"

William Fly brought his nosegay to his lips before dropping it over the edge of the scaffold into the hands of the crowd.

"Yes," he said so that we could all hear. "I would advise the masters of vessels to carry it well to their men, lest they should be put upon doing as I have done."

Reverend Mather darkened. The whole purpose of this public display was to show William Fly brought to heel. To crush him before the might of God and the colony of Massachusetts Bay, the distant backwater outpost of the throne of England, ruler of the seas of the world.

"Such stupidity!" Mather shouted. "Will you now, at the hour of your death, at least offer forgiveness to them that have brought you to justice?"

"I will not," Fly said.

"Come, your compatriots have forgiveness in their hearts! They have said they wish to disavow the sinful ways which have brought them to this unfortunate pass!" one of the other ministers prompted.

At their cue, Cole and Greenville stirred, nervous. Both had much greater signs of repentance upon them. The ministers led them in prayer, while Fly only looked on with a grim smile. Then the prayers were over, and the time of pleading was at hand.

"Take warning by us!" Cole shouted.

"Here it comes," Mary said to Sarah and me. My pulse quickened, and around me I felt the thrill of horrified excitement innervate all of us on the dam.

"Don't profane your souls with swearing!" Cole beseeched the mob. Mary laughed, and she wasn't the only one.

"Aye! Don't curse! I wish I'd never cursed a day in my life!" Greenville added as the ministers looked on with an attitude of satisfied dignity.

"D—n his eyes for a liar," Sarah said, while some in the mob shouted examples of the sort of curses Greenville should most abhor.

I knitted my fingers together and brought them up under my chin, my heart beating hard in my throat. I shouldn't have come. I didn't want to see after all. But there were Mary and Sarah on either side of me, laughing and whooping, and dozens of strangers all around us, doing the same, like we were playing games at harvest day. I wanted to run away, but I was stuck out here on the dam. There was nowhere for me to go. And if I covered my eyes with my hands, they would all see.

"Forsake drunkenness!" Cole shouted to be heard over the jeering of the crowd. "I early accustomed myself to profane swearing; and blasphemous language; and excessive drinking; and I frequently stole liquors from my master, for the satisfaction of them who hired me to do it. I bitterly regret it!"

"And me!" Greenville added.

I looked around at the faces of all the youths on the dam with me, their eyes shining, their mouths open, with crumbs of bread and cheese on their shirtfronts, some with teeth stained red by stolen wine. I read in a few faces the glimmer of uncertainty, the passing shadows of second thoughts. But we were all trapped here together. Any minute now. The moment I had both yearned for and dreaded would arrive.

"I abandoned myself to criminal pleasures, to drinking, dancing, whoring, and the rest!" Cole shouted.

"Sounds good by me!" cried a mill boy on the dam to scattered applause and laughter.

"All seafaring men! Take warning by my ignominious and miserable death, to which I am now brought by the enticements of the wicked!" Cole's voice cracked. "I be justly condemned, and I offer an abundance of thanks, for the assistance of these good ministers, whose wholesome instructions and holy directions they have given me."

The lower rims of my eyelids began to burn. I determined to keep my eyes open. I couldn't abide letting the others see me cry.

Greenville was watching him and broke in, not wishing to be outdone. "Yes! And Sabbath-breaking! Keep the Sabbath holy!"

The apprentice boys on the dam with us clapped and hooted. The prisoners may have heard how their repentances were being received, for they added testaments to their apparent belief in the justifications of the court and praised the justice of glorious God.

"I have hope." Cole swallowed a sob. "Hope of entering into heaven, by the blood of my glorious Redeemer!"

I wondered if the ministers could find the strength in their hearts to pardon these miserable men. Hard-used, unloved, forsaken by God. Would Reverend Mather really take pleasure in their death? What would the use of their deaths be to anyone? Why would Jesus deign to love them in the world to come if he had forgotten them in this one?

My fingers tightened under my chin. My knuckles cracked.

"Let us pray," Reverend Mather said, raising his hands. He led the crowd and Cole and Greenville in a sonorous recitation of the Lord's Prayer. The rhythmic words lathered up the crowd into a frenzy, rising to such a pitch where God would be sure to hear them and approve. So loud and pious were the prayers of the mob that the seagull wheeled away crying.

Only two sets of mouths did not speak the ancient words.

One belonged to William Fly.

The other belonged to me.

I was frozen in place, my eyes wide with disbelief. Petrified. If I only refused, if I didn't say the words, then the proceedings might not go forward. I could freeze this moment in time, in which the three pyrates still breathed, could still smell the perfume of violets.

Did our eyes meet in that moment of silent refusal?

"Will you relent, William Fly? Go to meet your maker with forgiveness in your heart? Welcome into your soul the benevolent goodness of Christian charity? See the devotions of your compatriots on the present occasion, see how they pray!" Reverend Mather screamed, enraged. "Happy would our seafaring people particularly be if the crimes and the ends of some whom they have seen drowned in perdition might effectually cause them to beware of the faults with which they may any of them charge themselves!"

Cole and Greenville were both trembling, their hands clasped, their mouths making the shapes of the prayers as the hangman stepped behind each one and fitted his neck securely into the noose.

Fly received these exhortations with apparent amusement and placed his noose around his neck himself.

I whispered, "Oh no," but I don't think any of my friends heard me.

"The Lord shall trouble them this day," Reverend Mather boomed over the murmuring sound of prayers and pleading. "The Jews have a charitable fancy that on that day, he saw an end of all his trouble, and that in the world to come, he shall have no further trouble but be found amongst the penitent and the pardoned. With the malefactors, who die penitent and pardoned, it will be so, but the infallible judgment of who are so is what none but God, the Judge of all, can determine."

William Fly looked out over the mob and in a low voice said, "Masters of vessels. Carry it well to your men. Lest they should be put upon doing as I have done."

Then the trapdoors gave way and they all three dropped together.

My reason rebelled that the moment had come. I wasn't ready. It was too fast. It wasn't even a moment. It was less than an instant. Almost as if it hadn't happened at all.

In the sudden shocked silence, we heard the creaking of the hemp as it stretched under their dying weight. Cole's purpled tongue poked through his mottled lips. A trickle of black blood dripped from Greenville's nose. Their bodies turned in the mild afternoon ocean breeze.

William Fly had twisted in the fall, and now hung with his back to us. His handsome head leaned at a sickening angle. He swayed left, then right, then left, a pendulum marking the passing of the final instants of his life. With each sway, his body turned by some degrees, until he came to stillness gazing out over the heads of the crowd at something seen only by himself.

William Fly's eyes were wide open.

Above his head, in the softening breath of the coming evening, the black flag curled, its white skull grinning down at the darkest joke of them all.

Chapter 3

~

I saw it," Mary was saying.

"You didn't," I told her. I rubbed under my hot eyes with a fist.

"His knees trembled. He clearly wanted to be thought a brave fellow," Mary insisted. "But I saw his knees shaking. Just at the end there. Didn't you see it?"

"I didn't," Sarah said.

"I did," one of the boys following behind us on the dam said.

"The hell you did!" I shouted at him, and the boy cringed away from me.

We had tarried on the dam for the rest of the afternoon, telling ourselves there would be no fighting through the crowd anyway, so why bother. Two of the boys had given us some of their food, and some good Barbadoes rum, which does as well for cooling the body on a hot day as it does for warming one on a cold night. We loafed on the milldam with our heads in each other's laps, chewing our bread and cheese, watching as the purpling sky turned the millpond and lazy curve of the Charles a silvery pale gray. The warmth of the day softened, and our sweaty brows dried. We watched the hangman slice through the ropes one by one, dropping the bodies like sacks over his shoulder and heaving them one atop the other into the hay cart. Only a few dozen onlookers remained on the flats, and the tide was creeping in, sneaking closer to the scaffold and stage.

"Well," said Sarah as she coiled her fingers through my hair. I had her mistress's straw hat over my eyes against the setting sun, and my hands were stroking her ankle through her layers of linen. "We'd best be going."

Here was Sarah's ankle. A warm and living being, Sarah. Something that made this ankle Sarah's was inside her now. Whatever had made Will Fly's ankles belong to Will Fly had fled in the moment the length of hemp stretched taut. I had been there, but I hadn't seen it go. Where had it gone?

I softly said, "Going where?" But no one heard me except the inside of the straw hat.

We started across the dam back homeward all the same.

The sun dropped closer to Charles Town, throwing our shadows long and painting the shipyard in black silhouette. Below us, on the narrowing flats, the wagon wheeled slowly away with its gruesome cargo. I wondered where they were taking them. Not to the old burying ground. But where?

"If she's locked you out, come by the Red Lion and you can bundle with me," Sarah said with her arm around my waist. She liked to flirt with me, and usually I let her.

"Forever?" I said, and Sarah laughed and touched the tip of my nose. She knew as well as I did that the Red Lion was no different from Ship Tavern. Just on a different street.

We idled in the shadow of the Baptist meetinghouse, watching the passing faces of strangers disappearing into the gathering dusk of Boston. I wondered how many sailing masters would be surprised to hear how it went. How many crews would arrive back aboard in their tenders with hard looks for their boatswains and dark plans in their hearts.

After a time, Mary said, "I suppose he mightn't have trembled after all," while looking at her fingernails.

"I would've," Sarah said.

I said nothing. I was thinking about Will Fly's eyes settling on me and wondering where he was now. Was I bringing some piece of him along with me, secreted away, in the look that he had given me, and that I had taken into myself, for myself alone? I had almost nothing of my own.

"All right, then, girls," Mary spoke the benediction of the day. "I've got just enough rum in me to make it back."

We embraced in a threesome before each setting off along a different cobbled alley, Sarah trudging down Salem Street with a rummy lean, Mary tripping away down Middle. I delayed long as I dared, until a passing stranger cast his eye on me long enough for me to understand what his question was, and I shrank myself even smaller to avoid his notice and scuttled back for home.

I sleep in a garret in Ship Tavern, on a pallet tucked into an attic, with no window. I didn't relish the thought of sneaking in the kitchen door, creaking my way up the winding back stair, dodging Mrs. Tomlinson and her innumerable children, only to lie down in a thick miasma under the roof beams and stew. The attic in summer is always too warm, but after a few hot days all together, it is unbearable. I determined I would prefer to sleep in the hayloft of the barn and take my just deserts the following day. It was sure to be a sound desert too. My back ached already at the thought of it.

The barn is usually empty, as most of our custom pours in from the wharf side, and Mrs. Tomlinson has a horror of chickens and livestock. She prefers to buy or trade for all our goods, and she is too disorganized in her business to rent the stalls out. It's drafty in the winter, with gaps between the boards wide enough that snow blows in and makes pale frosted molehills along the floor. But in summer its colander walls keep out the rain while letting through the ocean breeze, stirring the spiderwebs and abandoned tackle and blocks and coils of rope. It's been my habit to settle in the hayloft, strip down to my shift and hang my dress on a crossbeam to air out, and awake in the morning late, refreshed, smelling of sweet dried grass and dust, enjoying my few stolen moments alone. I enjoy only the occasional passing mouse for company, except on the odd occasion when I invite someone to stop with me. But that night I craved solitude. I wondered if, when I was finally alone, I would give myself leave to cry.

I slipped through the barn door, left open as there was nothing inside worth stealing, and drew it closed. The hour wasn't late, but exhaustion made me drag my limbs as though they were made of lead. The hangings had left me wrung out and jittery. Hands shaking. My stomach felt sour and twisted, either from hunger or worry about what lay in store on the morrow.

The image of his handsome face hanging at an angle, eyes open and empty, arose whenever I closed my eyes.

I must have been there. It must have happened.

This is all ridiculous.

I heard rustling in the hay overhead as I mounted the ladder to the loft. That would be the patchwork cat on her nightly hunt. I sometimes left lobster legs for her in a dish in the yard, between the corridors made of drying sheets and underthings hung on lines. Perhaps she would sleep with me that night. I hoped so. She did sometimes. Never close enough to touch but near enough for me to hear her breathing, or feel the soft brush of her whisker on my cheek, and know myself not alone.

I pulled myself into the hayloft, arms shaking under my slight weight. It was dark under the rafters, and warm. A comforting smell of dust and wood and straw and mice. The horse blanket I had left was still there, and I felt a sweet rush of warmth and safety. I wished I had carried some of the dam boys' victuals with me, as my belly was gnawing on itself. But there was nothing to be done about that. I unpinned the cap on my head and tossed it aside, scratching out my tangles of hair. I started to untie my skirt and pockets and unlace my dress, relishing the loosening of air about my damp ribs.

A blur of motion. The loft exploded in a starburst of hay and before I understood what was happening a hand clapped over my mouth and a wiry arm snagged my waist, holding me fast. Naked terror flooded my chest and heart and arms and legs. I tried to scream but the hand over my mouth crushed away any noise.

"Shhhhh," I heard hot in my ear.

"Mmmmmf!" I screamed muffled into his hand.

We struggled. My loosened skirt fell around my ankles and I kicked it away. I dug my fingernails into the hand over my mouth. I threw my weight back and rammed my assailant against the rafter. He gasped and

I found the pad of his thumb and bit, hard. I tasted copper. He sucked in his breath with pain.

"Let me go, you b—d, let me go!" I screamed, ripping at his arms and bucking like a drowning cat.

"Shhhh!" he hissed, breath on my neck. "Shhhh! Stop, stop! It's me!"

I whipped myself to and fro, like a terrier breaking the spine of a rat. My elbow cracked into his ribs and I broke away, gasping, hands on my knees.

Standing in the scattered heap of hay, his hands cradling his tender ribs, I found the boy from the week before. The sandy boy who had rowboated to Clark's Wharf from some brig or other in the harbor, in company with his laughing friend. The arrogant one who was from somewhere not Boston, but not Jamaica either.

"You," I exclaimed. I'd certainly never thought of seeing him again. I'd guessed correctly about their willingness to pay, and after delivering them their squabs the next time I meeched by their table I'd found the plates licked clean and the chairs empty. And I won my peach and a half.

"D—n you, for a sharp elbow," said the boy, rubbing the spot where I had hit him.

"D—n you up one side and down the other," I returned, my terror instantly replaced with something close to rage at being made to feel terrified. "What do you mean, hiding up here and grabbing people who just want to sleep?"

"Have you got anything to eat?" he said. "I could eat a horse, so I could."

"Eat?" I repeated, baffled that he wouldn't even say he was sorry for having led me to think I stood to be molested or worse. "What?"

"Yes, eat." He looked up at me, and in the waxing moonlight I saw that his freckled cheeks looked sunken, and he had purpling bags under his eyes. "I can pay. A little."

"I never have anything to eat," I told him.

He sat down heavily in the hay, bent slightly to one side.

"Pity," he said. "Every night I'm dreaming of lamb. And punch with lemons and rum. And apple cobbler. Even lobster, I'd take lobster."

Well did I know the insidious way hunger could infect my dreams with elaborate fantasies of feasts served in the dining room of my imagination. Even now, just listening to his list was bringing water flooding into my tired and hungry mouth. I always had to content myself with what the kitchen could spare, which was never much, or what I could glean in my travels. Cornmeal hasty pudding, maybe with some molasses. Though I was handy with a crabapple.

I kept a wide gap of space between this strange boy and myself. I didn't know what he wanted from me, or why he was here. Whatever it was, it was no business of mine. And I was tired. I wanted him to go away. I wanted to be alone with my regret. I wanted to rest alone and safe in the hay and prepare my back for the rigors of the morrow.

"I don't know you," I said with as much authority as I could muster standing in only my shift in front of a stranger. "You have to go."

"I can't," he said.

"You must, and you will," I told him, using a phrase I had borrowed from Mrs. Tomlinson.

What if he didn't leave? There was a pitchfork left leaning on the wall behind the trapdoor, if I could only put my hand on it. Pitchforks could be useful for convincing people of things.

"I can't," he countered, "and I won't. Not till the day after tomorrow."

"Get out of here!" I shouted, not that anyone would be passing by to hear me, or would be concerned with me if they were.

"You can beat me if you like," said the boy. "But I'm not leaving. Because if I leave, they're like to find me, and if they find me, then I'm dead. That is, if I don't starve first."

This was not what I had expected him to say. "You can't starve in only a week," I told him.

He may have tried to laugh, but it was hard to tell.

"Says you," he said. "You ever gone a week without anything at all? Not even a crust?"

I didn't see any reason to answer such a stupid question as that. I could reach the pitchfork in two steps. Maybe three. My stockinged foot crept around the trapdoor.

"What if you went and found us both something to eat?" he suggested with something akin to brightness. "I'd give you some money."

Oh, indeed, what if I did? The scoundrel. "I don't work for you," I retorted. "Go yourself."

"I told you." He grunted in pain as he shifted in the hay pile. "I can't. Day after tomorrow, I've got a berth on the *Reporter*, for the Azores. Cabin boy." He lifted his shirt to examine the darkening bruise I'd given him. He was nearly as skinny as me. His ribs stood out through his papery skin. "I'll leave then. And not a minute sooner. And with any luck, I'll not come back."

"You'll leave now," I said, making my voice as even and menacing as I could. He looked up from tending himself to find the center tine of the pitchfork in my hands, leveled at his reddened eye. "Or the *Reporter*'s shipping a blind cabin boy."

The boy paled.

"Please," he said.

"Get up," I told him, an unaccustomed rush of power bringing new strength to my shaking arms and legs.

Slowly he rose to his feet, his palms open, watching me. The moon had risen, casting flat silver light in the stable almost bright enough to read by, if I could read. The light made him look paler, sicker, hungrier, and more afraid.

"No, listen," he said, his voice thick with fear. "Please. You don't understand."

I lowered the pitchfork so that the rusted tines were aimed at his tender throat.

"By all means," I said. "Explain."

He worked his mouth, trying to bring moisture back into it. But he didn't speak.

"Start by telling me who you are," I instructed him. "And then finish by giving me your money." That would teach him to frighten people who were trying to go to sleep in peace.

"My name," he said. "Is. Is . . . Billy Chandler."

"Is it, now," I teased him, drunk with my newfound authority. "Are you sure?"

He nodded, too fast.

"And who wants you dead, Billy Chandler?" I mocked, scraping the pitchfork tine softly along the whiskerless skin of his cheek.

"Everyone," he said quietly. "Everyone wants me dead."

I was beginning to sympathize with everyone's point of view.

"Why?" I pressed. "Besides the obvious. That you're a scoundrel and a rogue, not worth the crabapple I'm not stealing for you."

Billy's countenance had gone waxy. "You wouldn't understand," he said, his voice gone small like a little boy's. In his accent I heard the tatters of a soft drawl from somewhere south. New Orleans? Maybe he was younger than I thought. Younger than me, even. We could have been two children playing soldiers in the attic and giggling, instead of what we were: two children, too starved and tired to trust. Billy was unsteady on his feet, and I realized he really hadn't eaten since I sat him and his compatriot by the door helping them to rob us. That was a whole week ago.

I straightened, but kept the pitchfork aimed just in case. "Where's your friend?" I asked with suspicion.

A darkness swam across Billy's pale eyes. He said, "They gave him this. Thinking him me."

He reached into the waist of his pantaloons, held up around his jutting hips with a tied length of rope. From this hiding place he withdrew a piece of paper, folded up small.

"I can't read," I informed him impatiently. "You'll have to tell me."

"There's nothing to read," he said, holding it out to me between two bony fingers.

I hesitated. Letting go of the pitchfork with one hand would make it easy for him to take it from me. But seeing him standing there like a half-dead mule waiting to be put down, I thought the last of his strength must have expired when he leapt out of the hay to subdue me. Right now, it looked for all the world like I could tip over Billy Chandler with a goose feather.

I took the paper from him and unfolded it.

It was blank.

"What is this?" I waved the paper at him, annoyed. "There's nothing here."

"Look closer," said Billy quietly.

In the chilling moonlight, I held the paper closer and saw that it contained a small ink circle, filled in.

A dot. Smaller than a baby's toenail.

Billy read the confusion that must have bent my face.

"It's the black spot," he said, his voice breaking. He took the paper back from me, folding it and tucking it away into his boot so that he didn't have to keep looking at it.

"It isn't," I said, disbelieving.

"It is. Authority might want me, but it's not the hangman I fear." Billy's face was tight with terror, and I knew then that he was telling me the truth.

I peered at this strange boy in my hayloft with renewed interest. "You were with them," I exclaimed. "You went pyrating with William Fly. That's why you knew all that was said, and who said it, and how it all happened!"

Billy collapsed in the straw with his head in his hands. "I'm so hungry," he moaned. "Please. Don't you have anything? A crust?"

"But how did you escape?" I demanded. "I thought he surrendered, and Boston jail held them all."

Billy stared at me. "A crumb?" he pleaded.

I finally saw this broken boy for what he was—a child. Afraid. Starving. A coward who had run and hid while his fellows went to the gallows. The hangman waiting for him on one side, and his betrayed shipmates stalking him on the other, which was somehow worse. The black spot. I always thought it was a fairy story told to waterfront children, to keep us trembling in our beds. I'd never known that it was real. Now I'd actually touched one. I wanted to wipe my hands on my shift, to cast off any residue of evil that might be clinging to me.

I set aside my pitchfork. "Come on," I said. I tried to make myself sound friendly. "Get up."

Night had settled in the hayloft. Billy's face was turned away from me. I heard sniffling.

"We can go to the kitchen," I said, trying to reassure him. "They'll all be asleep. Or nearly so."

"My head," Billy said through sniffs and tears. "It hurts so much."

"It's all right," I assured him. "There's cider too. Come on. Let's go."

I found his hand in the dark, rope-hardened despite its youth as mine was scrub-hardened despite mine, and helped him to his feet. He felt so light that he was brittle, and his other hand grasped my shoulder. I was just in my shift, bareheaded and barefoot, hair a mesh of tangles. But we'd only be gone a little while. Then I'd return to take my ease and sleep at last. Would I let Billy hide for the night with me? Maybe. I'd make him promise to tell me about pyrating until I fell asleep.

Somehow we made it down the ladder, the patchwork cat vanishing from her meal of mouse when we appeared in the stall where she'd been stalking. I led Billy gently to the barn door.

"Wait!" he cried, hanging back. "I can't go outside."

"It's just through the yard," I said. "There's no one there."

Waves of terror vibrated off Billy in the darkness, so thick I could taste them. "How far?" he asked in his little boy voice.

"It's that window there," I said. "See? Where the candle's burning?"

I cracked the barn door and pointed. Clotheslines crisscrossed the length and breadth of the narrow courtyard, hanging sheets and shifts and pantaloons and blouses and stockings making a labyrinth of shifting corridors and rooms, glowing almost blue in the moonlight. We heard a distant shipboard bell dong the hour. Eleven o'clock and all's well. The forbidding brick back of Ship Tavern faced us on the other side of the network of laundry, with a narrow wooden door and one small window of leaded diamond-shaped panes winking over the yard. I knew where Mrs. Tomlinson kept the meat pies and jars of sugared rhubarb and molasses. She hid sweet things from her horde of avaricious child-locusts, but we all had a genius for finding them no matter how cleverly concealed.

Billy stared down the aspect of the ropes of drying clothes.

"We'd have to run," he said. "But I'm so tired."

"Come on," I said, jostling his shoulder in what I imagined was a sisterly way. "I know where the limes are too."

I took his hand and we stepped into the lee of a sheet that billowed up on the breath of the sea. I batted it away from my face and ducked underneath it, and I pulled Billy along behind me. The wind off the harbor picked up, and the corridors realigned around us, here a path opening, then disappearing behind a wall of lifting and falling shirts. We turned this way, and then the other way. Somewhere I lost Billy's hand. The wind whistled in the clotheslines, pulling at my hair, and I ducked below a voluminous ruffled blouse and found myself concealed alone in a tiny room of sheets. Under the howl of wind and flapping linen, I heard footsteps.

"Billy?" I called. "Where are you?"

The footsteps drew nearer. A sheet fluttered, opening a corner like a doorway into a long hall of white.

"Hurry," an unfamiliar man's voice growled, close by.

The footsteps quickened.

"Billy!" I shouted.

"Who's that?" another man's gravelly voice barked.

A terrified cry ripped through the night. "Hannah!" Billy screamed. "Hannah! Run!"

I fought aside a screen of stockings, unsure which side of me the men were on, and fled, my hands before my face, floundering through cloying walls of wet cotton. "Billy!" I cried. I heard something sing through the air and then a wet thud.

"He's got a girl with him," Gravel Voice said.

I froze. I was afraid my heartbeat was loud enough to give me away. It boomed in my ears, hard as a bass drum on muster day.

The men stopped moving too. Our ears hunted for each other through the night.

"Oh, Hannah!" the first man sing-songed. Something metal tinked against the yard cobblestones.

Tink. Tink. Tink.

They couldn't have been more than ten feet away from where I stood, motionless as a headstone. The wind softened, the linens going slack. I breathed through my mouth so they wouldn't hear the terrified panting through my nose.

"Where is she?" Gravel Voice said.

"Oh, Hannah!" the other called. "Come here, my girl. There's nothing to be afraid of. God's my witness."

The wind breathed again, and a few linen shifts belonging to Mrs. Tomlinson's eldest daughter lifted to reveal poor Billy Chandler. He lay sprawled across the cobbles on his stomach, arms and legs splayed like a starfish. He was completely still, eyes open and glassed over in the moonlight, his mouth slack, teeth reddened with blood. An oily black pool spread below his head, creeping into the crevices between the stones. The back of his neck had been opened, and I saw a white gleam of bone. Bile rose in the back of my throat and my eyes flushed hot.

"Oh, Hannah!" the singsong voice came again. Some feet away from me a cutlass glinted in the moonlight over my head and fell on a clothesline, sighing a whole corridor wall to the ground.

"Come out, come out, wherever you are!" coaxed the singsong voice.

I flung aside a sheet and disappeared into the shadow of the kitchen door. I flattened myself into the doorjamb as though I could disappear into the bricks. One by one, the cutlass glinted and the lines fell. The moon hung overhead perfectly round, clear and bright in a cloudless sky, surrounded by a meshwork of stars. Cold blue and silver light illuminated the entire yard except for crisp black shadows. I could see every detail of the brick doorway where I trembled in hiding.

In a moment they would see me. Three more lines.

My mind tripped at a horse gallop as I tried to figure out what to do. If I opened the tavern door they would hear the creak, and then go rampaging at me through the kitchen. The worktable and barrels and baskets and pots scattered everywhere meant I'd never escape. I'd die hacked to pieces in the fireplace.

Another clothesline fell. "Hannah! Oh, Hannah!" Singsong Voice called.

"We'll take good care of ye, girl," Gravel Voice added.

On silent cat feet, breath coming high and fast in my chest, I vanished from the doorway, keeping low behind the last line of woolen stockings and kerchiefs and caps. Around the corner, I dashed into Fish Street, the long road of Clark's Wharf stretching out into the black harbor, licked into white-topped waves by the wind. D—n that moon. A coil of rope wouldn't hide me. The nearest moored boat was too far for me to swim by half. Fish Street was a wide avenue, paved with bricks that gleamed in the moonlight. I was exposed. Nowhere to hide. The cutlass men would follow me around the corner any moment and see me standing here, gasping, alive with fear. Would they dare to slice me in two in the street?

Outside the front door of Ship Tavern, which was closed and barred for the night, full of drunk and snoring sailors wrapped up in each other's arms, I spied the empty apple barrel where I used to sit and smoke.

I was inside, folded up as tight as the black spot Billy had shown me, the lid drawn down over my head, when the heavy footfalls with the tinking cutlass came around the corner.

"D—n your lubber's feet," said Gravel. "Where'd that kitten get to?"

"You don't see her?" Singsong said, all false mirth fallen from his voice. Their voices came to me muffled through the wood.

"She can't be far," Gravel responded.

The barrel stank of rotting apples, a stench almost overpowering. I breathed through my mouth, grateful for once for being so slight. Rotten apple mush rose between my toes. Rancid cider soaked my back.

"You think he told her?" Singsong asked. I heard the chink of the tip of the cutlass tapping against the bricks.

Gravel Voice grunted. "Hard to say. But he'll want her found."

"That he will," Singsong agreed grimly.

"Or we'll be the worse for it." Gravel sounded angry.

"It's a small town withal," Singsong assured him. "No way in or out but the Neck. We'll put a man there, and then we'll go street by street. We'll turn her up."

"A black spot for the little girl," agreed Gravel. "And a piece of eight for anyone should see fit to bring her forth."

Singsong laughed once, a cruel-sounding bark. "We'll drown your kitten before the sun passes the yardarm tomorrow," he said. "I'd lay money on it."

"What money?" Gravel laughed back, their voices growing fainter as they moved away.

I'm not, as I've told you, one who usually made much time in my day for prayer. But alone that long night in the apple barrel, all but naked, my knees pressed to my chin, all blood and feeling flattening out of my feet, tears streaming down my dirty and terrified face, my mouth moved in silence saying things I cannot repeat for fear that I might never be forgiven such deep and true hypocrisy.

Chapter 4

~

*L*ife returns to the waterfront well before the dawn. I knew I had to make a plan before the people started to stretch and wake to find me in terror, alone in the street, naked, and worth money if they would give me up to pitiless men. The distant ship-bell kept me apprised of the time, donging away the last hours of my life. By four o'clock and all's well, I could scarcely move from the strain of keeping myself knotted up so small and tight. Apple miasma filled my nose and mouth and eyes and ears and I feared would make me drunk just from breathing it. I had neither food nor money nor clothes nor shoes and a price levied upon my head.

Those men with the cutlasses knew my name.

And they knew where I made my home.

Silently, I lifted the barrel lid a hairsbreadth and scoped the wharf. A few lamps were glowing in shipboard cabin skylights on the brigantines and sloops resting at anchor in the harbor or moored up close to the wharf. Somewhere nearby a cow lowed to be milked. The roosters would stir before long, and the sky was already beginning to think about paling. The stars looked tired. The moon had set. In a few minutes the first sleepy servants, apprentices, and fishwives would pad out to the privy and back to the kitchen and stoke up banked embers and set things to boil. Another day in Boston would begin.

I didn't have much time.

I pushed aside the lid and pulled myself out, my legs instantly cramping, toes flushing angry and red with pins running up and down my legs. My shift clung wetly to me. I staggered on numb feet to the waterside. The tide was up. Rowboats strained at their mooring lines, water sloshed inches away from my feet. I got up on a piling and quick as a flash dove into the water like a cormorant after a fish.

My first thought had been that I would swim to Dorchester and flee from there on foot into the countryside. But as the cool water closed over my head and I spun in the silent bubbling blackness, my hair fanning out and my shift ballooning up like a jellyfish, I knew my plan was folly. I would drown. If I was lucky.

My lips broke the surface and I gasped for air. Overhead on the wharf a sleepy young sailor trudged past and I clung to the piling underneath, hiding in the shadows, listening to his receding footfalls. Barnacles scraped my palms, stinging in the salt water. The boy didn't look round. I peered out from under the wooden planks to see if I knew him. In his sailor's loose blouse and breeches and kerchief and bare feet he could have been any one of hundreds of anonymous boys who wash ashore in a different port, hardly aware that they are anywhere but far from home. He could have been anyone.

Or no one at all.

I pulled myself dripping from the water and ran, hunched down, dashing from shadow to shadow until I reached the yard behind the Tavern.

The laundry was nearly dry, what little the pyrates had left hanging. White sheets had stiffened, woolen stockings crispy. The brickyard was a heaped expanse of white and flax, like a softly rolling meadow of clover in bloom, marked only by the awful form of what had once been poor starving Billy Chandler sprawled on his empty stomach, his reddened teeth grimacing at me, wreathed in freshly beaten sheets.

I couldn't look at him. I was afraid of the accusation I might see in his open eyes. Afraid that, in trying to smuggle him to the kitchen, I had instead delivered him into the hands of the Devil. Afraid that now his soul sat in torment because of me.

When this broken boy's body was found, there were sure to be screams and a rush of commotion and onlookers and summoning of the constable. I had best be well gone by then.

Shivering in the thin early morning light, I stripped away my ruined shift and left it on the line, stained and mottled and soaked, the damp harbor air chilling my naked gooseflesh. I grabbed a blouse and pulled it over my head and then a pair of breeches that might have been just small enough and a pair of woolen stockings, hopping on one foot, then the other to roll them up over my knees. The sky was paling faster, and the distant ship-bell warned me that dawn was nigh.

I needed shoes.

I knew where I could find one pair that nobody else would miss. My skin crawled at the thought. I hated to do it. But I had to. I edged nearer the still form of Billy lying in the heaps of sheets, half expecting him to move or sit up, as though disturbed from a deep sleep. But he didn't move at all.

I crouched next to his lifeless body and pushed aside my fear and disgust and hurriedly started unlacing his boots.

"I'm sorry," I whispered as I yanked off one. His body jostled, limp and yielding. Blood filled the crevices between the cobbles, outlining them in black, like oakum.

I tried the other boot. It wouldn't come.

Fear buzzed in my ears. Any minute now we would be discovered, and I might be taken for a murderess and hanged within the week. "D—n it, Billy, give it to me!" I begged, pulling harder until it finally came away, shifting Billy's body's attitude on the ground. His cold foot lay inert across my lap, but I saw that his head had not moved from its resting spot.

The cutlass had taken it clean off.

I scrambled backward on my hands and feet in horror like a panicked crab, grabbing up the loose boot under my arm, rolled to my feet, and sprinted away from Ship Tavern just as the first rooster on the barn stretched out his lustrous wings and opened his throat to crow.

⚬

WHEN THEY CAME, just after the rising sun kissed the windows of Boston pale pink, the screams and shouts shuddered the waterfront. Bells clanging, rushing feet and people saying, "What is it? What's happened?" and "A boy, I heard. A stranger, in the alleyway." "Was he robbed?" "He must've been, for he'd nothing on him at all. Not even his shoes."

I was crouching near the town dockyard, by Long Wharf, loitering since I couldn't very well hide. Billy's shoes were too big by half, and I had to hold up the breeches with a line of hemp, the blouse sleeves rolled up to my elbows. I'd tied my hair in a pigtail and rolled a stolen kerchief about my neck. I'd found a half-eaten heel of bread and was gnawing on it in the shadow of a blacksmith's shop, my eyes darting this way and that like a hunted animal cornered in a glade.

"Here, you," a man said.

I stared up at him, cowering with the bread heel in my hands. He wore a soot-smirched leather apron and had massive blacksmith's forearms folded over his chest.

"Mmmf?" I said, my mouth full of stale bread. Nothing I had eaten had ever tasted so good.

"Move along." The blacksmith shooed me away. "I'll not have you idling here."

I stared at him like a cornered cat.

"Go on," he said. "Get to your ship, or I'll flog you myself."

I stuffed the end of my bread into my shirt, confused, but touched my knuckle to my forehead. Playing along. "Yes, sir," I said to the man in the apron, crumbs tumbling out of my mouth. "Thank you, sir."

I clopped into the crowd on the town dock landing, most of them going about their morning business, some of them trying to make their way to Clark's Wharf to see what all the commotion was about. I looked curiously into each face as I passed, reading it for signs of recognition. Many were folk I recognized, from Sabbath meeting or the market, faces that formed familiar features in the landscape of my life. There was the fisherman with the long gray beard. There was the old woman in the plain coif and collar of a generation ago. There was the man in the ramillies wig who was handsome despite his perpetual squint. There was the half-Wampanoag man who worked at the cooper's, with his pepper-gray hair. But now they were as strangers to me. Their eyes slid past me or looked over my head. I was invisible. Like all the anonymous hungry boys who rolled off the ships and rolled through town and then rolled away once more, never to be seen again.

A cluster of girls approached, all of them bound out like myself, all of them my confederates. They carried market baskets over their arms, and their heads leaned in close together, whispering and giggling and mocking. One girl shoved another in play, and the second shoved the first back, and the first's cap slipped from her forehead and I saw that it was my friend Sarah Wildes.

I let out a low whistle, wanting to talk to her without drawing too much attention to myself. "Pssst," I said, waving a hand to try to catch her eye. I imagined the look of shock and then the laughter when she beheld me in my new rig. I yearned to laugh with her. I wondered what she would say, when I told her about the cutlass men.

My whistles worked, and Sarah looked square at me in the street. But her face showed no glimmer of knowledge, no light of surprise or mirth. Instead, she pulled her cap back in place and retied it under her chin, glared at me, and showed me her profile as she moved away, while the other girls whispered behind their hands.

"Sarah!" I started to say. But she and the others were already gone.

I felt for all the world like I was in a waking dream. Like I were invisible as a shade, or a spirit sent out to do dark deeds in the night. I held my hand up before my face, unreasonably, testing to see if I could still see myself. There was my hand, fingers flexing in the morning air. I was still flesh and bone. I lived and breathed. But I blended into the crowd at the town landing as surely as a doe can disappear into the leaves of a forest, though standing only two yards away.

I couldn't have asked Sarah for help, not really. Not and brought the curse of the black spot down on her innocent head. And what could she have done, anyway? Hidden me in her attic? And then what? But it felt strange to find myself so thoroughly unknown. Like I was become an illusion defined only by whom I am seen.

As I pondered my newfound invisibility, I determined to make a test of it. I strolled over to the ropemakers' alley and went up to the first boy I saw. He was bent over, splicing, absorbed in his work.

"Ho there," I said.

He didn't look up. "What," he said.

"You know where I might find the *Reporter*?" I asked.

The boy's hands moved lightning quick, his eyes nearly unblinking. "Fruit packet. For the Azores?" he said. "Long Wharf, starboard side. All the way at the end."

I lingered, marveling that he didn't look at me twice. Did he not see I was a girl? Could he not hear it in my voice? Was I not as much the coquette as Mrs. Tomlinson would have me believe?

"Leaves tomorrow, I think they said," the boy continued, his hands never stopping. When at last he looked up at me, his face betrayed no remark or curiosity.

"And all full up," he added.

"Right," I said.

But I happened to know they were down a cabin boy.

I hurried out of the ropemakers' alley, tripping lighter as my soul sang in triumph. I found it! A way out of Boston that didn't take me by the Neck, where the pyrates lay in wait for me! I could escape! Maybe. If I was careful. If I could make myself be what they wanted to see.

Long Wharf, if you've never seen it, is like a city unto itself. Wide enough for horses to ride down it three abreast, so long it nearly has its own horizon. The length of Long Wharf is crowded with sail lofts and victualing houses and coffee houses and ropemakers and barrel makers and counting houses and stampers and engravers and chandlers, every-thing that is needed for kitting out ships and the men who sail them. I'd never spent much time there, in truth. Each wharf was its own country. Sometimes on a hot summer night we would go down Clark's and sit on the bitter end with our feet dangling over the water. When I first arrived with Mrs. Tomlinson I used to like to throw pebbles in the water to watch the pale blue sparkles of phosphorescence trace their bubbles into the deep. If you have your own wharf, why go all the way over to another one? I moved down Long Wharf a stranger.

The city of Long Wharf was bustling even as the morning began to threaten rain. As I clopped in Billy's loose boots looking for his ship I felt an electric tingle along my scalp, the eerie lightening in the head from a sudden drop in barometric pressure. I scented the coming rain, a sharpness and blackness in the air. The wind kicked up, and women's hands flew atop their straw hats to keep them from rippling away. A few young men appeared topside in flapping oilcloths. The gentle waves of the harbor rose into sharp black peaks whitened with foam.

I stopped at what seemed a likely ship, a great barque sparkling with fresh paint, several boys and young men busy on her deck. But when I made my inquiries, I was met with riotous laughter.

"Carry on a little farther," one of the young men urged me while the others exchanged glances. "You can't miss her."

Well, they were right. When I finally found my salvation, berthed stern-to and half-heartedly lashed to the piling with hemp lines hairy from hard use, I confess my resolve faltered. She was a shabby schooner, not even a hundred tons, two masts, paint chipped, worm-eaten, creaking where she lay like a tired tree that would snap at the first big blow. A few panes missing from her stern glass and skylights. No one was about. The scrollwork was sun-faded and peeling, but I could make out *RE OR ER* in faint shadow letters across the stern.

CAMBRIDGE

"It just cuts off like that?" Marian looked up at the student sitting across from her desk.

"It's not only the cover," said Kay. "Some pages are missing too."

Marian thumbed through the sheaf of yellowed paper resting atop a scattered mess of student research papers written in interchangeable sweet looping script. She'd been ignoring the papers for weeks. She didn't even remember which class they were for.

"They're not just sewn out of order?"

Kay said, "I don't think so. I've read the whole thing. It largely seems to be in order. I think. Just, here and there, some of it's gone. Cut out or lost. I don't know."

Marian said, "That's unfortunate." It was worse than unfortunate. It was a fragment.

"There's not that much missing," the undergraduate insisted.

"But there's no way to know how much," said Marian. She sat back in her swivel chair and propped a knee on her desk. A tuft of lint turned up on her slacks leg in the yellowing beam of late-afternoon sun. Marian plucked it off.

"Keep reading," said Kay.

Marian eyed the student perched across from her in the only office chair not heaped with books and papers, her young feet folded at the ankles like they tell you to do in charm class, one saddle shoe jiggling. Kay Lonergan wasn't the sort of student Marian usually noticed, not that Marian put much notice on the undergraduates as a rule. What the Harvard boys would call a "nice girl," she was a stolid young woman with Irish cheeks and a New Jersey home address. Slept with pins in her hair. No moth holes in her cardigan. Slim tweed skirt. Admired Myrna Loy and thought Jean Harlow was fast. Signet ring. Kay Lonergan would be the sort of girl who busied herself in the Radcliffe library and sang in a choir or two and went to lots of student meetings that felt very important at the time. She would collect her degree without honors and disappear back to New Jersey. She would date largely interchangeable boys who took her to football games and thought swallowing a live goldfish on a dare was the height of comic genius. If she majored in history, it would be so she could teach school in Montclair until she got married. Then, in the years to come, as she gazed out the window over her kitchen sink at her children playing under a red-leaved maple tree, she could close her eyes and conjure a perfect image of the court in Tudor England, draped in tapestries and redolent with the smell of roasting venison. And then she'd put the lunch plate in the drying rack.

"Look," Marian said, pushing the manuscript away. "You have to know that it's probably fake."

Kay's eyebrows went up in the middle, but she said, "I don't think it is, actually."

"First of all," Marian thumbed back over the pages she had briefly read. "How is it a true narrative written by herself if she's illiterate?"

"I mean," Kay said. Her foot kept jiggling. It was maddening. "She wrote it later. People learn to read and write their memoirs later."

"Sure," said Marian. "But they also invent stories too wild to be true to sell books. Even in the eighteenth century."

"I know," Kay said.

"Captivity narratives." Marian was bored. "Conversion narratives. I'm guessing that's what this manuscript winds up being—a conversion narrative. Have you even taken my class?"

Kay's thumbnails clicked together.

"It was probably written by a man," Marian continued. "Look."

She licked a thumb and riffled back a couple of pages. The paper was thick and heavy, wavy with water damage and browned with foxing. The manuscript certainly felt old enough. And the type looked consistent in font and spacing with other eighteenth-century books, with a title page claiming publication and sale by a printer that sounded plausible, in a street in Boston known for printing, even if it wasn't an imprint Marian had heard of before. But those details wouldn't be too hard to ape. Handwriting that actually belonged in the eighteenth century was much more difficult to fake. But not impossible.

Marian pointed to the passage in which Hannah addresses her friend Sarah in the street, and Sarah doesn't know her.

"Come on," said Marian. "She'd just seen her the day before. The text has implied that they weren't just friends but lovers. They'd bundled together, it said. What sort of male fantasy is that? Not that it didn't happen, but the idea that she'd put it in writing is preposterous. And if it were true, how could Sarah possibly not know her in the street?"

Marian realized how harsh her dismissal must sound, and she inwardly chastised herself for being so blunt. She always forgot how sensitive the newly opened petals of intellectual curiosity could be, delicate and flush, easily shriveled by the hot glare of disapproval. She supposed she couldn't fault some gullible teenager for feeling romantic, wishing her discovery to be what she imagined it was. Marian was no stranger to the seduction of thinking you have found exactly what you are dreaming of finding in the archive. She had had her heart broken more than once in more than one special collection. For Marian the broken promises of the archive were second only to the disappointments of a lover when they were finally revealed in all their inconsistencies and incompleteness and shortcomings. But just as no one person could possibly hope to contain all passion, and meaning and truth and understanding and patience, and hope in one frail and fallible human body, so too no text, no matter how dusty, could possibly embody the fantasy that Kay Lonergan thought she had found in this one.

Marian looked with some tenderness at the part in Kay's hair, as the undergraduate's head hung before her professor's curt dismissal. Everyone dreams of escape. Even sweet freshman Cliffies from New Jersey. Perhaps especially them, as they've stepped off the train in Cambridge with their valises and their fresh notebooks and their embossed stationery for their letters home. Marian often forgot that. And the truth was, almost no one gets to escape. Some mornings Marian beheld her dripping face framed in the medicine cabinet mirror over her sink, cheeks reddened with hot water, eyes purpled with exhaustion, papery lines etched on either side of her mouth, unable to believe that she had done it herself.

"I've thought about that," said Kay. She had been rummaging in the satchel at her feet and now pulled out a small framed photograph and slid it across the desk. She hadn't been chastised at all. Her face was smooth with seriousness. Marian also sometimes forgot that no one could be as arrogant and self-assured as an undergraduate who didn't know what she didn't know.

Marian picked up the photograph and looked at it.

The snapshot showed a row of six boys in baseball uniforms, grinning goofily into bright sunlight. Skinny and happy-looking, lined up by height on a bare dirt pitching mound. Blousy knickers and long socks and white buttoned shirts with dark sleeves smirched with dust. One of them held a bat over his shoulder, another one had a beaten leather glove tucked between his folded arms.

"Which one's me?" said Kay.

Marian glanced up at her, unable to conceal her surprise. Now it was Kay's turn to sit back in her chair. The saddle shoe finally stopped jiggling.

The kids in the picture all looked basically the same, though ranging slightly in size from largest to smallest, with a couple of twins mixed in to cause confusion. They could have been brothers. Upon reflection, they probably were brothers. Well, brothers and a sister, apparently. Apple cheeks. Freckles. One had slightly longer curls peeking out from under his hat and was noticeably shorter than the others. Marian put her finger on him and said, "That one."

"That's Mikey," said Kay. "He's the baby."

"Huh," said Marian. She peered closer and put her finger on one who seemed maybe slighter than the other five.

"That one?"

Kay smiled. "That's Joey. He and Sam are the twins."

Marian looked again but was damned if she couldn't tell which one was Kay and which one wasn't. The smiling adolescent faces all looked almost the same.

"I was thinking about it," Kay continued. "Haven't you ever bumped into someone at the pharmacy that you know from school or wherever and had no idea who they were because you didn't expect to see them there?"

More than once Marian had found herself flummoxed to hear a young voice exclaim in surprise, "Professor Beresford!" as her hands accepted her paper-wrapped pound of ground beef at the butcher's, or as she sat under the dryer at the hairdresser's turning a page of *McCall's*, or as she read the advance notices on the back of a book at the co-op, only to look up and be baffled by her interlocutor's face. In turn her students often reacted to seeing her out in the world, freed from behind her lectern, as though they had seen a ghost, or a reanimated corpse set loose amongst the living. As if she passed the hours between Tuesday and Thursday afternoons in suspended animation, only breathing with life when the students were there to observe her.

"People see what they expect to see," Kay pointed out, as though able to overhear what was passing through Marian's mind. "In the places they expect to see them."

Marian eyed this earnest Cliffie with renewed interest. She drew a cigarette from the box on her desk and offered one to Kay. Kay waved a hand to decline. Marian leaned forward to spark the lighter on her desk, drew on the cigarette, and exhaled twin streams of smoke through her nostrils.

Kay didn't cough.

"Interesting," said Marian.

"Usually people only see our context," Kay said. "Not ourselves."

It wasn't impossible, what Kay was suggesting. It was a stretch, but it wasn't impossible. Especially in 1726. A time before tomboys and women daring to wear slacks, like Marian herself. A time when gendered clothing choices went unquestioned.

"What's she supposed to be, seventeen?" said Marian, tapping her ash into a teacup. "What about her breasts?"

"She's starving," said Kay.

"Yes, but," Marian objected.

"My roommate doesn't eat."

"Nobody's roommates eat," said Marian.

"No," said Kay. "I mean, she really doesn't eat. She drinks hot water with lemon and has one peanut butter sandwich that she eats slowly all day. Crust first."

"Really?" Marian was surprised. Even for a girl on a strict reducing plan, that sounded extreme. Marian had had her reducing years, of course. She didn't know any woman who hadn't. Not until she turned thirty had she embraced the word "statuesque" and given up on the spring-loaded exercisers and hand weights that were all now in a box under her unmade bed.

"Really," Kay insisted. "The other night she came home from a date practically in hysterics. I asked her what was the matter, and she told me that this boy she'd been going steady with, this Yalie? They'd been neck-ing in his car after going to the movies."

Marian stiffened. Undergraduates often liked to confide in their woman professors. She wished she had left her office door open so that a colleague might stick her head in and ask to borrow the *American His-torical Review* or a cigarette or maybe to ask Marian to light her garters on fire. Anything to end this story.

"Things were getting pretty heavy, and she was trying to decide how far she'd let him go, and he kept reaching under her sweater, and he told her he loved her, and she thought she really loved him, so finally she let him. But when he got to her brassiere, he started laughing," Kay said.

"Laughing? Why?" Marian asked against her better judgment.

"Because he discovered she'd filled her brassiere with cotton balls."

"She . . . What?" Marian knew she shouldn't laugh. She definitely shouldn't. It sounded awful. She mostly succeeded, not laughing, but it was hard.

Kay leaned her elbows on her knees and said, "She has no breasts at all. None. She's starved them away. She doesn't want anyone to know, so she fills her brassiere with cotton balls. The only reason I know is because we share a room the size of a postage stamp. We can't change clothes without basically sitting in each other's laps."

"That's . . ."

Now that she thought about it, Hannah made sense. The spectral ribs poking through the skin. The way that hunger etches itself into the human body. A childhood of malnutrition could easily have imprisoned this hypo-thetical teenage Hannah in what, to a twentieth-century eye, would look like the body of a child. A tenacious, smart, wiry child. Starving would have dried up her menses too. That's another impossibility, solved. She'd been about to point this out to Kay, that a woman disguised as a man, or boy, in this instance, on board a ship would inevitably have had to contend with her monthly period, and surely that would be impossible to do in close quarters without being found out. But a starving woman, or a starving girl, rather, doing hard physical labor all day long would be all muscle and sinew and not enough fat. She might not have even begun to menstruate at all.

A pool of warmth spread at the base of Marian's neck as the nicotine settled into her bloodstream and her thoughts grew clear and without her acknowledging it was happening, a glimmer of excitement flamed to life somewhere in the animal stem of her brain.

"All right," said Marian at length. "Okay. I'll bite."

"Just you wait," said Kay. The jiggling foot started up again. Excitement, it seemed, not nervousness after all.

Marian plucked a loose crumb of tobacco off her lip and said, "Where did you find this again?"

"Keep reading," said Kay.

Marian touched the wavering page edges. "How much do you think is missing?"

"Just keep reading. You haven't even gotten to the best part yet." Kay's eyes crinkled at the corners. Her eyes were the green of fresh spring water.

Marian riffled back through the pages to find the spot where she had left off, where Hannah found the schooner with the name *RE OR ER* painted on the stern.

"And what part's that?" she said around the cigarette now parked in the corner of her mouth.

"The part with the treasure."

A backwash of smoke scorched Marian's lungs and she coughed, hacking until the phlegm cleared and she could collect herself and grind the cigarette out in the teacup. "What?"

Kay leaned forward, her hands gripping the arms of the swivel chair across from the desk in Marian's office. She gave Marian a conspiratorial smile.

In a low voice, Kay said, "Look at me."

Marian did. A curl had loosened itself from its pin and brushed the girl's delicate Irish eyebrow.

"I'm sitting right in front of you," Kay said. "And I'm the one holding the bat."

⌒

THE WIND KICKED up and the *Reporter* heeled over and I did my utmost not to scream. I must have failed, because a Black man of about three and twenty with a pink scar cleaving his eyebrow and cheek shouted, "Lively now, God d—n you!" And so I closed my eyes and pulled harder on the rope until I felt like my shoulders and my back were on fire.

"Madness," grumbled a barefoot rogue dragging on the line behind me. "Who leaves Boston Harbor in a squall?"

My stomach dropped into my feet as the wind seized the foremast topgallant and heeled us well over, my boots scrabbling for purchase on the deck. The ship groaned, rising like a tired beast over a rolling swell, pointing its bowsprit into the blackening sky, and then landing hard in the trough, tossing sea spray over us as thick as if we'd been doused with a bucket.

"D—n your one good eye, Seneca!" the barefoot sailor behind me bellowed.

The young man with the scar laughed and shouted, "Oh, do I offend you, Orne, you right Marblehead b—d? Come pluck it out!"

The barefoot one, Orne, laughed too, even as the wind screamed through our hair and the first needles of rain lanced into our cheeks, and I saw that they knew each other already. Probably quite well. Somehow I hadn't considered that a crew on a worm-eaten fruit packet might not all be strangers to each other.

Perhaps they were only strangers to me.

What if they weren't strangers to Billy Chandler either?

The wind whistled in the lines and the terror seizing my heart drove my petty worries well away as the larboard rail plunged near to the rising chop in the harbor. I pulled harder on my rope, teeth grinding with effort, when the man on the helm shouted, "Come about! Come about!" One point off starboard bow winked the guiding flame of Deer Island light, a sputtering beacon guarding rocky shoals that would open our belly and claw off our rudder given half a chance.

"Ready, ready, ready!" shouted Seneca as some sloppy company of my new shipmates scrambled to the high side and took up the slack sheets. The strain in my arms and back deepened as there were fewer hands to hold the line with me, and my heels dragged inch by inch across the deck, and each passing moment I was sure a zephyr would shred the mainsail into rags and we'd all go plunging into the deep. Dead, my first time on a ship since leaving Beverly, which I didn't even remember. Dead before even getting out of Boston Harbor. Could I swim to one of the islands? Only if the rigging didn't tangle around my feet and drag me down. The first thing to do once I found myself in the water, a strange calm voice in my mind instructed, would be to kick off these God d—n boots.

"Helm's a lee!" came a cry from the stern of the boat, and all at once the ship caromed onto its starboard ear, and I was being dragged facedown along the deck, boots knocking on the wood and my chin drumming *bump, bump, bump, bump* until I heard Seneca shouting, "Let go, you God d—n b—d, let go!"

My hands obeyed even if my brain didn't, and then I was free of the line and someone was pulling me to my feet by the armpit and propping me roughly against the rail. My chin smarted, and my palms were raw, but we were now cutting smoothly toward the Narrows on a larboard tack, sails well trimmed and the frothing shoals of Deer Island dropping behind us. I wrapped my arm in desperation around the rail, clinging to it for all life, my hair dripping, my eyes singed with salt water. I panted from the hard labor of it, and here was us, only just setting out.

At the wheel in the stern stood a man of indeterminate age, well older than I, hardened ageless by work as all of us were. He was English, sandy-looking with a broken nose, badly set, zigzagging across his face like a Z. I'd heard him called Edward Low. He strained at the wheel in the building wind, squinting at the sails as if taking the measure of them. Behind him I spied the blur of Boston dropping farther away, as successive curtains of rain fell around the *Reporter*, closing away the stage on which I'd played the first act of my life. The squall softened and the ship settled into her course, riding up and down the swells, and as Boston dropped farther behind me I felt relief flow through my veins like sweet wine. I had escaped! Let those murdering pyrates beat the bushes for me all they liked. Let them double the bounty on my head if they wanted!

Hannah Misery was gone from Boston.

Hannah Misery had disappeared.

Edward Low wasn't the master of the *Reporter*. He was sort of the first officer, if we could be said to have one. The master somewhere below, a beefy, corpulent character with a sour smell to him who had barked at us to make sail while the tide was with us, irrespective of the weather, and then disappeared into his cabin to be alone with his rum. I didn't even know his name. He'd taken less than no notice of me, so I didn't ask. The better for me to be invisible, a shadow in the hold, scuttling by as unnoticed as the rats.

But as the sails unfurled one by one after we piloted away from the wharf, the building wind and threatening skies filled not only me with a creeping unease. Even the others, sea dogs all of them, looked askance at each other and at the sky and at the disappearing back of the master as he grunted down the companionway after slurring, "Make way, then, time and tide and all that," while drawing a vague circle in the air with one finger. The grumbling about this command was already noticeable, and we'd been under weigh less than an hour.

Another mesh of wet air fell between the *Reporter* and my home, and Boston receded to a lumpen horizon with only the steeple of the new North Church to mark the entire world I had ever known. It seems strange to recall it now, for I had valued that life so little and thrown it over so freely. But now as I saw it dropping away from me, vanishing into mist like a dream, I felt all at once overcome with sorrow and regret. For a wild moment, I imagined jumping overboard and flailing back home. I craved the boisterous squabbling of Mrs. Tomlinson's children and the tolling of the steeple bell and the soft straw of my private hayloft and even the old sots in the settle by the fire, nodding off over their bowls of pudding. My friends would never know what had become of me. Sarah would never know.

As I leaned on the rail watching the North Church steeple disappear by slow degrees into the gathering mists, I felt hot water pool in the corners of my eyes, and my nose flushed, and I rubbed my face with my fist.

I was still lost in sorrow for my disappearing home when the schooner approached a rocky outcropping, too mean to be properly deemed an island, called Nix's Mate. It stands in froth at the mouth of the Narrows between Gallops and Lovells Islands.

The sails bellied as the ship adjusted course to draw nearer, which even I, who'd never left the land, could see was something the schooner shouldn't do. I tightened my hold on the rail, nerves humming, watchful.

Then Edward Low pulled himself up tall and doffed his hat. Seneca did too. The other men in the crew put their heads together murmuring and then a few more hats came off. Kerchiefs swept off foreheads where hats were not in evidence. I didn't understand what was happening, but I pulled my stolen kerchief from my forehead to my neck just in case.

Presently the mists breathed apart, and Nix's Mate loomed into view. An eerie silence settled over us all on the deck of the *Reporter*. Even the wind grew quiet.

I wanted to ask what was amiss but didn't know yet who amongst our company could be trusted with my questions. But the answer became apparent as we drew slowly abreast of the rock.

On the lonely heap of gravel and guano stood a rough wooden scaffold, shaped broadly like an inverted L. From the end of the scaffold arm, I was horrified to behold the dangling body of a man, stiff and swollen in death. He was wrapped round and round in heavy chains, a few crows standing sentinel atop the scaffold and the unfortunate man's shoulders, eyeing us jealously as we coasted past. The body swayed slightly in the slackening wind, and the sound of the clanking chains came clearly to us over the water. One of the crows took off cawing as the body turned, and all at once we beheld the chained man's gruesome visage. The body's hair hung like tangled seaweed, and the nose had been eaten away. The cheeks were yellow and sunken and putrid, lips grimacing away from long yellow teeth in a slack jaw, giving it the grotesque semblance of a man laughing out loud. The horrible face's hollowed-out eyes were black holes, but all the same, I saw that this dreadful body, this *thing*, had once been my William Fly.

I had never spoken to him. But watching how he had been so broken, how authority was using his body to terrify us all, filled me with such confused rushes of feeling that I couldn't speak. Waves of feeling submerged me, first of pity, then indignance, then crushing sorrow and despair, and maybe something close to love. Each wave changed the shape of my heart, as rushing water wears away at stone. My heart grew tender but also hardened as we drifted past.

I wanted us to stop and cut him down.

I wanted him to know that I was sorry.

This is all ridiculous, Will, I said to him inside my mind. The rotting face laughed silently back at me. No sound reached my ears but the licking of the surf along our bow, the cawing of the crows, and the *clank clank, clank clank* of William Fly's chains.

"Now, why'd they have to go and do that," murmured the one called Orne, whose grizzled face betrayed something that might have passed for real sadness. "The miserable b—d."

On the scaffold above William Fly the black flag stitched with a grinning white death's head that had witnessed the moment of his execution was nailed. A truer warning of terror I could not imagine.

"Aye," said another man whose name I didn't know, also English and younger than Orne. "Now I'll have to stitch me up another one."

The one called Orne laughed. "Do us up a better one," he said in a low voice, and then he looked over at me. I stared hard at the disappearing horizon behind us, the tears on my face disguised by droplets of salt water and mist, making no sign that I might have been listening to them, or even that I might be a living thing at all.

Our stern pulled silently past Nix's Mate, and as the vee of our wake vanished into the waves the crows alit once again upon William Fly's shoulders.

"All right, Ned," said Seneca soberly. The crew on deck stirred to life, kerchiefs mopped over faces, hats back on and tilted against the beams of sun just breaking through the parting thunder clouds, lighting our way like an angel's path to heaven.

"Coming about," called Ned, and all hands moved smoothly to the high side of the *Reporter*, lining up next to me along the rail, lines all in our hands and ready, pulling together as we made sail for the open sea.

Chapter 5

I was certain I was going to be sick.

Finally, after the longest day of work of my short lifetime of long days of work, my watch was dismissed, and I was allowed to collapse my weary bones for four hours in a canvas hammock that smelled like another man's vinegary feet.

Never in all my days had I craved sleep more, and never had I been surrounded by such racket as my new shipmates snoring. Like sawing wood, a rasping and gasping and rattling of phlegm in the backs of open mouths from men felled by the twin hammers of exhaustion and rum. My hammock hung so slack I was bent almost in two. Back in my pallet at Ship Tavern, I could sprawl on my stomach or stick out my legs or lean my feet up the wall if I so desired. I yearned for the hayloft with its sweet grass smell and its soft breathing cat and even the mild itch of hay down the back of my shift. In the hammock I couldn't turn over. I could only lie still, my arms folded over my chest as they will be some day in my coffin, feet together, Billy's boots in a heap on the cabin sole beneath me, being all I owned in the world. I had no blanket nor any other clothes to wrap myself in, but the air was so close between decks that I had no need for it. My shipmates hung in hammocks on both sides of me, the whole of us swaying together with the motion of the ship. Rocking, as a cradle might, though it was hard for me to imagine that the rogues and blackguards abandoned to sleep around me had all once been innocent babes, rocked to sleep and loved by God.

For the most part.

"You should sleep," the man pressed into my starboard side said softly.

"I know," I answered. I couldn't see the speaker, though he was lying as close to me as a lover. My hammock rose on either side of my head like blinders, locking me in a crowded sort of solitude.

"Four hours will pass like four minutes," he said. I recognized the even-tempered authority of Seneca's voice. He had twice saved me from my bumbling ignorance. If he hadn't told me to drop the line, I might have been pulled to my death overboard or slammed into the mainmast with all my teeth shattered before you could say "Jack Tar." And it was surely he who propped me up against the rail to collect my wits after we came about. But I couldn't think why it might be so. Ned, the first mate, paid me no notice. And none of us had seen the master since before the tenders were even shipped. He was holed up somewhere in the aft cabin, with the nautical charts and instruments and, it was whispered, some very fine silver plate.

"Seneca?" I said after a time. Snores around us, and the creaking of rigging and wooden ribs and the occasional soft scratch of rat paws.

"Mmmmm." He sounded half-asleep himself.

"Can I ask you something?"

"If you must," he said, but I could hear a smile in his voice.

"Are you an Indian?" I asked.

I'd heard there was a tribe of that name somewhere out west. Stalking through the ancient wilderness where the woods were peopled by those Reverend Cotton Mather called devils. I'd often see those devils on market days in Boston with their babies and children giggling and playing tag between the apple barrels and sacks of flour.

A long silence unfolded in the hammock next to me, and for a time I thought the young man who seemed to be our second lieutenant had fallen asleep. But I heard air passing through a nose and felt a soft jostling through our hammocks, as though my shipmate were stifling laughter deep in his chest.

"No," he said at length.

That seemed all the answer I was likely to get, and I must content myself with it.

Then he added, "I am a philosopher."

I didn't know what a philosopher was. I don't rightly know now either. It somehow seemed improvident to ask. So I said nothing. Saying nothing is rarely the wrong choice, in my experience.

"And what about you, William Chandler?" he asked after a time. His voice took on a gently teasing tone. "Are you an Indian? Because I see you're no sailor."

I tucked my hands more tightly under my arms and considered if I, too, could have fallen asleep in time not to have to answer this question. On my other side an unseen man muttered some nonsense in his sleep and jostled me about as he dreamed.

"That's your name, right? Billy Chandler?" I felt my lieutenant's body against mine, the ropy tautness of his muscles. I wondered how he got that pink scar across his face. I wondered how Ned Low's nose was shattered.

My mouth had gone dry, and I didn't remember when I'd last had any water. I licked my lips, which were cracking from the salt. Whenever I closed my eyes, I saw the hideous yellow rotting grin of William Fly. If I opened them, I saw the wooden beams close over my head, swimmily lit with a lamp that swayed when all our bodies did, folding my stomach in on itself, and, oh my God, I was going to be sick.

Don't be sick, the strange calm voice inside my head instructed me. *Answer the man's question. You're Billy Chandler, aren't you? You're a cabin boy. Been a cabin boy forever. Cabin boys don't get sick.*

I swallowed thickly and said, "Not Billy. It's Will."

William Fly's spectral grin laughed long and hard in my ear. *Quiet*, I told him.

"Will," Seneca repeated, sounding tired. "Just as you like."

Something in his voice made me certain he knew I was lying. But it didn't seem to matter. *I accept your lie*, he didn't say. *You're safe amongst a company of liars. Liars one and all.*

Presently, I felt Seneca's body slacken, and before long heard the soft whistle of air through his sleeping nose. On deck overhead there were some muffled shouts and oaths and the beating of feet, and the schooner groaned over, sounds of canvas flapping, and shuddering all through *Reporter*'s beams as all of us in hammocks swung from one side to the other. My hand flew to my mouth to hold the vomit in, but a bilious burning flooded my nose.

I struggled upright, worming my feet between the hammocks under Seneca's unconscious haunch, and slid down until my bare feet touched the cabin sole. In a crouch I hurried to the forward companionway with its promise of fresh air and the head where I could void my guts in peace.

The air on deck, cool and fresh with dew, lightened my breath with relief. Lanterns winked on the quarterdeck and mainmast, and I saw the vague shapes of the skeleton crew at work keeping us trimmed and on course for wherever it was that we were going. Overhead the sky had cleared to reveal a tapestry of stars, bending down in every direction and touching the black surface of the ocean. I was accustomed to feeling small. But I had never felt myself to be a tiny speck floating at the center of a glittering infinity. My heart swelled at the beauty of it, feeling myself this warm speck of life within the eternal reach of time.

The bowsprit extended out into the blackness, carrying only a pale jib floating like a moth wing in the soft night air, framed on both sides by hemp webbing. My hands gripped the webbing and I bent double, a silent shudder waving through my body as the contents of my stomach flowed from my mouth and splashed into the water below. I hocked and spat and wiped my ragged lips on my wrist and lay for a time in the netting, watching the water curl away from the bow glimmering with blue phosphorescence, spattering the figurehead of a woman in eerie sheens of light. Just like the phosphorescence that traced the pebbles I threw into the harbor as a child.

I heard a whimpering, like a child lost, and wondered if the sound could be coming from myself. If I was so undone by fatigue and strangeness and hunger that I had lost the very sense of myself, of where the world ended and Hannah began.

"Quiet," I said aloud.

The whimpering continued from somewhere close by.

I clambered back to the bow, feeling better now that I was empty and the salty breeze had swept the sweat off my brow. There was some kind of argument happening in the stern, near the wheel, but it didn't concern me, so I paid it no heed. Instead, I listened for the whimpering, wondering if I could have happened upon a stowaway.

In the shadow under the starboard rail, behind a heavy coil of anchor rode, I discovered a thin and wiry cur with askew ears, cowering. When my hands found his warm and breathing sides trembling with life he yipped, and I discovered he had a paw snarled in some line. His hind feet scrabbled, trying to free himself, but he was caught fast.

"Hi, you little ratcatcher," I said to him softly, rubbing his ears before setting to work freeing the paw. He gave my hand a lick as I worked, his tongue warm and soft. Some shouts from aft reached us, but I didn't hear what was said.

"How'd you get yourself into this fix? You can't get far without know-ing the ropes, you know," I remarked, echoing something Orne had told me in a quiet moment on our watch. He'd named every single rope and line and sheet to me, pointing and explaining, but I had forgotten them almost as quickly as he named them. The complexity of the rigging was as baffling to me as if each gossamer thread of a spiderweb had its own useful name and purpose.

I had come into a small knife somewhere along the line and used it now to saw away at the coil that had ensnared the dog, trusting it not to be affixed to anything important.

"Then get them up!" a drunken voice slurred, the first words I'd heard clearly from the ongoing argument. It was the master, raining abuse on Ned, who was still at the wheel all these hours later. I didn't understand Ned's reply, but I clearly heard the master answer, "God d—n you, I said get them up!" then the unmistakable sound of the cocking of a flintlock pistol.

Instantly on the alert, I glanced up at the sound of the cocked ham-mer, just as my knife sliced through the last filament of line. Suddenly free, the dog bolted away, just as a rain of sparks and smoke filled the quarterdeck and a tongue of fire spat from the barrel of the pistol in the master's hand. Shouts exploded across the water, and without warning, the *Reporter* rounded up into the wind. Booms swung loose overhead and the jib on the bowsprit flapped slack, the sheets all jumping like frightened snakes. The wheel had been left to spin.

"He's shot!" someone screamed. I heard scuffling in the dark, as the sleeping watch down below swarmed to the deck at the sound of trouble. Someone must have grabbed the wheel, as we came sloppily about, but when the crew tried to trim the jib it sailed forward like a pale angel, its clew waving free.

In freeing the little cur, I had sawed the jib sheet in half.

Fear flamed hot across my cheeks as I realized my mistake, and I ran double time to join my shipmates, my knife hidden in the waist of my stolen pantaloons, my feet bare. I fell in behind Orne and some others, shoving and shouting, someone giving orders, and someone else countermanding them just as fast. In the chaos I trusted no one would cotton to my being the culprit.

"Is he dead?" cried Seneca. The stern lantern had shattered, leaving a guttering flame on the deck, and we were lit only by the lamp hanging on the mainmast, which was swinging wildly with each roll of the *Reporter* in the open ocean.

Someone lit another lantern and held it up. There, sprawled on the quarterdeck in a halo of blood, lay Ned Low. Red-black spatters crossed his face and neck and shoulder. His eyes were open, staring at us on the larboard rail.

Seneca crouched next to him, touching his forehead.

"Ned," he said.

The master was held fast by two of the crew, his arms pinned behind his back. I could smell him from here, the same sour stink that clung to all the most pickled regulars tweaking my apron strings when I passed them in the Ship Tavern dining room. His blouse was undone at the throat, and his face shone with drink and sweat. The pistol had fallen to his feet.

"I gave him an order!" the master bellowed.

"Shut up!" one of the crew holding him cried, a squinty-eyed fellow with a kerchief on his head. The master bucked and struggled, but his captors overcame him when one delivered a blow to his belly, and the master groaned and fell quiet. I was hiding behind Orne's elderly bulk, my eyes leaping between the man who was supposed to be in charge of our ship and the helmsman he had laid out for no reason. Was Ned also going to die before my very eyes?

"Will!" Seneca shouted. "Tie his hands."

I was staring goggle-eyed when Orne jabbed me with an elbow. "Go on, boy, do as you're told," he said.

Will. Me. I'm Will. I'd forgotten.

I found myself confronted with a stark and probably fatal choice.

If I did as Seneca demanded and tied up the sailing master, then I could be tried for mutiny when the ship reached port and the log was read by whatever syndicate had backed the voyage. That is, assuming the master put the rebellion down and the voyage continued as planned. If the master put the mutiny down, and authority learned of my betrayal, I would be hanged. But on the other hand, who knew what might become of me in this moment if I refused? I thought about the glittering infinity around us, the complete desolation and cold of the blackest heart of the sea. How long would I survive, after they threw me overboard? I could swim, sort of. A skill that I now saw would only serve to prolong the agony of my death in the belly of the whale, as alone and forsaken as Jonah.

In half a second I determined it was better to be dead at some vague future moment than dead right now, and so I leapt to obey. I looped some rope once, twice, three times around the master's struggling wrists. My hands shook as I made the knot fast, and I kept my eyes down, my shoulders hunched up to make myself invisible.

"You little b—d," the master snarled at me, his breath hot and sour in my face. "You think you'll eat again, on this voyage? I'll tip your grog over the side while you watch, you son of a motherless w—e."

I made him no answer, but Orne quietly said, "Good boy," when I returned to my place at the rail with my shipmates, and an unseen hand clapped me roughly on the back. I was welcomed warmly into this ignominious mutiny. To think I was barely days away from a time when my darkest crime was the scuttling of Ephraim's favorite mug.

Seneca was bent over the prostrate form of Ned Low, and the little cur that I had freed turned up nearby, watching the proceedings with soft brown eyes. The wheel spun this way and that as the schooner wallowed in irons, mainsail flopping, boom swinging over our heads like a pendulum.

A groan came out of the first officer's mouth, and his pale eyes fluttered.

"Ned," Seneca said gently. "You're shot."

"Humnnngh," Ned groaned.

His lieutenant holding him by the shoulder, Ned Low rolled to seated. He gingerly touched his neck and shoulder, probing, exploring, and looked curiously at his fingers when they came away red. He pulled the shirt off over his head and used it to wipe his face and torso, which served only to smear the blood around until he looked painted for war. The whites of his pale eyes shone dreadfully in the lanternlight.

When he had taken the measure of all that had transpired, Ned Low said slowly, "Help me up."

Ned wasn't tall. He might have been nearly as short as me, though more stockily built. He flexed his arm a time or two on the wounded side, testing it for soundness. Then he rolled his head back on his neck. We all heard the crack. His wound seemed superficial, as though the ball had only grazed him. Or maybe even missed him completely, and the raw and oozing wound was a burn from the wadding. His naked chest was streaked with blood and sweat and grime, and his hands hung loose at his sides, empty. His gaze settled on the master's face and grew hard. With the change of Ned Low's look and carriage, a strange energy shot through all of us assembled on the deck. I didn't understand how I knew, but I perceived that the situation was no longer under control.

Perhaps sensing the same thing, the prisoner paled.

"This is madness!" the sailing master shouted. "We're off course! I gave him an order! I . . . We're heading due south! Due south, I say! See for yourselves! It's . . . We needed all hands! I told him to . . . I said . . ."

"A knife," Ned Low quietly commanded no one, holding out his open hand and waiting for his will to be served.

"Unhand me! Wickham, Granger, take hold of this man and clap him in irons and I'll double your rations!" The master screamed. His struggles against his captors took on renewed urgency.

"Give him your knife, boy," Orne hissed in my ear, and I was too transfixed with fear to argue. I set my rigging knife, hilt-first, in Ned Low's waiting palm.

His gaze didn't move from the master's terrified face.

"This is madness! Mutiny! You'll hang, the lot of you! You'll hang, by God!" the master's voice rose higher. "I'll see you hanged before God and all that's holy, and the lot of you cast into the flaming pits of hell where Satan will have you for his footstools!"

"You talk too much," Ned Low informed the master of the *Reporter*. The knife blade flashed, so quick I didn't see it move.

A gasp of horrified silence seized the crew. Then one by one, my shipmates started to laugh. Fingers pointed. A high-pitched scream, like the whistle of life being boiled out of a lobster, pealed out of the master's open, reddening mouth.

At first, I didn't understand what had happened. All the master's teeth were bared, his mouth red and gaping as though he were hysterically laughing. Blood began to drip in a steady stream off the end of his chin.

"Here, you little beast," Ned Low said to the dog. "Come."

The dog trotted over, wagging his stump of a tail.

Ned Low bent as though to offer it something from his hand. The master's scream became a guttural cry of horror, and the laughter amongst the crew increased.

"No, no, Ned, not the cur. He craves finer meat than that!" An unseen man shouted from amongst our number.

Then I understood. And when the understanding came to me, I was seized with unreasoning panic.

Ned Low had sliced off the master's lips.

A dizzying lightness swam through my head, and I was grateful that my stomach was already empty. I glanced around quickly, reading the expressions of my shipmates, most of whom were laughing like they were watching a tremendous joke. Some few of them wore on their faces the same grim disbelief, denial, and panic that I felt, and I wondered if they, like me, were weighing the theft of a tender and how likely we might be to survive alone at sea if we tried to row to safety.

The answer, I saw immediately, was not likely at all. I was trapped here, in the middle of the ocean, party to a mutiny, being led by a man of a cruelty I hadn't imagined possible in a soul that could still be called human.

Ned said, "Right you are. Let's give this fine gentleman a last meal to fill his mouth before his send-off."

He stuck the tip of my rigging knife into the tongue of flame burning on deck within the winking shards of the shattered lamp. A grotesque smell of roasting meat drifted through the air. He pulled the knife out, blew a coil of smoke away from the two shriveled worms of flesh, and thrust it into the red hole at the center of the master's face, forcing his chin closed with a hand until he swallowed. One amongst us bent and vomited, but I didn't know his name. I tried to make my face impassive, impenetrable, but I am certain that I failed.

"All right," said Ned Low. "Toss him."

"No! No, please! I have money. There's plate in the cabin!" the master screamed, bucking between the two sailors who were holding him prisoner, his words distorted with blood and the loss of the letter *P*. "For all that's holy, untie my hands at least! No! No, please!"

Ned Low smiled the grim, sharp smile of a wolf and said, "Nobody's holy here, sir."

I had never witnessed a grown man so alive with terror as the sailing master in the eternity of time that yawned between the moment his feet left the deck to the moment we heard the distant splash of his body hitting the water. At once the screams vanished, and I felt a bump through my bare feet that must have been the master's body driven under the keel of the wallowing ship. Most of my shipmates were laughing. I could not make myself laugh along with them. I could only stand mute, wondering what might become of me, delivered as I was into the hands of a madman.

"Enough," said Ned Low sharply. "Let's get to it."

A few of the sailors hung back together, murmuring nervously, men who presumably thought they'd signed on to a fruit packet for an easy voyage and a steady wage. Their options, like mine, had disappeared when the unfortunate master—I never did learn his name, for after that night he was never spoken of again—was swallowed by the deep. The rest looked to Seneca for guidance, who split us into gangs and quickly set us to work, one man bringing the wheel under control, some others putting their hands to lines, a few more climbing out along the bowsprit to bring the flapping jib to heel.

Someone had gone below and brought up a cask that looked to have been liberated from the master's cabin, with some pewter and a few silver cups. I'd never touched a silver cup before. It felt heavy and fine when it was placed in my hands, and I yearned immediately to keep it for myself. The cask was staved in with a knife hilt and red wine splashed out into cups and mouths and down the fronts of shirts. Someone beside me rubbed some wine into my hair, laughing. The frightening feeling of surging anarchy receded by degrees with every swallow of wine down our throats.

"Three cheers, for Edward Low!" cried Orne as the cups were passed from hand to hand then up into the rigging and fore and aft until everyone had one, and some had two. "From here on out, we only drink wine when we run out of rum! Hip hip!"

"Hurrah!" the sailors shouted.

"Hip hip!"

"Hurrah!" They shouted louder, my own hesitant voice amongst them this time.

"Hip hip!"

"Hurrah!"

The sails caught the wind and the Madeira moistened my mouth and soothed my stomach and warmed my feet as the *Reporter*—was she still the *Reporter?*—settled into her course, cutting sharply through the star-glittered night, heading due south. I may have even been smiling when a quiet voice said, "Here."

It was Ned Low, handing me back my rigging knife with a cold smile.

NEW YORK

Somehow they were already in Connecticut. Marian realized she must have fallen asleep, rocked against the window by the *clack clack, clack clack* of the train. She yawned and rubbed her eyes and looked around. A few men reading newspapers and smoking. Some college boys in sweaters with the letter *Y* on them, laughing and shoving each other. So they'd just passed New Haven. Not too long now, about forty-five minutes. The face she found in her compact had puffy eyes and the pink impressions of the train window curtain pressed into her cheek.

Marian hated to travel and generally found reasons not to even go into Boston. Perhaps because of the looks she would get, though more women wore slacks now. And wearing a dress was no better. She felt like a frump in costume in a dress, with the skirt length hitting at just the right part of her shin to make her seem shorter and wider and awkwarder and generally more laughable. Add a tiny hat and the whole thing was just a disaster. She knew, in a real sense, that most people in the world outside Cambridge (or in it, for that matter) were too absorbed in their own affairs to notice an uncomfortable woman of a certain age stumping along in heels and struggling with her suitcase. But the committee of strangers she imagined meeting daily to pass judgment on her life lived inside her own mind, weighing in hourly with their whispered chorus of disappointments. It was sitting with her on the train even now. She knew she was being irrational, knew that for all intents and purposes she didn't exist. Certainly, to the Yalies, but also to just about anyone else besides herself.

"Bridgeport!" a conductor called, walking up the aisle and collecting ticket stubs and helping a matron down with her hatbox. "Bridgeport next!"

Out the window Marian gazed on rolling golden marshlands dotted with nesting boxes—herons? She didn't know—and the occasional sailboat with sails furled. Beyond the marshes the quiet inlets of Connecticut drew apart along shallow sandbars before opening into the Atlantic Ocean—well, no, she supposed it was Long Island Sound, but really, it was all the same to her. A great blue-black expanse of nothing. Marian didn't care for the beach any more than she cared for traveling. There were sharks at the beach, for one thing. And whoever thought swimming in wool was a good idea? The clinging, and the wet, and the sopping, and the standing in the clinging and wet. It was always either far too hot or far too cold.

Marian considered if there was time to swing by the restaurant car, and though she determined yes, there was just enough time, she decided against it. Her Hamilton wristwatch read almost four o'clock. Her appointed meeting was at six.

She wondered if he would ask her to stay for dinner. Something masculine and exotic no doubt—swordfish? Probably. But then, it was just as likely he would have double-booked, standing up brusquely halfway through their conference to indicate that the time for their meeting was over, and what a pleasure it had been to see her. He would then excuse himself for a standing engagement with some gentlemen who were getting up an expedition to the Arctic, or to Grenada, or to the Yucatán, or to wherever he felt like lavishing his money these days. In that case she would have to dine alone. She wondered if the Columbia faculty club would take her without a letter. Surely, they must. Mustn't they? Assuming they admitted women.

Barnard then. She could dine at Barnard.

It was cold for early autumn, though it would be warmer in the city, but she'd only packed one pair of gloves and her cloth coat. The marsh grasses blurring past the train window were touched hard with frost, and she wondered what happened to those forgotten sailboats when the winter snows blanketed the seashore. It was amazing, and yet not amazing at all, that the ocean could swallow so much snow.

Kay's manuscript rode on the seat next to her, buckled into a leather satchel. As Marian gazed out over the chill expanse of water, she thought of Hannah Masury. If there was a Hannah Masury. There wasn't, of course, which was why her steady, predictable reappearance in Marian's thoughts was so irksome. Marian hated wasting so much time thinking about someone who didn't exist. But what might Hannah have felt, trapped on a tiny wooden dot surrounded by the desert nothingness of ocean? The very idea gave Marian the creeping horrors. Being a sailor, Samuel Johnson had noted, was like being in prison with the added possibility of being drowned. It was, Marian could confidently say, the only thing that she knew about sailing.

Her watch read nearly five by the time she dragged her suitcase up the brownstone steps of the American Association of University Women building in the East Thirties. It was only a short yet frightfully expensive taxicab ride from Pennsylvania Station, the echoing cavern of glass and steel through which Marian passed, one tiny black dot amongst an ocean of tiny black dots all on their way somewhere quickly. The AAUW felt comfortable and genteel and manageable, with a worn rug in the entryway and a bored-looking woman of indeterminate age paging through the afternoon *Herald-Tribune* behind the front desk. On a side table, tea in a samovar, with a halo of sliced lemons arranged nicely on a plate.

"Dr. Marian Beresford," Marian said to the woman behind the desk.

"Ah." The woman bent over a logbook and ran her hand down the page. Her finger waves didn't move. Marcelled as well as if they'd been carved in agate. "Here you are. First time?"

Marian said, somewhat stiffly, "Not in New York. But yes."

The woman's smile grew uncertain, but she presented a key on an awkward wooden fob and said, "Well, in that case. Welcome back."

"Thank you," said Marian, wondering who was going to carry her suitcase up the stairs. The brownstone was small and narrow and clearly had no elevator.

They stared at each other for a long moment, the check-in woman's smile faltering before she continued, "Your room's just at the top of the stairs there," and pointed.

The suitcase bumped hollowly on each step, hitting Marian's heels as she went up.

The room was pleasant enough and clean, with a twin bed and a pitcher of water on the end table and a small sink and mirror and a framed print of a building at Bryn Mawr and chintz curtains. Marian peeked through the blinds behind the curtain and found her view to be of some kind of air shaft.

Well, then. Time to go uptown.

She opened the clasps of her suitcase and looked down at the tweed skirt suit she had packed to wear to this meeting, with its silk flower corsage and the small fox stole meant to be worn round her neck, its dead paws clutching its own luxuriant tail. The stole's sewn-closed eyes made it look like a weasel had curled up and fallen asleep in her clothes.

Marian closed the suitcase, slung the leather satchel with Kay's manuscript over her head, and left.

SHE EMERGED FROM the Interborough Rapid Transit line, crowded with tired people on their way home to the Bronx, carrying newspapers and lunch boxes and studiedly ignoring the hobo who came shambling through the car in flapping shoes stuffed with newspaper. At the top of the stairs Marian emerged on 110th Street just as the bells in the unfinished cathedral started to toll through the deepening darkness. St. John the Divine stood over the neighborhood like a broken medieval palace that had had one tower lopped off by a giant, or the shattering of a bomb. A monument to false history, begun only thirty-odd years ago. They'd run out of money, just like everyone else. Now in the garden next door a modest Hooverville had taken root, with lean-tos assembled of castoff plywood and tarpaulin.

If the bells were tolling it was already six, and Marian was late.

He hated when she was late.

She hurried, holding her lapels closed against the sharpening wind. When she finally arrived at the door of the Explorers Club her cheeks were reddened with equal parts windburn and aggravation, and her hair was askew.

"Good evening, sir," said the gentleman who held swept open the door, and who saw his mistake as soon as Marian shrugged off her coat, betraying his awareness of it with a nervous fluttering of eyelids.

"Good evening, Warwick," Marian said, laying her coat and gloves over his arm and brushing her hair back with a gesture borrowed from Marlene Dietrich, which she had yet to perfect. "It's nice to see you again."

"Indeed," he said, mildly appalled while straightening the gloves. "Welcome back."

"Do you know where I can find him?"

"Of course, Dr. Beresford," said Warwick. "You can find Dr. Beresford in the lounge."

"Thank you," Marian said.

"And your pocketbook?" Warwick asked.

"No," said Marian, her grip tightening around the satchel. "Thank you."

Marian moved down a close wood-paneled hallway tinted with tobacco smoke and passed through a doorway framed on either side by mounted, massive elephant tusks. She brushed a fingertip along the pitted ivory as she went by.

The lounge of the Explorers Club was, as the evenings grew late, a sometimes notorious place in which women were not customarily admitted. But this early in the afternoon it was still quiet, with a few men in deep leather armchairs reading under framed photographs of themselves, or men identical to them, smiling into the sweltering tropical or frigid midnight suns of fifteen and twenty and thirty years ago. Stained expedition flags hung from the ceiling, and out of the shadows of heavy oak paneling loomed grizzly bears, their teeth bared in frozen snarls, claws poised ready to destroy. Somewhere it was rumored they also had a stuffed dodo, though Marian had never seen it.

On one side of the room a pleasant fire crackled in an ornate stone fireplace, and extending from one of the leather wing chairs, angled away from the door, Marian observed a familiar pair of long legs, with feet in worn oxfords crossed at the ankles. A small end table nearby held a tumbler containing one thick finger of Scotch, decanted, Marian knew, from a private stash maintained in the row of wooden lockers behind the bar. The floor before the fireplace was warmed by a splayed tiger skin, its taxidermied face staring glassy-eyed and open-mouthed at Marian, its great paws pinned under armchair legs.

"Hello, Papa," Marian said to the back of the wing chair.

"Hello, Monkey." A weathered hand dropped to the Scotch glass and picked it up, but her father didn't stand.

The wing chair was not paired with another one, and Marian had to retrieve one from a grouping a few feet away and drag it across the tiger skin to sit next to her father by the fire.

"It's seven past," said the elder Dr. Beresford.

Her father had gone gray before Marian was born, and for a time the juxtaposition of his relative youth with a shock of steel-colored hair had added to the vague sense of excitement and danger that suffused the air around John Beresford. No, "danger" wasn't the right word. Her father was in no way a dangerous man. Remote with his children rather than overbearing or unpredictable, slim and hardened with the exertions of mountaineering and yachting and whatever else he did when he was not at home, which was most of the time. But still, "danger" was the word that came to Marian's mind first, when thinking about her father. Even now, when the crags and furrows of his face had finally begun to catch up with his hair, which had faded further from steel-gray to cotton-white with the passing of the years, as he lounged carelessly in an armchair sipping Scotch from 1919, there crackled about him an imprecise and uncomfortable air of risk.

"I'm sorry," she said. "I hope you weren't waiting too long."

He put down the tumbler. "Well," he said, but that was all.

A long, awkward moment unfolded between them, which Marian filled, as had long been her habit, by withdrawing a slim cigarette from the little silver case, lighting it, and blowing twin streams of smoke from her nostrils as if she were a detective in the movies.

Her father emitted a carefully calibrated cough.

"So," he said when he was finished expressing his wordless disapproval. "You're looking well. Where are you staying?"

"The AAUW," said Marian, in a tone that came out sounding more defiant than she intended.

"If you won't stay at the house," her father said patiently, "you could at least join the Colony. Your mother . . ." He didn't finish his thought. "And it's so much more . . ."

Marian waited to hear what her late mother's society ladies' club was so much more of. Appropriate? Elegant? Acceptable?

"Convenient," he finished.

"John?" a man in an outdated sort of hacking jacket happened by and stepped into her father's field of vision with his hand extended before Marian could answer, not that she had an answer in mind. While her father stood to shake hands and exchange a back slap and some laughter and discussions of some trip or other that they either had both been on, or both intended to take, or both would never take again, Marian unbuckled her satchel and withdrew Kay's manuscript. In the raking firelight she saw that the cover had at one time borne a gilt impression, or drawing, but the gilding had long since been worn away.

Her father sat down again after some minutes, still laughing, saying, "Hah hah hah, oh. Elk," as if Marian had been paying attention to their conversation and was in on the joke. She smiled thinly.

"Yes, well," said Marian.

"Indeed," her father said.

"This is it," she said, patting the water-warped bundle of pages on her lap.

"Ah," said the elder Dr. Beresford. "May I?"

She passed it to him and leaned back in the wing chair, feeling the warmth of the fire press against her cheek. When the waiter came by she pointed at her father's Scotch glass and held up two fingers and said, "Thank you."

John Beresford opened the manuscript with delicate hands. Marian tried to read his face, following along with where he was, divining which fragment he was digesting of Hannah's unbelievable story. The crags were hard to decipher.

Her Scotch appeared, and Marian sipped it while she watched her father slowly turning one page, and then another. One of his hands reached thoughtfully into an interior pocket in his jacket and withdrew a pair of half-moon spectacles. The lenses caught the reflection of the fire.

He was about a third of the way in when he closed the book definitively and handed it back to her.

"It's a fake," he said with authority.

Even though he was only articulating what Marian herself had insisted to Kay, she felt deflated. The warmth of the Scotch on the back of her neck took away some of the sting. But even so. She had wanted him to say something different.

"What makes you so sure?" she said.

"Well, for one thing, Edward Low died in 1724. And William Fly was hanged in 1726. Simple enough mistake. Probably thought no one would notice, since the years are so close together."

"Who thought?" said Marian.

"Why, the fellow who wrote it," said her father.

A few other dusty-looking gentlemen came in together through the door between the elephant tusks. They hesitated long enough to catch John Beresford's attention, and to communicate by finger pointing and tipped thumbs that they would be getting drinks and waiting for him at the table in the corner, nearest the taxidermied polar bear growling over its meal of taxidermied seal. Her father lifted his chin and conveyed through signs that he would be over shortly, he was just finishing a meeting and would only be a few more minutes, and then Marian knew that she would be dining alone.

"I'd believe it was written in the eighteenth century," her father continued, "or maybe the early nineteenth. But I'd say it was a work of fiction. Thought he'd put in one of the most notorious pirates in history to sweeten it up and sell more copies."

"That's what I thought," Marian began.

"Well, of course. You've read *The Pirates Own Book*, I suppose?" Without waiting for Marian to confirm or deny his assumption, John Beresford continued, "After a career of infamous cruelty Edward Low's men finally mutinied aboard his ship the *Merry Christmas*, which had been a merchantman from Virginia, in retribution after he murdered some poor underling in his sleep. They'd had enough and set him adrift in the Caribbean without food or water. He was rescued, only to be hanged by the French at Martinique. In 1724."

"Yes, but," Marian said.

"Still and all," her father continued, "he did live in Boston for a time. So he's a good enough choice, if you're going to get the story wrong."

"Yes, but," Marian said again. "Johnson says something different."

"Oh? And what's that?" Her father looked at the corner where the men were waiting for him, and Marian knew that the time in which she could command his attention was drawing to a close. How long had he allotted her? Fifteen minutes? Twenty?

"*A General History of the Pyrates* is more contemporary to Edward Low's time than *Pirates Own Book*, which was written a hundred years later. Johnson says he was last seen in a ship called the *Fancy*, raiding off the Canary Islands," Marian told him.

"Indeed," he said. "And when was that written?"

"1724," said Marian. "That's why it doesn't mention William Fly."

"Well, there you go," said her father.

"It doesn't say anything about Edward Low being set adrift or hanged. It says nothing had been heard of him for some time, and he was presumed to still be alive, possibly active off Brazil."

"But it also notes a rumor that he was lost at sea, with all hands," said her father, as though he had played her into a corner at chess.

"That only proves that nobody actually knows how Edward Low died. Or when. The *Fancy*," Marian pressed, "was an eighty-ton schooner, probably fore-and-aft rigged, which Edward Low used to harass New England fishing fleets beginning around 1723."

"And?"

"And the author of this manuscript"—Marian couldn't quite bring herself to name Hannah Masury as the author of the manuscript, but even so, *someone* was the author—"describes the *Reporter* as being a schooner, of less than one hundred tons."

"My dear—" Her father was patient. "Fishing schooners of less than one hundred tons were among the most common vessels operating on the Atlantic coast in the eighteenth century. That's hardly a coincidence."

"But she also describes it as worm-eaten, as though it hadn't been dry-docked in a long time. Maybe ever. That's the kind of damage an oak ship might endure if it's careened in tropical shoals instead of hauled out of the water," Marian pointed out. "Which is how pirates typically maintained and refit their ships. Since they'd be arrested and hanged in port. They'd find shallow shoals in the tropics where no one was looking for them and use anchors to heel them over on one side, and then the other, to clean the bottom and do basic repairs."

Her father had been on the point of swallowing the last mouthful of his Scotch as a prelude to standing up, which was his habitual way of drawing discussions with Marian to a close. But the tumbler paused before it reached his lips.

"But the *Fancy* was captured," he said. "By the Royal Navy. Low mistook a naval ship for a whaler and they beat him up one side and down the other in 1723. That's why he wasn't in it during the mutiny."

"No," said Marian. "That's a common mistake. I checked. The *Ranger* was captured in that battle. A sloop that was part of Edward Low's fleet. The *Fancy* escaped. Golden Age pirates often sailed in fleets with the ships they captured. Not in one lone pirate ship like Captain Hook in *Peter and Wendy*."

Her father caught someone's eye over her shoulder and signaled that he would be a few more minutes.

"The author also mentions that the name *Reporter* was almost worn completely away," Marian went on. She could tell his interest was piqued. She had always been closely attuned to the rare instances when she could command her father's attention. "The manuscript describes the name on the stern as being spelled *RE OR ER*."

"All right." A gleam shone in John Beresford's eye. The earpiece of his spectacles tapped a tooth. "I'm listening."

Marian pulled the stub of her train ticket out of her jacket pocket.

"What if," she said, opening a pen, "instead of the name being worn away, it was hastily painted over?"

She wrote *RE OR ER* in block letters across the blank end of the ticket stub. Her father leaned in to watch what she was doing.

"How many lines does it take," Marian said, drawing carefully, "to make *RE OR ER* from something like . . . *F NC EY?*"

She managed to do it in only six.

Chapter 6

∽

*W*ho amongst you is a married man?"

We stood assembled on deck in the violet light of dawn, many of us the worse for wear. Hammers played a merry tune in my temples from the night's exertions of wine. The sails were well set and we'd picked up the trades, so for the first time since our mutiny, there was little sailing work for us to do. After some hours of splicing and coiling and scrubbing and cooking up salt beef and eating it and then a few rounds of singing and dancing, and after conferring with Seneca over the charts, Ned Low had summoned us all together to address us as a body.

A few hands went up here and there.

"I won't have married men in my crew," announced Ned Low. A palpable tension thrummed around the few men whose hands were now rapidly disappearing from our midst. "But I've no quarrel with you, who've stood with me." Barely audible sighs of relief. "You'll be off-loaded at the next port. Sen?"

"New York," Seneca said. He had taken charge of the navigation instruments and charts from the cabin of the murdered sailing master, which, together with the few arms aboard and the master's silver plate service, were the sole items of value apart from a small shipment of lumber in our hold. "You'll all be well fixed to find another berth, or make your way back to Boston, as you prefer."

"With what pay?" a voice called from within our number.

"You'll have your pay," Ned Low promised. "But we've some business to take care of first."

Those of our number who had sailed with Ned Low before smiled and murmured amongst themselves. The others, like myself, felt our stomachs twist with worry. No business of Ned Low's could be good.

Now that my fate rested wholly in his lip-slicing hands, I had begun to pay closer attention to the mate who I had at first taken for little more than an overworked helmsman. Near as I could fathom, Ned Low was actually many men imprisoned in one compact sailor's body, with never a sign of which one might be shown to the world at any given moment. He was one minute laughing and swallowing Madeira in his open mouth, spraying it in the air like a mermaid, and the next cracking one of my shipmates across the jaw for laughing too loudly. He'd returned my knife to me with a look that bordered on thanks, then shouted at one of the men who'd helped him subdue the master for standing too close to him. The only creature aboard who seemed insulated from his wrath, apart from Seneca, his second-in-command, was the stump-tailed stowaway who'd passed much of the foregoing night carried about in Ned Low's arms being fed rum-soaked bread until it was wobbling drunk and fell asleep. I was used to scenting the danger on certain men when I passed them by. Indeed, I had accustomed myself to sniffing for it whenever someone unknown to me sat down in the tavern and waited to be brought his dram. But Ned Low's danger was unscentable to me. Which only made me more wary. I kept as much space between myself and him as I was able.

Seneca too had so far escaped his wrath, though whether that was a matter of affection or utility or something else—debt?—I was powerless to divine. He was certainly as hard and pitiless as Ned Low, but less mercurial. Seneca presented himself as a man who would not easily change his mind once he had weighed one's character and made his determination for himself. Though the weighing and the determining might take some time, and he had not entirely decided yet about me. I observed my shipmates subtly jostling for his attention and approval, saw the way they watched him to learn which way the wind was like to blow. As though Sen were the Ned charmer, or the barometer that could tell us when a storm was gathering beyond our sight over the horizon.

"First, it's time we elected a captain," Ned Low proclaimed.

"Isn't he the captain now?" I whispered to Orne. Orne had quickly become grandfather to us all. His face was seamed from a lifetime in weather, his knuckles bent permanently into a grip for holding fast. I stuck close to him, watching, listening to him sift out tidbits of knowledge and understanding. He was patient with all my "Orne, what's this?" and "Orne, who's that?" and "Orne, how does this go?" I gathered I was not the first hapless cabin boy to apprentice himself to the old sailor from Marblehead.

"Not yet," Orne told me. "When you go out upon the account, the captain is chosen by popular acclaim. The people give him the authority, and the people can take it away."

I couldn't hide my surprise. I had never found myself in a company such as this, where anything was done by popular acclaim. Not since I was a child on the wharves in my few and precious idle hours, playing with the others, but even then, popular acclaim somehow always aligned with the interests of those children who were biggest.

"I vote Ned Low," proposed Granger, a reedy fellow who'd worked in the Charles Town yards, and who had landed the blow on the belly of the murdered sailing master.

"I'm for Seneca," said someone behind me, a young fellow named Jacob with a cauliflower ear.

"Hasn't he got a family name too?" I asked Orne.

"Sure," Orne eyed me with amusement. "And if you want to be run through with a cutlass, you'll ask what it is."

"All right," said Ned briskly. If he was irritated that he didn't win by default of being unchallenged, he didn't show it. He folded his hands under his armpits, standing with his sturdy feet wide apart. "Show of hands. Who's for Sen?"

Some hands went up. Not quite half, by my tally. I hesitated, then inched my own hand partway up, only as high as my shoulder. One of the fellows whose name I didn't know yet, but I knew was from the Cape Verde islands, tallied up and said, "That's eleven."

"And who's for me?" Ned lifted his chin when he said this, which was the only indication I could see that he actually wanted to win.

Just about every hand went up, but not all. I looked left and right and then mine went up too.

"That's twenty," said the tallier. I think there were twenty-four of us on board. So I wasn't alone with my hedged bets.

"Twenty takes it. Captain I'll be, for the time being, and I propose Sen for quartermaster. Who's with me?" Ned's cold blue eye gleamed in well-concealed triumph.

"Aye!" everyone shouted.

I stood by amazed as they quickly established who amongst our number should be doctor (a Spanish Creole called Jimenez with a barber for a father); mate—that was Orne, my grizzled interlocutor, as popular with the others as he had already proven to be with me. Gunner in charge of the meager few cannon and arms shipped aboard was given to a shaggy character named Bartholomew, called Black Bart though he was paler than water. And boatswain would be a skin-and-bones carpenter's mate named Wickham who was only twenty. I recognized Wickham as the one who'd bemoaned the loss of his flag. A hangdog fellow named John Somethingorother was already down one leg, moving about with a broomstick lashed to his stump. He'd been brought aboard as cook, and cook he remained, with plenty of jokes thrown his way about the fineness of his cuisine and the years he spent in France learning to fricassee rabbit whiskers and flavor them with squid ink and air.

Our company as a whole were largely English, if our citizenship could be fixed to any single spot on any single map, though sundry others of us hailed from Spain, America, France, the West Indies, and the western coast of Africa. But in truth, none of us were citizens of the lands where we were born. To a man each of us, save me, had lived on board ships longer than we had lived any one place on land. Orne had passed more of his days in St. Petersburg, on the northern coast of

Russia in the eerie light of the midnight sun, than he ever did in Marblehead. Jimenez spoke better French than Spanish, owing to his time in Louisiana, though he was born in Spanish Florida. We all belonged to a shadow realm, subjects of no monarch, in constant motion, touching down here in Port-au-Prince, here in Madagascar, beached in Shanghai, locked up for a night in Saint-Malo, passing by Fastnet Rock in a blow, drifting by St. Helena in the doldrums, losing all our money in Port Royal, catching the fever in New Orleans, running aground off Cape Cod. The ocean was our country, our authority, and our home. Our allegiances were as shifty and ephemeral as the wind that carried us at present into the cloudless blue Atlantic day, all sails set, hull skating over the rollers, rising and falling in a merry shower of spray.

We had not been free people. We had been press-ganged into the Royal Navy and fled, sold ourselves to a merchantman, gone unpaid, mutinied, fled again, secured a letter of marque to turn privateer, gone raiding trusting the flags of truce would not make us criminals. A mistimed raid is all it takes to turn pyrate. Or a mutiny. Then, in the narrow, fateful time between going out on our own account and authority building the scaffold to make examples of us, it would be a merry life we would lead, with ease and liquor and fairness of spoils. And government by popular acclaim.

A merry life, and a short one.

Well, so be it. Mine was bound to have been short anyway.

Off the larboard rail the water bubbled to life as something marbled and massive arose like a Leviathan from the deep. It was then that I spotted my first broaching whale. A heavy fluke lifted lazily from the water, dripping, arcing downward and vanishing whence it came, to tangle in the arms of the kraken. It felt for all the world like a benediction from God, who had seen fit to set us free.

As for me? I, Will Chandler, would be cabin boy, equal in dignity if not duties to an ordinary seaman. The more useful I made myself, and the handier I became, the greater my share might grow. I would make it my business to go aloft in the rigging at the first chance, to hand, reef, and steer and be rated able as soon as I could.

You are probably wondering if I feared for my already-threadbare honor at this moment. Perhaps I should have. We had, almost all of us, passed through the ranks of the Royal Navy at one time or another, with its infamous rigors of rum, buggery, and the lash. Buggery is a hanging offense in the Navy, and for good reason. A boy like me would be as likely as any to catch the eye of men long at sea and thirsty, even with the threat of death dangling in a noose overhead. In weighing this possibility, I considered that it would be wisest to submit and keep my secret and maybe even earn some special regard from whoever it was my suitor might be. It was a sin, to be sure, but so was everything else. It wouldn't be so different from the tavern life I had already known. But I discovered that life aboard a pyrate ship unfolded along a delicate balance of self-determination, uneasy trust, barely restrained violence, and something like faith. Our obligations to each other were spelled out clearly, as I was about to learn, and woe betide anyone who dared to violate them.

After establishing our corps of officers, such as it was, and organizing us into watches for sleep and work, Ned and Sen introduced what they called "the Articles," delivered unto us with all the gravity of Reverend Cotton Mather reading us the Word back at North Church. For some of my shipmates the reading of the Articles was as close as they were like to come to the inside of a meetinghouse for their entire sorry lives. Indeed, they might never hear the Word read again until it was recited to them on the gallows. To these dictums we all had to agree, putting our hands or marks to them as we were variously able. For my mark I chose a line curled back on itself, a spiral, like the patterns I'd seen in the stars overhead.

The Articles were as follows:

> I. *The Captain is to have two full Shares; the Quarter Master is to have one Share and one Half; the Doctor, Mate, Gunner and Boatswain, one Share and one Quarter.*
>
> II. *He that shall be found guilty of taking up any Unlawful Weapon on Board the Privateer or any other prize by us taken, so as to Strike or Abuse one another in any regard, shall suffer what Punishment the Captain and the Majority of the Company shall see fit.*

III. *He that shall be found Guilty of Cowardice in the time of Engagements, shall suffer what Punishment the Captain and the Majority of the Company shall think fit.*

IV. *If any Gold, Jewels, Silver, etc., be found on Board of any Prize or Prizes to the value of a Piece of Eight, & the finder do not deliver it to the Quarter Master in the space of 24 hours he shall suffer what Punishment the Captain and the Majority of the Company shall think fit.*

V. *He that is found Guilty of Gaming, or Defrauding one another to the value of a Royal of Plate, shall suffer what Punishment the Captain and the Majority of the Company shall think fit.*

VI. *He that shall have the Misfortune to lose a Limb in time of Engagement, shall have the Sum of Six hundred pieces of Eight, and remain aboard as long as he shall think fit.*

VII. *Good Quarters to be given when Craved.*

VIII. *He that sees a Sail first, shall have the best Pistol or Small Arm aboard of her.*

IX. *He that shall be guilty of Drunkenness in time of Engagement shall suffer what Punishment the Captain and Majority of the Company shall think fit.*

X. *No Snapping of Guns in the Hold.*

These all sat well with me, especially the eighth article, promising the best small arm to anyone who first spied a likely target. The sooner I could be armed with something fiercer than my rigging knife, the better I would feel. I supposed my hidden silver cup was in a manner of speaking a violation of an article or two, but as it had come from the master's cabin, and as I knew my shipmates to have held on to theirs as well, I worried little over the indiscretion. Pleased I was as well with Ned and Sen's immediate reshuffling of the watches such that we were all given six hours off at once instead of four. The *Reporter* sailed well with only a few hands, given her rig, so as few as six of us at a time could be on deck if the weather was fair. I already had plans to find the stump-tailed cur and name him and then take him into my hammock with me when I abandoned myself at last to sleep.

"Hi, you, Will! Get down below. I've got a hole in my stomach. Go see if the cook has got a horse for me to eat," said Orne when the assembly was adjourned, giving me a neighborly cuff on the ear.

My bones cried out for sleep, and many from my watch were already going below to the waiting arms of their hammocks and drunken dreams of mermaids and cowries and shining pieces of eight.

"But, Orne," I started to object. He froze me with a sharp look.

"You're the cabin boy," he told me. "You go and do where you're needed. Mutiny's hungry work. And we'll raise New York before you know it."

"Yes, sir," I said. "All right, sir."

I was doubtful about the wisdom of sending me to help with any cooking, given the blur of fatigue already bending my eyes. He'd be lucky I didn't poison the whole crew, if asked to do anything more complicated than stir. But so be it.

The galley was located aft of the gun deck where we slung our hammocks, near to where the master's cabin lay hidden behind sliding doors. The doors stood open now, as instead of taking it for himself, Ned slung his hammock in amongst the rest of us on staggered watch with Sen so that one or the other of them was always topside. I hadn't seen the inside of the master's cabin yet. When thinking on it I'd imagined sumptuous comforts, like something from the Arabian nights. Pillows? Hookahs? A feather bed? A chandelier? Gold, frankincense, and myrrh?

Well, the bed wasn't much, more a man-sized wooden cradle hung with rope, though it did have a pillow. And the cabin had glass stern windows, with a few panes missing, letting in a cool breeze and the sound of surf churning away from our rudder. The cabin had a skylight, too, making this the cheeriest spot by far belowdecks, with some unlit lanterns and mostly a lot of nautical charts and instruments that I didn't understand, scattered over a table with chipped paw feet. Its only nod to luxury was a small brass chandelier, with all the candles melted down, hardened wax hanging from it like frozen tears.

When I got below I smelled roasting mutton and heard the stumping of John Somethingorother's missing leg and the tuneless humming of a man at work. I hadn't exchanged a word with him yet. We'd eaten on the voyage once or twice, but between the gale and the murder of the master, I didn't even recall what it was that had been handed to me and poured down my gullet. And we'd all spent the past many hours fueled by excitement and the master's liberated Madeira.

"That you, boy, come to help me?" the ship's cook called when he heard the footfalls of Billy's loose-laced boots.

I stopped short outside the galley.

I knew that voice.

It rumbled like his throat was full of gravel.

I felt the folded paper that held Billy Chandler's death sentence, the black spot, crumpled into the arch of my foot, and became aware of my heartbeat pulsing in my throat. What if it hadn't been a blade that I had heard tap-tapping against the cobblestones back in the yard of Ship Tavern, one million years ago? What if it had been John's wooden leg? Was his sing-songing confederate also amongst our company on the *Reporter*, his cutlass still stained with Billy Chandler's blood?

The galley door drew open and a merry face flush with stove warmth smiled down at me. A few teeth were missing from one side of his mouth, though he was not as old as his ragged throat would have you think. John Somethingorother was probably thirty, a ruddy Englishman with a kerchief tied sideways on his straw-colored head.

"Smell that," he said. "If that don't set your mouth a-watering, why, nothing will."

"Aye," I agreed in a hurry. "I haven't had mutton in a dog's age."

"Get you down some trenchers and we'll start ladling it out," John told me. His face betrayed nothing but pleasure in the meal to come. He basted the mutton leg with drippings and gave an appreciative sniff.

I did my work quickly, ferrying hot roast slices up the companionway and passing them from man to man, each face lighting up with delighted hunger at the feast I was delivering to him. Pretty smart of Ned Low to feed us well at the outset, and lucky for me to be the bearer of good food when my shipmates were most keen to have it. I got my share of thanks and head tousles and shoulder-knocks as I worked, which made me feel well placed amongst the company. Will Chandler was shaping up to be a decent enough cabin boy. He was a better cabin boy than I had been a girl of all work, anyway. Maybe he wasn't as lazy as I was.

By the time everyone had his ration I went back to the galley, half expecting to be given pan crust and leavings for my own breakfast. But instead I found a nice thick slice of meat waiting for me. John was already chewing, looking pleased with the result of his efforts. I fell on the meat like a hungry dog, gnawing it between both my hands.

"Slow down, boy, you'll choke," said the cook affably.

I wiped the grease from my chin and licked my fingers. "It's good," I said around the gristle filling my cheeks.

"D—n right it is," agreed the cook. "What's your name, lad? Not Jim, is it?" He laughed at a joke known only to himself.

"Will," I said, hoping I sounded like I believed it.

"Will what?"

My ears were on the alert, for tests, or for suspicions. But I didn't think he was asking me out of any set purpose. It sounded for all the world like John Somethingorother was making idle conversation. But even so. My stolen last name would surely make him look at me askance, given that he had murdered me already.

"Just Will'll do," I said lightly, keeping my eyes down.

The cook laughed, licking grease from his thumb. "Smart boy," he said.

We ate together in silence, my lie sitting as easily with John as it had with Sen. If anything, my willingness to dissemble seemed to have made them trust me more. A sign that I was of a pyrate stripe. Out on my own account.

"John?" I asked, running my fingers around my plate to get all the juices up and into my mouth.

"Hmmm." He was doing the same, peg leg extended out between

us. I observed that it had a coin nailed to the bottom, like a horseshoe in miniature. The coin gleamed silver in the firelight. It would certainly have made a metallic tap on cobblestones.

"Why won't Ned Low have married men in his crew?" I asked.

John eyed me with a knowing smile and said, "You should ask him."

"I'm asking you," I said.

"Ha." John laughed. "All right. He was married, he was. Ned Low had him a wife and child."

I must have shown my surprise, because John added, "He fair doted on 'em, he did."

"Are they in Boston, then?" I asked. It seemed impossible, that the man I'd seen slice another man's lips off for sport before throwing him to his death could have once cradled a baby.

John looked down. "They were. His wife died," he said. "It like to broke him. She's up on Copp's Hill."

That was the burying ground that Sarah and Mary and I had dashed through, where I'd left the skin of my knee on the gravel.

The cook got up, taking my empty trencher and busying himself in the galley. "I knew him before," he said. "In the yards. When I still had my own two feet to stand on, by God. And I'll say the Ned Low I once knew has been dead ever since. I'll sail with him. But this man? This man's no Ned Low."

"What happened to the child?" I asked, drawing my knees up and wrapping my arms around my shins.

"He weren't in no kind of shape to care for it," John said. "He put it with some of his wife's people and went to sea."

I never imagined that I could feel pity for a murdering b—d like Ned Low. But I thought of the lonely slate headstones with their grinning death's heads and crossed long bones. Maybe he had buried all his goodness with his wife, where it would be safe and sleeping until the Resurrection.

"That was ages ago," John continued. "But it's a known fact he'll set ashore any man as is married. Thinks they ought to go home and be with their people rather than ride shellback to the gallows with him."

As I chewed the fat of my mutton, I considered that this affectation might not mark Ned Low as having a tender side after all. Anyone who dreamed of one day returning to hearth and home might have reason to hang back in a fight. Might surrender his shipmates to authority to save his own neck. Might have his loyalties divided in a way that no pyrate master could abide.

No, Ned Low's refusal of married men wasn't a sign of any tenderness he might nurse in his secret heart. It was just the opposite. Ned Low knew how to guarantee himself a crew of men with nothing left to lose.

I swallowed my last lump of meat and felt my stomach pleasantly distended from good warm food. I belched and picked a morsel from behind a tooth, wondering where that dog had got to and how many hours of hammock I could still count on. Five at least. My heart sang at the thought of it.

"All right," John said, heaving himself up and balancing on his uneven legs, made in turn by God and man. "You scrub those up real good, and we'll do it all again come suppertime."

He clapped me on the shoulder and stumped away, leaving me with a stick with a rag on the end and a pile of trenchers slick with congealed sheep grease. I bent to my labors, my hands falling to scrubbing as they had known their whole lives how to do.

Chapter 7

〜

$\mathcal{I}$ was nervous of our arrival in New York, fearing that authority would be waiting on the docks to haul us to the gaols in chains to await the Judgment of our Maker. But I needn't have been, as most of us didn't go ashore at all.

A quarter of the crew didn't dare set foot on Manhattan lest we be taken for absconded property and sold on the block. Better to stay on board, idling and owed one share apiece of whatever we might take when under weigh once again. Ned Low certainly wasn't going ashore, as the elected leader of a band of criminals, and a murderer to boot. Seneca wasn't either.

In the few days' easy passage around Montauk and then inward bound to New York Harbor, while at work sorting lines or keeping sails trimmed, watching, and listening, and eavesdropping, and trying not to ask any direct questions, I had slowly pieced together that Seneca had liberated himself from somewhere, though no one would tell me where or how or when. He had taken a philosopher's name in place of the one that he'd had before, which anyone who knew him knew better than to use in his presence. Even lacking any further details, the scar splitting his brow and cheek and robbing him of one of his eyes told me enough.

The *Reporter* anchored in the shallow inlet by Port Richmond, just inside the Narrows with their squirrely currents, away from the heaviest traffic of barks and pirogues ferrying vegetables and passengers between

Staten Island and Brooklyn. When we came to anchor and had the sails furled and all the lines put away, they had loaded those of us who were married—or, at least, those of us who admitted to being married—into a tender pointed in the direction of the Battery and waved goodbye. We lost only four or five of our number to Ned Low's rule, including one of the fellows who had helped him pinion and murder the master, who perhaps was mindful of the limits of his luck, and determined to escape before the world learned of our crimes. Each departing man had been issued his payment from Sen, who had tallied the value of the lumber and silver plate we carried on board and divided that value into shares of which we all owned one piece.

I did consider, fleetingly, if a boy as young as I was pretending to be could credibly claim to be married. Wouldn't it be wiser to slither free of this company of murderers and throw myself on the mercy of honest Christians? I could even bring the magistrates the news of our mutiny, to prove my bona fides, and collect the thanks of the syndicate whose purse was at risk with the seizing of the *Reporter*. All I'd have to do is present myself as a boy of twenty, from the country, with my young cousin for a wife, pining for my return. Surely that would be the wiser course. Get out now while the getting is good.

But no one would believe that I was twenty. Not with my whiskerless cheeks and slight build and high voice. I'd be a lad of fourteen, and if I claimed otherwise, they'd see my plan as plain as if it were published in a broadside and read aloud in the market square, and I would probably be dead before I reached the Battery. And anyway, where was I going to go in New York? Even with a coin or two in my pocket, my lot would soon be even sorrier than it had been with Mrs. Tomlinson. I didn't relish roaming the streets of an unfamiliar town alone, friendless, penniless. Sleeping in doorways with no coat or hat. And with no way of knowing if John's singsong friend was still back in Boston, offering a price to anyone who delivered my head.

Instead, I sought the example of some of my shipmates. While they were getting up a party of suitably English-seeming men to go ashore on Staten Island and barter some of the lumber in our hold, I filled my contraband silver cup with rum and took the little cur up in my arms and lay myself down in my hammock and got blind drunk.

I named the cur Jonah. It was probably bad luck, in retrospect, and Orne would have cuffed my ear but good if he heard. But Jonah he was called, and I knew it was the right name for him because he cocked his askew ears immediately when I said it and consented to stretch himself across my neck like a muffler as we settled in my hammock.

I was no stranger to rum, of course, or small beers or ciders, though I rarely tasted wine and didn't entirely care for it when I did. But I was altogether too hard-used in my former life to have time or opportunity for real drinking. Drinking like the ministers warn us against. Drinking like I meant it.

First, I drank until I was no longer afraid. That took a little time. I discovered fear lurking in corners of my body where I'd never even thought to look for it. In my elbows, or behind my knees. In my jaw and even in my earlobes. Sip by sip I found where the fear was dwelling in my body and drank until the spot was numb. Then I drank until I was sleepy, my head lolling over on my shoulder, my cheek resting on the cur's warm belly, my eyelids heavy. And then I drank some more. I drank until I felt myself in motion and found that though the ship rode at anchor and my hammock hung still, the spinning I felt was inside my head. And then, not long after that, I drank until I was sick.

I leaned over the side of my hammock and heaved, to a general exclamation of dismay by some of my shipmates, spat, and lay back down, and Jonah licked my face. I sighed and felt a soft curtain of black collapse about me, like the felt hangings on a bed in the dead of winter, where all within is softness and blackness and warmth and heavy labored breath.

I don't know how long I lay there. Longer than my watch, to be sure. At times I heard voices whispering nearby, or felt the soft pressure of another body slinging his hammock next to mine. At other times I thought I heard laughter or felt swaying or the creaking of the ship around me, but I knew not whether it was real or a dream.

"Let him be," I imagined someone say. I heard some soft yelping and Jonah's paws on my chest as he leapt to the sole, my half-dead body swaying from the pressure of his escape. Once I felt a nudge as someone tried to lift my silver cup from my curled fist and I had wits enough to snarl, "That's mine," and the thief withdrew laughing without my even opening my eyes.

For a time, I dreamed of my mother. Not my mother, exactly, for I barely remembered a time when I could be said to have one. Perhaps I mean the memory of what a mother might have been. A cool hand resting on my moist brow, smoothing away a floss of hair caught in my lashes. A tucking in of a coverlet, a gentle chafing of the back of my hand. A sweet voice saying, "There, there, sweet baby. Sweet, tired baby. Rest."

I reached out to touch her soft skin, but my fingertips found only coarse canvas, the edge of my hammock curled in and resting against my cheek.

I sat up. A few shipmates swung in their own dream worlds nearby, arms and a foot dangling from their hammocks, but I could tell from the slant of light down the companionway that it was late morning, and most everyone would be up on deck, busy at his labors.

I held my head gingerly as I made my uneasy way up the companionway and into the glinting daylight.

"He lives!" cried Black Bart, the gunner so pale he was almost translucent, like glass. He had disassembled the stern chaser and was working it over with an oiled rag.

"Ho there! Have you heard the good news? He is risen!" agreed Wickham with a grin. The boatswain lounged in the stern with Bart, barefooted, sending a needle through a length of bright sailcloth while they laughed at me. Another of our number was taking his turn at the helm.

I put my hand to my temple and grimaced.

To my shock, I found that we were well out to sea. I scanned the ocean around us, seeing no land anywhere, only blue-black water extending to infinity in every direction, giving me the uncanny sense of having no idea where I was, or in which direction we were heading. The sky was bright with soft white clouds, a few high above faint and trailing like maiden hair. A gull followed us, crying every so often like a beggar, but he was the only sign of life apart from the *Reporter* in the great empty expanse of ocean and air as far as I could see.

"How long was I out?" I asked no one in particular.

My shipmates exchanged a look and Wickham said, "Sen told me I could have your cup if you were dead."

Bart smirked.

"Well, I'm not," I told them, and stalked to the bow to use the head.

I settled myself bent over and bare in the webbing above the figurehead, up by the bowsprit, and relieved myself hidden only by the blousing of my shirt. No one paid me any heed. Most everyone was on deck, idle, some leaning on the rail, a few occupied with the miscellaneous work of cleaning or lashing or splicing, and a few had food in their mouths. I didn't see Sen or Ned anywhere, which was unusual. Generally, one or the other was among us on deck, and often both together. They could have been below, in the master's cabin, studying navigational charts and making plans.

When I was finished, I put myself back to rights and idled in the rigging, watching the water churn away from the bow. There didn't seem to be any task for me, and no one was shouting my—that is, Will's—name. Within the blurred swell of water below me, I glimpsed a silvery flash. What was it? I stared hard, making out a flicker of tail, and all excited I exclaimed, "It's a mermaid, by God!"

But the animal diving and playing and surfing along the curl of water didn't have the body of a woman or breasts or hair or anything like that. I've since learned it was a porpoise leaping with its brothers as we all skated over the surface of the sea.

I watched, entranced, as the blue-gray creature played about below me. It turned an eye up to me, curious, and though I was nowhere near enough, I reached my hand down through the webbing as though I would touch its sleek and perfect head. Then, as swiftly as it had appeared, it was gone, leaving only the imaginary echo of a siren singing in my ears.

I lifted my face into the wind, drinking in the fresh ocean air with my hair coiling away from my back. If I squinted my eyes in just the right way, far away on the horizon I could observe a faint gathering grayness. A squall. I didn't know then how to guess how long it would be before the weather would have the *Reporter* in its teeth. For now, it looked very far away. I watched, fascinated, as the squall darkened and then a flash and flicker ripped it apart as a bolt of lightning shot through the clouds, still too far for me to hear the rumble.

In the momentary illumination of the lightning bolt, I spied something hidden within the squall. It was dark below and pale above. It could have been part of the cloud, or a trick of the light playing on the surface of the water.

Another white zigzag shot through the gathering darkness, and the silhouetted shape was now unmistakable.

It was a ship.

Alone. Undefended. Heeled well over in the building wind, doubtless so absorbed in saving themselves from the weather that the crew would have had no time to clock our appearance on the horizon.

"Sail ho!" I shouted.

"What? Where?" Thumping feet beat on the deck behind me as I kept my hand and eyes trained on the distant speck of what would become our quarry. I thought of the good arms I would be owed, for finding her first. What might I get? A flintlock? A blunderbuss? Behind me, my shipmates crowded onto the bow, all wanting to see what riches might lie in store. But none of them could see it but me.

"Where away?" demanded Sen. He was instantly beside me in the bowsprit webbing. He held a narrow brass spyglass to his one good eye, leaning forward like a man hungry for the meat he is slowly roasting on a spit.

"Two points to starboard," I said. "Just there."

Sen followed my finger with his glass, adjusting it minutely. Around us, our shipmates waited for his determination.

"What are you congregants praying to now?" Ned Low said behind us. The people stepped aside, making way for him, keeping their heads down. If they had been wolves, they'd have kept their tails low between their legs at his approach.

"A pink," said Sen. He passed the glass to our elected captain.

Over the past few days, Orne had been schooling me in the different kinds of ships we were likely to encounter. I knew some from my life on Clark's Wharf, when I had kept the sailors from getting too sober in Ship Tavern. But there was always more to learn. Narrow-sterned and fast, square rigged to our fore-and-aft, a pink would do us well in the shallow, shoaly waters of the Caribbean, which is where most of us on the crew expected we were headed. We would take it for our own and bend its crew to our will and make them join us, or set them adrift in their tenders if they would not. We might take the pink and burn the *Reporter* to the water line, or we might take both and travel in convoy, a two-headed Hydra of terror. In any case, it promised to be a rich prize. If we could take it.

Ned stood with a foot planted on the bowsprit and screwed his eye into the spyglass. We all waited for him to make the call, our nerves thrumming.

"That's it," said Ned. "Make sail. Wickham, no colors till we're abreast of her. Bart, you creeping b—d, get the chaser ready and moved amid-ships. If there's no balls aboard, we'll load up with grapeshot. All the lot of you, get your whetstones and get to work."

The crew scattered, each man to his post, chattering excitedly amongst themselves, eyes agleam with avarice and ready to taste blood.

"Who spotted our rose pink?" Ned asked Sen. "Some beast with d—n fine eyes he must be."

Sen indicated me with a look, the spyglass tucked under his arm.

"You, boy," said Ned, with an edge to his voice that made me instantly watchful and nervous. "You sober?"

"Yes, sir," I said. So even the captain knew I'd been three sheets to the wind for who knew how many days. Fortunately, no one seemed to care if my stupor had robbed me of my usefulness. But being blind drunk during a raid was something else. Were I too drunk to stand shoulder to shoulder with my shipmates when we sailed down upon the pink, according to the Articles, I'd be punished in a manner determined by the collective will of the crew. I could be lashed. Or worse.

"Good. Get you ready. Knife sharp, wits sharper. Right?" Ned said in a low voice. It was plainly a warning. I took it.

"Yes, sir!" I shouted. If I was to do my part to pillage the pink with nothing but my rigging knife in my hand, it had better be as sharp as I could make it. And I had better be ready to do my worst. I must be prepared to open the neck of a stranger and bleed him to death like a pig while looking him square in the face. I must be ready to destroy.

"What's your name?" Ned Low demanded. I had up until this moment been largely invisible to him. Just the cabin boy scuttling about, getting barked at and lolling in indolence whenever I could.

"He's Will Chandler," Sen said. His tone was mild, yet in its very mildness, I heard his understanding of my lie.

Something changed in Ned Low's face. Some glimmer of calculation in his otherwise empty eyes. I knew then that I was right to be afraid.

"Is he now," Ned Low said.

I dared not look away. The pyrate captain's eyes were the chill stone blue of pebbles hardened by frigid winters. I stood my ground, meeting his stare. I wouldn't think about how he had sliced off the master's lips, roasted them, and fed them back to him. I wouldn't flinch. If he chose to strike me, I would take it like a man.

He moved his face nearer to mine, near enough that I could smell his breath. Or I would have been able to if he were any other man. Ned Low continued to smell like nothing to me. Like air, or like the back of my own wrist.

The look he gave me lasted long enough that I felt a bead of sweat form in my hairline and trace down my temple. I could see the texture of the scars pocking his cheeks, the pale bristles on his upper lip, and the blankness behind his eyes where a soul should have been.

He didn't strike me. But two lines formed between his pale brows.

Presently he dismissed me with a curt nod and went off to make his own preparations. I discovered that I had been holding my breath only when I let it out again after Ned Low's back was turned.

Seneca watched all this unfold with his measuring eye. If he had thoughts about Ned's examination of me, he kept them to himself.

"Better hurry. If it goes our way, you'll be well armed before the day is through," Sen told me as he moved off on his own business.

Over his shoulder, he added, "Will."

NEW YORK

"Massachusetts, please," Marian said into the receiver. Outside the telephone booth a crush of men at the coat check line talked together while waiting to surrender overcoats and mufflers and be handed tickets so they could go enjoy their snifters and reminisce in peace.

"One moment, please," said a nasal young woman on the other end of the line. A click, and another click. "I have Massachusetts for you."

"Can you please connect me to Trowbridge, 87935?" said Marian, twisting the telephone cord around her thumb.

"And who shall I say is calling?" asked another young woman's voice, this one clearly born in Dorchester.

"Just say New York," said Marian.

"One moment." A few clicks, several rings, and a girlish voice answered, "Hello?" In the background, Marian heard the chatter and bustle of what could only be a dormitory hallway overflowing with teenage girls.

"I have New York calling," said the operator. "Go ahead, New York."

The answering Cliffie squealed, "It's long-distance!" and many voices could be heard talking all together.

"Yes, hello. Kay Lonergan, please," said Marian, feeling foolish and adult.

"KAY!" the girl on the other end shouted with a clunk as the receiver was left to fall and dangle. "Is Kay in her room? KAY!"

Whispers and chatters came down the line while Marian tallied up what this call must be costing the house committee of the Explorers Club. When she arrived at her not-inconsiderable estimate, she smiled.

"Hullo?" said a girl who sounded slightly out of breath, then with her hand over the receiver, to someone standing behind her, she added, "I've got it, I've got it."

"Kay?" Marian asked, not at all sure.

"Yes?" said the girl on the other end of the line.

"It's Professor Beresford," said Marian.

"Oh! Hi." Marian heard a soft clattering, and then the background behind Kay grew duller, as though she had stepped into a closet. "So what did he say?" Kay asked.

"Well . . ." Marian hesitated. "He thought about it. And first he told me it was a fake. Which is pretty much what I expected him to do."

"It's not."

"It could still be."

"It isn't," said Kay.

"That's what I told him," said Marian. "So we went back and forth, and I told him some of what you and I were discussing at our last meeting, about no one knowing for sure when Ned Low died or how. And about how the *Reporter* could have been the *Fancy* in disguise. And then . . ."

"I can't stand it! Tell me what he said, please please please!" begged Kay.

"Well. Then he said . . ." Marian drew it out, enjoying the suspense.

"I'm dying right now," said Kay.

"They'd back us," Marian said, unable to suppress the smile in her voice.

"NO." Kay's response was perfect.

Marian laughed, drawn in by Kay's breathless enthusiasm and inappropriate familiarity and the giggling and girlishness of the background. It was a good feeling, that cahoots feeling, one she had almost forgotten, or maybe just pushed aside, stuffed into a memory box with a dried corsage and two lost jacks then slid under the bed of her soul. She spent so much of her time trying to be taken for as mature as she felt she should be, that she had become self-serious. She had tamped down some of the chaotic exuberance in herself that innervates spaces that are crowded with girls, the confidential giggling, the puppy dog hijinks, the tendernesses, even the jealousies, the rages, and the tears. The truth was, Marian was barely past thirty. Ribbons of girl still unrolled inside her, somewhere.

"Yes. I mean, it's not a ton of money," Marian said. She didn't want to crush Kay's hopes, but it was barely a thousand dollars. Enough for their train tickets and the hotel and not much else. "And he insists on coming with us." That last part annoyed her. But there was no way around it. If she wanted the club's backing, a club member had to be along. And she, herself, was not a club member.

"Who cares?" Kay cried. "An Explorers Club–backed expedition! Like . . . like . . . Sir Edmund Hillary!"

Marian laughed. "Sort of. Only with less chance of freezing to death. One hopes."

"When do we leave?"

Someone banged on the telephone booth door and Marian made a kissy face at him, waved, and turned her back. "Well, that's the trick of it," Marian said.

"We could go on spring break. Or summer; I can start my job late. Summer might be better." Kay was talking so fast, Marian could barely understand her.

"Kay," Marian said.

"Do you think I could get course credit? Like as an independent study? Ooh, that would be fine. Imagine! Hunting pirate treasure! Don't you think the other girls will be green when I tell them!" Her voice rose until it was loud enough that Marian felt pretty certain all the girls on her floor would know the news already.

"Kay," Marian said.

"Can I wear a pith helmet? What about jodhpurs? I'll look swell in jodhpurs!"

"KAY."

"What?"

"I think our first order of business," Marian said patiently, "will be to figure out where exactly we are going."

A pause on the other end of the line. "I guess you're right." Kay sounded despondent. "Spoilsport."

"Don't worry," said Marian. "We can talk more later when it's not costing a fortune, but I have a pretty good idea of where Hannah wound up."

"I have some theories too," Kay said.

"It's got to be the Florida Keys," Marian told her.

"You think?" Kay didn't sound convinced.

"I do." The man was back tapping on the glass and pointing at his wristwatch. Marian widened her eyes and batted her eyelashes at him with her most gamine expression. He mouthed some words that Marian didn't care to understand.

"What makes you so sure?" asked Kay.

"Everything I've read says that the Dry Tortugas hosted a ton of pirates during the Golden Age," said Marian, growing more excited. "The Dry Tortugas are a small chain of islands just west of what we now call the Florida Keys. It might take some doing for us to figure out which one it's on. Probably some sandbar whose name has changed a dozen times over. But Hannah's treasure is there, or I'll eat my handbag."

"Spring break in Key West!" Kay exclaimed. "How glamorous. Mother will be so scandalized."

"Anyway. I wanted to let you know. We've got our backing. If Hannah is real, and if she's telling us the truth, then there's no reason we shouldn't be able to find what we're looking for." Marian thought about Hannah. Pictured her. A skinny thing, sunburnt, long tangles of hair. In some strange way, Marian had started to feel like Hannah wanted her to do this. Wanted her to find what she had hidden.

Kay scoffed, "Of course she was real."

The certainty of youth. How Marian envied it. There was a time, she felt sure, when she too knew things as certainly as Kay professed to know them.

They hung up with plans in place to meet again upon Marian's return to Cambridge amid Kay's breathless speculation about when they would be leaving and how long they'd be gone and how much treasure would be there. But really, would it be under a giant *X* marking the spot? She didn't even seem curious about the other, older, more famous Dr. Beresford, who would be along on their adventure. Marian supposed he didn't really exist, as far as Kay's mind went. She was a girl in an adventure story, the heroine of her own imagination. A Lost Boy, a Tiger Lily, a

Billy-Bones-His-Fancy. Marian barely existed herself, to Kay. The under-graduate was in a fantasy world that was oceans away from her mother's lace curtains in Kearny, New Jersey.

Of course, it was entirely possible they would get there—wherever "there" was—and find nothing.

Suppose Hannah was real. And suppose she was telling the truth. Neither of which was at all certain, or even probable, if Marian set aside her fantasies and looked at the evidence with the cold eyes of an aca-demic. But suppose there were just enough clues in the manuscript for them to piece together where, of all the desert islands in the world, Han-nah would have found herself alone in a band of pirates with her hands on a treasure that she needed to hide. And suppose their expedition got there. Who's to say the island hadn't been swept clean ten times over since Hannah's time? Anything could happen in two hundred years. Sandbar islands could bubble up out of the Caribbean, sprout palm trees, and be stripped naked by the next hurricane. Castaways could land there. Or fishermen. Or smugglers. Bootleggers, bringing boatloads of rum from the islands and smuggling them into Florida and Louisiana to slake the thirst of Americans bored by Volstead. She and her father and Kay could get there, if there was a "there," and find nothing but empty rum bottles and trash.

The man was back again, banging on the glass doors.

"All right, all right," Marian snapped, opening the telephone booth door. "Where's the fire?"

"I'll thank you to let someone else use the telephone," the man said behind a pinched pair of spectacles. Marian read the disapproval and distaste in his face as he looked down at her, and she considered naming it to him, bringing it out in the open to embarrass him with his own discomfort. But she was too tired. Anyway, whoever he was, he probably knew her father. And she didn't want any trouble. Especially not with an Explorers Club imprimatur on her coming wild goose chase.

Her wristwatch told her it was just past seven, and her stomach was rumbling. Marian decided that she would as soon dine alone on dry chicken and thawed peas in the Barnard faculty club dining room as she would throw it all over and take a job as a taxi dancer in Coney Island. In fact, Coney Island sounded more appealing.

Outside on Cathedral Parkway, Marian considered trudging back into the flattening autumn wind all the way to the IRT. In her head she heard her father's voice calling her insistence on taking the train a proletarian affectation that impressed and convinced nobody. And who, after all, was Marian trying to convince? Where was the panel of judges now, with the wind nipping at her ears?

Marian stuck out her hand and got a cab on her third try.

"West Fourth Street, please," she said, and when she named the exact address, she felt a familiar, long-dormant flutter of rebellion breathe to life in her chest. The taxi driver half turned over his shoulder to look at her, perhaps to see if she was serious. Instead of answering his questioning look, she presented him with her profile, pulled out her compact, and inspected her face.

"Have it your way," muttered the cabbie as they pulled away.

Under the flickering stripes of the passing streetlights, Marian found herself in the compact mirror appearing younger than she remembered, softer, and her eyes looking a little more daring around the corners. Like a Marian she remembered but hadn't seen for a while. The Marian of ten or fifteen years ago. The perfect Marian for a trip to the Mad Hatter.

She wondered if Jimmie would remember her. Jimmie remembered everybody.

"You got your three pieces on?" the cab driver said around his cigar, his eyes on her in his rearview mirror.

Marian ignored him. The cab driver chuckled to himself, and the taxi picked up speed through the dizzying lights of Broadway, streaking down to the Village.

It was still early. No one was standing guard at the Mad Hatter's front door. When Marian entered the tearoom, the same rush of thrill and danger vibrated through her chest that she had first felt when she came here in her late teens. A time before she went away to school, when there was still an outside chance that one of her mother's society friends on a slumming mission might see her and report back. They came to the

Village sometimes, the society swells, on excursions as if going to the zoo. They liked to see the artists and would-be artists and the Bohemians and the weekend-only Bohemians in their wild clothes with their wild dancing and their wild music. They liked to drink up their measure of perversion in the tearooms and slides before going home with their clean hands to lie on their clean pillows bathed in their clean consciences.

The front room of the Mad Hatter was narrow and crowded with small tables and spindly bentwood chairs and little candles under lamp-shades, with women sitting in groups of two and three and four over teacups and plates of sandwiches. When she came through the door a few eyes, some rimmed with kohl or peering through lace, others under newsboy caps and homburgs, looked up and traced over her, and then returned to their tables. It was frowned upon to look too long at some-one you didn't already know. And most of the women Marian knew probably weren't here anymore. At the end of the room sat a smoky fireplace in a brick wall that had been plastered over and painted with gestural drawings of the White Rabbit and Alice, the Caterpillar on his mushroom smoking a hookah and looking lazily out at thoughts known only to himself.

The restaurant felt shabbier than Marian remembered, its tin ceil-ing darkened with cigarette smoke, and scuffs on the wooden floor. To the rear of the dining room, a curtained doorway led to another room from which the muffled sound of jazz could be heard, just a three-piece combo, a bass and a saxophone and a drum.

Perched on a stool near this door was a smallish familiar person, somewhat older than Marian, in a short bowl haircut and an artist smock and boots, reading a book. So nothing had changed after all, Marian noted with some satisfaction. What was the special pleasure of going back to a place distantly remembered and finding it essentially the same? Was it from a hope of finding a shade of her former self, the bold girl in slacks and smocks, full of certainty and unafraid? Marian missed herself sometimes. But if she was anywhere, that girl might be here. Her mother might be long dead, her father a self-satisfied cipher, their townhouse a tomb where Marian largely refused to tread, her career uninspired, her Cambridge apartment empty save for piles of books and one orchid barely clinging to life, but the Mad Hatter was still here, and here no one would look twice at Marian. Unless she wanted them to.

"Jimmie," said Marian. She put out her hand and the proprietor of the tearoom looked up with some surprise and a slow smile and took it.

"As I live and breathe," said Jimmie. "Dr. Beresford, I presume. How are ya?"

"Oh," said Marian. "You know."

"I do," agreed Jimmie. "Go on in. Good set tonight."

"Thanks. Can I get some sandwiches? I'm starved," Marian said as she shrugged off her coat.

"'Course," said Jimmie. "Shouldn't take more than a week or two. I'll send out the carrier pigeon."

"Excellent. You know just what I like." Marian smiled.

"That I do, that I do," said Jimmie. Jimmie's name had once been Eliza. But not for some time.

Marian passed through the heavy velvet curtains into the secret back room that wasn't really a secret at all. In one corner behind some blue footlights, three musicians down from Harlem dressed in tired tuxedos played "If I Had You," a slow song, moody and languid. As they played, they looked at each other, for the changes, or down at their shoes. Here and there couples danced together, marcelled heads resting on suit jacket shoulders, arms wound tightly around necks and waists. Some couples retreated to the shadowy corners, to booths lined in velveteen, away from the light.

A bar stretched along one side of the room, softly gaslit and mirrored. At one end of the bar, everyone clustered together wearing pants and button-down shirts and jackets, their hair short. Some were dressed up for the evening in pressed tuxedos and cummerbunds, some fresh from work in suspenders and tweeds and boots, some more artist types with paint flecks in their hair. A few of these patrons nodded at Marian, edging over, moving their drinks, making room at the bar. In the Mad Hatter, everyone knew where she stood.

At the other end of the bar, tittering and whispering, sat women who dressed themselves in a more feminine mode. They were waiting. To be bought drinks, to be introduced, to be asked to dance. Maybe to be asked for other things. A few of them looked a little rough around the edges, blurred lipstick or a shiner over the eye artfully concealed with makeup, but many of them were flawless: luscious and watery in satin dresses skimming over their hips, copied from ones they'd seen in the movies, their lips rosy, their wrists heavy with bangles. Others were in their work clothes, simple skirts and sensible heels, but most had gone home first, gussied up, dabbed perfume behind ears and on wrists and maybe, just enough, a delicate trail in the soft smooth groove between their breasts. Here, Marian could look at them all she wanted.

As Marian watched, one of these glittering Village butterflies crossed one knee over the other, revealing a smooth length of calf under the ripples of a burgundy satin dress. She gazed at Marian under lowered lids and smiled. Heavy brunette waves, thick brows like a Modigliani painting, her hair in a rich coil at the nape of her neck.

The woman slowly unclasped her pocketbook, withdrew a single cigarette, put it between her darkened lips, and smiled.

Marian sidled up to the bar next to the Modigliani, hoping she remembered how it was all supposed to go.

"Well, hello," the woman said.

"Hello," said Marian. She pulled out her lighter, sparked it, and held it lightly to the tip of the woman's cigarette. The Modigliani cupped her hand delicately around Marian's, leaning in close. Her nails were lacquered the same burgundy as her dress, her hands free of rings, tender and naked. The cigarette ember glowed, illuminating her stark brows and the planes of her cheeks. Her perfume smelled like tuberoses. Marian leaned closer, inhaling the aroma of the perfume mingled with the musky newness of the stranger's hair and her skin.

"So"—the woman exhaled twin streams of smoke from her nostrils while Marian lit a cigarette of her own—"what's your story, morning glory?"

Marian felt a rush of pleasure and adrenaline and freedom tripping through her blood, dizzying her with possibilities.

"My name is Marian," she said. She looked levelly into the Modigliani's dark, playful eyes and smiled. She lifted a fingertip, drew it softly along the Modigliani's jaw, and added in a voice just above a whisper, "And I'm a pirate."

Chapter 8

We were all standing at the starboard rail, and every one of us, even John Somethingorother with his wooden leg, armed to the teeth. We clenched our knives in our mouths. Those of us with pistols or cutlasses held them at the ready in our hands, those others of us bare-handed, ready at the lines or at the few arms at our disposal, all of which had been rolled or hauled or otherwise maneuvered to the starboard side. Each one loaded and aimed, wheels shipped against recoil, ready to fire. Jonah had been given a bone to gnaw and urged to stay below.

"Steady now," muttered Sen.

He stood amongst our company, twin flintlocks slung at his waist, hands by his sides. One jittering finger kept returning to the stock of his pistol as though to reassure himself that it was there. Orne was on the helm; as the eldest and the longest-lived at sea, he was thought to have the steadiest and subtlest hand at the wheel. Ned Low stalked back and forth next to him, his face a mask of avarice. John stood near me, clutching a butcher knife in one hand and a carving knife in the other. Wickham was at the stern, Black Bart was issuing instructions to those of us charged with firing the cannon. He'd loaded the chaser with forks from the galley when not enough cannonballs could be found in the hold, though some few had been discovered amongst the ballast stones, been chipped free of their rust, and brought above to do their duty.

The distant gale harassing the pink had blown on by without leaving so much as a drop of rain on us, as though a gift from Davy Jones. They were making very little way as we glided swiftly down upon them. We flew the flag of Massachusetts Bay from our stern. Sen made ready with a speaking tube to address our prey. They were only about a half a mile away.

The plan, as Orne had explained to me in the hasty moments of whetting our blades and retying our pigtails, was that we would approach under the pretense of offering them aid. Pull up alongside, make ourselves known, and give them the chance to surrender without a shot fired. Depending on how cooperative they were, we would offer them quarter if they would join our band, or set them adrift if they would not. Oftentimes, Orne had assured me, folks would be so seized with terror at the mere suggestion of pyrates that they would drop their arms and surrender without a drop of blood being spilt.

This was my fervent hope. If I let myself think too long on it, I shrank from the ugly work that lay ahead of me. But as I stood amongst my shipmates, my teeth gripping the hilt of my sharpened rigging knife, my hands twitching with tension, I knew that if the pink should offer up any resistance, there would be no choice.

A hypocrite, in addition to a liar, I silently begged God to make the pink full of people as cowardly as me.

"Steady," Sen said again.

The pink was wallowing, and as we drew near we saw that her top-gallants were hanging amidst a spiderweb of snapped rigging. We saw no name on her slim stern, but she carried what remained of a French flag. A few exhausted-looking figures could be seen at the helm or edging their way out along the yardarms to cut the ripped sails down, the wallowing of the ship sending the masts seesawing, so that the crew aloft had to work not to be flung into the sea. Two tenders floated behind them on long lines, as though they had been making ready to abandon ship. The tenders were loaded down with provisions and barrels of water, but no people.

Sen brought the speaking tube to his lips just as we drifted past the first of the empty tenders.

"*Allo!*" he called. "*Avez-vous besoin d'aide?*"

I often heard other languages spoken on the streets of Boston, but I never ceased to be amazed when a person I knew spoke something other than English in front of me. It was like the card tricks some people can play, where they pull the two of diamonds out of a pack of playing cards on the first try.

"Brilliant," I whispered to myself, and a shipmate standing beside me, whose name I no longer remember, a rangy fellow so sunburnt he looked like dried beef, growled, "Oh, aye. He can d—n your soul to hell so well, you'll look forward to the trip."

A moment of deadly silence unfolded as we all awaited the pink's reply.

"*Non, non, merci!*" a distant voice called. We observed the figures in the yardarms hurry down the ratlines hand over hand and anxious motion on the deck.

"*Nous vous aiderons avec plaisir!*" shouted Sen through the speaking tube across the rapidly narrowing expanse of ocean between the pink and the *Reporter*. "I insist!"

Sen then caught Ned Low's eye, and Ned whispered an order in Orne's ear, and the word was passed for us to spill the wind from our sails to kill our speed. Orne's delicate touch on the wheel brought us right in line to draw our starboard rail within a hairsbreadth of the pink's larboard side.

Panic and shouting seized the deck of the pink, and a puff of smoke bloomed from the ship's narrow stern. Someone shouted, "Down!" and a whoosh of heat threw me onto my back and then a boom shattered my eardrums and my knife fell hard from my teeth.

"That's it, fellows, let fly!" shouted Ned Low, his voice muffled under the ringing in my ears.

The world wound down slow, and I opened my eyes. I saw my shipmate, the one who had just told me how fluently Sen could d—n someone, who had been standing shoulder to shoulder with me. He lay sprawled on the deck, a starburst of blood and brains and bone where his head used to be, and behind him, a ragged hole punched through the deck where the two-pound cannonball had splintered us. My eyes saucered in horror as Sen shouted, "John, get you down below and check for damage. Will! Boy! On your feet!"

From our stern, in place of the Massachusetts colors, we now flew a pitch-black flag stitched with a dancing skeleton in scarlet red. Our sails billowed and a quick cannonade of gunfire rippled from our starboard side, forks and bullets and grapeshot singing through the air and landing with wet thuds.

"On your feet, I said!" an enraged voice bellowed in my ear, and then a white burst of pain exploded across my face.

Sen had struck me.

The pain brought me back into my body, and time sped up again, my ears now full of screams and gunfire and shouted orders. I scrambled to my feet, my knife back in my teeth, my hands and boots climbing with my shipmates over our starboard rail, sliding down lines held fast by grappling hooks to the pink's deck. Men were locked in combat on every side of me, grunts and shouts in French and English and Spanish. Flintlocks spat flames and bullets zinged by. Splinters erupted with each impact, clouding the air with flying shards of wood. A few of the pink's crew lay splayed on the deck, one of them pepper-flecked with blood from the grapeshot, another pinned through his cheeks and neck to the mainmast by forks warped with cannon heat.

I saw Jimenez, our nominal doctor, who'd gently set a shipmate's dislocated shoulder as we lay at anchor in Port Richmond, now crazed with malice, his hands wrapped around the throat of a Frenchman whose face was purpling, eyes starting out of his head as he gasped his last breath. Wickham, who'd stitched our flag with the close care of a spinster at her needlework, sank a cutlass into the thigh of another Frenchman, withdrew it dripping in blood, and sank it again with a laugh. Sen fired one pistol, then the other, dropping one French crewmember under his exploding jaw and another in the belly who clutched at his opened entrails with screams of horror as he fell at Sen's feet.

I determined to make my way to the hold. I figured every able man would be on deck after such a gale, and certainly now that we sea rovers had set upon them. The gun decks and cabins would be empty. Keeping low, I sprinted along the length of the pink, ducking, weaving, heading for the companionway.

I got to the trapdoor and flung it open to find the terrified face of a grizzled man with his upper teeth all missing. He reached out for me with a snarl. My rigging knife was in my hand and then it was in his eye, blood running over my hand as the man clutched his face screaming and fell down the companionway ladder. I was quick down the ladder after him.

The gun deck was dark and close and smelled of unwashed men. All the gun ports were closed, the cannon shipped and still. We had caught them completely unaware. I needed to find the captain's cabin, which I assumed on a pink would be like on our schooner, near the stern and containing items of value belonging to the captain or any wealthy passengers they might have aboard. I'd let Sen tally the value of whatever cargo they had in the hold. Lumber was good money, but it didn't excite me. It was booty I wanted. Riches that would buy my worth in the eyes of Ned and Sen.

I stalked, silent in Billy's boots that had finally started to feel like mine, knife at the ready. I heard voices and presently came to a sliding door, pulled closed. This would be the captain's cabin. Inside, three voices argued in French. I put a hand on the latch to slide the door open, but it was locked.

I stepped back, readying to break down the door with my boot, but as I let my foot fly the door slid open and my boot met the chest of a young well-dressed man with lace ruffles at his throat. In an instant I was upon him, my knees pinning him to the cabin sole, my hand in his hair, forcing his head back and baring his throat to my blade. I was screaming at him to shut up, shut up, shut up, and he was screaming back at me. We struggled, locked together, and I heard someone else in the room scream. The fancy young Frenchman's hair pulled out of his pigtail and his hand tried to grasp my ear to tear it off.

I shouted oaths at the ridiculous popinjay and belted him hard in the jaw with my elbow and he spat blood. His face was powdered, and sweat was melting rivulets through the talcum caked on his skin.

I pinned his head under my weight and pressed the rigging knife to his neck, drawing out a pinprick of blood.

It was enough. He froze.

We both breathed raggedly, inflamed with rage, staring into one another's crazed eyes.

"*Arrêtez! Arrêtez!*" Someone was screaming in the cabin, with someone else echoing "*Arrêtez!*" in an awful squawk, and without looking round, I shouted, "Shut up! Just you shut your mouth!"

The screamers obeyed.

"All right," I said to the fancy young Frenchman. "Get up."

I climbed off him, menacing him with my rigging knife so he wouldn't try to cross me. He said something in French, pointing, and I said, "Stop it with your frog talk, God d—n you, and get against the wall."

"*Arrêtez!*" came the squawk voice again, and I shouted, "Shut up, God d—n your eyes, shut up!"

The Frenchman backed away slowly, his palms open, and moved over to stand next to the other person in the cabin I hadn't bothered to notice. The sole was littered with scattered letters and nautical charts and overturned chairs and a brass chandelier hanging at a dangerous angle, dripping hot wax on the floor. Somewhere water trickled in from a crack wrought by the passing gale. I spied the squawker—a parrot—the likes of which I had never seen before, dangling in a spinning cage of polished brass. It was a fierce scarlet red, with a long shimmering tail, and it watched me with one lizard eye, the curve of its beak looking perversely like a smile.

"*Arrêtez, arrêtez,*" it said, stretching its wings out and flapping before settling itself again.

My other prisoner proved to be a young woman, probably only a little older than me, but curled and pressed and laced and dressed. I stared at her without meaning to, my lips parted, seized with an unreal surge of envy. I'd never been so close to a woman of quality before. Her sack dress was so fashionable I had only seen drawings of the like in Boston, worked in light gray silk with box pleats at her shoulders and patterned in tiny flowers over an incommodious set of hoops. Her hair was heaped up in a crown of curls held in place with something that glittered, but in the violence of the storm she must have been tossed about, as a few locks had loosened and now rested on her forehead and her décolletage. Her skin was perfect. I have never seen such perfect skin, before or since. I didn't think skin could be so perfect, like the surface of a bowl of heavy cream.

"Please!" she screamed in heavily accented English. "Don't touch me! You touch me, I will kill myself."

I was taken aback, for an instant forgetting that I was Will. But because I had been Hannah, I knew what she was afraid of.

"Well, we can't have that," I said. I couldn't stop staring at her. This girl wouldn't have deigned to set foot in an ordinary like Ship Tavern, where I worked for my bread. She was so far above me that I couldn't even imagine a world in which she barked an order my way. In every plane of imaginable existence, we would have been utterly invisible to each other. And now here we stood.

The young Frenchwoman took hold of her companion's arm so tightly that I thought she might fling him at me to defend herself.

I moved closer to where they cowered against my approach. I spied a chain looped around her neck, on which hung some sort of locket, probably gold. Her ears flashed with something heavy and bright and red—rubies. I had heard of this gem before but never seen one. I felt an unaccustomed rush of power, and my lip curled in an avaricious smile. The fancy girl saw the power flood my face, and she paled.

"Here," she said quickly, a hand going to her delicate earlobe. "I give to you. You let me go, I give to you."

Her compatriot exclaimed in a long string of French but the young woman silenced him with a few sharp words and returned to her project of placating me.

Her hand unfastened one of the earrings and held it out to me. In the soft sunbeam falling through the cabin skylight the ruby glinted like a prism, casting bloodred shards about the room. I took it from her hand

and held it in my palm. The gem was in a teardrop shape, held to a loop of gold wire by shining filigree with tiny chips of something white and sparkling—diamonds. It was heavy. Why are rich things so heavy?

I heard footsteps approach and a familiar voice say, "Well, what have we here?"

I turned to find Jimenez, our murdering doctor. He was a Creole, a born pyrate, spending his sordid youth piloting smugglers through the bayous to dodge the customs man at the Balize. That meant he spoke French. And if he could speak French, he could make these two fancy fashion dolls tell us where their treasures where hidden.

"She's offering me her rubies if I spare her life," I told him. "And her honor."

Jimenez said, "I bet she is."

He said something long to her in a kind of French that didn't sound entirely like hers, in the way that my English didn't sound entirely like the English of my shipmates from England. She responded with evident distaste, and something she said made Jimenez laugh heartily.

"What is it?" I demanded. "What did she say?"

"Says she's a duchess." He could barely contain himself. "Duchess, my eye. Check her pockets."

I moved in close, my face inches away from hers, close enough that I could breathe in the jasmine scent of her perfume. I could see the errant hairs in her eyebrows, the one overlooked whisker on her otherwise flaw-less chin. She watched me, her expression darkening. I lifted my hands, privately marveling that I was about to touch someone as perfect as she. I snapped the locket from around her neck and helped myself to her other ruby earring and her rings and bracelets, my fingers brushing against her skin, moving between her fingers as I gently twisted the gold rings free of her knuckles. Her skin felt as soft as it looked. I wondered what it must be like, having hands that have never scrubbed or basted or stoked. To have the skin of your knuckles feel as soft as the skin of a cheek or a lip.

I was sure she could see every detail of me too. I must have stunk of sweat and oakum and maybe a cloud of rum in the miasma of my breath.

My hair unwashed and greasy in its long pigtail. Boils scattered over my dirty forehead and cheeks. The skin of my hands rough against hers, as rough as a man's.

I slowly slid my hand under one of her pleats of silk, rummaging in her loose sack dress to find where her pockets were tied. Her folds of linen and lace felt warm and soft, and my hand luxuriated in them, unhurried. I moved the back of my hand along her waist, trailing it down the hidden slope of her belly, and when my knuckle brushed lightly against a part of her that she probably thought I didn't know about, she audibly gasped. Shocked at my own audacity, I dared to look at her with laughing eyes. At last, I found the hidden pocket, my gaze holding hers while I helped myself to a few more rings and necklaces and tidbits that she had secreted there.

When my hand reappeared clutching its bounty I smiled in triumph. Her face contorted in naked rage, and before she could d—n my b—d soul to hell I laughed, and, head buzzing with my newfound power, I kissed her on the lips.

I had just enough time to register the supple softness of her mouth, the sweet taste of her tongue, before she recoiled, spitting on the floor between us after I broke away. I laughed in delight at my boldness and stuffed her jewelry into my pantaloons.

She tasted like rose water.

"Will, you sly dog," teased Jimenez. He had helped himself with a few quick flicks of a knife to the brass buttons holding the young Frenchman's doublet together, a signet ring, and a few odds and ends from his pockets. He even took the Frenchman's shoes, heavy with two great silver buckles. The young man stood, red with rage, in white silk-stocking feet.

"I've never seen a creature so fine," I remarked to Jimenez, still staring at the French girl, whose glare was so hard and cold, it could freeze the blood in my veins.

"That dress'll be worth some good money," said Jimenez, eyeing the possible duchess of wherever in her *à la mode* fashionable silks.

"Not if it's bloodstained and cut to ribbons," I pointed out. "She gave up her rubies of her own accord. I guess that's all she'll give up without a fight."

The duchess watched us talking. I suspected she spoke enough English to understand what was under discussion. Her face was white under its artful powdering, her eyes darting between the swamp doctor and me.

The sounds of struggle above deck had subsided. We could hear shouted demands as Ned Low berated the remaining crew of the pink to join us or be left to die, but no more blows or running feet or gunfire.

We still had work to do.

"Ask them where the rest of it is," I said to Jimenez.

He spoke a long string of New World French to our prisoners. Both responded with apparent defiance and rage, shouting over each other and at Jimenez and me and probably at God too.

"They said we'll get not a sou more," said Jimenez genially. "And then she called me a very unflattering name. But I bet we can persuade them. Come on."

"*Arrêtez!*" called the parrot from its cage as we shoved our prisoners ahead of us out the sliding cabin doors.

We prodded the fashion dolls to walk before us through the gun deck to the narrow ladder leading topside. Jimenez leered up the duchess's skirts as they climbed, urging them on with rough looks and French words. Her shoes were the same gray silk as her dress, with elevated heels, and the hoops were difficult to force through the trapdoor. I had to stuff her up, her masses of linen and silk in my face. It was a wonder she could move at all.

We arrived on deck to find our shipmates gathered around the mainmast, many of them the worse for wear, with ears crusted with blood or torn shirts or blackened eyes. None, that I could see, were dead, apart from the shattered body of my shipmate back on the *Reporter*. Not so the crew of the unready pink, half a dozen of whom lay in twisted piles of flesh and bone, their eyes glassed and empty. Some few others stood lined up, their hands tied before them. The surviving crew were being forced to stand by as observers while Ned Low persuaded the captain, what was left of him, to give up their riches.

If I thought I had seen Ned Low's cruelty on display when we over-threw our sailing master, I was sorely mistaken.

The captain had been stripped naked and tied to the mast. His back was ribboned red with lashings delivered by Wickham, standing by breathless with his cat-o'-nine-tails by his side. The captain's hands were bound out straight before him, arms around the mast, ropes looped fast around his wrists, with rags snaking between his outstretched fingers. He was sobbing.

"Where is it, God d—n you!" Ned Low shouted, smacking the captain hard in the face. His head rocked back on his shoulders and clocked against the mast.

"There is nothing," the captain slurred through pulped lips. "You have it all, there is nothing else."

"Liar!" Another blow cracked the captain's jaw so hard we all heard it dislocate. Several of his crew tried to object, but Ned shouted, "The next man who speaks will taste salt water!"

"Wait," said the duchess quietly. "Wait. I tell you."

In shocked silence the whole assembled company, pyrates and French crew both, stared at the splendid creature who they now found standing in their midst. I'm sure none of my shipmates had ever been so close to a lady of quality either. I wondered if they found her nearness as intox-icating as I did.

Ned stalked over to her like a hungry animal, his face a mask of pure fury. "Where?" he said coldly.

If the duchess was afraid of the hard men now surrounding her, she did not show it. She was taller than Ned Low and carried herself with an air of untouchability. Like a woman accustomed to being obeyed. Her evident authority created a space around her, which even we lawless sea rovers hesitated to pierce. She drew herself up and said, "In Jean-Pierre's writing desk. In our cabin. You look there. You find what you desire."

Ned stared hard at her. Then he growled, "Will, Jimenez. Get it. Sen?"

Seneca, standing by, his blouse soaked with another man's blood and blackened with gunpowder, looked momentarily perturbed.

"Sen!" Ned shouted.

Our first lieutenant hardened his face and softly commanded, "Do it," to one of our other shipmates who was stationed near the pinioned captain, holding a flint.

My shipmate struck a spark. The captain screamed in terror and some few of us put our hands over our eyes as the oil-soaked rags coiling around his fingers instantly caught fire. I felt the sudden heat pressing into me and cringed away.

"Well?" Ned barked at me, his back to the display. "Hurry up."

I was staring, transfixed with horror. "Yes, sir," I said. I glanced over at the duchess, who watched the captain's hands and arms engulfing with flame with the impassive gaze of a woman accustomed to unimaginable things. But even she could not fathom the cruelty of Ned Low. I saw plainly that she didn't understand the true depth of her danger. She thought her carriage would save her. But no one would be saved.

"Captain," I hazarded.

"What?" said Ned Low as the pink captain's screams rose in pitch.

"She gave up her jewels to me. I've promised." I worried my hands together. They were stained in the toothless Frenchman's blood.

"No one will touch her," he said, but the hardness in his eyes belied his words.

It was short work for Jimenez and me to find the cabin where the duchess and her lover—at least I guessed that's what he was—were quartered, and from there to discover the small wooden writing desk bound in brass and locked away safe, stashed in a cubby under some sailcloth. It was heavy. Jimenez and I struggled with it together, heaving it on our shoulders through the trapdoor and onto the deck.

"Well, now," said Ned Low, his eyes gleaming. He turned to the cringing, half-dead captain, who had collapsed to the deck when his wrist ropes burned to cinders. His arms were now bloody and blackened stumps, still smoking. The air smelled singed with melting fat. "God d—n your eyes for a liar, you son of a b—h," Ned said to the captain.

"I suppose you are wanting the key?" the duchess said quietly. Her expression unchanged.

"Yes, Madame. If you please," said Ned Low.

The duchess lifted one perfect hand and drew it down her throat. We all watched her, rapt. Her finger traced a delicate line down the soft swell of her décolletage, disappearing into the lace ruffles just out of sight below her neckline. Why hadn't I thought to look there? She stirred about in that soft spot, hunting. Her face impassive, she slowly withdrew a long length of black satin ribbon, at the end of which hung a tiny brass key.

"Here is the key," she said, dangling it from her hand.

Then she took three quick steps.

She was over the rail before we knew what had happened. We heard the splash, and we all rushed to the rail.

The young duchess flailed in the gentle waves, her dress and hoops pooling out around her, gathering water, weighing her down. She gasped, and her perfect face dipped below the water, her hands held out flat, pressing down on the surface of the sea as if she would push herself out.

She didn't scream. She didn't cry out. She didn't beg us for a line or to jump in and save her. She didn't speak at all.

It only took a few minutes. She slipped below the water, her heavy silks dragging on her, her rosy lips gulping like a fish, her eyes open. Her arms stilled and she drifted softly in the current, before sinking, slowly, by tiny degrees, a bubble or two loosed from her nose, her curls floating softly free, before she slipped out of sight into the depths. Then she was as gone as if she had never been here at all.

"Well. I hope you got all you could from her," Sen said darkly. He was next to me at the rail.

"Aye," I said. I was still too stunned to move. She chose to die. Her power would stay absolute. I could still taste her rose water on my lips.

"That was a brave thing," I said quietly to him. At least I think I said it to him. Perhaps I only said it to myself.

"Was it?" Sen looked down at me. "I'd say it was a stupid thing."

I looked at our quartermaster with questions in my eyes.

"Ned always sets women adrift," Sen told me.

"Is our captain a gentleman, then?" I asked, doubting it could be so.

"Thinks it bad luck to have them aboard. Leads to infighting," Sen said. So no, not a gentleman at all. "The insurance company would have made her whole for her losses. Most times we can take a ship like this without a drop of blood, as everyone knows the insurance company stands behind the cargo. Anyway. Where's the strength in giving up, when you can fight, and live to see another day? You can fight like a man. Or you can die like a dog."

I was on the point of answering when Sen added, "There's the desk already broken open."

Someone had taken a cutlass hilt to the lock and bashed it in, spilling gold and silver coins all over the deck. She must have been a duchess after all, to be traveling with such a fortune. My shipmates were laughing and raking their fingers through the hoard, and Ned had sent someone down to the galley for strong drink. Two of the pink's crew had elected to turn pyrate with us, and the remaining few had been set in the tenders, cut loose, and pointed toward the Carolina shore. The dead had been dumped overboard. The duchess's handsome young lover had joined them with a quick slice to the throat from one of my shipmates, leaving his velvet breeches and doublet behind to join the pile of spoils. The pink was ours. One of our number had even liberated the parrot, a blur of red who flapped from shoulder to spar and back again, squawking, "*Arrêtez! Arrêtez!*"

"God's my witness," I said softly to Sen, watching as the spirit of victory innervated my shipmates. One had started singing a shanty, clapping and stomping the beat, while some others danced arm in arm and joined in. "I've never seen so much money in all my life."

Sen laughed a short laugh. "It's not nothing," he said. "But it'll not hold a candle to what William Fly stole from us. And us with no insurance company backing our booty either."

William Fly. I froze. I didn't dare let Seneca know I had anything to say about William Fly.

"William Fly," I said, keeping my voice light. "He was a confederate of yours?"

"That he was," said Sen. "Did you know him?"

"Oh, no," said I.

"You did say you were from Boston," Sen said.

"Me? No, not Boston. I'm from Beverly," I said, probably too fast.

It was true. Sort of.

"Huh." Sen watched as drink poured freely into the mouths of our shipmates. The two French recruits were having brandy poured down their throats until they started to choke, and one of them bent double and voided his guts to the general laughter and approval of everyone.

"But I saw him hang," I said in a low voice.

"So did I," said Sen, just as quietly.

"Ho there!" shouted Ned Low, his face gone blurry with drink, all hint of cruelty vanished from his face as though he weren't stepping over the scorched circle that had moments ago held the roasted body of the French captain. "Sen, did you give him his just reward?"

"Not yet," Sen said. There was a tightness in his voice that I didn't remember hearing before. To me, he added, "So, have you decided?"

"Decided?" I asked.

"You're the fellow who first spotted our *Rose Pink*," he reminded me. "D—n sharp eyes you've got. I could barely see it, even with the glass. That means you get first choice of the arms aboard, as your own. Well deserved too."

My ears flushed with pleasure. "Oh," I said.

"The captain had a flintlock with a pretty fine stock. Ivory, I think it is," said Sen, leaning on the rail. "Or you can have his cutlass, if a flint-lock's too precious for you."

I eyed him, watching his scarred face for clues. "Which would you choose?"

Sen thought, turning his opinions over in silence while two of our shipmates threw punches at each other disputing some imagined slight and then collapsed in a scuffling heap on the deck, only to be pulled apart and given more drink.

"I'd choose the pistol," he said at length. "That is, if you can fire one."

I was on the point of answering him when Ned Low arrived at my side, a cup of brandy in his hand. "The French," he slurred. "And their God d—d brandy. Here." He roughly poured some in my mouth, most of it dribbling over my chin and down my chest. I coughed and swallowed as best I could.

"Now," Ned Low said, draping his arm over my shoulder as if we were boon companions. I stiffened, instinctively on watch for a sudden burst of rage. I never saw a man so changeable as Ned Low. Something in Sen's face that had been open while we were talking in confidence had slid closed when Ned approached. That was the first time I considered that Sen might have held opinions in reserve that were his own, and secret. "We'll be outfitting the *Rose Pink* and sailing in convoy. Sen here will assume command of the pink and you're to ship with him. All right?"

"All right," I agreed. My eyes met Sen's, and though I can't be sure as I recall it now, I think we both felt some relief.

"There's just one thing you've got to do first," Ned said. All at once, the drunken merriment drained out of his voice. His arm tightened about me like a vise. I felt my rigging knife, a lump secreted in the waist of my pantaloons, and wondered if I would have time to reach it.

"Name it," I said. "Sir."

I knew I must make Ned believe I was his unquestioning shipmate. To make Ned Low believe I would follow him to the bottom of the sea.

Our pyrate captain leaned his mouth in close to my ear, so near that I could feel his breath. But I still could not smell him.

"Tell me your name," he said with such a delicate softness that he might have been the Devil offering me a sixpence for my soul.

I froze, my terrified eyes jumping from Ned to Sen and back again. Was I found out? How could I be? I'd done everything a cabin boy does. I'd cooked, I'd scrubbed, I'd fetched, I'd carried, I'd gotten drunk and shirked my labors and been called to task for it. I'd kissed the duchess, for my own sake partly as one long resentful of my betters, but also so that Jimenez would tell everyone I was as much a rogue as any of them. I'd stabbed a man to death through the eye! My soul, none too clean to begin with, was stained forever, dipped in blood, all in service to Ned Low. The flames of hell licked at my heels with every waking moment, because of him. Well, because of me. Because I was more a coward than the duchess of wherever, I suppose. Though here I stood, one of God's creatures, for all I was a sinner, breathing still, my heart still beating like sparrow wings in my chest. And where was she? Heaven, I guess.

"Sir?" I said, trying to make my voice as innocent and dumb as a lamb's. "I thought you knew. I'm Will Chandler."

Ned and Sen exchanged a look, and Ned started to laugh.

"Ach, you poor b—d," said Ned Low. He released my shoulder and stood on one side of me, arms folded over his chest, while Sen stood on my other side, still leaning casually on the rail, though blocking any means of my escape.

This is all ridiculous, William Fly's skeleton skull cackled inside my head.

"Billy Chandler, you see, I happen to know, is dead," said Ned Low in what almost passed for a friendly tone, smiling out of one side of his mouth as he observed our shipmates' drunken dancing.

"And Billy Chandler," Seneca added slowly, gazing out over the shimmering Atlantic waters, his back to the dancing and merriment on board, "was from Jamaica. And as Black as the night is long."

Chapter 9

Jamaica! That lying, thieving b—d in whose boots I was presently quaking. What a tale he had spun for me, as if he were an innocent lamb walking alone through the valley of the shadow of death. Who was he, then? So Billy Chandler was the rolly-gaited Jamaican boy with the hearty appetite for squab. The sandy boy from New Orleans who I found hiding in my hayloft fearing for his life wasn't Billy Chandler at all. He was a boy who would let his friend die in his place and steal his name to save his skin. And try to send me out on errands for him while he hid in my hayloft in perfect safety. To think I'd wasted my pity on him! And apologized when I stole the boots from his sorry, lying corpse.

Whoever he was, he had gone pyrating with William Fly. That much I knew. And now I come to learn that William Fly had stolen from Ned Low and fled. And Ned Low had chased them all to Boston, then lain in hiding while authority took Will Fly and his shipmates prisoner, though the sandy boy had somehow escaped. Sen had been at the hanging. He'd have known the sandy boy wasn't amongst their number on the gallows, and so they sent John Somethingorother and a confederate out to find him and exact their revenge.

They'd found him, hiding with a girl for his protector. Some protector I proved to be. They'd killed him dead in the yard. And the girl had gotten away. My mind tripped along as fast as I could make it go, scrabbling for a story that I could tell that they might believe.

But what was there to believe? The lying New Orleans b—d was dead. Why should he have been anything to me? The version of me that was Will, that is. There were dozens of hungry boys like Will awash in the streets of Boston. I could be anyone. I had nothing to do with any of it.

"Oh," I said easily. "Is that a fact?"

"It is," Ned Low said, watching me with his blank blue eyes. "So if you would be so kind as to tell me your name. I would know who serves as able seaman on my *Rose Pink*."

I was too busy calculating my next move to pay sufficient attention to what Ned Low had just said. If they didn't want me here, I reasoned, I would be dead already. It would have been easy enough for Sen to dispatch me while we conferred by the rail. Or anytime, really, if they had known I was an impostor before we even left Long Wharf. But many kinds of desperate men go out upon the account. Not all of our number had been on the fateful cruise that saw William Fly abscond with Ned Low's treasure. Others of us thought we were shipping out on an honest fruit packet and were as new to the pleasures and horrors of pyracy as I was. Those two Frenchmen vomiting their captain's brandy all over the deck awoke this morning thinking themselves honest seamen bringing rich passengers safely through a gale, and now look at them. They'd hang with the rest of us and make no mistake.

No, I could be anyone. I *was* anyone. I had nothing to fear from my connection to that dead sandy boy. Under the flexing toes of my left foot, I felt the folded square of the boy's black spot crinkle.

"It's Will," I said with enough conviction that I started to believe it myself. "That much is true."

Sen and Ned exchanged another look, one that I couldn't wholly read.

"And how did you come to be aboard the *Reporter*, Will-That-Much-Is-True?" Sen asked, his one good eye resting evenly on my face.

I was aware of his nearness to me, as I had been our first night at sea, when his body was pressed up against mine in a row of snoring hammocks. I found Sen's nearness calmed me, though I couldn't explain why. I'd certainly seen him do dark and pitiless work. Even now his blouse was stiffening from another man's blood. But just as Ned Low's nearness set me instantly on a knife edge, Sen's gentled me down. Ned's eerie lack of scent left me watchful and suspicious, as though he were a predator disguising himself to draw close for the kill. But Sen smelled well to me, even at our foulest, after our longest days of work. He was redolent of pine tree sap and rum. Now I stood sandwiched between them, my back against the rail with nothing behind me but the open ocean.

If I could show them what they expected to see, I might raid with them in perfect safety. Well, not perfect. I would end on the gallows if I didn't die dashed to pieces on shoals or in the belly of the whale with all my shipmates after a gale blew us all to dust. But until we reached our inevitable end, whichever gruesome death God saw fit to send my way, my task was to live to see another day.

"I'm a thief," I said. The lie sprang so easily to my lips that Mrs. Tomlinson would have despaired over my soul. "I was apprenticed to a pewterer, and his wife put me out of doors when she caught me. Boxed my ears and denied me my wage, and even the clothes on my back. I was hungry, on the streets, and friendless. Sleeping in doorways. Stealing to eat. No shoes. I heard some other boys on the wharves talking of a fruit packet set to sail the next day, so I presented myself in hopes the *Reporter* would have me. And I praised God Almighty when the real Billy Chandler never showed."

It sounded good. I would believe myself if I were listening to me.

Would they?

"What did you steal?" asked Sen. His one good eye, darkly watching me. I wondered what that eye might look like when he smiled. Had I ever seen Sen smile? I'd seen him laugh, but always drily, never with a smile. Maybe that's not something philosophers do.

"Apples," I said, thinking of my terrible night folded up tight in the apple barrel while John Somethingorother and his unknown confederate hunted the streets ready to slice off my head. The coin on the bottom of John's peg leg tinking against the courtyard bricks, counting away the minutes of my life.

"Apples?" said Ned Low. "Wouldn't your mistress be bound to feed you? How's that thieving?"

"I stole them to sell," I said. "I kept the proceeds for myself and spent it all on liquor. Liquor and w—res."

Ned and Sen both laughed. "A lad of what, fourteen? Balls not even dropped?" bellowed Ned Low, loudly enough for all and sundry to hear. "Well, if you weren't born a pyrate."

I smiled tightly.

"All right. Let's make ready. Sen, you'll choose your crew. Keep one of the Frenchies who knows the ship, but not both. Don't want a mutiny on our hands," said Ned Low. He went to the group of shipmates drinking and tussling together by the pink's mainmast and barked, "Make ready!" One of them was too drunk to stand, and, with a roar, Ned's good humor vanished faster than morning dew, and he landed a boot in the drunken man's ribs.

If Sen was troubled by our mercurial captain, he made no sign.

"And what's your family name, Will-That-Much-Is-True?" he said when we were alone again.

I'd thought they might let me get away with being nameless. Most of us went by only one name. Seneca first amongst us all.

But I didn't think fast enough. I blurted out, "Masury," before I could stop myself.

"Will Misery," he said. "If you say so."

He lifted his weight off the rail, tired from the day's exertions, and made as though to move away. But he stopped and said, "So what did you decide?"

"Sir?" I said, but my thoughts remained on how I had escaped. By a hairsbreadth, perhaps so narrow, I couldn't even see it. But here I stood, still breathing.

"Your arms. For spotting the pink. What do you choose?"

My lies made me bold. I felt an unaccustomed surge of power.

"I'd have both," I said, wearing my boldness on my face. "The cutlass and the pistol. The one with the ivory stock. And to prove my worth to the people, I'll add these to the common haul."

I pulled my pantaloon leg out of my boot and emptied out the clatter of jewels I had lifted from the duchess of wherever. They filled my hand, the locket swinging from my still-bloodied fist. The rubies glinted in the late afternoon sunlight.

For the first time in my short days of knowing him, I saw Sen look at me with surprise. And then, with a slowly dawning smile. He still had all his teeth too, even and younger than his face under his pink scar. His smile made his one eye glitter and filled me with such sneaking warmth that I smiled too.

"Well, well," he said, impressed. "A bold fellow is this Will Misery. So he'd have them both, would he? Thinks because he sweetened our pot so well that we'll reward him justly? As long as no one of the people objects. It can't hurt to have an able seaman well armed on the *Rose Pink*."

"Able?" I flushed with unaccustomed delight.

I was a lowly cabin boy no more. I, Will Misery, late Will Chandler, née Hannah Masury of Boston, Beverly, and points north, was rated able and would be paid as such.

Sen laid the flintlock pistol in my hand. It was heavy. The ivory stock was worked in the pattern of a mermaid with naked breasts and a split fish tail, her hair flowing around the grip like seaweed.

"Once we're under weigh, I'll teach you how to fire it," said Sen. "Can't have you blowing off anyone's head. Unless you mean to."

"Thank you, sir," I said, my cheeks aflame with pleasure. I weighed my prize in my hand, held it out, and squinted down the barrel, pointing it first down the length of the deck at the shipmate who had taken the helm, then up at Wickham, who was dragging the grappling hooks back aboard the *Reporter*, and settling finally on the scarlet parrot who sat preening himself in the shrouds.

I was so absorbed in my new toy that I didn't notice Sen seeming to linger as though he were about to tell me something further. Whatever it was, he must have thought better of it.

"Your cutlass is below," he told me. "Now, let's make ready. Jimenez!" he shouted to the swamp doctor. "Get the others and tell them to get to their posts. We're headed south."

"South, Sen?" Jimenez said, wiping the brandy off his chin.

"Due south," Sen said.

One by one we unfurled the newly bent-on sails. When the fresh main dropped into place with a whoomph, the scarlet parrot abandoned his post in the shrouds for a spot on the starboard rail, squawking, "*Arrêtez! Arrêtez! Arrêtez!*" A shimmering tail feather left behind to drift on ocean breezes, caught up and carried out over the sparkling water and coming to rest just where the duchess had vanished under the waves.

"Will!" someone shouted.

CAMBRIDGE

"Now, see, this is the part that doesn't make sense to me," Marian said from behind her hands. She was leaning forward with her elbows on the table, her palms over her eyes, her head throbbing.

"What do you mean?" asked Kay. She looked just as tired and wrung out as Marian felt. Her saddle shoes were off, her bobby-socked feet folded under her in the library chair. Fortunately, the map department in the library was empty. Marian slipped her own oxfords off under the table and reached down to massage one stockinged foot.

"I mean all of it," said Marian. "First off, all the other primary sources talk about the taking of the *Rose Pink* as happening in the Azores."

"Yeah," said Kay wearily. "I know."

"So, what is this source doing, implying they were off the coast of the Carolinas?" Marian wondered.

"I know," Kay said again.

"And secondly, the dates are wrong," said Marian. "The other sources all have the *Rose Pink* taken in 1722 or 1723."

"It's so close, though," said Kay. "When was the Julian/Gregorian calendar switch? It was about then, wasn't it? That could have us a year off."

"Only through March." Marian frowned. "And anyway, the calendar switch in England and the colonies was in 1752."

"Oh," said Kay. "I thought it was 1725." She laid her head down on her folded arms.

Marian stared down at the nautical chart under her elbows. To her, most nautical charts from the age of sail looked like a whole lot of nothing. It was hard to imagine the time and care it would have cost, taking soundings with a lead weight and wax and noting down the depth, and where the shoals were, the specific qualities of sand. Five fathoms, six fathoms, nine fathoms, ten. And then, blankness. The early eighteenth century was only a few decades away from maps of the world naming *terra incognita*, with engravings of sea serpents and the warning *Here there be monsters*. Monsters, indeed. It was a wonder anyone knew anything about the sea bottom at all. It was as close and omnipresent and alien and unreachable as outer space.

"Maybe it's hyperbole," said Kay into the tabletop. "She's being literary. They could have taken the pink off the Azores, like all the sources say. Maybe Hannah saying that they sent the tenders toward Carolina meant they pointed them in a hopeless direction, assuming they would drift to their deaths."

"Could be," Marian said.

It was true that Hannah didn't give any sense of how much time had passed from their leaving New York before they took the pink. But it didn't seem to be enough time. Hannah suggested that she got blind drunk and didn't sober up until right before she spotted the ship. It was impossible she could have been unconscious that long. The Azores were practically off the coast of Africa. She'd have had to be drunk for, what, a month? At least? No, they must have been off the coast of the Carolinas after all. Plenty of pirate activity off Cape Hatteras. It made sense. Could the other sources be wrong?

"I mean, they murdered everybody else," Kay continued, speaking into her arm. "They could be the kind of pirates who set people adrift with no hope."

"Except the two who joined the crew. They didn't murder them. And a lot of what we know about Ned Low came from a diary by a fisherman he kidnapped who refused to sign his articles. Philip Ashton. He tortured him, and he starved him, but he didn't murder him," Marian said.

"Right. Hannah says they didn't murder the two Frenchmen. But she never tells us their names," said Kay.

"There's a lot she leaves out," agreed Marian.

The more closely she looked for these details, the more Marian felt creeping doubt. Maybe this account was a fake after all. But it didn't feel like a fake. Marian could poke holes in parts of Hannah's story, but somehow the holes themselves felt consistent with the kind of fragile tissue paper tears that open in the memories of our own lives: dates mixed up, locations made composite, stories burnished and embroidered in the retelling. Could Marian recall the exact year she first dared to visit the Mad Hatter? It may have been 1915, but it could have been 1914, or even 1916 if she wasn't as sophisticated a teenager as she imagined herself to be. Could she tell the month, day, hour, and moment that her roommate in college first touched the back of her hand? Could she recount the substance of the last conversation she ever had with her mother?

Marian switched feet under the table, rubbing under her tired big toe with a thumb.

Kay was examining a length of curl pulled out of her ponytail and using it to tickle her own nose. She had worn eye makeup to the library, and a corner of it had smudged. "Not that much," she countered. "There's a lot of description, anyway."

"Sort of," said Marian. "How come she never tells us what kind of coins they found?"

"They were French," said Kay. "The duchess said they wouldn't get a sou more."

"Yeah, but that's also a common expression. Just a figure of speech. 'Not worth a sou.' 'Won't get a sou.' People even say that now, and the franc supplanted the livre in 1795," said Marian. "A duchess traveling with a lot of ready cash in the 1720s would probably have had a mixture. Spanish, French, some Portuguese, maybe even English. Pieces of eight were the commonest currency in the world."

"How would Hannah know what all those kinds of coins looked like?" Kay pointed out.

"True," Marian said. "Though she worked at an ordinary. People would have paid for their room and board. She'd have seen Spanish reals all the time."

Kay shrugged without lifting her head from the library table.

Due south, Hannah said they were headed. Due south from where?

Marian shuffled one chart away and pulled up another. It was titled *A chart of the coast of America: from New York and Philadelphia to the Strait or Gulf of Florida, and from thence to the Mississippi*, and dated from around 1850.

"Maybe we should be looking at a modern one?" Kay suggested. "I bet with modern technology those maps would be more complete."

"Maybe," said Marian.

Her gut was telling her to look at older ones. Ideally, Marian wanted to look at the charts that Hannah would have looked at, or failing Hannah herself, whoever it was in charge of navigation. Seneca, probably. Marian had to laugh at that one. A Black contraband pirate naming himself after a Stoic. He had to be made up. She had read plenty of Stoics, but doubted anyone in 1726 did, or at least, not anyone outside of Harvard College, with its studious teenage Yankee boys bent over their Greek and Latin and Bible.

All the same, there was a line that had stuck with her, back when she was in school. How did it go?

Sometimes even to live is an act of courage.

Marian was accustomed to looking at maps like the ones in a regular atlas, where north was always up, the frozen poles at the top and the bottom, the Americas in the middle, with oceans on either side and Asia cleaved in two. But some of these charts, especially the ones of the Atlantic coast of the Americas, were oriented with *terra firma* at the top, and the shoreline stretched out sideways, with north roughly to the right (though not exactly) and the south off to the left. This chart from the 1850s looked like that. The unaccustomed orientation rendered the East Coast of the United States into an alien and mysterious landscape.

Kay got up and wandered off in her stocking feet to the stacks without saying anything. Marian watched her go, and then returned to staring at the chart of the Eastern seaboard where Hannah would have gone pirating.

To the right, New York Harbor looked treacherous, with soundings of three and four feet—or would it have been fathoms? Did the 1850s use fathoms? She didn't know—no, it must have been feet, as they marked a deadly shoal off the coast of Brooklyn. In addition to the depths the chart noted the quality of the sea bottom—yellow sand, yellow-gray sand, and one mysterious area marked *Mud Hole*. Near the bottom of the chart the soundings and descriptions petered gradually out—*Gravel* was noted somewhere, and then a white expanse of no information at all. In twenty-four feet of water, *scattered shells and sea eggs*. Then thirty-three feet of water, and then nothing until a few directional arrows pointing left and the notation *cold southerly current*. No wonder that mariners would have kept a weather eye out for mermaids in such unspeakable expanses of emptiness.

Marian's eyes traced to the left along the contours of the shoreline, moving down roughly to what she imagined Hannah's route must have been. Hannah noted in the manuscript that they were out of sight of land when she woke from her bender and spotted the pink, which made sense—they were mutineers, probably twice over, if Hannah's story about Ned Low was correct. They would have wanted to avoid notice at all costs. Better to stay away from shipping lanes and busy ports and any place where they were likely to attract uncomfortable questions. Also better, if they were going to raid, to do it in an area where other ships would be less likely to come to the victims' aid. That would explain why they only saw the pink and no other vessels.

Where would the pink have been going with a noble French passenger and her lover and her jewels? Hannah hadn't bothered to ask anyone in the manuscript, or evince any curiosity about it, and Marian had no idea. New Orleans? Maybe. Or possibly Haiti. Haiti would still have been Saint-Domingue in 1726. Brutal, sweltering, a ruthlessly efficient plantation slave system producing cane sugar and coffee for rich European tongues. Hannah remarked on the supposed duchess's impassiveness in the face of Ned Low's torture of the pink's nameless captain. If she were a white slaveowner from Saint-Domingue, that would account for her apparent comfort with brutality. Just an idea. But none of those theories suggested where Hannah and company were headed after the pink was taken.

There was Cape Hatteras. The chart noted the dangers of the shoals around the Carolina coast and remarked that the course of the Gulf Stream varied according to the prevailing winds, with westerlies driving the stream farther from the land and easterly or southeasterlies driving it nearer the shore. Did that matter?

"Bermuda?" she wondered aloud to herself.

"That's southeast," said Kay, who had wandered back to their table with a modern atlas in her hands and sat down. "Not due south."

"Right," said Marian.

The chart also said that the Gulf Stream moved at about three miles per hour. And that it was warmer than the water on either side of it. Marian wondered how they had figured that out. She tried to imagine sailors' hands in the water. Sailors' feet. Sailors who had fallen overboard. The thought made her squirm, and she pushed it aside. What was the singular horror of drowning? Was it the solitude? Was it the darkness? Was it the certain knowledge that it must take a given length of time?

Marian didn't like to interrogate death too closely. She supposed she wasn't alone in that regard. She was as horrified as Hannah had been when she read of the duchess's abrupt suicide. Not that Marian was especially sorry now that she had a credible hypothesis for where that duchess came from. But even so. An unwelcome image arose in her mind of the duchess's body suspended in the deep, drifting at a steady three miles per hour. Marian had read that there was a trench in the middle of the Atlantic Ocean so deep, no human or machine could plumb its depths. That the pressure of the water would crumple a submarine like a tin can. That the pressure made the water subfreezing but still liquid and perfectly, completely dark, too deep for sunlight to penetrate. Any animals living there would be blind and alien beings, their bodies knit of gossamer water. She pictured the dead duchess drifting down into this trench, vanishing into darkness by slow degrees, frozen, preserved like a specimen in formaldehyde, eyes open, hair still, sunk into a kind of suboceanic hell.

"How about Bimini?" Kay said brightly.

"What?" Marian snapped out of her reverie of horrors to find the undergraduate tucked into the chair opposite her and looking at a map of the Caribbean that had been published recently by the Army Corps of Engineers.

"Bimini," Kay said again, pushing her atlas across the table to Marian and pointing. "It's due magnetic south from a few points off Cape Hatteras. If I'm reading this correctly. I mean, so is Grand Bahama, but I'd say it's too big even in 1726 for any serious pirate shenanigans."

"Shenanigans?" Marian smiled.

"What?" Kay said. "Should I say tomfoolery instead? Fine, pirate tomfoolery."

Marian looked at Kay's atlas page, and then back again to her nineteenth-century chart, the earliest she had been able to find in her hasty map collection search. The chart did show *N. Bemini* and *South Bemini*, with a different spelling. But here was something—on Marian's 1850s chart, the Bemini Bank seemed to be ringed with tiny islands.

"Cat Key," she read to herself. And farther down, "Orange Kays," with many dots in between. She checked the chart against the contemporary atlas. Cat Key was there, and so was Orange, but the scale of the atlas was smaller, and so the tiny dots didn't appear.

"What do you think?" Kay asked, leaning a cheek on her hand.

Marian rubbed her fingertips over her eyebrows. From behind her hands, she said, "I mean, maybe. But it's nothing more than a guess. I don't think we can get the Explorers Club to support a research trip on a wild guess. We need Hannah to give us something more."

They settled in silence, staring at the nautical chart and atlas.

The Gulf Weeds are larger and in greater quantity on the outer Edge of the Stream than within it, the antique chart informed her.

Marian frowned.

"Library's closing in fifteen minutes!" an unseen voice called into the stacks where they were working.

"Damn it," said Marian.

"I can't come tomorrow," Kay told her as she started closing books and packing her schoolbag. "I have an exam."

It was midterms already. The elm leaves in the quad had deepened into reds and golds and started to fall, and Marian was giving an exam herself tomorrow, in her senior seminar on Concord in the nineteenth century. She hoped that the rumors of a network of secretly filed papers and exams in the plush lounges of the private sororities weren't true, as she was going to give the exact same exam tomorrow that she had given last year, and the year before that. Then again, if they didn't care to actually learn the material, well, what difference did it make? What were any of them going to go on and do, anyway? Were they going to be history professors?

She eyed Kay, who was buckling closed her satchel and stacking a tidy pile of call slips. There was an efficiency to Kay's method of work, and to the way that she liked to drive to a simple answer. Maybe lacking in some nuance, but Kay didn't let herself get lost in hypothetical backwaters like Marian did. She wasn't quite brusque, but almost. For all Kay's occasional girlish humor, there was a straightforwardness to her, a clearing away of nonsense, that Marian had started to appreciate. A word arose in Marian's mind in connection with Kay: "modern." As the young woman wound her scarf around her neck and tucked her curls under a brown woolen cloche, Marian scrubbed aside the kitchen window in Montclair in which she had first trapped her imagined Kay of the future, a thwarted romantic living through her fantasies of the past to dull the stultification of her present. Down a bustling New York City street strode an entirely different imaginary future Kay, a modish and sophisticated Kay, in perfect gloves and a streamlined brooch, indifferent to the admiring glances of all the fedoraed businessmen parting ways for her on Fifth Avenue. Who was this Kay? Some sort of curator, perhaps, or a writer, a woman serious but livened with a twinkling of fun. Marian envied this future version of Kay. This Kay drank cocktails in tiny, elegant glasses and danced to jazz in clubs without secret rooms. This Kay swanned through hotel lobbies in fur and went to the opera and actually enjoyed herself.

"Well?" said the actual Kay, her bag over her shoulder, bundled against a walk home in the biting Cambridge dusk.

"I just can't get over it," said Marian, frustrated and strangely embarrassed by the story about Kay she had just been telling herself.

"I know," said Kay.

Marian clasped her hands on top of her head and moaned, "Why couldn't Hannah have just saved the drawing of the map?"

"I know," said Kay. "I know."

I HUNG MY head over the side. The water was so glassy and smooth that I could clearly see my face reflected, surrounded by a corona of sunlight that moved with me if I turned my head. I was sunburnt and my hair had begun to bleach. My stolen blouse was grayed from lack of washing and my overall aspect was of a boy growing to manhood, being weathered out of youth by salt and drink and sun. Though still no whiskers, and a voice unbroken.

The water sloshed softly against our hull. We were barely moving at all. The sea was a rich lapis blue, and our bow combed through seaweed as thick as though we were sailing through the hair of a submerged giant.

"Somebody give him something to do," I heard Orne complain about the Frenchman who hovered at his elbow by the helm. *Rose Pink* had been under weigh for some days, I don't remember how long, but the Frenchman who had joined us had affixed himself to our sailing master like a remora fish the moment our convoy turned south. The more Orne harangued and abused him, the nearer the Frenchman clung. I didn't know his name—Jean something, probably; they all seemed to be called Jean something—and he never tried to speak to me. He had made Orne his protector when his confederate crewmate was mustered to serve on the *Reporter* with Ned Low.

I gazed out over the water and spied the *Reporter* as a distant blur on the shimmering horizon, far and away off to port of us. They had very little weigh too, but without intending to they had pulled away from us, being swifter bottomed than we, or possibly better sailed. We required more men, being square rigged, and the *Reporter* sailed well with only a few able hands, but our numbers had been evenly divided as Ned Low wished to keep us under his influence and control.

"Ach." Orne peered aloft at the sails. We had every stitch of canvas out, and most of it hanging in the airless afternoon like drying laundry. Jonah the stump-tailed cur had stowed away with us and dozed now in a ball atop a coil of lines. I gently shifted one of his paws away from a bight, and he kicked in his sleep. He'd catch his foot again if he wasn't careful. After more than one colorful scuffle of flying fur and feathers he and the crimson parrot had reached an uneasy truce, with one taking a watch on starboard side, and the other on larboard, then switching at eight bells.

I heard the telltale *drag* and *chink*, *drag* and *chink* that meant that John Somethingorother was approaching. Presently he leaned at the rail next to me, squinting into the distance, a three-cornered hat that he had discovered forgotten in the gun deck of the pink perched rakishly on his head. He had outfitted the dented hat with a shimmering red cockade crafted from a couple of the parrot's tail feathers. The parrot himself sat in a crimson ball, dozing, his head under a wing as he perched on a water barrel lashed to the deck. I had tried to approach him more than once and gotten a sharp beak to the thumb for my trouble.

"'Bout ready for supper making," John said. "Thought I'd get me a breath of air first."

It was hot in the galley always. I didn't care to be summoned to duty just then, or really anytime, in truth. It was unpleasant duty, hot and tiresome, and I hated the scrubbing up afterward, but above that, I felt better keeping more than an arm's reach between me and the man who had at one time wanted me dead, even if he didn't know it. Whenever possible, I found other duties to absorb my labor and my time that kept me on a different deck entirely from John. But despite my rising fortunes in the crew, John still outranked me as cook, and if asked I must go below.

"Aye," I said. "Not much air to be found up here, but . . ."

"God d—n your eyes, you snail-breathed son of a w—e," Orne swore. "I'll not have you for my greatcoat!"

The Frenchman smiled his unsettling smile and didn't move from his station by Orne's elbow.

"You reckon he thinks to take the helm?" John asked me with an eye on the Frenchman. "Drive us back to shore in revenge?"

I didn't know what I reckoned, but I knew if he angered Orne much more, we'd certainly be down a Frenchman.

"Take it where?" I replied. "There's not even enough air to tack."

John grunted his assent. I missed my clay pipe and hemp from the tavern, and not for the first time. Maybe I could make myself one with a whale tooth or a walrus tusk, if I could find one lying about. I wondered what had happened to it. At times, I dreamed that Sarah had somehow found it, and when she slipped it between her lips, she thought of me.

"That's enough!" Orne bellowed. "John, you take this frog below and boil him for supper. Will! Take this God d—d wheel before I rip it out of the deck and cast it into the sea."

Orne let go the wheel without even waiting for my assent, and the ship slowly wallowed, making like it was going to round up, bringing us to a standstill in the middle of the ocean. Orne stalked off in a rage, the Frenchman close at his heels. John was laughing, but I hurried to the quarterdeck, buzzing with significance. It was my first time at the helm. For the next many hours, the *Rose Pink* would be mine.

My hands closed around the spokes of the wheel, and I eased the helm back into position. What little wind we had pressed softly into the sails so that they no longer hung slack, and the *Rose Pink* settled herself, resuming her silent, painfully slow progress. I peered at where the *Reporter* had been, and she had grown even smaller on the horizon. If I wasn't careful, I might lose her. I swore softly to myself and set my sights on her, steering as straight as I was able.

The sleepy afternoon wore on, the sun making its lazy way across the sky, the parrot ruffling himself awake and flapping over to the stern rail for a preen and to observe me at the helm as I minutely corrected and watched the sails. Jonah rolled onto his back in the ropes, showing a pale belly to the tropical sun. I couldn't figure it out. The *Reporter* was now a mere dot. I was sailing as close to the wind as I could, but it felt as though we weren't moving forward at all.

Salt pork stew was handed around for the midday meal and someone passed me a hard biscuit to gnaw on. The parrot waddled over to help himself to the crumbs that fell from my lip. Sensing opportunity, Jonah trotted over and nipped at the parrot's heels, sending him squawking to the stern rail.

"Quiet, you," I said to him.

I felt the pressure of the current on our rudder but couldn't sense the answering pressure from the wind.

A few hours into my watch, Sen ambled to the stern to check in with me.

"Well?" he said, leaning on a barrel strapped nearby, his arms folded across his chest.

"I see why Orne went off in a huff," I said, hoping that the reference to our sailing master would suggest that if we were off course, it wasn't due to some error of mine.

"I don't see them," he said, scanning the horizon.

"Over there," I said, pointing.

Sen pulled out the spyglass from under his arm, following my sight, and checked the position of the *Reporter*. Upon observing her great distance from us, Sen swore fluently.

"We're being set by the current," he told me with evident irritation. "And *Reporter*'s rig can carry her closer to the wind. There's no way we can stay this course. At this rate the current might carry us all the way to England before we can raise the islands."

So the information gleaned from my hands on the wheel was accurate. We weren't moving forward. We were moving sideways.

Sen still hadn't told any of us where we were going. He and Ned Low had settled on a rendezvous point before the two ships uncoupled and set off, and only the two of them knew where it lay.

"What would you have me do?" I asked. I couldn't tell if having Ned

Low sail over the horizon away from us made me feel more at ease or less. Perhaps both at once. I worried over losing sight of our elected leader when our command was to stick close to him. But I breathed easier knowing he wasn't on board the pink. I found it easier to sleep. I think the rest of my shipmates did too.

Sen frowned out over the water for a short time, thinking. "Pass the word," he said at length. "Fire two shots off the port side in double time. Blanks."

The word was passed and in moments we heard two gunports swing open and the *boom, boom* of first one, and then the next two-pound cannon, startling the parrot, who flapped squawking back into the shrouds. Plumes of smoke breathed from our hull, but no balls were launched. We waited, Sen staring hard through his spyglass.

After a few tense moments we heard a faint *boom*, and then another *boom*. The *Reporter* answering. Sen kept his good eye trained through the spyglass, waiting for confirmation of our message.

After a time, he said, "All right. They've come about."

They were heading back for us. Though they'd be sailing into the current. The ocean might decide to push us apart no matter what we might will or choose.

My hands were cramping from long hours on the wheel as the sun settled into the western ocean and painted the evening sky in pinks and violets. I had kept a weather eye on the *Reporter* all afternoon, and though they hadn't winked out of existence over the horizon, they didn't seem to be getting any nearer either. In the gathering dusk I thought I saw a lantern glitter to life on their mainmast, but it wouldn't be enough to guide us to them in the dark.

I had passed so many hours looking between the *Reporter* and the sails and back again that I hadn't taken the measure of our surroundings in some time. As I rolled my head on my tired neck, bones cracking, I spied for the first time a small sail in the distance, well away off to starboard. The light was fast disappearing from the east, the stars beginning to open their cold eyes to gaze upon us in our silent pool of seaweed and black water. The ship was hard to make out in the rising darkness. No point to raising the alarm, I supposed. Was there?

"Ho there," I called to Jacob idling on the main deck. "Pass the word for Sen."

By the time my captain had mounted the quarterdeck again to join me, a soft navy darkness had settled completely on the eastern horizon. I thought I had my eye still on the sail, and that perhaps it had illuminated some running lights. The faint glimmers I saw could have belonged to falling stars.

"What is it?" Sen asked me, plainly tired.

"Sail on the horizon," I said. "Could be a fishing vessel."

I pointed, and he scanned the waveless expanse of open water along the length of my outstretched fingertips.

"I don't see it," he said.

I moved closer, my chin just over his shoulder, aiming my arm alongside the spyglass. I steadied myself with a light touch on his hip. "Just there," I said. "A light, moving left to right. Very faint. Can you make it out?"

I felt Sen stiffen away from my touch, and he looked down at me with a strange expression that I didn't much like. I moved back to my place at the wheel and said, "Sir."

He looked at me for a tense moment and then returned to his spyglass.

"Maybe," he said. "Hard to say."

I looked hard at nothing, one ear flushed red. I hadn't thought anything of touching him. All of us shipmates were too close together all the time. I thought nothing of a shipmate's hand on my shoulder, or an elbow in my ribs to urge me out of the way, or even a knee in my back as we went up and down the companionway. But I had never touched him on purpose before.

Then I realized that, to my knowledge, Sen had never intentionally touched me.

My captain rubbed a tired hand along the back of his neck and said, "We'll see if she's still there at dawn."

I kept staring straight ahead, my face a mask. "Yes, sir," I said.

"*Arrêtez*," the parrot agreed from the mizzen shrouds.

A bell donged, telling us that our watches were turning over. Sleepy men on deck with me checked their lines for fastness and then shuffled off, as shadowy figures emerged from below chattering amongst themselves. Someone approached with a lantern to spell me at the wheel, and I surrendered it with gratitude, cracking my knuckles and stretching out my hands.

"Will," Sen said gently, "you needn't be wearing it at the ready all the time."

He nodded at the cutlass, which I had slung about my hips with a handsome yellow and blue sash liberated from the duchess's cabin. The sash was long and soft and silken and ended in golden tassels, and I had never held anything so fine or beautiful before, much less could I say that it belonged to me. I loved the weight of the cutlass blade flat against my thigh, I loved the scrape of its blade catching the wood when I turned too quickly. It was cumbersome, but it was mine. And I would be d—d if anyone might take it from me.

I touched the hilt and said, "I like it."

Sen, patient, said, "You'll cut a man's leg off. Stow it below with your hammock." Then, as though sensing my hesitation, he added, "The people all know it's yours."

I supposed he was right. When I first appeared with it on, I had enjoyed many back slaps and brotherly jeers, as each of us had privately tallied what his share of the duchess's jewels might be. Riches unimagined and an awful lot of very fine rum. And all because I had spotted the pink with my uncanny farsighted eyes.

"Yes, sir," I said.

We moved down the companionway ladder, Sen waving me to go down first so as to keep well clear of the blade swinging behind me like a dog tail as I went. Down below, the gun ports were open to catch any whiff of breeze, but the deck still felt stale and hot from the sultry summer afternoon. The clearance was low enough that I had to duck under the occasional beam, and Sen, who was a head again taller than I, had to hunch himself over to walk.

"Long watch. If you can spare an hour's sleep, I'll show you how to work the pistol," he said.

"All right," I said, happy to have a reason for his attention, and also knowing that we could make use of the aft cabin, which had windows for air and light, and a chandelier with new candles hung high enough to clear my head when I sat down.

A table and some ornate French chairs decorated with gold leaf sat in the center of the cabin, and the table was covered with charts, a compass, a stylus, and other tools of navigation that I didn't understand. In a corner the empty parrot cage swung gently with the motion of the boat, and the candles cast a warm and friendly glow in the cabin. We could almost be friends bending together over a table in the corner of the small dining room at Ship Tavern, which I'd heard described more than once as like the captain's quarters on a brig, roomy and full of good things to eat.

"Sen?" I asked as he busied himself with taking apart the flintlock pistol with the carved ivory mermaid for a stock.

"Hmmm?" he said, pulling out a soft rag to polish away salt and grime. He nodded at one of the delicate gilt chairs and I sat in it, worried that even my slight weight would prove too much for its insect-thin legs.

I looked upon the charts in untidy piles on the table. Here was one, showing almost nothing except some depth soundings in numbers and what I guessed might have been notes on current, as there were words within a confusing network of arrows. Here was another chart, showing *terra firma*—Orne had taught me how to recognize that phrase above all others, saying it meant the mainland—and a few islands with names that were not legible to me. One was marked as having a population of wild pigs good for eating, or so I gathered from a drawing of a pig on it, and a spot with a handwritten ink notation over the symbol for shoals. I supposed that was a careening ground. A few of the islands, the chart noted in drawings, were populated with unfriendly Caribs, for here and there a small skull and crossbones suggested that death would surely wait for anyone who dared to put in uninvited.

"Where are we going?" I asked as he set each piece of the disassembled pistol down in front of me.

Sen settled his tired body in the other gilt chair, unconcerned that it might fall to splinters beneath him, and said, "In truth? I don't know."

"You don't know?" I exclaimed.

"Well, I know in general," he said. "Here."

He pulled a chart from beneath the others and spread it out before us. It showed a chain of islands arranged in a crescent, each island smaller than the last. The crescent islands looked to be an atoll in a similar pattern to the one on the chart I had just been eyeing, with the pigs and the Caribs and the careening ground, only this chart was larger, with more details. Many of the islands it showed where smaller than the nail on my smallest toe. Some were as minute as an eyelash. The chart was covered with writing, but I couldn't tell what any of it said. I didn't see *terra firma*.

"It's a favorite spot of Ned's," Sen told me. "Look here." He pointed to the shoals and said, "Here's where we'll careen the ships. It's sheltered and shallow enough that we can pull them over and clean the barnacles off and make any repairs we need to make, and the Royal Navy will never trouble us. There's fresh water here"—he pointed to one of the larger islands in the chain—"and pigs here"—he pointed to the pig island I had noticed already. "Have you ever had coconut?"

I shook my head. I'd heard tell of coconuts, and once I'd seen a dried one brought home as a curiosity by one of Ship Tavern's custom. It looked like a perfectly round brown stone with eyes. I couldn't imagine it would be good to eat. The old salt who'd showed it to me said that they floated on the water like driftwood, and if you split one with a cutlass the flesh inside was as tender as a newborn lamb, and sweet.

"Well, there's coconut palms on all of them," said Sen, and he may have even sounded excited. "And other fruits as well. All different kinds, some you've never even seen before."

Water sprang to my mouth as I dreamed of fresh fruit, visions of cornucopias overflowing lemons and limes and apples and berries rising immediately to my fevered mind. I hadn't had any fruit in weeks, not even preserved. We had discovered none in the *Rose Pink*, and some amongst the crew had muttered that they didn't throw over their lives ashore to go pyrating and risk the gallows just to get loose teeth.

"And will we . . . live there?" I asked, uncertain. I had not yet broken free from the idea that I might have a home to go to. I still believed that I was on a journey, away from one home, en route to another.

Sen looked at me strangely. "Live?" he asked.

"Yes. Do we each get a house of our own? Can Jonah stay with me?" As I recall this conversation, I see what a child I still was. I didn't understand that my life was never going to be at rest. I had become a citizen of a world in constant motion that would be stilled only by my death.

"No, Will Misery," he said, but his voice was gentle. "I don't blame you for wanting a place to call your own. I used to dream of such things too. A hearth and bed stuffed with feathers. Ease and safety. It took a long time for me to find my home."

"But you did find it?" I asked him, my voice small with hope.

"I did. Eventually." He sounded tired. Bone-weary. A weariness deep in his very soul.

"Where is it?" I asked. I wondered if I could make my home there too. Wherever it was. A place warm. And safe. With lots of fruit.

"Here is your home now." He tapped me gently in the very center of my forehead. "You carry it with you wherever you go. You can visit any time you close your eyes. There's no roof. It is open to the stars. Inside, you are completely free. It is yours and yours alone, until God calls you to go and be with Him."

"Oh," I said. I could tell I was supposed to find his words reassuring. But instead, I found I had never felt more friendless and alone.

Sen returned his attention to the charts before us, considering them with his chin in his hand. If he knew how crushed he made me feel, he gave no sign. "We'll tarry there awhile and make the ships ready. We'll load up with food and water and we'll retrieve what William Fly took from us, that thieving son of a w——e, and once it's found, we will terrorize the seas until we have all the riches we can carry," he told me quietly.

"And what then?" I asked.

"Then?" Sen seemed confused, as if he had never allowed himself to dream that far.

"Yes, when we have all the riches we can carry, what then?" I said. I trusted Sen to have an answer.

He hesitated, looking at the chart. "Maybe we'll go to St. Mary's," he said, but his voice sounded unsure, like he didn't know whether he was speaking of a real place or no. He said "St. Mary's" the way I had just said "house," as the place of safety dreamed of but never attained. I dared not ask where or what St. Mary's was.

"The trick," Sen continued, "is that I don't know where Will Fly stashed what he stole. And Ned doesn't either. It could be here." He pointed to one of the tiny islands. "Or could be on this one, which is near to where he lay at anchor on *Fame's Revenge*." He pointed to another.

"What did William Fly take?" I asked.

I wondered what the chart had to say about all these mysterious islands and the sea around them. I had never been much bothered by being unlettered. I had had enough Bible and hymns and *Pilgrim's Progress* poured into my head by Mrs. Tomlinson that I could spit out verses on demand, and anyway, what time would I have had to learn, or practice, or read anything beyond the Word? And the Word was brought to me whether I wanted it or not. No, I never felt much call to read. But now, looking at all scribbles and notes on the chart, I wished that I had my letters. I would have known what all of it said. I would have known how to calculate our position by looking at the stars, how to make note in the log of our position and the weather and the taking of *Rose Pink*, how to sign the name I had taken for myself to the articles under which I now lived.

Sen leaned his head back in his hands, his elbows splayed out, and I heard his back crack. He said, "Around one hundred thousand Spanish dollars, plus four pounds of gold dust."

"One hundred . . . what?" I couldn't grasp the vastness of the sums that Sen had just named. It seemed like more money than there was in the whole world. In fact, when I tried to name the sum aloud to myself, I failed.

Sen saw my astonishment and said drily, "So you see why we must go looking for it."

I nodded, mute, and looked upon the chart again. The atoll swam before my eyes, a near infinity of tiny islands, and any one of them could have hidden more wealth than was in all of Boston. A man would commit any number of horrors to put his hands on such a sum. He might betray his confederates, as Will Fly had done. As I imagined the lengths to which a man might go for even a fraction of such a sum, the quiet, reasonable voice within my mind reminded me of an interesting fact.

When the treasure is found, I will own one share.

How many of us were there? Around twenty-five, with extra half shares to our captains and officers. One twenty-fifth part of one hundred thousand Spanish reals and one twenty-fifth part of four pounds of gold dust, not counting what the duchess of wherever's hoard of jewels and coins might add to the total, meant that my part was . . .

It was . . .

I was as unnumbered as I was unlettered. But I knew that it was more than I would get in a lifetime of whatever I was liable to have done when my service to Mrs. Tomlinson was to end.

A soft tingling awoke in my fingertips, and I knew we must do anything we could to regain the treasure stolen from us.

Good luck. Will Fly's spectral skull laughed in my ear. *You'll never find it.*

Hold your tongue, Will, I told him inside my head.

This tongue? he asked me, opening his empty skeletal jaw, and the imagined sound of his laughter rose.

"And you don't know where it is?" I said, my voice too loud in the quiet cabin as I tried to drown out Will Fly's mocking laugh.

Sen started reassembling the flintlock pistol without even having to look at his practiced hands. "All the men who know where it is are dead," he told me. "Three on the gallows before my very eyes. And one in Boston at the point of a cutlass."

I was sitting very straight, my feet flat on the floor in not-Billy's boots, my fingers splayed on the table over the charts as though to keep myself from falling over.

"In Boston," I repeated. I felt words bubbling up in my chest, words too dangerous to say. But by now, surely Sen must trust me. Had I not proven myself to them? Was I not a worthy shipmate? The cutlass weighing at my hips said that I was.

"Behind a tavern," Sen said. "Before we could shake the answer out of him. A costly mistake, all told."

"Behind a tavern, you say," I echoed.

"That's right," said Sen.

"Was he a boy?" I asked before I could think better of it.

Sen gazed on me with one of his steady, calculating, unreadable expressions. "He was," said my captain.

"Sir," I said thickly, hoping my gamble would pay off. "I believe I stole his shoes."

Did I expect Sen to be surprised by this information? I don't remember. But Sen as a rule was not a man to register his surprise. Instead, he just said, "Did you?"

"Aye," I said. "I was put out without shoes. I was desperate." The lies tumbled out of me easily, one after the next. I was, indeed, becoming a capable and practiced sinner. "When I came upon him in my wanderings at first, I thought he was lying there dead drunk. Then I thought the poor fellow had been set upon by thieves and beaten unconscious. I approached him and presently I saw that there was no help for him, and he had no further need of boots nor anything else on this earth. So I took them."

Sen looked at my feet.

"Did you happen to take anything else of his?" he said quietly.

"Only this," I said. I unlaced the left boot and withdrew the small paper that had been crumpled beneath my toes for lo these many weeks.

I ironed the paper out under my hands on the tabletop. On one side was the tiny black spot that not-Billy had told me was the death sentence that had been delivered to him. Sen peered closely at it and said, "Ah."

He turned the black spot over to examine the back of the paper. It seemed to have some smudging, doubtless from its many days being ground under my great toe while I did my pyrating work.

Sen took the paper up in his hands and held it aloft, over his head, bringing it near to the candles in the chandelier to get a clearer look. As we spoke darkness had swallowed the corners of the cabin. We were sitting together in a confidential circle of candlelight.

With the light behind it the paper appeared nearly translucent, with only the black spot in the middle. But as Sen and I watched, something exceedingly strange happened.

When he brought the paper close to the open flame, a rippling seemed to overtake the paper. Out of the white blankness a dark brown line bubbled into existence, scoring itself across the black spot. At first, I thought the paper must be scorched, but the bubbling brown lines quickly resolved themselves into a shape. And the paper was not catching fire.

"What the Devil," exclaimed Sen, as astonished as I. He moved the paper delicately so that each corner of the slip was exposed to the warmth of the flame in equal measure. As he did so, more brown lines swam into focus and resolved themselves before our eyes, forming here a tracing of what seemed to be parts of a map, and there a line of brown dots of varying shapes and sizes. When the paper had revealed all that it seemed capable of, Sen laid it on the table before us with fascination.

It was a map. Or rather, it was a tracing of a nautical chart. It seemed to show the same crescent moon of island atoll that we had just been considering moments before. But over the heart of the paper, blotting away the tiny black dot of the boy's death sentence, the secret brown lines formed one large capital letter *X*.

"I'll be God d—d," said Sen. "That Jim Hawkins wrote it down after all."

So that was not-Billy's name. The sandy boy from New Orleans was called Jim Hawkins. I recalled my first conversation as cabin boy with John Somethingorother, when he'd asked my name, and wondered aloud if it was Jim. A private joke, I suppose, as John had opened the back of Jim's skull with his cutlass days before.

John, and some other man who spoke with a singsong voice when he called out my real name in the night.

Sen hurriedly pulled the nautical chart of the atoll back to the top of the pile and compared it with the hastily scrawled map in his hand. The paper was thin enough that the dark ink lines of the chart could just be made out through the message. Sen moved the paper around, trying it this way and trying it that, before he stopped and said, "There she be. Would you look at that."

I looked. The two maps aligned perfectly. It was almost as though Jim had overlaid this very chart to make his tracing with whatever secret ink he had had. The vortex of the capital letter X lay directly atop a small smudge of a dot of an island, two islands west of the one rich with pigs. I couldn't see that this island had a name. But at least it didn't have a skull and crossbones on it.

"Well, Will Misery," said Sen. "I'll say that was a nice piece of thievery you did."

And that was the first time that Sen ever reached over and took my hand.

CAMBRIDGE

"Invisible ink," Marian muttered. She still couldn't get over it.

Kay had proposed one theory when Marian first voiced her utter disbelief.

"Didn't you do Campfire Girls?" Kay asked, incredulous.

Marian looked at her blankly.

"You know. Campfire Girls. You do crafts, go on hikes, wear Indian headdresses," Kay explained. "Sleepover camp. You know. All that stuff."

Marian had tried to imagine the late Mrs. John Beresford, née Livingston, permitting her daughter to do any activity that might have encouraged her any further in the direction in which Marian had so clearly been inclining when she was a small child. Mrs. John Beresford would have presumed that tomboyish activities like camping and hiking would only have made Marian worse, no matter how fancy the headdresses involved. Instead, Marian had stumped her awkward and reluctant way through ballet and dancing class at her indomitable mother's insistence, determined as she was that Marian's dangerous tendencies be nipped in the bud, only brought to a merciful end at the tactful suggestion of the dancing mistress.

"I'm unfamiliar," Marian said.

"Oh, it's fun. We had a ball. And one of the things we did my Bluebird year was writing messages with invisible ink," Kay said, a curl coiled around one freshly manicured finger.

"Your Bluebird year?" Sometimes Marian thought of Kay as a visitor from another planet. That planet being the real world as it began in earnest, the moment one set foot across the Hudson.

"It's a cinch. All you do is use lemon juice," Kay said brightly.

"Lemon juice? That's it?" said Marian.

"Sure. Then when you bring it close to a heat source, the lemon juice oxidizes. It's too fun. We did it with a clothes iron. I used to send secret messages to my baby brother when he was a Webelo." Marian hadn't the least idea what Kay was talking about, but she got the larger point. Lemon juice could function, incredibly, as invisible ink.

Now Marian sat in her office, looking down at Hannah's manuscript. Lemons and limes were in high demand in the age of sail to guard against scurvy. Ships would often keep some citrus fruits aboard for just that reason. It wasn't impossible to imagine that Jim would have had access to a lemon. Or even a discarded lemon rind and a quill nub, or the tip of a finger, to note the exact location of the most important secret of his young life.

An *X*, though! *X* marks the spot! It was preposterous. But also perfect. Less ambiguous than a circle or an arrow. Why wouldn't Jim want to have that information at his disposal to bargain for his life if he needed to? But when John and the other mystery pirate came upon him, there hadn't been any time for bargaining. The way Seneca described it, killing Jim may have been a hasty mistake. Violent men like Ned Low's pirate band could be blunt instruments, ill-suited to the sometimes-delicate tasks of negotiation and persuasion. They would be prone to making deadly mistakes.

"Dr. Beresford?" asked someone from her office door.

"Hmm?" Marian didn't look up.

"Oh, sorry. I was just wondering if I could maybe talk to you about my grade on the midterm?" said the undergraduate.

"Make an appointment," Marian said, still absorbed.

"Oh. All right." The student sounded perturbed, but obediently turned on her heel and walked away.

Marian got up, shut her office door, shot the dead bolt, and then returned to her desk.

A crescent shape. Like a crescent moon. That was the image Hannah kept going back to when talking about the atoll. It couldn't possibly be Bimini, no matter what Kay's Campfire Girl map-reading training might suggest. Bimini was in an atoll that was shaped like a zigzag. Though in her reading Marian had discovered that Edward Teach, better known as Blackbeard, had used the keys around Bimini as a raiding ground when he wasn't terrorizing Cape Hatteras. So it would have been attractive for other pirates too.

Maybe Marian's first instinct was right. Maybe it was the Dry Tortugas?

She pulled out the contemporary atlas that Kay had retrieved when they were working in the map room and opened the page that showed the Florida Keys.

There, just to the west of Key West, Marian observed a smattering of tiny seemingly nameless islands. And then, a bit farther west, the Marquesas Keys.

Was that a crescent shape?

Marian turned the atlas to the side. It was more of a ring. But Marquesas Key itself was definitely a crescent shape.

Marquesas. Hmmm.

She turned to a different section in the atlas, riffling through pages. Hannah talked about seaweed as thick as a giant's hair. And they weren't able to sail due south from Cape Hatteras because they were being set by the current—presumably the Gulf Stream. Pushing them east.

The telephone on her desk rang and Marian picked it up, irritated. "Yes?"

"Dr. Beresford, there's a young lady here wanting to speak to you about her midterm?" said Edna, the history department secretary, a serious woman of indeterminate age who had been in her position since, it was rumored amongst the undergraduates when Marian was one herself, approximately the Civil War.

"Tell her to come back during office hours," said Marian.

"Dr. Beresford, aren't these your office hours?" said the secretary mildly.

"Are they?" Marian put a hand to her temple.

"Shall I send her in?" the secretary said in a tone clearly meant to suggest to Marian that that's what ought to be done.

"Ah," said Marian. "Yes. I mean, no. Please have her come back next week. Thank you, Edna."

Edna expressed her disapproval with a split-second interval of silence before saying, "Yes, Dr. Beresford," and hanging up.

Moments later the telephone rang again, and Marian snatched it up and snapped, "What?"

A pause at the other end of the line, followed by a clicking sound, and then a young woman's voice said, "I have New York calling for Dr. Marian Beresford. Go ahead, New York."

"Monkey," said her father.

"Oh," said Marian, leaning her forehead in her hand. "Hello, Papa. How are you?"

The elder Dr. Beresford sounded amused. "Better than you, I gather. Just calling for an update. You know. The committee . . ."

"Yes, yes. You mentioned."

"Well, they'll be meeting next week. We need to know what, if anything, we're proposing to fund. What's the word?"

Marian glared down at the atlas. Why couldn't Hannah have just reproduced the damn map? Even without any names, she would have been able to compare it to atolls all over the world and found the right one quickly enough. No, that would have been far too convenient. But how many other places could it be? It was certainly in the Caribbean Sea. It wouldn't be in the Lesser Antilles, or down by Trinidad. They'd have had to be within close reach of the Eastern Seaboard, if William Fly betrayed his confederates and then fled back as far as Boston. The pirates were traveling in the thick of hurricane season. They would have wanted to dodge the Royal Navy, but be close enough to safe harbor in the event of a huge storm. The eighteenth century didn't have the weather prediction wherewithal that they enjoyed in the twentieth, with hours of advance notice before a hurricane might hit. And experienced mariners knew when the dangerous seasons were. They'd have guarded against it as best they could, even a slapdash pirate operation like Ned Low's.

"I've got it," she said, the words tumbling out before she had a chance to second-guess herself. "You can tell the committee. We're going to Marquesas Key."

"Are you sure?" her father's voice sharpened, with the keen interest and attention that Marian usually only heard when he discussed his own exploits.

"Hurricane season ends November thirtieth," said Marian, looking at the calendar on her desk. "Final exam week ends December sixth. We'll set out December seventh. Not sure if we're taking a steamer or the train."

"December seventh," he repeated, as though writing it down. "All right. Excellent. I'll be in touch."

"Love you, Papa," said Marian.

Dr. Beresford had already rung off.

Marian sat listening to the silence on the other end of the line, then tapped a finger on the receiver to get a fresh connection. While she was waiting for Edna to pick up, she heard a gentle rapping on her office door. A woman was silhouetted in the pebbled glass of the window.

Marian hurried to open it, wanting to tell Edna to price out travel options for the day after grades were due.

"Edna," she said as she pulled open the door. But instead of the unflappable mien of the department secretary, Marian was confronted with a serious-looking undergraduate with a notepad tucked under her arm, her hair hidden under an unfashionable pompom hat.

"Yes? Can I help you?" Marian said, irritated.

"I hope so," the undergraduate said. "May I come in?"

Marian saw it was the same young woman as before, with the question about her midterm. She didn't look at all familiar. She was stocky and ruddy-cheeked, in heavy snow boots and thick eyeglasses. Marian knew she hadn't necessarily been the most engaged professor this semester. Or last semester. Or really for the last couple of years. But it was unusual for her to not recognize a student of hers even slightly. A forgotten name, sure. But Marian generally grasped their faces. After a minute.

She opened the door more widely and swept her arm in invitation. "Have a seat," Marian said.

She deliberately left the door open. She wanted the meeting to be brief.

"Great," said the young woman. She bustled in importantly and sat down without taking off her coat. "My name is Allison Bosworth-Jones, and I'm a reporter for the *Radcliffe Daily*. I just have a few questions."

"For the . . . what?" Marian was perplexed. "Isn't this about a midterm?"

Allison licked the tip of her pen, flipped to a fresh sheet in her notebook, and said, "Not as such. First, your name is Professor Marian Beresford, is that right?"

"You already know it is," Marian said. "And failing that, there's my name on the door there." She pointed. As she did so, her body flooded with adrenaline, so abrupt and intense that her finger began to shake. What could this person want from her? She hadn't done anything. Had she? What could this be about? They couldn't know about her private life. In Cambridge, she had none, essentially. She was what she appeared to be: a spinster, married to her work, in sensible shoes. And in New York, well . . . what would they care? Even if they did know, which they couldn't possibly.

Unless someone had seen her.

Had someone seen her?

Marian settled behind her desk and affixed a mild smile to her face while she waited for Allison Bosworth-Jones to continue. Behind the false smile, the back of her mind flipped through face after face that she had seen at the teahouse, or on the street, or waiting for a cab, or at the AAUW, or at the train station. She reviewed every single face at the bar, she pored over every set of eyes lowered over the flickering candles in the dining room. None of them had stared too long. None of them had evinced the sort of shock that one might expect of a student spotting a professor in a place neither of them was supposed to be. At least, not that Marian had noticed.

All at once the adrenaline gave way to a scorching rush of rage. What business was it of the *Radcliffe Daily's*, anyway? So what if she'd gone to a teahouse? What were they going to do, have her job for it? Over her dead body. She'd sue them. She'd sue them so hard Radcliffe would have to close and reopen as a God-damned secretarial school. Marian's hands trembled on the desk blotter, and she slowly curled them into fists.

And then, just as quickly, the rage devolved into trembling fear. She should never have taken the Modigliani back to her room. What a stupid blunder. But it had been so late. The front door was already locked for the night, and whoever was supposed to be on the front desk was dozing in the back listening to Fanny Brice on the radio. And anyway, whoever cared if women were alone together in a room, and laughing late at night? She wasn't the only person in the world to bring a flask out of her pocketbook, to invite a new friend into her confidence, to do other things when she was alone in the city and away from home.

The reporter didn't seem to notice. She was reviewing a set of notes.

"I've been told," Allison Bosworth-Jones said officiously, "that your father is the famous Dr. John Beresford, who was on the Frans Blom expedition to Palenque, mapping the Temple of the Jaguar. Is that correct?"

"That's my understanding," Marian said, forcing her voice to remain polite. "But you'd do better to ask him yourself."

"Uh-huh," the reporter said. "And is it true that you've secured his backing for an expedition to be mounted this winter that's going to be led by Kay Lonergan?"

"Excuse me?" Marian said.

"Kay Lonergan. She's a student of yours? I'm just referring to the press release. I need to confirm a few of the details," said the reporter.

"The press release?" Marian was baffled.

"Yeah. We're going to lead with a headline, something like 'Cliffie on the Hunt for Lost Pirate Treasure.'" Allison looked up, adjusted her heavy glasses, and smiled. "It's pretty exciting stuff. My editor thinks it might get picked up by the *Globe*. And then, who knows? I'm hoping I can get you on the record with some of the details."

"Your editor?" Marian, her hands twitching with tension, reached mechanically for a cigarette from the box on her desk but found the case empty. She snapped it closed.

"Yeah. I only have a few more questions. When are you leaving? And where are you going? And how exciting is it to have a student doing this kind of innovative research? How does your father feel about it? Do you think you'll find the treasure? If you do, do you think you'll be as famous as him? What do you think Radcliffe will do with the money? Or do you think you and Kay will get to split it?" The young reporter looked up and said, "Kay said it was all very hush-hush when I talked to her. She didn't give me a lot to go on."

"First of all," Marian said, "Kay isn't leading this expedition. I am. We'll be going after finals next month. I can't tell you where."

"Huh." Allison flipped through her notes. "That's interesting. But isn't it true that Kay's the one who first learned of the treasure's existence?"

"Yes, but," said Marian.

"And is it true that it was her idea that you should approach the Explorers Club for backing?" the reporter pressed.

"Well, I suppose, but," Marian said.

"She's going on the expedition, right?" Allison raised her eyebrows.

"Sure, but the other Dr. Beresford is too," Marian objected, but somehow the objection failed to minimize Kay the way she had intended to.

"Sounds to me like Kay Lonergan is really the driving force behind this expedition. I mean, you wouldn't be going to look for any treasure without her, right?" said Allison.

Marian allowed, "I suppose not." She wasn't sure why she felt com-pelled to argue with this reporter. Everything she was saying was correct. Sort of.

"So, how much do you think it'll be worth?" Allison said, scribbling while she spoke. "And when you say 'treasure,' what are we really talking about here? Is it gold, is it silver? Jewels? What?"

"There's no way of knowing," Marian said. "If we do find it, which is a big 'if.'"

Allison nodded. "Right, right. Is it in a 'treasure chest,' and if so, do you think it'll be under a big *X* marks the spot?"

Marian said, "You can't be serious."

Allison looked up and without cracking a smile said, "That part was a joke."

Marian said, "Oh."

"So how does it feel," Allison pressed on, "having a famous explorer for a father? Did you always want to be like him when you grew up? Did he take you along on his big expedition to Palenque? I heard they found a jade mask in the temple complex. That must have been crazy. Is this your big chance to finally be seen on the same level as him?"

"What?" Marian got to her feet without consciously deciding to stand.

Allison looked up at her, unconcerned. "Is it?" she said.

"No, he didn't take me along to Palenque. The truth is, I saw him very rarely when I was growing up. And anyway, that's not what this is." Marian was confused. How had she gotten herself into this conversation? How could she possibly get out of it?

"So, what is it?" Allison pressed.

"It's . . . That is . . . Kay brought me an interesting source." Marian groped for the right way to explain. "And we're following up a wholly hypothetical and probably nonexistent research direction as part of an independent study that she has applied to complete, with me as her advising professor. It's a school project. That's all."

Allison wrote at a furious speed. Her shorthand was a sight to behold.

"Right," she said. "And do your undergrads usually have projects that get the backing of a famous consortium of world-renowned explorers?"

Marian said, "No."

"Great." Allison got to her feet. "Thank you so much for your time, Professor Beresford. One last question. I'd love to come along on the expedition. You know, to file reports. It could be like a series, notes from the field? I'm sure the university would let me do it as an independent study too, and anyway, I want to be a stringer. If you find something, I bet the Boston and New York papers would eat it up. Maybe even the wire services too. The publicity would be huge."

"What a generous offer," Marian said. "I'm so sorry I have to decline."

Allison capped her pen and folded her notebook closed. "I think," she said, "you don't understand how good this could be for you, Professor."

Marian was slightly shocked. Every year the undergraduates seemed more bold and self-interested, but this really took the cake.

"Am I," said Marian tightly.

Allison said, "I'll send you my copy for fact-checking, but it should be in the paper the day after tomorrow. Thanks and good afternoon."

The student reporter was halfway out the door before Marian said, "Wait. Who sent you the press release?"

Allison turned in the doorway and said, "If you don't even know that, then I don't know what more I can tell you."

The door clicked shut behind her.

Marian sat down heavily behind her desk, reached mechanically for a cigarette, then remembered the box was still empty. She knitted her fingers together instead. Kay, obviously. Kay must have sent the press release. Why would Kay send a press release? Moreover, why would she send a press release that touted her involvement and then refuse to answer questions about it? That didn't make any sense. What did that girl mean, that Marian wasn't understanding how good this could be for her?

For the first time, Marian felt the stillness of her office in the history department not as a prison, or a cupboard in which she had somehow stored herself in anticipation of being needed at some distant point in time. Now she felt as though she were standing alone in the still and strange calm at the center of a weather system only beginning to stir into existence. The eerie sharp moment of heavy heat and sun when the barometer has just begun to fall, and though no clouds are on the horizon, the storm is definitely approaching.

Chapter 10

$\mathcal{I}$ took up my watch early the next morning, and I'd never known what the doldrums could feel like until I came up on deck into the shimmering heat of complete stillness. The current had gone slack, and though we continued in something like a southerly direction, the sails hung lifeless, and the air was heavy with moisture. The *Reporter* was a distant blur through the heat on the horizon, and the ship I thought I had spotted the night before was nowhere to be seen.

"I don't like it," Orne said at the rail next to me.

Here it was not even full day, and he was mopping the sweat on his brow. The crimson parrot rode watchfully on his shoulder, smiling its beaky smile at me.

"Don't like what?" I asked.

In the dense air I could smell myself for the first time I could remember since I first fled down Long Wharf stinking of rotted apples. My blouse clung wetly between my shoulder blades as I leaned at the rail. I felt ripe and sordid. The water below us was glassine and inviting, a perfect crystal azure, with tufts of seaweed and coral in white sand, far in the depths but seeming close enough to touch. I wondered if our pace was slow enough to permit of a swim.

Orne glared at the sky. The heavens were a tropical blue with only the faintest paintbrush streaks of cloud, high above, and the sun hanging fat and low in the east, hot enough to set the ocean aboil.

"Just don't like it," Orne said before moving away to relieve the sleepy shipmate at the helm. Orne's Frenchman shadow followed along on his heels.

The morning wore on hotter, and everyone in the crew carried himself as though his teeth were on edge, though none of us could properly name why. Two shipmates threw themselves at each other over some imagined insult that none of us heard and had to be pulled apart, but not before one of them relieved the other of his ear with a quick slash of his rigging knife, splashing a dark puddle of blood across the deck. Jimenez had to tie the sniveling unfortunate's head with long bands of rag that did little to stanch the bleeding. John spooned up cornmeal gruel with neither molasses nor salt for our morning repast, and when we all complained, he pulled a pistol from his waist and allowed he would open the bowels of the next man amongst us to speak one single word, so help him God. I went to offer a spoon lick to Jonah and he thanked me with a sharp nip at my thumb. Even Sen, our usually even-keeled post captain, gave off waves of simmering rage so palpable, I could almost taste them. For the first time I felt myself ill at ease in his proximity, and more than once I caught him glaring at my back when I was busy at my labors. I did wonder how I could have offended him, but valued my neck too much to ask. Instead, I did what I always do, which was keep my head down and holystone the deck as a make-work to forswear anyone from asking me to do anything else.

That's when we heard the cannon fire.

We'd seen nothing on the horizon, no signs of life nor ship, only a few hazy lines of islands in the distance, ones we were doing our utmost to avoid. Our lookout had gone idle in the doldrums, as we moved with the ponderous pace of a box turtle on a summer afternoon, and so none of us were stationed anywhere with a spyglass when we heard the first booms. Some of us hit the deck, conditioned to save our hides before anything else, but presently our folly was clear when no balls caromed overhead, and we got up sheepfaced. The distant booms continued, *boom, boom, boom, boom*, a real broadside they were, and that's when I heard someone shout, "Ned!"

We all rushed to the larboard rail, but no one had his hand on the spyglass.

"Where away?" said Sen, sounding tense.

Orne pointed, his hand held out like a paddle. We followed the direction of his arm and there I spied on the far horizon the distant specter of our sister ship, the *Reporter*, alit all along her side with tongues of yellow-and-orange flame, and surrounded by a darkening cloud of cannon smoke. As the current steadily pushed us closer together, we saw more details come into view. Her opponent proved to be the little ship I had spotted the night before, the one swallowed by the dusk. I'd taken it for a fishing vessel.

How wrong I was.

She was a man-of-war. I don't remember what kind. She may have been a brigantine. Royal Navy colors flew from her stern, a long trailing pennant from her mainmast rode the waves of heat from the cannon like the tendrils of a jellyfish.

"Come up, come up," shouted Sen, but there was no air, and the wheel spun fruitlessly under the helmsman's hands. Sen swore long and fluently, and as we watched the two distant ships pass each other through the deepening smoke, the mizzenmast of the brigantine swayed, and then gave way. It fell in an eerie slowness, its sails sighing into the water like ghosts, a few men dropping after them, rigging collapsing. We heard distant cheers erupt from the deck of the *Reporter*, and I knew that in moments, the brigantine would be awash in blood. Perhaps that was what had soured us all on this dreadful, sun-drenched day. Perhaps we'd had a premonition of the evil deeds to come.

Just then a zephyr danced across the back of my sweating neck. The breeze should have refreshed and enlivened me, but instead something about it blackened my soul with a formless dread. The same unease bent the faces of my shipmates too: Jimenez standing at the rail next to me looked stricken, as though I'd just told him his mother had fallen to her death. Even Orne's pet Frenchman wore a look of inchoate horror. The strong gust filled in our sails as if blown from the puffed cheeks of Poseidon and the *Rose Pink* heeled over.

"Come up!" Sen shouted again, and this time the helm obeyed, the *Rose Pink* stirring to life and setting a course to intercept our confederate. The *Reporter* was outgunned but fighting with greater malice, and her opponent was already partly dismasted. Only after our ship began to move did I turn to look in the direction from whence came the freshening wind.

At first, I didn't understand what I was looking at.

Well to stern of us and rising from the water I saw what looked at first like the wall of a castle. Not that I had ever seen a castle, but I had heard stories about them, and I had imagined them often enough, and when I pictured them, I imagined walls of solid stone built up so high that only giants could ever think of scaling them. I stared, uncomprehending, wondering insanely how a wall of stone could have erupted from the ocean without anyone, neither God nor Devil, breathing a word. But presently I understood that it wasn't a wall of stone I was seeing. It was a wall of storm. A solid bulwark of rain and wind. Moments away from slamming into us.

"Reef!" shouted Orne. "Reef, God d—n you! Will, go, go! Jacob, Bart, the lot of you! Go aloft now!"

Instantly my feet were running on the deck and my hands were on the ratlines up into the rigging and I was climbing. The strengthening wind ripped at my hair and my blouse and my breeches, snapping the sails and pushing us over and over and over.

"Hurry!" Jacob shouted. In the doldrums we'd had every stitch of canvas hanging, gasping for air, desperate to catch any passing puff of wind. Now out of nowhere we were in the teeth of a gale. Not a gale—a toothed Charybdis, a vortex of terror, and if we didn't bring the sails in right now the sea was bound to yawn open like the mouth of a terrible serpent and swallow us whole.

High wind in rigging screams like a siren. I edged along the footropes with my arms wrapped around the yardarm, fifty feet up in the air, my shipmates moving like ants over the deck far below my feet. I dared not look down. I reached over the spar to grab fistfuls of sail and tried to battle it into my arms. It fought me, beating my chest against the spar, spreading bruises across my breastbone and chin. Jacob struggled too, shouting something at me that I couldn't understand. Afar down below us on deck the jibs had been struck, and all around the ship waves were building and beginning to foam. They rolled up behind us, lifting us up, as high as a house, then higher still, and we surfed down their face with the narrow stern going squirrely as the helmsman fought to maintain control. Those of us aloft clung in desperation to the yards or the mast.

"Will!" Jacob screamed.

I was trying to make the topgallant fast, sloppily bunched in my shaking hands, the wind filling my ears and nose and mouth and eyes, trying to peel the skin from my face. I looked up from my hopeless work and saw that my shipmate had lost his footing on the footrope. A massive wave rose, built, lifted us up and up and up, and the *Rose Pink* heeled over. Jacob's bare feet swung free, kicking at nothing, but he held fast to the yardarm, his eyes saucers of fear. "Will!" he screamed again. "Help!"

Before I could even think what to do, the next massive wave slammed into our starboard side. The masts tipped over, over, over, and I clung to the yardarm for all love, staring in terror at the surface of the ocean rushing to meet me. The calm and steady voice that sometimes lived inside my mind instructed me that there was nothing to be done, I would soon be in the water, and when I felt the water close over my lips, the wisest course would be to be a duchess about it. Just close my eyes, let my body go limp, breathe the water in, and give myself to the sea. I held tightly to the yardarm, the footrope under my feet, my cheek pressed to the reefed sail, my eyes squeezed tight. I supposed I might have prayed if I'd thought it would do me any good.

"Help!" my shipmate screamed. "He—"

And then he was gone.

The yardarm tips dipped into the waves, shedding Jacob with a shrug. My shipmates at the helm wrestled the wheel into submission as another giant swell lifted us up, sailing me through the air as I clung to life, the wind ripping my pigtail free and my hair streaming behind me.

I know not how I got from the yardarm back to the deck. I can't remember. I didn't fall. I must have slid down the ratlines, but the next thing I knew, I was back on deck and being sent below with the others just as a solid wall of rain closed around the *Rose Pink*. The rain did not come in drops, or rivulets, or even sheets. The wall of rain that shuttered us was so solid that for an instant I could swear I was standing with one half of my body underwater, and the other half of me dry as if I were in the dining room of Ship Tavern. It happened so fast, it's a wonder we got the sails in at all.

I didn't hear anyone suggest we try to go back for Jacob. I don't even know if any barrels had been thrown overboard so that he might try in vain to save himself. He was there, and then he was gone and instantly forgotten. I hadn't really known him, beyond idle chatter over a meal. I hadn't even known his last name, or if he'd gone pyrating before, or if he was one of those who thought our fruit packet was really a fruit packet. And now no one would ever know what became of him. If he had any family, they would eventually stop wondering. Or else they never would.

I cowered in the gun deck with Jonah trembling and damp in my arms, listening to the distant reports of more cannon fire. The storm had come upon us first, but it would set upon the *Reporter* and her quarry soon enough. A Royal Navy ship wouldn't have anything on board worth plundering beyond food and arms. But it would have good arms. More cannon than we had between the two ships in our convoy, and all the men aboard would have swords or cutlasses and pistols. Orne had whispered to me that Ned Low would leave not a single man amongst them living, except perhaps those rogues who had been press-ganged and wished to throw their sorry lots in with us. Being a Navy ship, the brigantine had the right to try and hang us. They had the right to arrest us and bring us ashore in chains. They could flog us until our flesh hung off our backs in ribbons. They certainly would warn maritime trade against us. Their very danger to us signed their death warrant.

Merchantmen, when confronted with pyrates, often preferred to let us have our way with their cargo and leave their ship and crew largely unmolested. Merchant sailors knew the job lay with the insurance company to make the syndicate whole, not with the common mariners at the points of our blades. Why should they risk their lives and ships to save the insurance company's money? Much better to give us what we wanted and go on their way. But a Navy ship was something else. A Navy ship had the will only to terrorize and destroy when coming upon a pyrate. For this, I knew Ned Low would give them no quarter. I shuddered to think what no quarter from someone as brutal as Ned Low might look like. The distant booms echoed in my ears, and I closed my eyes against the images of what would happen once the two ships were locked together, and Ned Low and the crew swarmed over the rail to board the brigantine, knives in their teeth. It would be kill or be killed. And Ned Low, I had learned, was one for killing.

The *Rose Pink's* cannon were all double lashed in place when I made it below, but as the ship was pitching with such violence, I feared what might happen if one of the cannon were to break loose and roll free. Any one of them, once rolling, would flatten a man, and might even punch a hole in our side and send us plunging into the deep. My shipmates clustered together, each wedging himself in as best he could against the terrible motion of the waves, more than one of them bending double and voiding his guts, filling the air with the sour stench of bile and semi-digested liquor.

I got to my hands and knees and crawled to the empty aft cabin with Jonah squirming in my shirt, the cabin sole pitching and rocking beneath me.

In the aft cabin I found the chairs and table stowed, the navigation instruments and charts stuffed away, and the chandelier was extinguished, swinging wildly with the pitching and yawing of the ship. The brass birdcage swung too, and with some surprise I found the crimson parrot had stowed himself back inside. The cage door hung open, but he sat on his perch stoically, his clawed feet holding fast as the cage veered like a pendulum, once crashing into the wall. We all feel safest in our best-known prisons.

The wooden cradle-like bed that had once been the captain's hammock rocked to and fro, nearly striking me a deadly blow to the skull before I took it in both my hands and tumbled myself and Jonah into it in a tangle of arms and legs and fur. Once inside I folded my hands under my chin in a prayerful attitude, cur held tight to my chest, and screwed my eyes closed. The hammock continued back and forth, back and forth. It would have been soothing if each rock hadn't marked the rolling past of a wave that could pitchpole the *Rose Pink*, barrel-rolling us in circles through the waves and foam until we hit the sandy bottom and broke into a million pieces. I thought of the nursery rhyme I had heard Mrs. Tomlinson sing to her youngest son, eons ago, in my previous life, something about babies rocking in treetops and breaking and falling and death.

I don't know how long I lay there. An hour? Two? The waves kept coming, as did the screaming of the wind in the rigging, and the tearing of the *Rose Pink* through the waves under bare poles and only a scrap of sail. I think they finally hove to and fashioned some kind of sea anchor so that we bobbed on the surface of the ocean like a wine cork in the maelstrom. Some of my shipmates had told me stories about the great storms that swirled to life in the center of the blue Atlantic, roaring into shore with the fury of a thousand banshees. I was no stranger to nor'easters, the blows that would sometimes flatten Boston and rip the limbs from the trees and peel the shingles from our roofs. But I had never known a storm with a rage like this one. I huddled into myself, my body coiled around the trembling warmth of Jonah, both of us wet, small, and afraid.

I stayed like that for a very long time.

Then all at once, the ship fell silent.

I opened my eyes a crack to see sunlight streaming through the stern windows, spilling across the floor of the cabin.

Jonah and I peeked suspiciously over the edge of the wooden hammock. The crimson parrot spied me, opened his wings, and said, "*Arrêtez!* You b—d, *arrêtez!*"

Someone had been teaching him English, it seemed.

For a moment I wondered if we were all dead. Through the skylight I saw the familiar perfect tropical blue sky of the morning, cloudless and calm. I listened. For what, I knew not. Choirs of angels? But no, they wouldn't be singing for us. If we had all been sent to Davy Jones's locker,

I doubted very much that heaven lay waiting on the other side. No, for us, the journey would have only just carried farther down, into the belly of fire at the center of the earth.

I heard a few voices topside and sensed bodies moving about in the gun deck, readying themselves to emerge.

"Stay here," I said to the cur, who seemed happy enough to remain curled tight in the wooden cradle. His hind legs were still shaking.

I crept out of my hiding place, distrusting the sudden calm, the warmth of the sun, the sparkling sky, and the stillness of the deck under my worried feet.

As I moved through the gun deck, I stopped by the corner where I had stashed my meager belongings. I traded dead Jim's cumbersome boots for my bare feet and grabbed up my cutlass and looped the sash around myself, tying it tight, and stuck the flintlock into my waistband. I felt better with the pistol's weight on me, with the cutlass hilt close at hand. The uneasiness of the day refused to leave me, so that even when I ought to have been celebrating our deliverance from the maw of death, I found myself watchful, waiting.

When I emerged from the companionway, I found my shipmates clustered together near the helm, assessing the ship and themselves for damage.

"—wonder it wasn't worse," Orne was saying to Sen. They were soaked through, as they had both been in the skeleton crew that stayed topside during the greatest extremity of the storm. Sen's shirt clung wetly to his chest and somehow was missing a sleeve. His eyes, both good and scarred, were ringed purple with exhaustion.

"Should change out the storm sails," Orne continued, "and there's a crack in the mizzen I don't like at all. But beyond that, I'd say we're sound." His French pet stood close as a shadow, both hands on Orne's shoulders.

"We're not through it yet," Sen said grimly.

Along with my shipmates, I stared in sickening wonder. Where we stood in the water, the *Rose Pink* rode safely, and though the sea around her was still angry, choppy and touched with foam, we were at the moment, incredibly, stirred by no wind at all. But before us, and on all sides, and to the stern of us too, we were surrounded by the solid wall of the storm. I didn't understand it. We were as in the center of a cyclone. And when I looked straight up, I found the masts pointing into a nearly perfect circle drawn around a calm blue sky.

"The eye," Jimenez said softly.

"What eye?" I said.

"We had a storm like this when I was a boy," he said. "At the Balize. It washed away my father's house with my two sisters inside. I thought I was lost, clinging to a tree branch, washed into the teeth of a live oak tree, and I grabbed hold of it while the waters rushed around me. Then all at once, the heavens opened and the sky was a perfect crystal blue. Like this."

It seemed unreal. The calmness and beauty of death.

"And then what happened?" I asked, my voice small.

Jimenez looked hard at me. "What happened? The back of the storm came for us, with the wind blowing in the other direction, and the water that had been pushed onto the land was forced back out to sea, taking my father and mother out with it. That's what happened."

Sen heard this and said grimly, "All right. At least we know what to expect. Orne, take some of the people and ensure the lines are all fast and the storm sails set. Bart, check the cannon and make double sure they're fast, then see how much water we've taken on and man the pumps."

"In the Tejas province of New Spain," Jimenez said quietly to me while Sen continued issuing our instructions, "in the old days, the priests used to try to ward these storms off with the consecrated host and prayers to the Virgin of Guadalupe."

"Did it work?" I asked him, my gaze fixed on the slowly moving wall of water and wind that was encircling us, and creeping ever nearer.

"What do you think?" he said before moving off to join the group securing the cannon and checking the hold.

My hand fell on the hilt of my cutlass, but it failed to reassure me.

"Well?" Sen barked at me as I loitered at the rail, staring into the jaws of my coming death. I still didn't know what I'd done to make him so angry.

"Sir," I said. But before I could say anything more, the wall of the storm advanced enough to unveil our sister ship, three points off our larboard bow. The *Reporter* joined us becalmed within the terrible storm's silent eye.

We had run before the wind for some time, during the worst of the blow, and so made up much of the distance between ourselves and our confederates. We were now perhaps only a quarter of a mile away from them, across open choppy water. We could clearly see the *Reporter*, even without a spyglass. She was locked together with the nameless Royal Navy brigantine. The Navy ship's colors and mizzenmast had been stripped away, by weather or conquest, we knew not which.

Sen saw them at the same moment that I did. But I don't think he was aware that he spoke aloud when he said, "What in the name of God Almighty."

I didn't know Sen to be a religious man. None of us were. How could we be? We knew too well the hard truths of man's lesser nature. We didn't judge ourselves for it. Pitilessness and cruelty were a fact of life out on the account.

Sen knew cruelty. His missing eye told me so. And I knew he could mete out tortures of his own, when called to do so. I knew also that he was loyal to Ned Low. I never did understand why. But now, I saw something change in Sen as he beheld the full measure of the horror that Ned Low had wrought upon the hapless Navy brigantine.

Some of my shipmates had described to me the way that certain serpents in the tropics will coil themselves about the necks and bodies of their victims to choke them to death before swallowing them whole. The coiling turns them into one hideous organism of predator and prey locked together, melding together as the prey ceases to struggle and then slowly disappears down the opening snakelike maw. Others had told me tales of giant sea monsters, krakens, wrapping their clinging tentacles about giant whales and rolling together until the sea foamed red with blood. As we drifted nearer the forms of the *Reporter* and the brigantine, locked together with webs of lines and fallen masts and collapsed rigging, both these stories arose in my mind, though at first it was hard to tell which was the devouring serpent and which was the victim.

The sails on both ships had been flayed to ribbons by the storm. The man-of-war was riding low and listing; in the blow she must have taken on water or had a hole punched in her side, perhaps by the collapsed mizzenmast, which floated alongside her like a deadly battering ram still lashed by the rigging. She was surely sinking. Neither of these details would have drawn Sen up short, crumpling his face and bringing him to lean unsteadily with his hands clutching the rail. No.

Sen's unaccustomed appeal to God came when we both saw what was hanging from the yards.

Silent and agape, we all beheld swaying from the *Reporter*'s yards and masts and rigging the stilled, shattered, hanging bodies of men. I counted ten or twelve, all forms motionless, some hoisted up by the neck, their heads bent down at right angles, hair hanging in their faces. Some others had been hoisted aloft by a single foot, and they dangled with their arms and legs splayed, looking for all the world like giant starfish dragged up gasping from the bottom of the sea. A couple of the bodies were charred and black, as though they had been doused in oil and set afire before being hauled screaming into the air to burn in the wind. All of them swayed softly with the motion of the ship in the waves. The silence of the eye and the silence of their hanging forms blared in my ears, as loud as if I had been screaming.

As we drifted ever nearer to the bizarre horror of the two ships locked together, we spied rivulets of dark red blood streaking down the hull of the brigantine like washes of paint. An oily plume of black smoke began coiling up from the Navy ship's companionway, the greasy column fouling the perfect blue of the storm's eye.

We were a scant three boat-lengths away when the eerie silence was pierced by an unseen man's high-pitched scream. Then we heard something else: the sound of laughter, rippling over the water. From the stern of the *Reporter* the black flag billowed, and the crimson skeleton stitched upon it seemed as though it were dancing.

Sen looked down at the water passing along our larboard side. A tremor passed through his shoulders. Each of us stood rooted in place, frozen by the realization of our own nightmares made real.

My hand was closed so tightly around my cutlass hilt that I was beginning to lose feeling in my fingertips. I finally understood what I had done. Perhaps it had all seemed unreal to me before that moment. Like playing a game. Even when I stabbed that old Frenchman in the face, and his eye burst and ran down his cheek and over my very hand, it somehow hadn't seemed real.

But it was.

I was here. It was all true.

Or rather, Will Misery was here. Will Misery had pledged himself to a demon made flesh and blood, going about on the oceans like a roaring lion, seeking what he may devour.

We the people huddled together on the deck of the *Rose Pink*, staring at the dancing bloodred skeleton on the flag of pyracy under which we had all agreed to sail, all of us having become death, destroyer of worlds. When we put our hands to the Articles with no thought but what ease and riches we would be owed, we had signed away our souls. We had written our names in the Devil's book. Now we belonged to him. I heard Will Fly's spectral laughter in my ears, rising, growing louder, growing hysterical.

It was then I decided. I had to get away from Ned Low.

Ned Low was not a man like us, driven to sea roving out of desperation or necessity. He didn't kill to save himself, or because the rigors of the raid required it. Ned Low killed because killing was what Ned Low was born to do.

"Great God in Heaven," said Orne next to me. All the others had stopped at their labors and were staring, first at the hideous Hydra with its laughing skeleton flag, then at one another, in shock and disbelief.

Seneca turned from the rail and looked at us. I had seen him enraged, and I had seen him determined, and I had seen him calm and unafraid, and I had seen him seized in fits of violence. I had even finally seen him laugh. But I had never seen this expression on Sen before. I struggled to determine what the word was, one that would define what I saw Seneca feeling.

I never found it.

All I know is that the next thing to come out of Seneca's mouth was, "Head down." He pointed off to starboard.

Chattering and commentary shot amongst the crew. Before the storm overtook us, we had signaled to Ned Low that we were coming to his aid. We had all signed Articles, each one of us, pledging never to stand down from a fight. If we expected to share in the spoils of our pyrating we must redden our hands alongside him. Never mind that he had taken the ship without our help; we were still honor bound to do our duty, to help our shipmates secure the cargo and arms and booty, if there was any, then dispose of the bodies and burn the brigantine to the waterline. To make certain our wounded shipmates were patched up, to ensure the seaworthiness of their vessel, and to relieve them from the *Reporter* if she had had holes punched in her sides by the Navy ship's mizzen too. There is honor amongst thieves after all, enforced by the hard justice of the will of the people, to which we had all agreed.

"Sir?" said the Cape Verdean shipmate on the helm, who was soaked through from his hours piloting us through the jaws of hell.

"Head down, I said," Sen said again, his voice stronger. "And set the storm sails. We're running before the wind."

We all looked at each other in confusion.

"Do it!" shouted Sen, his good eye sharp with rage.

Without waiting for our assent, he shoved aside the man on the helm and took the wheel himself, spinning it until our bow moved away from the wind as far as he desired, our scraps of sails filling as the back side of the hurricane's eye inched nearer. Our captain was running away from the *Reporter*. Leaving them behind. And at as many knots as the wind dared blow—running before the wind would blow us at the same speed as the storm, faster than terror, faster than any ship could go without shattering to splinters around us, wherever the storm desired. Heaving to would keep us still and relatively hunkered down in hopes the storm would pass over us, like a turtle hiding inside its shell. Running before the wind was a death wish. We could be dashed to pieces on a reef, we could be run hard aground, we could be overtaken by waves taller than two houses together. We would almost certainly, every last one of us, be dead within the hour.

The *Reporter* could be flush with wealth seized from their victims, or they could be sinking fast with a hull punched full of holes, or they could be both, but we weren't stopping to find out. Seneca would take our sorry lives in his hands, throwing away our portions and bringing down the unholy rage of a man given to torture and murder onto our sorry heads, all to get away from the *Reporter*.

That was how I understood that Seneca had determined to be finished with Ned Low too.

None of us dared to contradict Sen's order. I suppose we would have been within our rights to relieve him of his command. He served at the will of the people, after all, and there were certainly those amongst us who would be counting the money lost when our agreement with Ned Low was broken. I wasn't one of them, though. We had the duchess's stash of jewelry and coin on board the *Rose Pink*. And I knew where we intended to look for the treasure that Will Fly had stolen from us. If I felt a twinge of doubt about Sen's decision, it guttered away at the thought that if we could survive the next four hours or so with our pink intact, we'd have half as many people to divide the spoils with.

"Aye, sir," some of us said. We scuttled, heads down, to our stations to triple-check the lines and lashings. I joined a group that was setting the small, tough storm sails and making good the sheets and hammering down oilcloth over anything that looked like it might leak and let the water pour into the hold. All of us busy readying in the final moments before the hurricane opened its dripping jaws to devour us.

I don't know if Ned Low saw us approach. I don't know if he saw us draw near, stop, and turn away. I do know that the last thing I saw before the wall of weather slammed into us again were the open eyes of a Navy midshipman dangling by his shattered elbow from the mizzen yardarm of the *Reporter*, blood trickling from his nose down his baby-smooth cheeks, who looked to be about the same age as me.

FLORIDA

Marian thought she might still have been dreaming. All she could see was water, extending out to the horizon, blurring past. She felt as though she were a seagull, soaring low over the surface of the sea as it unrolled to infinity, lumpy and blue and alien. The water rushed past, almost close enough to touch, inviting her to dip and dive and soar up and swoop down, but for some reason she couldn't move her wings. She was trapped and for an instant, seized with unreasoning panic.

The rhythmic *clack clack, clack clack, clack clack* of the wheels brought her back. She was slumped against the window of her private compartment on the Overseas Limited, her forehead pressed to the glass. A woolen shawl had somehow tangled itself about her arms while she slept. Marian fought it off, finally kicking it to the floor. Her compartment was plush, lined in burgundy velvet with fringed curtains and dark polished wood, but in her struggle, she had knocked over her suitcase. Pants and blouses and shorts and gloves and sun hats now lay all over the floor, as though someone had broken in and ransacked her belongings. Marian leaned her head in her hands, trying to slow her breathing.

The train whistle blew, long and mournful over the ocean. Marian looked at her watch and saw it at least was still running; in fifteen minutes she would go to the restaurant car to have lunch with her father. And with Kay. A few hours after that, they were due to arrive in Key West. Finally. She felt like she had been locked in this train compartment for a month. It was comfortable and even a little glamorous, but she felt as trapped as a bird in an ornate and beautiful cage. The air was close and stale from her cigarette smoke, and Marian felt rumpled, dirty, and in need of a long bath. Her father would be unfazed by the strains of train travel. He wouldn't even experience them as strains, probably. Dr. John Beresford was accustomed to sleeping in tents, on camp cots under mosquito netting, glossed with sweat and unconcerned with snakes or scorpions. But what about Kay? How was Kay spending her time as the train rocketed over this slender, impossible bridge stretching over the long empty ocean miles between keys that Marian couldn't name?

Kay strode through Penn Station to meet them with a porter trailing behind her, wheeling a large, expensive-looking trunk on his handcart. She was kitted out like a movie star, or like a duchess boarding the Orient Express from Paris to Istanbul, wearing a smart, well-fitting suit and heels with stockings, a fur stole—fox? chinchilla?—and a tidy little hat. Her hair had been peroxided, but lightly, and her lips were painted in a flattering shade of mauve. The overall effect was to somehow make Kay Lonergan seem both older than she was, and also younger. Gone was the girl with the nervous jiggling saddle shoe. Gone was the battered satchel full of college books. This Kay carried a slim pocketbook under her arm and wore a pair of sunglasses that made her look haughty and blank. When the porter took charge of her trunk, she tipped him with five dollars.

"Well!" Kay had said, turning to Marian and her father and folding her sunglasses away with a bright smile. "What an adventure! You must be Dr. Beresford. Such a pleasure." She extended a gloved hand and Marian's father took it.

"And you must be Marian's student," he said drily. "How do you do." He had packed only a small leather valise, cracked and worn from hard use. He was underdressed for the New York winter weather, in a safari jacket and newsboy hat and worn trousers, with only a muffler tucked about his neck in acknowledgment of the reality of winter. Marian knew he was thinking only of the tropics. Trunks, he had remarked more than once to Marian, were for amateurs. But never within earshot of Marian's mother. Marian's mother had been the sort of woman who always traveled with a capacious trunk. How else could she pack enough clothes to look appropriate, regardless of circumstances? Dinner or luncheon? Snow or mosquitoes? Mrs. John Beresford, when she was alive, had styled herself as expert in appropriateness. Everything is easier when you know what is appropriate, she used to tell Marian. But even when Marian knew, appropriateness never came easily for her.

At his characterization of her as Marian's student, Kay's smile slipped.

"Hello, Kay," said Marian, putting out her own hand. Why did Kay's elegant traveling kit irritate her? The undergraduate probably didn't get to travel very often. Maybe Kay's mother had taken her shopping for traveling clothes special for the journey, the way she one day would usher Kay with great ceremony through the assembly of her trousseau at one of the middling Manhattan department stores. Kay was trying on a role, the role of the elegant adventuress. The explorer. She would dine out on her stories of a Christmas vacation hunting for pirate treasure for the rest of her life.

Marian herself was caught somewhere in between the two members of her party, alone in her discomfort and uncertainty. She hadn't traveled with her father since she was a girl, and then it had only been to go up to Boston to visit cousins and see some theater, and once to Bermuda when her mother was getting over her first bout of pneumonia. Never to any place that might be construed as a real journey, like this. Well, to Newport, she supposed, but that didn't count.

Marian had read about Key West, and had packed her summer clothes, and had gone to an outfitter for a pair of sensible boots, since she presumed that sandals and boat shoes wouldn't do for a treasure hunt in the middle of God knows what kind of island conditions. Her suitcase was overstuffed and too heavy, and she was dressed in a hodgepodge of clothes that would be equally wrong in winter in New York and summer anywhere else. She had turned her grades in the day before. She gave everyone a B. Bs were fine. No one would complain to the dean about getting a B.

"Hello, Professor Beresford," said Kay, her smile papering over any sense that she was aware Marian wasn't entirely happy to see her.

"Here, I have your tickets. Papa." She passed a ticket to her father, paid for the previous week with the money wired to her from the Explorers. As Marian passed the ticket into his weathered hands, it occurred to her that she was essentially handing him a ticket he himself had paid for, and the thought made her irritation more palpable. "And Kay." She passed one to Kay.

"I don't get a sleeper?" Kay's dismay was evident.

"You're young," said the senior Dr. Beresford. "You'll manage."

Marian managed not to smirk. "I think we should all get settled and then rendezvous for dinner," she said.

"Will they let second class into your dining car?" Kay said, not entirely petulant but close enough.

Marian was about to answer when a weedy-looking man in a fedora and rumpled suit flecked with grease spots, a camera slung around his neck, approached them and said, "'Scuse me, folks. This the treasure hunters?"

Marian said, "What?" but Kay's pique vanished as she said, "Why, yes! Yes, we are."

"Great," said the reporter. "Couple questions, if I may. How much you think you're gonna find?"

"Excuse me," Marian tried to break in, but Kay was already saying, "Oh, there's no way of knowing. We're excited to have some good leads. But we don't want to say too much at this point. All we can tell you is it was stolen from a pirate who was very notorious in his day. Edward Low. Famous for his cruelty. And if we find it, no one will have ever seen anything quite like it before. Who knows? There could be jewels or Spanish silver or gold. He was infamous, and he raided all up and down the East Coast and the Caribbean. He came from Boston, you know, and it's thought that he may have even spent time in New York."

The man nodded, scribbling notes in a small notebook. "Right, right. He have a hook for a hand and everything?"

Kay laughed as if she had never heard anything so brilliant and hilarious. "Not that I am aware of, no," she said.

"All right, all right. So where's this secret treasure, then? Where you headed?" the reporter said, rapid-fire and scribbling.

"Oh, we aren't at liberty to say." Kay smiled, one hand in the fur near her face, stroking it like a pet. "We've been backed by the Explorers Club, which as I'm sure you know is something of a private equivalent of National Geographic. We've promised to keep them closely apprised. We've a fiduciary duty to report any of our finds to them first."

The senior Dr. Beresford said, "Heh," but no one paid him any attention.

"Uh-huh. That's the train for Key West, ain't it?" the reporter said.

"Maybe," said Kay coyly.

"And who-all's going? You and what team?" pressed the reporter.

"Well, there's me. It's Kay Lonergan, *L-O-N-E-R-G-A-N*. And of course you recognize Dr. John Beresford, who was part of the team that found the jade mask at Palenque. And—"

"Pardon me," Marian's father broke in. "May we see some credentials?"

"Yeah, sure thing." The reporter flashed a card, almost too fast for Marian to read, saying, "Harvey Nymark, *New York World*. Lemme get a quick picture, if you don't mind."

Kay posed with one foot forward and beamed. The flashbulb dropped a curtain of white before Marian's befuddled eyes.

"One more, Miss Lonergan, if you don't mind," said Harvey Nymark.

"Like this?" said Kay, changing her attitude to look more sultry. Again, the flashbulb popped.

"Sir," Marian said. "Mr. Nymark. Listen, we—"

"All right, I got what I need, thank you," said the reporter. "You find anything good, you give me a call, let us know. We'll have a man down there, do a full feature. Pictures and everything."

"Oh, we shall," said Kay.

"All right, folks, thank you for your time. Miss Lonergan." Harvey Nymark lifted his hat and withdrew into the crowd.

"Kay," Marian started to say after the reporter had gone. "What—"

"All aboard!" The locomotive rumbled to life beside them, exhaling a cloud of steam over the platform. "All aboard, for the Overseas Limited!"

"That's us," Marian's father said.

Kay slid her sunglasses back into place and said, "Well. See you at dinner, then. Shall we say seven?"

Before Marian could answer, her student had turned on her stacked heel and strode toward the door for second class.

"So," said John Beresford when she was gone. "Shall we?"

Marian couldn't entirely believe what had just happened. "Was that the *New York World?*" she said as her father took her gently by an elbow and steered her to the first-class sleeper cars.

"I believe it may have been," her father said as he showed their tickets to the man at the door, then helped Marian up the first big step into the car.

"The tabloid?" Marian said.

"That's the only *New York World* I know," he said mildly. "Come along, Monkey. Let's get settled."

Their first dinner had passed in mostly uncomfortable silence. Marian knew her father couldn't be counted on to carry the conversation. In fact, he appeared at the table with a thick volume under his arm about a colleague's recent excavations in the Yucatán, and when it became apparent that neither woman was going to object, he opened it and read. He evinced no interest about the arrangements Marian had made for them upon arrival, and he certainly wasn't going to ask Kay all the dull questions that typically pass between newly acquainted people on board long-distance trains. Had Marian been alone with either of them, she could guess how the struggle to converse would have unfolded. With her father, she would have felt desperate to claim his attention from his book and would have launched into a meandering monologue about her recent research or reading or teaching, each anecdote sounding more pathetic than the last, waiting for him to evince some semblance of approval of her, or her thoughts, or her life as it was unfolding, one day after the other, one year after the next. He would have listened patiently before inquiring about her social life, probing to see if she might be anything other than the solitary spinster she pretended to be, and then he would have mused over the social advantages her dead mother had given her, and Marian would have become inflamed with resentment, and they would have ended the dinner in complete silence.

If alone with Kay, on the other hand, she would have felt the need to assume a sort of big-sisterly authority. To help her read the menu, to ensure her feelings were unbruised by her lesser train accommodation, to ensure the waiter brought her enough tea. She would have invited Kay's confidence with polite, and patient, interest, feigning the requisite enthusiasm for stories of undergraduate romantic drama, interpersonal rivalry, and intellectual growth. She would have monitored herself keenly, making absolutely sure that her comportment toward Kay was in every respect above reproach. She would not have touched so much as the back of Kay's hand. She would have stopped herself from admiring Kay's clothes, or commenting in any way whatsoever on Kay's appearance. She would have said almost nothing about herself, confining her remarks to books, to the project at hand, to the savagery of Ned Low, to Hannah and the ongoing, open question of her veracity and trustworthiness.

But as these two scenarios called for two entirely different Marians, she found herself unable to square the circle of which Marian she should be to make the conversation proceed, and so it did not.

Since that dinner their first night on the train, Marian had seen very little of Kay. They passed each other in the dining car once when the train slowed outside of Charleston, and Kay had smiled and greeted her like a long-lost cousin, and then waved and swanned back to second class. Once Marian had spied her through the window, standing outside on the platform with some other travelers, chatting and smoking and stretching their legs. She looked clean and relaxed, and seemed to have been engaged in an animated, excited conversation. Marian supposed she was telling any and everyone within earshot that she was on a break from school to go on a treasure hunt. And why shouldn't she? It was exciting. Marian was excited, or, at least, she felt certain she felt that way, if she could only discover the excitement hiding under her many layers of ambient anxiety.

She had entrusted a note to a porter, inviting Kay to join them for this lunch, and he had returned with an answering note in the affirmative. They needed to meet, all three of them, so that Marian could brief them on the arrangements she had made in Key West. Or tried to make—chartering a boat had proved a tricky prospect, and the truth was, she hadn't made any progress finding one when she had called repeatedly from her office in Cambridge. She had been assured by more than one somewhat unhelpful person at their hotel and at the end of various crackling telephone exchanges that chartering a boat would be no problem once she was there. In fact, there was very little else to do on Key West, apart from chartering boats. When making her inquiries, she had made it sound as though they all wanted to go deep-sea fishing. Marian, who had never been deep-sea fishing, didn't know what questions deep-sea fishing people typically asked when telephoning ahead for boat charters.

The train rocketed over a small key lush with greenery and, she thought, one or two coconut palms blurring by. Marian stopped repacking her wrecked suitcase and moved back to her window to get a better look, but even faster than it was there, the island was gone, and they were shooting along another expanse of lonely track over lumpy azure-blue water.

Marian went to the washbasin and splashed some water on her face. She looked closely at herself in the mirror, the single-filament bulb overhead casting her face in grotesque shadows. A tired woman peered back, with fine papery lines around her eyes and hollowed cheeks. Threads of gray in her hair. Errant eyebrows, wiry and unkempt, because Marian's hand moved too much in the swaying of the train, and the light in her compartment wasn't good. But her eyes held a steel resolve that was new.

She was on her way to find pirate treasure. Hidden by a hitherto unknown female pirate. When Marian's thoughts turned to Hannah Masury, her reflection smiled at her, and her gray eyes shone. A smile of secret conspiracies.

They might find nothing, of course. But what, Marian allowed herself to wonder, if they didn't find nothing? What if they got to Marquesas Key and everything aligned with the way that Hannah had described it? What if they went ashore and bushwacked through the mangroves and came to a sandy clearing and it was just the same, a bubble frozen in time as though two hundred years hadn't gone by?

Marian's eyes widened into a luscious daydream of tattered sailcloth hanging from two coconut palms lashed together in the shape of an X, and her hand pushing away warm golden sand. When the image dissipated in the mirror over the washbasin, Marian saw that her dripping face held a smile.

She reached for a towel and brushed her short curls into place, sort of, and put on a scarf, because why not? Then she headed for the dining car.

Her father was already there, reading a newspaper. The car was mostly empty, as they were both early. Tables freshly laid in white tablecloths with glassware rattling with the rumble of the wheels on the tracks, and small white gardenias in little silverplate vases on each table, sweetening the air with their perfume. It had taken a few days for Marian to get used to reaching for saltshakers that were always vibrating, but now she didn't even notice.

"Hello, Papa," she said, and sat down.

"Monkey," he greeted her. He rattled the paper and folded it into quarters, saying, "Have you seen this?" and set it on her napkin.

Marian picked it up. It was a short article about their excursion, under the headline "Treasure for Christmas." Not so many details, but it did say where they were going. The article seemed to appear in a society column, near a roundup of visitors from out of town and who they were visiting and how long they were staying. The item mentioned all three of them by name and featured a small photograph of Kay smiling in her sunglasses, a scarf knotted over her hair.

Kay hadn't been wearing a scarf when the *New York World* photographed her.

"Where is this from?" said Marian.

"Charleston paper," replied her father, taking a sip from the tumbler he already had at his disposal. "Yesterday's evening edition."

Marian looked at the paper again. "She told them we're going to Key West," she said, panic sharpening her tone.

"Mm-hmm." He placed a long finger alongside his temple.

"But why would she?" said Marian.

"Why would she what?" asked Kay, who appeared at the table looking fresh and pressed in light linen slacks and a well-fitted silk blouse. She seemed too elegant for the eighteen-year-old girl who had laid her head on the Radcliffe library table across from Marian a few short weeks ago, as though she had chosen her outfits from a society magazine feature about Palm Beach.

"We were just discussing this piece of yours in the *Charleston Advocate*," said John Beresford.

"Oh! That," said Kay. She sat down, and when the waiter appeared to take her drink order, she asked for lemonade.

"Now, Miss Lonergan," Marian's father began.

"May I see it?" Kay helped herself to the paper in Marian's hand and scanned it with a critical eye.

"Kay," Marian tried, but Kay cut her off, saying, "Hrm. It's not as long as they said it would be."

"And how long did they say?" said Marian, an edge of irritation in her voice.

"They promised a feature," said Kay, handing the paper back. "I'd call this more of a mention, wouldn't you? Well, that's disappointing. After I went to all that trouble."

"'Disappointing' is not the word I was going to use," said John Beresford. "Look, Miss Lonergan."

"Can we order? I'm starved," said Kay, looking around for the waiter tasked with bringing her lemonade.

"Kay," said Marian, reaching to put a hand on Kay's arm but thinking better of it, instead placing her hand in her lap. "Listen, we're just trying to help. You see . . ."

"Young lady," John Beresford said sharply enough that both Kay and Marian snapped to attention. "This has got to stop. All this bandying about in the press."

"Stop?" said Kay, unperturbed. "What for?" To the waiter placing lemonade down on a vibrating table she said, "Just the tuna fish sandwich, please. Thank you."

"The same," Marian said to him, handing over her menu.

"The roast beef," said Marian's father to the waiter. "Because," he continued in a lowered voice, against any listening ears as the dining car filled with couples and families chattering and excited about their imminent arrival. Some of them were planning to stay cloistered in their opulent sleeping cars upon arrival in Key West as they were moved with care onto a specially designed barge and then ferried across the Straits of Florida all the way to Havana. "For one thing, the Explorers will want to have a say in any publicity that results from this expedition. There's a right way to do these things. We don't know if we'll find anything at all. And if the odds are in our favor and we do find something, that will be the beginning of our work, not the end. We'll have to bring in archaeologists, we'll have to secure more funding. We'll need permission from the state to do the excavation work. We'll have to carefully catalogue every object and note down where it was found. We'll have to assemble a much larger team, a syndicate, really, and determine who has the rights to any artifacts we uncover. It's a yearslong process. Years. The time for publicity is after all that work is done, not before we even arrive."

Kay sipped her lemonade, looking at Marian's father over the rim of her glass. "Oh," she said.

"Look, Kay," Marian interjected, wanting to protect the girl from her father's special talent for meting out disappointment. "It's natural to be excited. We're all excited. Aren't we, Papa?"

Her father didn't respond.

"And your journal of this trip will make for a pretty fine independent study. Even if this is only the beginning of a complicated process, we understand why you'd still be excited to talk about it. Don't we?" said Marian.

Again, no response from her father, who was gazing out the window at the nameless key blurring past.

"But in this instance—" Marian softened her tone. To assume the big-sisterly voice that she imagined would be most effective with this effusive, dazzled young person. "Don't you agree it would be better, wiser, even, if we kept more to ourselves?"

Kay picked up her lemonade and took a long, slow sip through her straw. Then she set it down again.

"If you say so, Marian," Kay said, her eyes the cool green of coconut palm leaves on a tropical afternoon.

Chapter 11

~

*W*e were limping and lame as a horse needing to be shot. Our sails hung in rags. We had taken on so much water that we sat low-slung, sailing like a swaybacked cow, and leaning slightly to one side. We might have been sinking. Slowly, but the water always wins. I was riding the bow, straddling the bowsprit with my bare feet hanging through what remained of the netting, toes touching the fraying horse lines, ocean moving beneath me. I didn't need to be out that far, but I was pressing myself toward the land. The farther out on the sprit I could sit, the sooner I might see it. I dreamed of wading ashore through the crystal tropical water and throwing myself on the white sand, feeling the grains between my fingers, kissing it, and pledging before God and the Devil never to go pyrating again.

For hours I had seen nothing but empty horizon as I scanned through Sen's spyglass. I swept north, I swept south, I looked so hard, my eyes began playing tricks on me, mistaking first a glint of sunlight for our deliverance, then a floating piece of driftwood. My lips were chapped and peeling from the salt water and wind and rain and then the punishing sun that followed on the heels of the storm, as though a cruel Neptune sent us perfect sunlight so that we might better behold the horrors the storm had wrought upon us.

My spyglass swung past the point of the bowsprit, tripping momentarily over a black speck, and then skidding out over the shimmering water. We were riding far too low. A heavy rogue wave could topple us over. What a cruel jape it would be, to come through the maw of a storm such as that, only to be ended by the sighing past of a single rolling wave.

I swung my glass back to the speck. I squinted hard, trying to force it to resolve into the shape of something. Anything. The glass swung in circles around the speck, my arms were so exhausted that they trembled when I held the glass before me for longer than five minutes at a time.

I brought the spyglass down and shook out my arms and rubbed my eyes. The salt in my eyelashes made my eyes burn. I let myself sit, idle, just for a moment, the fatigue so deep in my bones that I might have slipped into a dream just as I was sitting there. Perhaps death wouldn't be so bad. At least then I would be able to rest. To sleep for as long as I liked. And when I finally awoke, perhaps I would see my mother again.

Something cool closed over my dangling toe, and my eyes drifted open again. We had dipped into the hollow of a swell, and the storm-shattered *Rose Pink* was now riding so low that my toe had touched the surface of the water. It wouldn't be too long now.

The sunlight scattered winking over the water, and I summoned whatever strength I could find to lift the spyglass to my eye once again.

The speck had resolved itself into a distant mound of green.

"Land!" I shouted. My throat was parched and ragged, and it came out a croak. "Land ho!" I shouted again, waving my arms over my head, and then pointing, my arm held out like a weathervane.

"Land!" My call was taken up by my shipmates on deck, and I felt the gentle movement of their bodies as they carefully urged the *Rose Pink* to head down a couple of points. The wind moved directly abaft of us, and somehow the pink liked this point of sail better. The bowsprit lifted and my feet were no longer within reach of any sirens who might happen by and decide to drag me down to cavort with them in the deep.

As we drew nearer to the island the water shoaled up into shallows and I could see an entire teeming city beneath my feet. Fish in colors I had never imagined hiding within waving seaweeds. Roseate tufts and starfish and spiny creatures with eyes on stalks. A lobster, looking for all the world like a visitor from Boston taking in the scenery. Shelves of coral rising up from smooth white sand, tiny bright fish scattering before the pressure of the water thrown off by our bow.

After another hour, we drifted past a larger island thickly covered in jungle, with some brightly colored open fishing boats pulled up on white sand beaches and stowed above the tide line. It wouldn't do to put in on an island that was inhabited. I knew from my interview with Seneca that we were bound for a tiny atoll south of this bigger key, one in a crescent shape. The atoll was empty. One of the islands would be inhabited by nothing but wild pigs.

When we reached the lee of the larger island, the swells flattened until the water was as smooth as a pane of window glass, and just as clear. The underwater cities thinned until we were gliding over expanses of naked white sand dotted with seaweed. Then I spied a small gathering of islands, some consisting of little more than a white sand hill in the shape of a teardrop, with a spouting of palms on the thick end and the sand tail disappearing into clear shallows. Two of the islands in the atoll were somewhat larger than the tiny cays, and these two were both thickly forested in palms and vines and greenery. Of the two, one arced around a slightly deeper bay, where the water was turquoise instead of clear, and I felt the *Rose Pink* shifting under my hips as my shipmates trimmed our ragged sails to make for this harbor of refuge. I heard the orders being issued, and I felt the wind spilled from the sails to bring us to an easy drift.

The *Rose Pink* crept into the sheltering arms of the turquoise lagoon, arced with pale sand and low sweeping coconut palms. We shed our speed, approaching the shore in silence. Then I heard the rattle and clatter of chains as someone let fall the anchor and paid out the rode. The splash of the anchor hitting the water soaked my feet. We were at rest. The pink settled into her anchorage as through she, too, were exhausted. I climbed from my post and laid myself down in the webbing, my arms folded around the spyglass, and curled myself up like a baby.

My shipmates were as shattered as I was. Rum was being passed around to fuel us through the last push of labors necessary to make fast the ship in our new port. John Somethingorother started up a shanty

usually used on the halyards, but it served just as well for putting everything away. John sang the words while my shipmates joined the chorus.

Oh they call me hanging Johnny, away, boys, away.

They says I hangs for money, oh, hang, boys, hang.

"Will," someone said.

"Hmmph." I didn't want to budge. I wanted to lie here and sleep for
eternity.

"Will."

It was Seneca. He was standing on the bow, and he shook the webbing where I lay, jostling me. "We're here." He sounded as exhausted as
I felt.

"All right," I said. I didn't get up.

"Listen. We'll go ashore when the ship is fast and set up camp," Sen
told me. "Then after a bit of rest, we'll careen her and start our repairs.
And while that happens, some of us will take a tender over there"—he
pointed at one of the islands in the chain just outside our lagoon—"to
get some fresh bacon for the people. While you and I"—he dropped his
voice so the others couldn't hear—"will go over there." He pointed to
an island so small it looked like the back of a porpoise, rising from the
still water, marked by two slender palm trees heavy with fruit. Seneca
allowed himself a conspiratorial smile. "And we'll see what Will Fly has
left us, eh?"

I sat up in the webbing, the mention of Will Fly's treasure renewing
me. "Will Fly," said I.

"The same," said Seneca. His face split into a merry grin, and I grinned
back.

We'll hang and haul together, away, boys, away.

We'll haul for better weather, oh, hang, boys, hang.

It was short work to make the ship fast, sails all put away and compan-
ionways propped open to let the belowdecks begin to dry out. I got my
wish when we landed the tenders onshore. I climbed over the gunwale
and splashed into the shallows and felt the soft shifting sand between my

toes. When I reached the beach, I fell to my hands and knees and petted the sand like it was the naked chest of my lover. I closed my eyes and whispered an apology to God that I had gone so far astray.

Some of the people laughed at me, but others of them were silent as they hauled the tenders far above the reach of the tide. Even Jonah trotted up the beach and rolled on his back with his heels in the air, merry with the warm sun on his ragged belly.

The lagoon was ringed on three sides by clean white sand, the tide line a tangled boundary of driftwood snarled with seaweed teeming with crabs. Here and there, palm trees leaning with heavy green fruit extended out over the sand, slender as swan necks, feathery leaves waving in the warm breeze. Above the tide line, the island was thick with vegetation, the likes of which I had never seen before. Giant waxy green leaves, tall palms of a different type, coiling vines thick enough to sit upon, blooming pink and orange flowers the size of my two fists together, perfuming the air with a sticky sweetness. The beauty of the island was unreal. I had the disquieting feeling that perhaps we had been sunk after all and found ourselves trapped in some demonic delusion designed to fool us into unawareness of our own death.

John and Sen and Orne and Black Bart and one or two of the others had been to the island before, when they were here with William Fly. They led us, trudging barefoot and exhausted, up the beach to an opening between the palms, a sandy pathway that wound into the jungle. I kept close to them. Not as close as Orne's pet Frenchman, but almost. The crimson parrot had weathered the storm in his brass cage, and then emerged with the rest of us when the danger was past and coasted into the lagoon riding in the shrouds. Now he perched on John's shoulder swaying with the motion of John's body as he swung his peg leg over fallen tree trunks. Jonah trotted at my feet, making a nuisance of himself. I put my hand on a coiled vine to help myself clamber over a trunk, but when I touched it, the surface of the vine moved and I found it wasn't a vine at all but a serpent as thick as my arm, with scales a strange pale pink. The snake watched me pass with a dead flat eye, its forked tongue tasting the air behind me.

We arrived at a narrow clearing of sand and scrub dotted with old split coconut husks and shaded by sea grapes heavy with fruit. Here and there some mean huts still stood, sort of. Palm frond roofs dried out and scattered, busted walls of heaped driftwood and broken spars tied with frayed hemp lines. From one of the trees a tattered black flag hung, sun-bleached and stained, stitched in the pattern of a grinning white skeleton holding an hourglass and a spear. The skeleton's spear aimed at a bleeding heart that had once been red, but which had faded from hard weathering into a pink as pale as the serpent that had startled me in the jungle.

"All right, fellows," said Sen. He peered up at the sky with his hand in his hair, taking the measure of the time. "Two hours' liberty. Then we'll have two companies. One for the careening and one for the pigs."

Everyone grumbled their assent and broke off in twos and threes, some heading for huts to gather fresh palm fronds to improve their shelter, some going to collect sea grapes to eat. Orne sent his Frenchman to a nearby tree to obtain coconuts, not that the man knew how to climb a trunk with no branches. Instead, he shook them down, and they fell with hard thumps in the sand. John Somethingorother set to kindling a fire in the charred remnants of a cooking pit in anticipation of the pig feast to come.

I beckoned to Jonah and whistled, designing that I could cuddle him as my pillow while I slept somewhere beneath a tree, but he ignored me and went to follow John, sniffing for something to eat.

"Come on," said Sen. He was talking to me.

"Where are we going?" I asked.

"That one." Sen indicated one of the huts. "It was Ned's."

Inside I found the hut surprisingly comfortable, sandy, and cool, with a soft pile of dead fronds on one side and a cache of coconuts on the other. I crouched on my heels in a corner, watchful. Sen split a coconut with one blow of a cutlass and broke it open with his hands. He offered one half to me. Inside the flesh was cold and pale, and I drank the water pooled in the hollow of it. I have never tasted anything so sweet and good.

"Told you," said Sen with an uneasy smile as he watched the sweetness take over my face, bringing rosy life to my sallow cheeks.

"You're right. I've never tasted anything so fine," I confessed. I dug out the tender coconut flesh with my fingernails, heaping it into my mouth. I felt moisture flooding into my lips and nourishment enlivening my blood. In moments, the coconut was scraped raw and empty, and I was wanting another one, and Sen had somehow known this already, splitting one and offering me half. When he passed the half to me, our fingertips brushed together, and we both acted like they hadn't.

We devoured coconuts until our bellies were round and then sleep overcame us. Our eyelids heavy, we lay down and dozed together on the pile of dried palm fronds, snoring softly. I plunged headlong into the velvet blackness of my exhaustion and was insensible for some time. A while later, I don't know how long, lost in the safety of sleep, Sen coiled an arm around my waist and drew me close. My head fitted under his stubbled chin, our knees drawn up together, his soft breath stirring the hairs on my brow, his chest pressed close to my back.

My eyes opened. I stared at a chink in the driftwood wall of the hut, waiting. I heard voices outside and saw Jonah trot by, stump tail wagging.

I lay still, stiff with awareness. I wondered if Sen had cottoned to my secret. Or if he had not, what would happen, when what was about to happen, happened. When he reached for me to hold me close to him, I understood why he had been acting so strangely. Why he had for days been anxious and short, curt and irritable whenever I was near. Why I sometimes caught him staring at me while I was busy at my labors.

A finger traced gently along the outer curve of my ear.

I'm not going to tell you how it happened. That is between Sen and me. And God, I guess. I will tell you that I gave of myself willingly, even hungrily, and that Sen and I became locked together in a conspiracy of silence, of things neither of us would ever name, to each other or even to ourselves.

Nothing was said. Everything was understood.

And then, everything was known.

When it was over, Sen lay abandoned in sleep, an arm flung over his eyes against the afternoon sun glinting through the chinks in the driftwood walls, sweat gleaming on his cheeks and upper lip and chest. His other arm was wrapped tightly around me, his hand holding my hip. My hair was matted with my own sweat, one of my skinny legs coiled around his muscled one, as though our bodies were braided together and could never be undone.

Now there was nothing about me that Sen did not know. If he was surprised, I didn't see it. There was no room, in that mean little hut, for surprise.

I lay awake humming with nerves, trying to decide what I should do. I determined that the best course of action was to affect ignorance. The Articles we had signed decreed that what had just happened was impossible. So, it would be impossible. If he said it didn't happen, and I said it didn't happen, then it didn't happen. Slowly, I lifted his arm away from my haunch by gentle degrees and brought it to rest on his chest. He snuffled in sleep and turned his head. I backed away softly, pulled on my filthy pantaloons and blouse, tied my damp hair back, and crept out of the hut.

The people noticed. They knew we had disappeared inside, alone. And each of them, except the one patched up by Jimenez still sporting a crusted bandage, had two ears. But no one said a word. No one gave me so much as a look. Every man was busy with his own affairs, boiling grapes in a still, stoking a cooking fire, hacking ineffectually at coconuts that rolled away when struck askance, dozing with kerchiefs or hats over their eyes. Even Jonah ignored me, gnawing on a coconut husk in a sea grape burrow he had dug in the sand. No one would admit that they suspected anything amiss. The conspiracy of silence blanketed us all. I was watchful, but the silence reassured me. I went over and picked some sea grapes of my own and sat outside the hut chewing them and keeping to myself. They were tart and full of seeds and I had never tasted anything so green and ripe and delicious.

After a time, Sen emerged yawning from the hut. No one dared look at him. If they looked, they would be showing him that they knew. If they knew, then Sen would have reason to ensure they forgot. So they knew nothing.

"All right," Sen announced. The people looked up now that he had told them to. "That's enough liberty. We'll form two companies. Orne, you'll superintend the careening. Choose your men."

Orne scratched under his hat and named those amongst our number who were ablest with lines and knots. His gaze settled on me momentarily, as though he were going to name me too, but then he glanced at Sen and seemed to think better of it. Those he had chosen gathered around him.

"The rest of you lot," said Sen, "except John, will go to Pig Island." He pointed through the trees around the clearing in the general direction of the smaller forested islands in the atoll outside the lagoon. "You'll need arms. Pistols, cutlasses, spears, if you can fashion them. Bring back as many as you can carry. At least three. We'll sup tonight and smoke whatever we can't eat to take with us."

Jimenez was in the pig group. He said, "And what will you be doing, Captain?"

"Leave me a tender," Sen said. "And you'll see."

John Somethingorother was tending the smoldering firepit with a dark look in his eyes. But he said nothing.

"*Arrêtez*, you b—d," said the parrot from his shoulder.

"Will comes with me," Sen continued. "And we'll rendezvous back here when the sun drops behind the tree line."

Many looks passed amongst the people. Orne glanced at me with what I imagine was something like fatherly concern, not that I had ever had that type of concern directed at me before. I half smiled at him, to show him I was all right. His unease grew doubtful, but he turned away to discuss the coming rigging and careening work with his company. Some of the looks cast at me were sour ones. I sensed that I may have made a tactical error, letting the people think Sen had any special regard for me. It never pays to be the favorite.

Favorites get cast out and find themselves standing alone.

"Orne," I said, thinking it would be wiser for me to join the careeners, thereby assuring my shipmates that I was only one amongst many, with one share just like theirs. No special favors. No airs put on. But before I could attach myself to them, Sen said, "Let's go."

I felt eyes on my back as we moved out of the clearing and down the sandy path to the beach. When I passed the firepit, I clearly heard John mutter, "Well, look at you."

A creeping worry grew in my mind as I followed behind Sen to the beach. Being free of Ned Low might not be enough. If I stayed here, having lost the goodwill of the people, it would be an ugly business. Uglier still if they knew my secret. It would doubtless end with my death, which was inevitable anyway. But what kind of death. That was the question.

I had to escape. I had to escape right now. Today. But how could I and take my share with me? The quiet voice that sometimes lived inside my mind pointed out that I was owed what I was owed. My share. Mine. I'd be d—d if they would take it from me.

Sen gave no indication that he noticed any hard looks amongst the crew, or even that anything had transpired between us that might have made it so. When we arrived at the tenders the beach looked as abandoned as at the Rapture, with no sign of life save the ruined *Rose Pink* resting at her anchor in the middle of the azure lagoon. We took hold of the smaller of the tenders, each of us on a gunwale, pushing the open boat together over the driftwood tide line and skidding it down the sand, soft and white as new fallen snow. I hopped in first, being smaller and lighter, and took up the oars as the tender met the gentle surf. Then Sen was with me in the boat, and I was pulling on the oars, piloting us into deeper water.

The oars were heavy, and I felt them working at my back as I rowed. Sen reached into his loose shirt and pulled out some pieces of paper and unfolded them on his knee. They proved to be the black spot I'd found in dead Jim's boot, with its secret map, and the nautical chart that the map matched. Sen peered down at them, and then up at the line of sandy islands separated by roiling blue currents and jutting lips of coral.

"It's behind that spit of rock," he said, pointing. "The tide's going, so steer to port to keep clear of the bricks." Bricks meant rocks hidden just below the surface.

I hauled harder on one oar than the other as I felt the current take us up. We were being washed gently out of the lagoon. Tides can play tricks like this. A current that feels soft and easy when it's with you can feel like walking into a wall if it's against you. We might be gone long enough for the tide to reach dead low, which would be slack enough to make the return row easy enough. Or we might be washed away to sea and never see the lagoon again.

I leaned on the oar so that we drifted clear of a spit of bright coral studded with rainbow anemones that I saw plainly through the water as they passed under our shallow keel.

Then we were out of the lagoon in deeper water with a bit of chop. The atoll was a line of seven or eight tiny islands, each of them a hillock of white sand ringed in pale sky-blue shallows, some with tangles of vegetation or a couple of spindly coconut palms blown ragged by the wind.

Sen studied the maps again, comparing them to the line of islands before us.

"That one," he said.

I looked over my shoulder at the island second from the last. It consisted of two even hillocks of white dune sloping gently down to the water, as smooth and unblemished as the breasts of a young English woman who has had plenty to eat. Nestled between the dunes was a hollow dense with jungle. Two skinny palm trees stood out from the low thickets of vine and mangrove in the hollow, one palm arched to the left, the other palm arched to the right. From our aspect in the water, the trees seemed to cross each other, making the shape of a large X.

My pulse tripped faster, and the oars sat more lightly in my hands as I pulled, and I pulled, and I pulled.

Away astern of us, I spied the larger tender emerging from the mouth of the lagoon, carrying Jimenez and the company of buccaneers, making for the most distant of the islands in the chain. Pig Island lay nearer the mouth of the lagoon than our nameless cay, and they reached their beach before we reached ours. From afar across the water, I observed them splash into the shallows and drag the boat onto the beach, and the glints of the sunlight flashing along their sharpened cutlass blades. I thought Jimenez may have stopped to stare across the water at us with a hand shading his eyes, but then he turned and followed the others into the jungle.

At last, I felt the scraping of sand on our bottom. I then shipped the oars, Sen and I splashing out, dragging our tender up to shore. There was almost no beach here to land on, the island was so small. We nosed the bow of the boat into a thick root work of mangrove, but the stern lay in the sand only a foot or so from the water. A rolling tongue of wave could easily take it away from us. But the tide was going, so the waves would be inching gradually down the beach. We wouldn't be trapped. I hoped.

"Not much to look at, is it?" I said.

"I haven't been on this one," Sen told me, his good eye looking critically at the mouth of the jungled hollow. We were met with a veritable wall of roots. There must have been a clearing within, or the palms wouldn't have taken root, but we were d—d if we could see our way to it.

"Maybe if we climb the top of the dune?" I suggested.

Seneca scratched a hand through his twists of hair, considering. Then he looked at me. "Sometimes," he said gravely, "the only way out is through."

He had his cutlass in his hand, and so I took up mine from where it hung at my waist and we hacked together, our blades singing through the air and crunching at the wood, until the roots gave way and fell apart. It was hot, sweaty work, and mosquitoes whined in close to my ears and sucked up welts on my neck and arms. Sen slapped at them too, leaving flecks of blood on his shirt.

After a time, we had cleared enough undergrowth to pass through the screen of roots, and we found ourselves inside a secret hollow, dark from shadow, cool, and wet. A small spring bubbled up from the tangled roots of the mangroves, seeping into the sand and making the smallest freshet trickling out to the beach. I felt as though the roots were growing so fast that I could see them, knitting themselves back together where we had just torn them asunder. My blouse was soaked through and clinging to my skin, so I knelt and put my lips to the bubbling water.

"Careful," said Sen, his gaze on my body as I bent down. He was sitting on a root nearby and mopping the back of his neck with a kerchief. "The wrong water can kill you."

"I'm dead already," I said softly, and drank deep of the spring, on my hands and knees like a thirsty dog. It tasted cool and earthy and without a hint of brine.

The undergrowth formed a network above us, creating a dim and sandy tunnel through which we could walk, if we hunched over. Our bare feet splashed in the shallow brook, twigs and branches snarled in our hair as we passed. I wondered if Sen was going to ask me about my secret. Surely, he would have something to say. Surely, he had been surprised. But then again, perhaps nothing could surprise Seneca. His carriage toward me was slightly more proprietary but otherwise unchanged.

The tunnel thinned and opened until we emerged into a sandy clearing, only wide enough for two men to lie down without having their feet in the mangroves. The two palms arched overhead, growing on opposite sides of the clearing, not actually meeting as they had appeared from the water. Dead fronds and bits of bark dotted the circlet of sand.

"God's my witness," I exclaimed as I stared into the clearing.

Sen laughed and reached over and tousled my hair. "There be Sam," he said. "Will Fly's mate. I wondered where he got to, the poor b—d."

At the edge of the clearing, against the trunk of one of the spindly palms, leaned what had once been a man. His flesh had almost all been eaten away, and his skull hung lopsided, his naked teeth and empty eye sockets grinning hideously at us. He was clad only in ragged pantaloons and a rotting kerchief knotted over his head, shriveled hair hanging down over the bones of his face and neck. He was secured to the palm trunk by several lines of rotting hemp, one of them hanging broken and frayed as though it had been chewed through before the man's strength finally left him.

This unfortunate shipmate would have died, of thirst, most likely, though he might have had wounds we could no longer apprehend, staring at the center of the clearing. There, at the exact center of the circle of sand, a long wooden handle stuck out of the ground at an angle, with a rag tied to its end. The rag might have at one time been a kerchief, dyed red, but it had since weathered into a filthy brown.

I heard soft laughter coming from Will Fly's spectral skull, so close I could have sworn I felt his breath hot on the back of my neck.

"Come on," said Sen.

The handle proved to belong to an iron shovel. It was short work for us to shovel the loose white sand out of the hole. Only a couple of feet below the surface, the shovel blade knocked against something hollow.

Kneeling, we used our hands to clear off the last sifting grains and brush them away.

The dead man was guarding a trunk. A sea chest, really, made of wood and leather and bound together with hobnails. A tiny fiddler crab scuttled away from the lock, snapping at me with its great claw when I reached for it. We tried the handles. The lid didn't budge. Locked, or else bound in place by the weight of the surrounding sand.

"We need to lift it out," I said, sitting back on my cracked heels.

Sen looked at the sky. The sun had slipped and was now hanging just behind the leaning palms, casting our skeletal comrade Sam into shadow. The sky was beginning to pale and turn pink around the edges. Sen wiped a wrist over his eyes, leaving a streak of sand behind.

"There's no time. The tide's going to turn. And anyway"—he rapped the shovel on the lid—"I doubt we could lift it, the two of us."

"How much might it weigh?" I asked. The chest was big. Bigger than I had imagined. Big enough for a boy my size to hide in. I remembered how heavy the duchess's writing desk had been, and it was only the size of a lap.

"Depends how much Will Fly left inside," he said. He looked over at the dead pyrate, who seemed to be watching us. In a quiet voice, he added, "Seems it could be a lot."

We stared at each other over the hole as gentle rivulets of sand ran down the sides and sifted onto the lid of the trunk. I wondered if he was thinking what I was thinking: that we should break open the lid with the shovel, dig out whatever we could carry in our shirts and kerchiefs, and keep it for ourselves. I was wondering how far we could get, sailing the leaking *Rose Pink* with just the two of us, and would it be far enough. Maybe he saw the avarice gleaming in my eye. I don't know. Maybe he knew better than I did how much stolen treasure lay inside. It was possible that our portion of all the spoils evenly divided amongst the people would be greater than whatever we could manage to carry in secret. Then again, it was also possible Sen had more honor than I.

Most people did.

"Tomorrow," he assured me, as though he could see my plans. "We'll come back with some of the others and get what's ours."

I didn't agree right away. Instead, I looked steadily at him. I let him feel that I was looking. My look told him that I knew his body as well as he knew mine. That I had seen his face scowling in pleasure. That I had held him while he slept. That I had gently traced a finger down the pink scar cleaving his bad eye and smoothed away the sweat from his brow and drawn circles in the soft gleam on his chest. My look told him that we were already in a conspiracy together. That I would not let him forget that we were known to each other.

He returned my gaze. His returned look told me that he was well aware of what had transpired between us. That he was not one to forget. That he was there, inside the conspiracy, with me. But he stopped short of bending to my will. We would not be stealing what we could carry and fleeing together that night.

"All right," I said at length, but I gave him to understand that there were other opportunities, hovering just outside of reach.

We left the hole open but took the shovel with us. When we returned to the snub of beach, we saw that the tide was at just about dead low, and if we hurried, the current would be slack and the row back to the lagoon easy. We pushed the tender down the sand, climbed in, and rowed for the mouth of the lagoon. Sen took the oars this time. He said nothing about it. As the lower-ranking of the two, by rights and custom, the rowing ought to have been mine. Instead, I rode in the stern of the tender.

The sun had slipped lower as we approached the sharp coral

outcropping that guarded the lagoon entrance. The sky glowed a deep orange pink, as rich as the sweet blooming flowers in the jungle around the camp.

When we rounded the outcropping half the lagoon had fallen into shadow, and low orange sunset stained the strip of beach. Sen paused on the oars, glaring into the lagoon, and my hands tightened on the gunwales.

It wasn't the light striking the beach that caught our attention.

There, riding at anchor close to the *Rose Pink*, battered and listing and with sails hanging it tatters, was the *Reporter*.

Ned Low had come for us.

Key West

Marian stepped onto the platform through parting clouds of steam breathing out of the huffing locomotive and beheld the Casa Marina Hotel, a sprawling complex of white stucco and gleaming glass and impeccable lawn dotted with coconut palms. The sun was slipping nearer to the Gulf of Mexico, coloring the sky in purples and oranges, painting the hotel's face in rose and gold. Tangles of bougainvillea knotted over a shady portico, and the arched glass windows along the arcade were all whitened by the setting sun, giving the hotel a blank and forbidding face. A perfect lawn rolled away from the portico, dotted with figures all dressed in white, with white straw hats, some of them crouched over croquet mallets. Now and again Marian could hear the crack of a mallet hitting a ball and peals of laughter.

Marian was looking for someone to help her with her bag. Her father was already on the platform, checking his watch, his battered case at his feet.

"Where's the girl?" he asked her. "I want to get checked in so we can get an early start tomorrow."

"I know," said Marian.

She felt as though she had stepped through a curtain of water. Summers in New York could be humid when she was a girl, but Marian had never known a humidity like this. She had thought the soft breezes of the meeting oceans would have swept Key West clean, lifting away mosquitoes and humidity and sand flies. Something bit her neck as she thought this, and she smacked it, her hand coming away smeared with a speck of blood. She said, "Ugh," and rummaged for her handkerchief to wipe it away.

The other chattering passengers gradually thinned and presently they heard a singsong voice call, "Halloo!" and there was Kay, chic and sun-glassed, waving to them from amongst a heap of luggage. She had changed clothes into a well-fitting tailored linen suit, with a fresh gardenia corsage on her lapel. She was standing in the company of a couple of men in rolled shirtsleeves and low hats. One of them was wearing a camera.

Marian sighed heavily and followed her father to join Kay and the reporters, who proved to be from the *Key West Citizen*. They were some-how already well informed on the plans of the tiny band of intrepid explorers who had just disembarked at the southernmost point in the United States on the hunt for long-lost pirate treasure.

THE STENCH OF gasoline was almost overpowering, and Marian was afraid she was going to be sick. She cowered in the bow of the long, low wooden boat, as far away from the outboard engine as she could get without actually diving in for a swim. But the bow skipped up over the swells and slammed down and skipped up and slammed down and Marian's head was rattling and she was definitely going to be sick.

"Why don't you sit to starboard, Monkey?" her father shouted over the propeller noise, and Marian crawled miserably out of the bow and parked herself on the right side of the boat, out of the wind, with her head hanging over the gunwale. The turquoise water swelled past her, foaming from the bow wake, but at least when her guts finally voided themselves, she was in the lee of the wind. The contents emptied into the water and not all over the boat and herself.

Someone was rubbing her back. She looked up, miserable, a rope of spittle swinging from her lip.

Her father.

"Fish food," he said with a gentle smile.

They'd had no trouble finding a boat to hire. After a bright and elegant breakfast in the Casa Marina dining room, with pressed napkins and fresh orange juice and softly humming tropical ceiling fans, they had ventured forth into a day of blistering white sunlight that gave Marian a headache almost immediately. Kay had skipped breakfast, and on the portico they discovered why: she stood in a bright glare of artificial light, waving into a whirring moving camera. Her lips were drawn on in deep red with an exaggerated bow shape, as though she knew how she might come off in motion and in black-and-white. She was in a man's white linen shirt with lots of pockets and rolled sleeves and beautifully flattering jodhpurs and had a straw hat tucked under her arm.

"Movietone," Dr. John Beresford said grimly. They had come upon Kay filming a newsreel. She waved into the camera, laughing, and looked demure and laughed again, and pointed and shaded her eyes and looked off into the distance, and turned this way, and turned that, leading with first one foot, then the other. She put her hands on her hips, and then positioned them at her waist, elbows aimed outward with her fingers pointed down, in the waist-accentuating posture of a starlet. This went on for some minutes while one of the men seemed to be asking questions and noting down answers that could be rendered on title cards.

"All right, Miss Lonergan," said the fellow with the list of questions as the one with the camera stopped the film. "That's all we need."

"Thanks, fellas." Kay beamed. "Here're the Drs. Beresford now. We're off! Isn't it exciting?"

"Sure is, Miss Lonergan," agreed the cameraman.

"You'll let us know the second you find something, won't you? Make a great follow-up. Maybe even a series," said the interviewer, or whatever he was.

"You bet I will," Kay promised.

Dr. Beresford looked pointedly at Marian. Marian made an apologetic face, but really, what was she supposed to do? She couldn't very well forbid Kay from speaking to the press. Last night, alone in her room, wiping Pond's off her face with cotton wool—it was too hot to imagine wearing cold cream, which clung to her face like molten wax—she considered that maybe Kay's apparent talent for commanding attention wasn't the worst thing in the world. Maybe it would encourage the Explorers to back them more. Maybe even National Geographic. Marian had stared at herself in the mirror, at the tired lines around her eyes, the gentle pudge around her middle that she had stopped trying to eliminate with reducing plans or girdles. Kay was young, she wasn't quite pretty, but close enough. Of course, her father wouldn't think these things mattered. But Marian's mother hadn't raised a fool. She knew that young women could command attention that older women could not. It just hadn't occurred to Marian until now that she was the older woman.

After the Movietone people withdrew, the three of them had walked into the heart of Old Town, moving through air as warm as bathwater, striped by shadows thrown by spindly coconut palms, their reflections swimming in the windows of buildings dressed in weathered clapboards. Here and there, men tanned dark as leather, gripping pipes between their teeth, lounged in chairs tipped onto their back legs and watched them pass from beneath sun-whitened signs advertising bay mullets and crawfish.

The previous night, after they checked in and sent their bags upstairs, John Beresford had lingered in the bar after "the girls," as he referred to Kay and Marian, had retired to their rooms and made the acquaintance of a handsome, jocular man with flushed cheeks and a trim mustache and a lot to say about sport-fishing. They shared some whiskey and the man—Ernie, he said his name was—questioned John closely about his expedition to Central America and his various safari trips to Southern Rhodesia. In return, John had gotten the Conch—that's what Ernie told him the locals referred to themselves as, Conchs: saltwater, if born on the island, freshwater, if they, like him, were late arrivals—to tell him where he could charter a boat and how much he should expect to pay.

They passed a warehouse that looked to Marian what an 1880s saloon must have looked like, except the plate glass windows were heaped high with wild sponges. Inside, men in rolled shirts and pants sorted them by size into different woven baskets or piled them up behind chicken wire. Despite the polished people resting in lounge chairs under the portico of the hotel, sipping their rum cocktails and betting too much at bridge, Key West still sifted out its living from the depths of the sea. Sponge warehouses nestled together with bait shops and sport-fishing enterprises, and they passed at least one storefront that advertised "Wrecking," which meant scavenging from the vessels that ran aground or foundered within a quick boat ride of the key. Wrecking had fed Key West for over a hundred years. As she and Kay and her father shuffled through the unthinkable heat of the early morning, Marian had time to wonder if the lost treasure they were hunting for wasn't lost at all but secreted away, one piece of eight at a time, behind the dim shuttered windows of the shacks and houses that they were walking past.

They'd found their charter captain, a desiccated figure with a low-pulled newsboy cap and a pipe, reading a newspaper in a bentwood chair in the back of Pepe's Coffee Shop. Copper samovars on a stovetop filled the air with the sharp smell of coffee, which somehow seemed sharper and more tropical here. His name, improbably enough, was given as Flint. Now he sat in the stern, silent, a hand on the tiller, paying equally no attention to Marian as she was sick over the side and to Kay as she pretended she wasn't.

"Is that it?" John Beresford shouted over the engine noise as Marian groped for her canteen of water.

Flint wore no sunglasses. His eyes were fixed in a permanent squint, burned in place over a lifetime of staring out over glittering tropical water.

"Nope," their guide said. He didn't elaborate. He didn't even glance at the island John was indicating.

"I think that's Boca Grande," Kay shouted, her hand on top of her straw hat. It was tied under her chin with a scarf, but the hand sat there anyway. She showed Marian's father a page in a map booklet she had procured from the concierge, and they leaned together to consult it.

It had never occurred to Marian that they might find a wrecker in a coffee shop. Much less a coffee shop situated next door to a storefront advertising *Curios*, which included a prehistoric-looking sunfish preserved and nailed to the wall, together with miscellaneous turtle shells and sponges for sale and nothing else. Good thing her father had such a penchant for drinking in hotel bars with loquacious men. Ernie the sport-fisherman had told John Beresford that Flint would be the one to hire, if there were wrecks from the Golden Age of piracy anywhere near Key West or the Dry Tortugas to be found. In 1825, he informed John over their third round of whiskey, Congress enacted the Federal Wrecking Act, which required that all items seized from wrecks in United States waters had to be taken to a United States port of entry. For wrecks in the Caribbean, that port of entry was Key West. Flint, John had been given to understand, had begun wrecking with his father when he was a boy, and his father had begun wrecking with his father before that, and he conducted his business by word of mouth only. He could be found, if they were lucky, at Pepe's, past the Old Spanish Fort.

Pepe's was at the end of a lane, not far from the ruins of a cigar factory that stood like the white marble remnants of an abandoned Roman temple, roofless and waiting to be consumed by grasses and scrub. Marian felt foolish and conspicuous in her brand-new boots and zinc oxide and hat as they stood in the door of the coffee house. Kay was too young to feel foolish, beaming at the grizzled locals with the benevolence of a visiting dignitary. Only John Beresford seemed to speak the language of blending in, looking as weathered and unconcerned as the men who watched them hesitate in the door.

Flint negotiated a price roughly twice what they were told to expect to pay. They paid it all the same, and he passed the wad of cash to a man behind a cash register—Pepe?—to hold as he said, "Awright. Right this way."

They followed him down through a weedy lot behind the café to a dock where half a dozen men sat mending fishing nets in shallow draft open boats essentially identical to the one they were riding in now. They climbed unsteadily aboard, Marian thinking back uncomfortably to tippy canoes on Rhode Island salt marshes in her girlhood. Flint pushed the boat away from the dock and started the outboard right up and eased on the throttle, peeling away from the wharf without even checking to see which direction he was headed. They skidded lightly over the glass-smooth water on their way outward bound, gliding along the surface like a pelican skating along the waterline ready to scoop up a fish. It didn't get hairy until they hit the swells. They'd bumped past Man Key and Woman Key, rising up and slamming down and rising up and slamming down, and Marian was counting the seconds, hoping that the next blur of green and white to appear on the horizon might be Marquesas.

"Isn't it exciting?" Kay shouted, her cheeks flushed, beaming. Her lipstick had melted a bit, running into the corner of her mouth, but instead of making her look sloppy the effect was almost passionate, of a happy young woman who had just been necking with her boyfriend after a football game in a very nice car.

Marian dabbed at the sweat under her eyes with her handkerchief and managed a miserable nod.

At last, in the distance, a knobby green silhouette heaved into view, looking for all the world like the back of a broaching alligator.

"That's it," barked Flint. He throttled down on the outboard until it dropped to a putt. The fishing boat settled down, tripping lightly over the waves instead of slamming. All three of them stared in wonder as the uninhabited island hove into view, and Marian could tell that even her father was excited.

They were approaching Marquesas from the back. Marian didn't know if there was a technical term she was missing, but in any event, the mouth of the lagoon seemed to open away from them. The water around them shoaled up into shallows, shimmering in pale shifting turquoise and azure, and over the side of the boat Marian could clearly see tufts of sponge and waving anemones dotting white sand, with no sense of how shallow they lay. The water played tricks, making them look almost close enough to touch.

"Do you see any palm trees?" she asked no one in particular, shading her eyes with a hand.

Kay had sunglasses on and could look longer. "No," she said slowly. "I'm not sure what all that is. Just jungle, I guess."

"'S mangrove," Flint said around his pipe.

"Oh," said Marian. From this aspect the island looked nearly impenetrable, the undergrowth was so dense and rich and knotted.

"Hurricanes," John Beresford said. He was standing in the bow in an active crouch, riding the motion of the boat with knees bending, as though he were standing on the back of a galloping horse. "They could easily have been blown away in two hundred years."

Flint said nothing.

Marian said, "I guess that's true."

They passed another open fishing boat, inward bound back the way they had come, carrying a couple of locals and two obvious tourists, already tired from a morning sport-fishing. As the boats crossed paths Flint waved a hand in greeting and the other waved in turn.

"Friends of yours?" Marian's father asked.

Flint didn't answer. Instead, he turned up the gas on the outboard, blurring them faster over the surface of the water until the enclosing arm of Marquesas began to open into the heart of a pale tropical lagoon.

A small island called Gull Key sat directly off the southernmost tip of Marquesas, separated from the larger island by a sluice too narrow and shallow even for their boat to traverse. The remainder of the lagoon—Mooney Harbor, it was called on the current nautical charts—was enclosed by five or six tiny keys, each of them consisting of little more than a tuft of green sitting atop a smudge of pure white sand.

Flint steered for the lee side of Gull Key, and as they rounded it, he cut the engine. They drifted in sudden silence into the heart of the lagoon.

The total absence of engine noise stunned Marian's ears, and she listened as the water lapped along the slowing hull of their fishing boat. They carried along, slower, slower, softly, until they felt the gentle brushing of sand along the underside of the hull and they came to rest a few feet up the beach. Flint's timing was impeccable. As though he had done the exact same trip a hundred times before.

The beach was perfect—stunning white sand, a few hermit crabs lazily crawling about their business. Not quite a crescent, the sand rose and eddied in dunes that gave way to a nearly solid wall of mangrove.

"Where do you think it is?" Marian said.

"The path?" John said.

Marian said, "Yes."

Her father scanned the tangled mangrove wall and after a time said, "Maybe it was there."

He indicated a slight thinning of undergrowth that marked a bubbling spill of fresh water seeping from the interior of the island down the beach to empty into the lagoon. It carried a few dead leaves, cutting a ribbon through the sand. A couple of hermit crabs plodded along the water's edge.

"The manuscript doesn't say anything about a freshet on the main island," said Marian. "Hannah wrote that it was on the island where the treasure was. In the atoll. One of those ones." She waved a hand at the nameless line of tiny, indifferent islands, each covered in a tangled mesh of green.

"Just because she doesn't mention it doesn't mean it wasn't there," Kay pointed out. "There must have been fresh water. They'd never have camped there otherwise. And what about the coconut palms? They'd need a freshwater source, wouldn't they?"

"I guess so," Marian allowed. No one would camp where there wasn't some fresh water somewhere.

Marian climbed awkwardly over the gunwale and landed with a splash, water immediately seeping into her new boots. She couldn't see any coconut palms. Not one.

Her father followed, and Kay was last into the shallow wash. Flint stayed in the stern of the fishing boat, his face impassive.

Marian slogged up the beach to the wall of mangrove and peered into the undergrowth. It seemed impenetrable. Dark, tangled, muddy, humming with mosquitoes, with a thick and loamy smell. She couldn't see any way in or out. She couldn't even spy the kinds of narrow trails carved by animals, like rats or pigs or whatever other animals might make their homes here. Next, she tried the thinner spot, a little way up the beach, her boots planted in the trickling fresh water. The brook was less than an inch deep, more a leak than a stream. Her father arrived next to her. Crabs probed their toes and then crawled away.

"This is our best bet, I think," he said, testing the roots with one hand.

He had brought a machete with him, with a wooden handle worn polished from long use. Marian had dismissed it as an affectation, but no, it turned out all her father's years in the Central American jungle weren't for naught. With a few quick slices of the machete enough roots fell away that something like a path opened. They stepped inside. But they didn't get very far before John Beresford had to wield the machete again, hacking at the undergrowth.

Marian didn't know how long they bushwhacked into the interior of the mangrove swamp. At least an hour. By the time they stopped, exhausted, to drink from their canteens and take stock of their progress, her shirt was plastered to her body and even Kay was looking like she had her regrets.

"How far have we gone?" Marian asked, leaning over with her hands on her knees to catch her breath.

Her father wiped his forehead on his sleeve and said, "I'm not sure. Maybe ten yards? Fifteen?"

Kay's hat was off, and her head was hanging between her hands draped over her knees. She didn't say anything, and she didn't look up.

All at once Marian felt a rush of understanding. There was no clearing here. There were no flowers. There were no pink boa constrictors. There certainly were no remnant pirate huts and flags.

Marian's father was breathing hard, and he sat heavily on a nearby root and stuck his machete point down in the mud. Marian realized, for the first time in a real way, that he was getting older. Marian didn't like to think of her father as a human person, beset by time as much as anyone else. But looking at him now, she saw his cheeks were pallid, and under his shock of white hair, his scalp was bright red from heat and exertion. Dr. John Beresford, the famous explorer, always ready to climb on the back of a camel or straddle the neck of an elephant or shine a light into the cave hidden behind the waterfall or pitch a tent on the edge of a crevasse, had somehow become a seventy-year-old man. She had dragged a seventy-year-old man on some damn-fool wild-goose chase in tropical heat that could be deadly even for men half his age. Marian felt an unaccustomed flush of shame and regret.

"Let's go back," she suggested. She half expected Kay to put up an argument, but instead both Kay and her father got mutely to their feet and followed Marian back the way they had come.

They found Flint dozing in the stern of his boat with his cap over his eyes and his fingers knitted across his chest.

"Flint," Marian said.

He ignored her.

"Flint," she said again, jostling the gunwale.

He awoke with a half snore and lifted his cap and said, "Yes, ma'am."

"Which one of those keys is Pig Island?" Marian asked, pointing at the atoll ringing the shallow lagoon.

"Ma'am?" he asked. His eyes, Marian noticed, were an unsettling ice gray, as if they had started out brown but been slowly bleached by the sun.

"One of those islands has a population of wild pigs on it," Marian said. "Or, at least, it used to. Which one?"

Flint looked over his shoulder at the line of scrub islands and white sandy beaches. "There?" he said. "Nothing on Mooney Harbor Key but more mangrove."

"What do you mean?" John Beresford asked sharply.

"Mangrove swamp. Some more mangrove swamp. That's it," said Flint, and something in his tone made Marian suspect that everyone but them knew this already. That Flint and the fishermen who'd passed them on their way outward bound, and all the men smoking and reading the paper in Pepe's, and the men lounging in chairs under overhangs, and the reporters and the concierge at the hotel and the sport fisherman at the bar and maybe even the dead sunfish in the curio shop knew this.

"No pigs?" Marian said. She already knew what he was going to say.

"No pigs," agreed Flint.

"Maybe they're all hunted and gone?" Kay said. Her hat was back on her head, but her face remained flushed from heat. Sweat gleamed on her cheeks, and her freckles showed where her makeup had melted off.

"Pigs? Pigs reproduce as fast as rats. They can't all be gone. All of them?" Marian said.

"Welcome to look," Flint said in the manner of someone who knows they will be wasting their time but who doesn't mind because he is being paid by the hour.

Marian stood on the sandy beach of this lonely, isolated tropical island paradise. A mosquito whined in and nipped at her ear, sucking up an angry welt.

No coconut palms. No coconut shells. No flowers. No snakes. No path.

"Flint," she said, speaking slowly so that she could hear herself over the sound of the blood rising in her throat. "How deep would you say this lagoon is?"

"Ma'am?" Flint's ice gray wrecker's eyes gave away nothing.

"How deep? At its deepest point?" Marian said. The longer she looked at it, the smaller the lagoon seemed. Small enough that she could swim across it in an hour or so. And she wasn't much of a swimmer. The bath-warm water was calm and blue, the sand on the bottom peopled with tiny bright-colored fish schooling around anemones and sponges. But not around coral.

There was no coral. There was no outcropping. Hannah had talked about the lagoon being guarded by sharp coral. Here there was only soft snowy white sand.

"I'd say," Flint spoke slowly around the mouthpiece of his pipe, "'bout nine feet."

"Nine feet," Marian repeated.

"At the deepest point, over there." Flint indicated a slightly bluer spot. "At flood tide. Most ways I'd call it closer to two."

Marian felt her head grow light.

"Two feet?" John Beresford said, hand tightening around his machete.

"It could have silted in," Kay began, but Marian held up her hand to stop Kay from saying anything more.

"Flint," Marian said, and she felt as though she were standing outside herself, watching her humiliation unfold. Of course, her father had to be there. Why had she agreed to bring him along? Why must he be standing right here, next to her, with his money and his reputation and his backing, his machete in his hand, the weight of all his years and his fame and the attention that his fame brought that reflected dimly on Marian, from which she had tried so long to escape? Her whole adult life had been spent being the other Dr. Beresford, a pale imitation of the original. A female version, and imperfect at even that, as her mother had never failed to point out. A failure at being a butterfly, and so electing to stay locked inside her chrysalis until the walls she had spun from her own flesh began to ossify and Marian became trapped by her very existence.

Why did Kay have to be standing there too, in her naive and trusting youth, with her fresh hat and her deepening sunburn and all her promised interviews to all her various press outlets, all the expectations she had stoked, that Marian had allowed her to enjoy? That Marian had pretended to disdain, but had really envied, when she was honest with herself, as she so rarely was, these days.

Wasn't it bad enough that Marian was standing here herself? Dr. Beresford, the younger, with her reputation on the line, and Radcliffe behind her name? Or forget Radcliffe. Forget her reputation. Forget whatever glories she might have imagined this project would bring her. Marian hadn't allowed herself to get that far, consciously, but surely there would have been some glories involved, the temptations of which had played about in the secret parts of her heart: attention, maybe promotion, maybe some money. Certainly acclaim. A story, of her own adventure, that she could tell over whiskeys to admiring people when she was old, too old to be admired for other things.

Marian Beresford, just by herself.

Marian Beresford, alone.

Humiliated.

That was bad enough.

"We told you we were looking for a shipwreck. From 1726," she said, her voice tightening. "That had sunk in the middle of a lagoon. By a crescent moon island. Surrounded by an atoll."

"Mm-hmm," Flint agreed.

"There's no shipwreck here, is there?" said Marian, glaring at the shallow lagoon, so clear and calm and warm that it contained no secrets at all.

Flint scratched under his hat and said, "Guess'n there probably isn't."

Chapter 12

~

$\mathcal{M}$y first thought was that we should run.

It must have been Sen's first thought too.

"Ned," Seneca said quietly, glowering at the *Reporter*, riding at anchor near the *Rose Pink*, looking so storm-shattered that it was a wonder it still floated at all. For its part, the *Rose Pink* was leaning sharply to starboard, having been partway careened ahead of having her hull scraped clean and repaired beginning the following day.

"I didn't think they'd weather the storm," I said. In truth, I had hoped that they wouldn't. Sen didn't answer, but I could tell that his thoughts had been the same. When we sailed away from them, he thought he was signing Ned Low's death warrant. He had almost signed ours, but that spoke to how keenly he was determined to break away.

We rowed in silence as the setting sun cast the lagoon into deepening darkness. The tender passed into the lee of the two anchored ships, disappearing into their shadows. From our momentary hiding place, we spied an orange glow rising from behind the tree line, casting the leaning palms into stark silhouette. The cooking fire was going, and it was a big one.

"I need to know. Will you back me?" Seneca said quietly.

I couldn't imagine that the opinion of a cabin boy would make any difference with the people if the question concerned Sen's abandonment of our elected captain at his most desperate extremity. My shipmates would be called upon to choose which side they spoke for. Any one of us would choose Ned, out of self-preservation if nothing else. It would be madness to choose otherwise, and risk Ned's mutilating wrath.

But I said, "Yes."

Before we drifted out of the sheltering darkness and up onto the beach gleaming white in the coming moonlight, I quietly added, "If you'll back me."

"All right," said Sen.

He found my hand in the darkness of the tender, wove our fingers together, and squeezed.

Our compact sealed, we beached the tender, shipped the oars, and without discussing it, left the small boat where it lay rather than pushing it all the way back up the beach above the waterline. I think both of us understood we might be needing it before the tide turned.

I followed close on his heels up the beach until we found the mouth of the path through the jungle that led to the clearing where my shipmates had set up camp. To the west the sky was stained bloodred, the kind of sky to delight the soul of any sailor, and yet it filled us—well, it filled me—with an uneasy sense of foreboding. As though the Devil were stoking up the fires of hell in readiness for our arrival.

The path wound dark and twisting through the jungle, and in the moonlight the occasional rose-pink serpent watched us pass from the forks of trees or the hanging slings of vines, their tongues tasting the air around our bodies. Presently the orange glow showed through the palm leaves, with the shadows of men moving around it. We heard the slurred sounds of drunken singing, *Fifteen men on a dead man's chest*, and smelled oily black smoke and roasting meat. The pig-hunters had found success.

We arrived in the clearing to find a bacchanal underway. A pig carcass was speared through the mouth and turning stiff-legged on a spit over a roaring fire, its skin blackened from smoke. The heat was terrific, filling the clearing with light from dancing flames, as though we were standing in the heart of the sun. Men were stripped down to their breeches and pantaloons, their chests gleaming, their heads bound in kerchiefs to keep the sweat from their eyes. A few lay in heaps with cups in their loose hands, their heads nodded forward on their chests. A barrel of rum stood on a stump, with one shipmate lying on the sand and another opening the tap into his mouth. Jonah romped by with a fat rat in his mouth, squeaking and kicking its feet. My bare foot stepped into a puddle of sour-smelling vomit.

At the center of the clearing, not far from the fire, a naked man stood lashed to a palm trunk, his flesh striped with smoke and blood. His head hung forward with his hair in his face so we couldn't see who he was, at least until the shipmate standing next to him grabbed his hair with his hand and forced his face up.

It was Jimenez, our swamp doctor. His eyes rolled back in his head, showing the whites, his face locked in a grimace of pain. I couldn't tell if he was alive or dead. The shipmate poured water on his face, and he coughed and sputtered. Alive.

John Somethingother barked, "Well, well. Look who's back."

The shanty-singing abruptly stopped as everyone turned to stare at Sen and me. I felt their eyes burning into my skin. Eyes of curiosity, or betrayal, or wariness, or malice, and in a few instances, eyes of pity. Pale blue and dark brown and gray-flecked and bloodshot.

A rolling billow of heat and smoke and sparks curled up from the bonfire, lifting the tattered black flag with its ragged skeleton aiming a spear at a pink heart, causing it to rise as though lifted by the hand of a ghost.

Someone shouted, "Ned!"

Out of the broken-spar hut roofed in dead palm leaves in which Sen and I had passed our afternoon stepped a man who had once been Ned Low. Our former captain looked crazed. His hair stood on end, greased and full of ashes. His shirt hung on his body in tatters, and his skin all over was blued with either bruises or smudges of ash and smoke. On a soot-darkened face his eyes seemed to glow, they were so pale.

"Well, now," he said, and even his voice sounded eerie and changed. "My hearties. What a relief it is, to see you here, home safe amongst our number. Welcome."

Jimenez groaned. Ned turned to him and said sharply, "See? You held your peace, through all of that. And for what? They came back all the same." The shipmate standing next to him dropped Jimenez's head and it fell forward.

My officer and ship's doctor—not my friend, exactly, but someone I had come to trust—had suffered this brutal treatment out of loyalty to Sen. And maybe to me. Jimenez's life was ebbing slowly out of the ragged openings in his skin, all because of his steadfast refusal to tell Ned Low which island in the atoll we were digging on. Blood ribboned down his legs and pooled in the sand around his bare feet. Guilt and shame burned in my chest, and I wanted to hide my face away, but I couldn't.

"Ned," Seneca said evenly. "You're alive. I'm so glad. I trust all our shipmates from *Reporter* are the same."

I didn't believe him. I wondered if anyone did. Ned smiled at us, the smile breaking open his grisly face made it look even more like the visage of a demon.

"Indeed, my friend. Alive I be," said Ned. "And our shipmates alive with me. Ready to die, but alive all the same."

The pyrates were closely watching this exchange, the tension thrumming across the clearing between Ned and Sen thicker even than the smoke from the cooking fire. It weighed in the air tasting of sulfur and brimstone. Even those too deep into their cups to stand were shifting about swimmily, lolling their heads so that they could watch what was about to happen. Slowly, in a circle, the people drew nearer, surrounding us. Here, Orne and his pet Frenchman. Over there, Wickham and Black Bart, who'd gotten even skinnier in the past few days. John the cook stood off-kilter, his peg leg sinking in the soft sand. On his shoulder the crimson parrot perched like a bright cockade.

"*Arrêtez*," it said, blinking a lizard-like eye at us.

Ned drew nearer. "So," he said to Seneca, "did you find it?"

Seneca was standing with his hands loose at his sides. I had my flintlock pistol charged and ready, tucked in the waist of my pantaloons, hidden under my blouse at the small of my back, and my cutlass slung around my hips. I dared not touch the hilt. I couldn't be the first to arm myself. I must watch Sen. I must wait. There was a chance that everyone was drunk enough that we might talk our way out of having abandoned Ned and the *Reporter*, leaving them all for dead in the jaws of the storm. A slim chance.

Touching the hilt of my cutlass would admit of my betrayal.

Seneca seemed to be calculating what the wisest next move would be. If he told Ned where Will Fly had hidden the treasure, they would surely kill us, as we had no further value and were still owed our shares. If he refused to tell, Ned would think we had deliberately betrayed him in hopes of keeping the treasure for ourselves. And they would likely kill us all the same.

A long moment wore by. It probably wasn't long at all, barely a second or two, but as I felt my very life hanging in the balance between the hard stares of these two hard men, time opened up and swallowed me down, like Jonah into the belly of the whale. As I slid screaming down the whale's maw, I had time to reprove myself for going pyrating at all. For spending my born days a sinner. I had time to wish I were back home safe in Boston, lying idle on the milldam with my head in Sarah Wildes's lap and the setting sun bright in my eyes. I had heard that life passes before the eyes of those who are about to die, and I even had time to reflect that they were right, as here was my life unfolding for my review. I found it largely wanting. I had time to pledge to God that if I could only escape this cursed paradise I would mend my ways and try to live an honorable and decent life.

That's when Sen started to laugh. Looks passed amongst the people, all of us surprised and confused.

"Aye," Sen said. "We did. And tomorrow we'll go together and claim what's ours. Now, I want some of that good bacon John's got cooking. John! How long before we eat?"

I had to admire Sen's courage. For an instant I thought maybe his ploy would work—that he might convince Ned that nothing was amiss, all was the same, we were all one body of common will.

"Not long now," John Somethingorother answered. I could clearly hear the coldness in his otherwise genial words. "Come over here and you can have the first taste."

"First taste for our first officer," agreed Ned. He joined us by the cooking fire, and aside said, "Put him out of his misery, would you?" to the shipmate standing next to the unfortunate Jimenez. The fellow said, "Aye, Captain," and lifted the doctor's head by his hair and drew his rigging knife along our compatriot's throat. An apron of blood poured glistening down Jimenez's chest, but he didn't cry out. God at least saw fit to have him out of his senses when the final moment came. Such were the pitiful mercies of life amongst pyrates.

Ned draped his arm over Sen's shoulders, and they walked together to the fire, which John was stoking, sending up coils of sparks into the night sky. I caught Sen's one good eye, and in his look, I read a stark warning. I stayed where I was, on the outskirts of the company, doing my best to blend into the jungle.

"Say, Sen," John asked without looking round, affecting a casualness that we all saw was a lie. "How'd you know just where that b—d Will Fly hid our spoils?"

"How?" Sen said in a transparent grasp for time to come up with an answer. He shouldn't have looked at me. He should have kept his eye down, or looking at the roasting pig, or up at the night sky, or anywhere, absolutely anywhere else, but instead his gaze came to rest squarely on me.

I felt the blood rise in my chest and heard its roaring rising in my ears, drowning away anything else that Ned or Sen might have been saying. The calm and rational voice that lived sometimes in my mind instructed me that I should ready myself. For what, the voice knew not. To run. To fight. To die, most likely.

John and Ned followed Sen's unwitting stare where it rested on my reddening face.

"I heard a rumor," John said, his voice low and full of gravel. "That you found a map."

"By happenstance and luck," Sen said. "So I did. Didn't I, Will?"

His words reached me slowly, muffled and wound down, as though I were hearing them through heavy waves of water.

I didn't know what would be the smartest thing to do. Agree? Play dumb? Was Sen throwing me to them to devour, like a bloody deer bone to a stalking pack of wolves? Would he so readily betray me like this? At this thought, I felt a strange quavering in my heart, the likes of which I hadn't felt since I was a small child.

But if he would, was I truly surprised? He was a pyrate, wasn't he? He'd sailed with Ned Low for years. Seneca had committed murder before my very eyes. Anyone who could do that was a cold, hard man, a brutal man, selfish and self-interested, and I was a fool if I thought otherwise. He would take me and use me for his pleasure and discard me without a thought. That's what my rational mind said. But I couldn't quite believe it was really true.

I searched Seneca's face and tried to read in it some reassurance or safety.

"Aye," I said slowly. "In some boots I stole. Off a dead boy."

John was glaring at me without bothering to hide it. "Right. Jim was his name," he said. "That boy. You remember, Sen. We were hunting that boy down in the streets of Boston. Weren't we? Split his skull like a ripe pumpkin, so we did."

The blood that was boiling in my head went ice cold all at once, and now I was helpless not to curl my fist around the hilt of my cutlass. The mystery of which murdering pyrates had hunted me through the streets of Boston was solved.

I hadn't left them behind me at all.

It was Seneca. Seneca had been the singsong man. Sen had called my name through the darkness, trying to lure me to my death at the end of his cutlass. Sen had sliced down lines of drying laundry, one by one, closing off my avenues of escape. Sen had scanned the street for my fleeing body as I hid in the apple barrel, terrified and afraid to breathe.

"Didn't I tell you two to kill that Jim and take away his black spot?" Ned said into Sen's reddening ear.

"I . . ." Seneca started to say. For the first time I read something like panic in his face. I had never seen Sen panic before. Afraid, in pain, in pleasure, but never not in control. When I saw his fear, I knew he was not forsaking me. He was buying time, trying to talk our way out of what was sure to come.

But I also knew we were surrounded.

"So you did, Captain," agreed John, holding a hot poker in his hand, stoking the flames under the pig carcass. "Only he fell in with a girl, didn't he? We got our Jim, but not his spot. And not the girl who helped him try to get away."

I didn't have time to think. I don't remember making the decision. What I do remember is the shower of sparks and smoke exploding in my hand, and the ear-shattering boom that ripped through the clearing. I remember the hot red spray across my skin and lips and hair and the look of shock in John's wide-open eyes as his hands flew to his belly and the way the surprise dissolved into horror when his hands filled with warm pulsing life as he slumped into the sand. A smattering of crimson feathers ringed his body as the parrot vanished into the trees.

The next thing I knew, I was fleeing through the jungle, panting, no sound in my ears but my own breath and beating blood. Night had spread under the thick waxy leaves, and I tore through vines and vaulted over fallen palm trunks, my chest bursting, the pistol still in my hand. My feet beat in time to my breath, and I heard crashing through the undergrowth behind me, and shouts, and the crack and boom of a pistol and a whizzing as the ball sped past my ear.

The moon had begun to rise, and I saw the shimmering white expanse of the beach opening through the screen of trees. Then I was back at the tender. The tide had turned, with gentle lips of surf licking at the stern of the boat, shifting it lightly on the sand, so it was short work for me to shove it into the water, a smattering of bright blue phosphorescence scattering along its waterline. My hands were shaking. I stuffed the pistol into my pantaloons and tried to unship the oars, but they were heavy, cumbersome oak things, and my palms were slick with sweat. I'd only just fitted one of them in an oarlock when someone exploded out of the jungle, sprinted across the sand, and splashed into the surf after me.

I screamed, lifting the oar to bring it down on my shipmate's head, but then I saw that it was Sen. He flung himself over the gunwale, gasping, "Help me up, please, help me," and kicking up spray with his feet.

I grabbed the back of his shirt and hauled him over the gunwale and into the hold just as Ned and the others burst out onto the beach. A hiss and boom and orange tongues of flame and a ball whizzed by and plopped into the water inches away from where Sen had just been. He scrambled to his knees, and we got both the oars unshipped and were hauling together for the *Rose Pink*, which was the closest to shore.

"Hurry up!" we heard Ned scream. "You lazy good for nothing b—ds, hurry!"

Our shipmates were trying to launch another tender after us, but it was slow going, as the other boats had been hauled clear of the water line and had to be muscled down the beach. Further, everyone was three sheets to the wind, stumbling drunk. By the time our pursuers got their oars unshipped and started pulling after us, we were already bumping against the *Rose Pink*'s starboard side and shinnying up the careening lines. The hemp was rough under my palms, stretched and wet, but my hands and thighs pulled together and in an instant my feet were safe on the deck.

"We've got to cut the lines," Sen cried. The careening lines held the ship fast to the shore and kept her tipped over at an angle.

"I'll slip the cable," I answered.

"No, the lines first," Sen said. The tender carrying Ned and the others, knives in their teeth and baying for our blood, pulled closer. The pink had been careened over at almost forty degrees. To get away in her we needed to cut all the lines holding her akimbo and cut the anchor free.

We heard the pursuing tender draw up to the starboard side, the same side we'd used to board, because the careening lines drew it so close to the water.

Sen cursed a blue streak, produced a flintlock, and fired. Orange flame and smoke and a boom and we heard a wet thwap, a scream, and a splash. One pursuer down.

"That was some shot, you son of a w—e," Ned shouted. "Avast, fellows! We're boarding!"

"Come on," Sen said, and he took my hand. We fled together to the forward companionway and slid down the ladder. Then we were on the gun deck and running for the stern.

"Come out, come out, wherever you are!" Ned shouted. We heard feet landing on the deck overhead and wicked laughter and running for the companionway after us.

"Wait!" I cried.

"There's no time!" Sen shouted, but I went to the starboard gunports anyway and unlatched them one by one. The ship was heeled over so far, and lying so heavy with water in the hold from leaking, that the surface of the lagoon lapped only an inch or three below the opening of the gun ports. Our pursuers were shinnying after us along the careening lines, dragging on them with the weight of two dozen men. Would it be enough?

"Let's go," I said, my quick work done. Sen and I were almost to the sternmost cabin when Ned landed hard at the foot of the companion-way ladder and fired a pistol at us, a cloud of smoke and flame roaring through the close confines of the deck, the ball zinging past my temple and shattering a lantern, raining down shards of glass like pinpricks of ice.

My face slammed hard against the cabin sole, Sen's weight on me, crushing out my breath as he cried, "Hannah!" and tried to shield me from the gunfire.

My real name.

Not that I'd forgotten it. But I hadn't heard it spoken since my feet stepped aboard the *Reporter* wearing dead Jim's boots. Of course Sen knew my name. He sang it out in the night back in Boston, a lifetime ago.

Ned Low stopped short, cutlass in one hand and smoking pistol in the other. Through the acrid gloom of the gun deck, I heard him echo, in an unbelieving voice, "Hannah?"

Sen and I stared at him, momentarily frozen. Something strange was happening to Ned's face. Usually bent and folded in a red Z of rage, now some ribbon of something smoothed him out, rendering him unrecognizable, at least to me. The flintlock in his hand dropped a few degrees, and he quietly said, "Did you say 'Hannah'?"

Sen pulled me to my feet, shouting, "Come on!" just as Orne and some of the others landed in the gun deck behind Ned. Up topside more bodies clambered aboard, throwing their legs over the rail. The *Rose Pink* shifted her cant slightly, under the added weight of men. Water lapped over the centermost gun port, as soft and delicate as a cat's tongue. The lap immediately became a trickle, which became a flow.

I was staring at Ned Low. And Ned Low was staring at me, an unreal wonder dawning across his face, even as water began to pool around his feet. "It couldn't be," Ned Low whispered, and when he did so, I saw that with his face smoothed out like that, unbent, unangry, something in the slope of his cheeks and turn of his lip made him look a little bit like me.

Sen shouted, "Now, Hannah, let's go!"

He grabbed my arm roughly and dragged me with him into the sternmost cabin. More men reached the gun deck, and the cant of the ship shifted, and then shouts filled the belowdecks as two more gunport lips slipped below the surface of the water, and the sea started to push in.

The cabin was a wreck of charts and hanging chandelier and overturned chairs and busted parrot cage. Sen looked around, his eye wild, grabbing up whatever charts he could see and stuffing them into his shirt. As an afterthought he picked up the duchess's writing desk under his arm. He took a compass and stuffed it down my shirt and then we were climbing up a rope ladder hanging from the stern skylight and we punched through the glass in a rain of shards and then we gained the quarterdeck, gasping and bleeding and trapped.

The pink groaned under the gathering weight of inrushing water. I saw some of my shipmates standing hip-deep on the deck, shouting and trying to get the men out who had gone below after us. Her masts leaned at nearly sixty degrees, and waves lapped over the rail scattering pale blue phosphorescent sparks along the length of the ship. Overhead, the first cold stars were winking to life. Then one of the last gunports must have opened, as the leaning gathered speed and the shouts became screams.

"What do we do?" I shouted. In minutes, the quarterdeck would be awash.

"Halyards," Sen said. Instantly I understood. The halyards are the lines that lift the sails up the length of the mast. They are fastened at the very top of the mast, with lots of length to play with.

It was short work to untie the mizzen halyard. We looped it around ourselves, fashioning a kind of boatswain's chair for us together. I held tightly to the line, and to Sen, and he held the box and the line and me.

"Ready?" he looked down at me. And he smiled.

"Ready," I said. I smiled back. And then, knowing the odds were good we'd be in the drink in moments and dead shortly thereafter, I pressed my eager mouth to his. I would die, I decided, with Sen's taste on my lips.

"Here we go," he said. Together we leaned backward, then jogged forward a few yards and our feet lifted off the quarterdeck and we swung free.

Our bare feet sailed through the night, and I saw only black lagoon water below us. The warm night wind whistled through my hair as we swung out in a wide, arcing semicircle. In a moment the bow of the *Reporter* was rushing to meet us.

"Now!" Sen said, and we let go.

I closed my eyes and felt my body fall. I expected any moment to feel the warm water close over my face, and for the weight of the compass and pistol and cutlass to drag my slight body down to the bottom of the lagoon, never to rise again. I lingered over the taste of Sen on my tongue, thinking that when I awoke to find myself sunk in the flames of hell, I would at least have the pleasure of his lips on mine to remember my sorry life by.

I landed in the bouncy rope webbing on either side of the bowsprit.

I opened my eyes.

Screaming ripped through the night from the foundering *Rose Pink*. Sen had landed hard on the bowsprit with one leg and was grimacing in pain.

"Hannah," he grunted through gritted teeth. "I think it's broken."

"All right," I said.

I left him there to sort himself out. First, I slipped the anchor cable. I knew the tide was coming, and if I didn't get a sail up immediately, the *Reporter* would be driven onto the beach. I heard splashes and cries as my shipmates threw themselves into the lagoon to escape the sinking *Rose Pink*. Some of them could swim, but most could not. They would all be flailing for the *Reporter* as we spoke, desperate to save themselves.

I found the staysail halyard and hauled hand over hand, grunting with the effort, dragging the sail up the mizzenmast. I made it fast, and the soft night breeze bellied into the small sail and the schooner started to spin.

I heard Sen groaning as he dragged himself onto the bow. Then I was at the wheel. I spun it until I felt the pressure of the wind answering on the rudder. The staysail had some holes, but it was less tattered than it could have been. A few of the topgallants were dangling like ribbons, useless. But the *Reporter* responded, moaning through a sloppy tack and aiming her bow where I asked it to go. We were outward bound.

I lashed the wheel to keep our point of sail and then went to try to raise the main. It was no good. It was too heavy. I strained, I hauled, I scrabbled, but it wouldn't go. I'd set a jib or I'd set nothing.

I ran to the bow and busied myself with a flying jib, stepping over a prostrate Seneca as I sorted out the lines. "The wheel," he moaned through teeth gritted in pain.

"Not now," I barked at him. Then the jib was up, and it was filling, and it was drawing, but my wheel lashing had slipped and we were making straight for the coral outcropping.

I flew back to the stern, taking hold of the wheel. Just then a dark missile sped by, no more than a yard from me, ripping a perfect hole in the staysail, and followed by a head-cracking boom and a splash. In the momentary burst of flame that lit up the lagoon I saw that someone had fired the stern chaser from the *Rose Pink*, whose yardarms were touching the water.

They thought to stop us, but instead the hole it punched in the sail spilled just enough air that the current pushed us down. My hands gripped the wheel, touching it gently, as I might touch the body of my lover, to coax him into doing what I wanted. The coral outcropping that marked the mouth of the lagoon loomed, a deadly line of perfect jagged black outlined in glittering blue at the waterline. I adjusted the wheel again. The bow aimed down another degree. The sails backed, dropping the air that was carrying us. I held my breath, as if making myself even smaller would make the schooner narrower too.

The jagged blackness swelled past, almost close enough for me to touch.

And then we were away. I adjusted the wheel, bringing the air back into our two pitiful sails. Off the bow I saw the line of the atoll, the island beaches glowing white in the rising moonlight, and I aimed the schooner for the deep black channel between the two largest islands.

I thought with some sorrow of Jonah, my stump-tailed cur, left behind in the camp with his fat rat to chew on, but at least I knew he'd have a pig carcass all to himself. I glanced astern, but the lagoon beach was hidden away by the enclosing coral outcropping, so I couldn't see the final moments of the *Rose Pink*. I could, however, hear the screams. They rose to a fevered pitch, cries of desperation, hardened rogues reduced to begging the heavens for mercy, and in at least one instance, I clearly heard someone weeping for his mother.

The last scream that tore the night might have been Ned Low, calling my name.

An answering scream arose from the shrouds of the *Reporter*. It was the hideous crimson parrot, who had secreted himself in the shrouds and was making an escape alongside us. As the screams from the lagoon died away, the parrot's screams quieted too. Presently the night settled into deadly silence, with no sound but the water rolling away from our bow and Sen's faint moans from the foredeck.

I kept my hands on the wheel until we were through the channel and aimed back out into the open sea, tracing our path along the shimmering road of yellow-white moonlight. I lashed the wheel and went to tend to

Sen, who was collapsed with his hands around his leg. As I made my way forward, I heard rustling and flapping and then I felt sharp claws sink securely into my shoulder.

"*Arrêtez*, you b—d," the creature said to me.

"Not on your life," I said. I made bold to scratch him under his chin, and the feathers of his cheeks bristled in pleasure.

The parrot answered by squawking something that might have been "*Pieces of eight*," but then again, maybe I was only hearing that inside my mind, in the same secret chamber where just then, and for the last time, I heard Will Fly laughing his spectral laugh of triumph that his treasure would never be found again.

Key West

Marian lay on her back, staring up through the tropical darkness at the ceiling fan as it stirred the lifeless air in her room.

She couldn't sleep. But she was too tired to get up. She was stuck in an in-between place. Always in between.

Even with the ceiling fan, Marian was hot. A sheen of sweat had settled between her breasts and clung to her cotton men's pajamas. Sweat dotted her upper lip and her hairline and collected in the backs of her knees. A droplet rolled down her armpit.

Frustrated, Marian flopped over onto her side, flipped her pillow over, looking for a cool spot, punched it into shape, and lay still.

Her eyes wouldn't close. Every time she tried to lower her eyelids, they drifted upward, of their own volition, pried open by her anger and shame.

Marian threw off the thin cotton blanket and found the air in her hotel room to be as hot as the air underneath it.

She stared at the clock on the nightstand. The second hand ticked. The clock read 11:56.

Marian rolled up to seated and put her head in her hands.

Then she snapped on the lamp.

Hannah's manuscript sat on a tea table near the French doors that led out onto a narrow terrace overlooking the croquet field. Pages thick and wavy from age and water damage. Whole chunks missing. Thick leather binding, probably rebound later, reassembled after whatever had torn the book apart the first time. Marian almost felt as though Hannah were there, in the room with her, sleepless too. Stalking back and forth waiting for Marian to figure out where she'd gone wrong.

It would be too simple to say that she felt like Hannah was trying to tell her something. Hannah had told her everything she had to tell, by writing the book in the first place. But there was something Marian was missing.

"Why couldn't you have just drawn the map?" Marian asked the empty room.

She opened the French doors and found the night air slightly cooler. Humid haze kept her from seeing much in the way of stars, but the moonlight was bright enough for Marian to see the ghost-white shapes of lawn chairs and the black silhouettes of palm trees lining the drive to the hotel portico. Someone was laughing down on the croquet field. A fat gibbous moon hung low, almost low enough to touch the coconut palms, and in the distance, Marian could spy the winking of green and red ships' lights as they moved through the straits, cutting their steady progress to Havana. The night air tasted briny and fresh, and Marian breathed deep, feeling the sweat lift from her skin.

She left the French doors open and sat in one of the gilt bamboo chairs at the tea table. Marian leaned her chin on her hand and opened Hannah's book again.

There was the beginning of Hannah's story. Boston, Ship Tavern, the dead boy Billy, who was actually Jim. She turned the manuscript over and riffled to the end. The *Rose Pink* sank. Hannah and Sen escaped. To where? Boston, probably. But there was no way of knowing what else had happened in Hannah's life. Marian could conclude she'd gotten away, of course. And somewhere along the line, she learned to read. After all, the book had been written. Who knew when or how or why. Well, the why was easy enough to guess—Hannah probably needed the money. She would have sold her story for profit, just as people did today. How much would a pirate story, privately printed in Boston at the end of the eighteenth century and sold from the printer's shop, glean for its author? Couldn't have been all that much.

Marian took the pages in her hand and bent them, intending to riffle back to the original description of the island, when the *Rose Pink* first arrived. She shifted the book so that she could read it in the light from the nightstand without turning on another lamp. She held the leaves gently, bent so the edges were fanned and could be paged with her thumb. But before she let the pages go, Marian hesitated.

"Huh," she said.

Illuminated by the raking light, the edges of the pages seemed to have been decorated. The patterns were very faint, faded from water damage and time, which presumably was why she had never noticed them before.

The manuscript's endpapers were patterned in a paisley-like oil swirl, which had at one time been yellow and orange and green on a reddish background, now grown peeling and dingy with years. Sometimes, Marian knew, the edges of pages of antique books were decorated in patterns that mirrored the oil swirls on the endpapers, or in red paint or gilding. Usually, those sorts of flourishes appeared on more elegantly bound books than this, though.

Marian lifted the book gently, tilting it nearer the light, and bent the pages in her left hand again so that she could get a better look.

"You have got to be kidding me," she said aloud. She listened for imaginary laughter inside her mind, the way Hannah kept hearing the whispers of Will Fly. But if Hannah was there in the room laughing at her, Marian couldn't hear her.

The pattern on the edge of the papers was invisible when the pages were aligned, as when the book was sitting unopened on a table or a shelf. But when Marian bent the pages, fanning them a bit, and held them in raking light, a clear image appeared. Or an image that had at one time been clear, very long ago.

It was a map. Roughly drawn, as by an untutored hand. It featured a larger island, in a vaguely crescent shape, a line of squiggling circles of decreasing size, something that looked like a fish with a rolling eye in the space that would have been the lagoon, and there, over one of the squiggled circles, stood two crudely drawn palm trees.

Marian's eyes widened until the whites shone around her irises on all sides, and she said, "I will be God damned."

It was unmistakable.

The palm trees were crossed in the shape of an X.

Marian threw on her dressing gown and dashed out of the room, Hannah's book clutched to her chest.

"It's ROATÁN," SAID Marian.

"What in God's name are you wearing?" John Beresford said.

Her guess was right—her father was still up, drinking in the bar. If the bartender was surprised to see a middle-aged woman with her hair in pins show up at the bar in a silk dressing gown, so hastily knotted that it had come undone and revealed light cotton pajamas that left little of Marian's shape or gradations of skin color to the imagination, he was at least good enough at his job that he didn't let on. Marian climbed onto the stool next to her father and said, "Look."

"Marian, really," he said, averting his eyes. Her father turned his profile to her, and he sipped his whiskey, staring hard at the painted odalisque lounging provocatively behind the arrayed bottles at the back of the bar.

"Papa," Marian insisted. "Listen to me. I've figured it out. It's Roatán Island."

"Excuse me, ma'am," the bartender said after a delicate clearing of his throat. "Did you happen to obtain a membership card on your way in?"

"A what?" Marian said, settling the book in front of her and helping herself to a candle to show her father what she had found.

"A membership card. For the club." The bartender gestured at the bottles of whiskey and rum behind him.

Marian stared at him, and then decided that he was wasting her time and so she didn't need to answer. "Papa," she said again, "I'm telling you, it's Roatán Island. Look."

She moved the book around, readying to show him the trick, only to have the bartender interrupt. "Fortunately I have a spare one here. If you would just like to sign your name . . ."

"Fine." Marian scribbled something on the paper in front of her and waved him away.

"What can I get you?" the bartender said, undaunted.

"Oh my God, would you—" Marian started to say, but her father interrupted.

"She'll have a whiskey. Neat. Thank you, Jarvis." To Marian, he added, "I realize we're not far from Havana, but really, darling, this isn't a good look for you."

Marian flushed and hastily relooped the belt of her dressing gown. When the whiskey appeared, she took a long swallow of it and then noticed that the few other patrons still in the bar weren't quite as unfazed as the bartender was. Eyes were settling on her, and a few whispers could be heard.

"Have you got a cigarette?" she asked, holding the dressing gown closed at the neck.

"Certainly," her father said. He produced one and then struck a match. She took the cigarette, but instead of accepting the match, she leaned down and lit it on the candle in front of her, drew a long drag of smoke deep into her lungs, and sighed it back out. Immediately she felt more in control. She let go the neck of her dressing gown and rested an elbow on the bar, crossing her legs at the knees.

After another drag, she repeated, "I've figured it out. It's not Marquesas at all. It's Roatán Island, in the Gulf of Honduras."

Her father didn't immediately respond. He turned his glass where it sat on a paper napkin.

"It's where Ned Low abandoned Philip Ashton," Marian reminded him. "In 1723."

Philip Ashton was a sailor from Marblehead, Massachusetts, who had been captured by Ned Low from a fishing vessel on the Grand Banks, and who had refused to sign the Articles and turn pirate with them. He had published an account of his year spent as a castaway when he escaped the pirates and hid alone in the jungle before hitching a ride home on a vessel out of Salem. It was, up until now, the most famous firsthand account of life under the notorious pirate Edward Low. Why hadn't she thought of Roatán before? Of course Ned Low could have gone back there with Will Fly. It was a safe harbor for watering and careening, and he'd have already known the dangerous outcroppings and patterns of current and tide. And Roatán was uninhabited.

Still the glass turned in her father's hands. "Philip Ashton," he said slowly, "if I'm not mistaken, wasn't abandoned. He escaped."

"Right!" said Marian excitedly. "Like Hannah!"

"Just like Hannah." Now John Beresford looked at her.

"So Ned Low must have returned to Roatán. It's got to be there! And look!" Marian showed him the trick with the bending edges of the pages, with the secret, sloppily drawn map. She expected him to light up with excitement and interest when she did it. His eyebrows rose a bit, but that was all. He lifted his glass to his lips.

"Neat trick," said the bartender. He was polishing a highball glass and obviously eavesdropping on them.

"Indeed," her father said. "It's quite a trick."

"I figure, we go back to the Explorers and see if they'll underwrite us for an expedition to Roatán," Marian spoke quickly. "I bet with all the interest Kay has drummed up, they'll want to do it. Maybe we even hit up National Geographic. We've got a map now! Just imagine! We can even loop in an archaeologist. We can—"

"Yes, about all that interest Kay has drummed up," her father cut her off. "Have you asked her where she found this miraculous story? Hmm?"

"Have I . . . what?" Marian said.

John Beresford met the eye of the bartender, who wordlessly refilled his whiskey glass. At a further look from her father, he refilled Marian's glass too.

"Asked her," her father said. "Where she got it."

"Of course," Marian said, stiffening.

"Well? Where'd it come from?" He looked at her.

Smoke coiled up from her cigarette nub, forgotten.

"It," Marian started to answer. Only then did she realize that, while she had certainly asked Kay the question, she didn't remember what the answer was. What had she said? She'd said something. Not the library. Where had Kay found it? Marian looked for a time into her whiskey glass, as if she might be able to find the answer in the bottom.

"Huh," her father said when she did not.

"I don't think . . ." Marian said, not sure what was going to come out next. Nothing came to mind.

She picked up the whiskey glass.

"Monkey," her father said gently. He placed a hand on the back of her fist where it sat on top of the manuscript. But instead of delivering a dismissive pat, his fingers curled protectively around hers and squeezed. And his other hand came to rest on top. "I think," he continued, "you should ask her. Before we go off half-cocked. Don't you?"

Marian was gazing into the middle distance, into some imaginary, fantastical space behind the idling bartender, at a desert tropical island peopled with foul-mouthed crimson parrots and coconut palms. She was thinking about Hannah. She had spent so much time thinking about Hannah over these past few weeks. Talking to her, almost. Painting her in her mind's eye. The Hannah in Marian's imagination had freckles on her sunburned cheeks, had long weedy hair in a pigtail down her back tied with twine. She was skinny and hard-edged and cunning, but sentimental too. Marian's Hannah was somehow both tiny and unafraid, her cutlass hanging heavy at her hips, almost as long as she was herself. Hannah had lain in wait for her when Marian got up every morning, laughing at all the ablutions twentieth-century women must put themselves through. Hannah draped herself over a chair in Marian's office, eyeing her while she marked her students' indifferent papers. She had stalked behind Marian in the library, astonished that so many books could exist in one place in the world. Marian realized how accustomed she had become to Hannah. To the Hannah-ness that had taken root and begun to bloom inside herself, urging Marian to risk, urging Marian to take action. Helping Marian be unafraid.

For the first time, Marian could imagine what the ghostly laughter sounded like when it pealed in Hannah's ears.

She tossed back her whiskey, put down the glass, and stood up.

"Yes," Marian said to her father. "Yes, I do."

She picked up the manuscript and clutched it protectively to her chest as her bare feet padded across the cool tile floor of the bar.

Marian's ears were hot as she hurried to the elevators, her dressing gown rippling behind her. She hit the "up" button with a thumb. Then she hit it again. And again and again and again and again and again.

The elevator crept up to Kay's floor. *Ding. Ding. Ding. Ding.*

The doors slid open.

Marian stalked down a hall swathed in shadow, sleeping doorknobs all wearing their *Do Not Disturb* signs hanging at angles. Here and there, peals of laughter came muffled through the doors, and as Marian passed one, she overheard a soft cry out and a sigh. She held the manuscript closer and rose to the balls of her feet to make herself silent as she passed.

Which room was that girl in? 604? No, it was 606. There it was.

This *Do Not Disturb* sign was up too, and behind the door, the room seemed silent. Marian couldn't see any light under the door. She rapped all the same, *bang, bang, bang.*

"Yes?" came a muffled voice. Not a sleepy voice. A voice interrupted in the middle of doing something else.

"Kay," said Marian curtly. "It's me."

"Just a minute." Still muffled. Marian heard shuffling and the sounds of hangers clattering together and then fumbling with a dead bolt.

The door opened a crack, and one palm-leaf-green eye peered out.

"What's up?" Kay said from behind the door.

"Can I come in?" Marian said. All at once she realized that she was in her dressing gown and pajamas, knocking on the door of her undergraduate's hotel room. She realized it at the very moment that Kay must have realized the same thing.

The green eye traveled slowly down the full length of Marian, from her pinned hair to her lined face to her translucent cotton nightclothes to her bare feet, before it came to rest on the book clutched to Marian's breasts.

"Um," Kay demurred. "Sure. I guess."

Kay swung the door wide, and Marian came in. Kay wasn't dressed for sleep. She was clean and tidy and pressed, in fresh traveling clothes. One of her suitcases lay open on the bed, vomiting up heaps of linen and cotton and hats and scarves. The others lay in an unstable pyramid near the door. A telephone sat on the nightstand, with depressions in the pillows and comforter, as if Kay had been lounging there, taking calls, her feet crossed at their slender ankles.

"What's all this?" Marian said.

"Packing," Kay said. She moved smoothly back into the room and settled in the pillows on the bed with one foot drawn up underneath her. "Shall I call for some tea?" Her tone suggested that Marian looked like someone who could use a cup of tea whether she wanted one or not.

"Packing?" exclaimed Marian. "But our train isn't for three more days."

"Yours isn't," said Kay evenly. "Mine leaves at five. So, in about"—she checked the alarm clock by her bed, which was identical to the one by Marian's bed—"four hours or so. I guess I'll probably just stay up. Maybe see if anyone interesting's in the bar. I'd ask you to join me, but . . ." Kay looked pointedly at Marian's state of undress and didn't finish her thought.

Kay was leaving. She hadn't breathed a word of her plans to Marian.

"You're going back to Cambridge?" Marian said. "But winter break isn't over for three more weeks."

"No," said Kay. She lifted a sweet short-sleeved blouse with a Peter Pan collar, and slowly folded it into a tidy square and laid it in her suitcase. "California. At least, for a little while."

Marian sat down heavily at the tea table that was identical to the tea table in her room, still cradling the manuscript in her arms. What if Kay insisted on taking Hannah with her? No, she wouldn't. Kay was done with her adventure. Somehow, Marian could tell. Kay was finished.

"I figured it out," Marian told Kay, her voice sounding hollow in her ears. "Where we went wrong. We're looking in the wrong place. The wrong island entirely."

"Oh?" said Kay, rolling a long pair of stockings into a tidy tube and tucking it into a side compartment of the suitcase.

"Don't you want to know where we should be looking instead?" asked Marian.

Kay smiled down at her. "I know you're dying to tell me," she said. Her hands lifted a gossamer silk scarf, floating it through the air, urging it into an imperfect, slippery square, and settling it down in the suitcase.

"I think I can get the Explorers to give us more backing," Marian said slowly. "But there's just one problem."

"What's that?" Kay didn't look round. Instead, she moved into the powder room and snapped on a light, casting a yellow rectangle into the center of the room, struck through with Kay's moving shadow. Marian heard the sounds of hair rollers and pins and brushes and bottles being gathered up and stuffed into a beauty case.

Marian looked down at the book in her arms. Weathered and water-stained. Grimy. Inside those pages dwelled a living, breathing soul, somehow imprisoned. Hannah. Hannah was a prisoner of her own story. Marian yearned to free her. And Kay must help her do it.

Marian said, "You have to tell me where you found this book."

A long silence wore by inside the powder room. Marian saw Kay's shadow pause, and then resume picking up bottles.

"Didn't I tell you?" Kay called, casual, singsong. Marian's eye roved over Kay's heaps of luggage and finery.

"No," said Marian flatly. "No, you never did."

Kay reappeared silhouetted in the bathroom door with her hands full of makeup brushes, the beauty case tucked under an arm.

"Where'd you find it, Kay?" Marian said. She rested a hand on the leather binding, guarding it almost, against whatever it was that Kay was about to say.

Kay eyed her for a long minute while she fit her various beauty items into crevices between the clothes and shoes overflowing the suitcase. Then she straightened and planted her hands on hips in the affected movie starlet pose that Marian had seen her adopt for the newsreel.

"All right," Kay said. Her green eyes cooled perceptibly. "If you really want to know. It came from the basement of Westmorly Court." She closed the suitcase lid with unexpected force and snapped the latches shut.

"What?" Marian was confused.

Westmorly Court was a Harvard undergraduate dormitory. One of the expensive ones, rumored to enjoy its own private swimming pool full of spitting stone dryads, like a Roman bath, where nude Brahmin sons disported themselves in the interest of manly good health. It contained upperclassmen who could afford to stay at school with a valet in tow. Radcliffe girls certainly weren't allowed inside.

Kay smiled. "Yep. They have a letterpress there. A really good one."

Kay disappeared back into the bathroom, leaving a dull silence thudding in Marian's ears. Marian lifted her hands slowly off the weathered leather binding.

"Letterpress?" Marian echoed in disbelief.

"Come on." Kay laughed from inside the bathroom. "You mean to tell me you really didn't know?"

Hannah. Sen. The dead boy Jim. All of it.

Marian's heart contracted.

"But the water damage," she objected. "The foxing."

Kay came back into the bedroom holding her straw hat and hunted up a hatbox to fit it, discovering it kicked under the bed. "Tea," she said, sounding smug as she stuffed tissue into the hat's crown and settled it in the box. "Worked even better than I thought. You soak the pages and hang them up to dry. And didn't you just love the map?"

Marian didn't answer. She felt sick to her stomach. She wanted to take Hannah into her arms and whisper into her hair that it wasn't true, that Hannah didn't have anything to worry about, that Marian knew Kay was lying. Wasn't she?

"I thought for sure you'd find it right off the bat. That was hard to pull off. I got the idea from Nancy Drew. My niece loves those."

Marian had no idea what she was talking about.

"But. The leather?" Marian said. She felt as though she were standing beside herself, watching the scene play out before her, watching some pantomime-Marian go through the motions with a pantomime-Kay. It was as if everything they said and did had already been written down and they were moving through the scene like automatons, unaware until just now that they were being manipulated, with as little control over their words or actions as a baby doll who cries at the pull of a string.

"Schlesinger Library," said Kay. "Special collections. Some poetry book, I think? I don't really remember." She waved a dismissive hand. "Not like anybody checks out half those books anyway."

Some antique artifact had been skinned and left for dead in pieces in the stacks. And for what?

She knew she should be angry. Actually, she should be furious that this girl would go to such Herculean efforts, not just to fool her, which would be betrayal enough, but to humiliate her too. Publicly. How much time must that have taken? Weeks. Maybe months. To invent the story and stain the paper and set the press and run the pages. An unreal amount of work. How did Kay even know all these things? How could she have made all this up? Made it so plausible? Marian did feel furious, in a dull and throbbing way, the way that pain comes later to a grave wound, but first comes shock that the wound has been inflicted at all. Only with the understanding comes the pain.

Even before Marian felt the pain, she felt the loss. A wave of grief crested and submerged her, dragging her down so deep that for an instant Marian couldn't breathe. The grief was for Hannah. For here, in this moment, was Hannah's death. Hannah ended not swinging on the gallows before the smug Boston ministers and gawking townsfolk, nor old in her bed, a forgotten curiosity surrounded by grandchildren, nor at the point of a cutlass run through her narrow hungry body, nor in a gale swallowed by enraged waves to drift to a sandy rest at the bottom of the sea. Hannah ended here, at this hideous tea table, in this hideous room, in this hideous hotel, because Hannah existed only as a story Marian had yearned to believe was true.

The lower rims of Marian's eyes burned hot as she tried not to cry.

"Why?" she said, her voice coming out barely above a whisper. "Why would you pretend to go on a hunt for pirate treasure when you know it doesn't exist?"

"But it does exist," Kay said, her voice hardening. "I've found exactly what I set out to find."

Marian looked up, baffled. Kay took a sheaf of newspapers from the nightstand and threw them on top of the manuscript on the table in front of Marian.

"Look at that," Kay said. "New York, at least three editions. Key West. Philadelphia. Charleston. Boston. New Orleans. Los Angeles. *Photoplay. Town Topics.* And those are just the ones I know about. What do you see in those papers?"

Marian looked down at the scattered pile of newspaper clippings and saw Kay's face beaming up at her in pixelated black-and-white, under headlines that read "Radcliffe Girl on the Trail of Pirate Gold" and "Intrepid Young Treasure Hunter" and "Who's Playing Pirates Now?"

"Me," said Kay with a fierce gleam. "I am. My name. My face. Next week, every movie theater in America is going to have a newsreel feature about me. And I'll already be in Los Angeles. Now do you see?"

The shock and grief vanished. Marian's breast erupted with a rising bubble of molten lava made of pure rage.

"I'll tell everyone!" Marian shouted, throwing aside the gilt chair, not even realizing she had gotten to her feet. Her hands balled at her sides, her nails digging into her palms. "I'll tell everyone you're a fraud! I'll call the papers, and I'll call Movietone. You just think about the headlines then!"

Kay was standing over by the French doors, which were identical to Marian's French doors. She eased one of them open and breathed in the night air. Something had bloomed in the moonlight since Marian stood at her own open door, and the air smelled sickly sweet. Without turning around, Kay quietly said, "No, you won't."

Marian's cheek twitched as if she had been slapped. "What makes you think I won't?" She stalked over to the French doors, her fists coiled in the belt of her dressing gown to make sure she didn't shove Kay over the railing.

"Marian," Kay said patiently, her green eyes almost seemed to soften in pity. "Think how it'll look."

"Look?" Marian spat. "It'll look like you're a fraud and a liar, that's how it'll look!"

"No," Kay said slowly. "Think how it'll look for you."

Marian froze.

"For me?" someone said softly, and it may have been Marian, but she couldn't be sure.

Kay leaned her head back into the white gauze curtain on the French door and gazed down her nose at Marian with her arms folded over her chest. "Sure," she said. "I mean. You're a big-time college professor, aren't you? You've got this famous dad and all his big-time adventuring friends, don't you? And they put up all that money. I mean . . . how was I able to fool someone as smart and savvy as you?"

The blood drained out of Marian's face.

"And beyond that," Kay lowered her eyelids and edged near enough to Marian that she could smell the tuberose soap that Kay had used to wash her body, and the hint of mint from her tooth powder, and the gardenia toilet water she had probably dabbed behind her ears. The lamp on the bedside table cast Kay's hair in tones of rose and gold, and Marian could just spy the shadow of her Irish freckles ghosting beneath the layer of dusting powder and rouge Kay had applied to her cheeks.

Kay held her gaze for a long minute and smiled. "I would hate," she said softly, "for the rumors to be true. Wouldn't you?"

Marian's mouth went bone-dry. She took a step back, away from Kay. Through the haze of fear and shame burning through Marian's blood she could stand apart, observe herself in this situation, and admit that she was impressed. The treasure they were fighting over wasn't a hidden chest of gold and jewels and pieces of eight, buried in the sand and marked with an *X*. It was only this: the power to be the one who decides how things are going to go.

Marian didn't answer. Kay was holding all the trump cards. Marian might as well lay her cards on the table and let Kay take them all without going through the charade of finishing the rubber.

The fight drained out of Marian as quickly as it had flared to life, and now all she felt was exhaustion. She yearned to be far away from this tropical island, to be back in her unassuming little apartment in Cambridge, in her own bed, alone. Safe. She leaned against the frame of the French window, staring miserably out into the warm island night.

"I can't believe you made it all up," Marian murmured as they stood together in the French doors, both casting long shadows onto the croquet field below. Somewhere, way far off to the east, across the sleeping midnight ocean, the horizon was beginning to pale.

"Yeah." Kay laughed. "Well, sort of."

"Sort of," Marian repeated with bitter irony.

Kay smoothed a loosened curl away from Marian's forehead. Her young hand felt cool and soft. "I found Hannah," Kay said, "in this book of diaries I had to catalogue last summer at the Beverly Historical Society for my internship. So boring. Who wants to read any of that stuff, anyway? Nobody cares. So, I took her and used her for myself."

"You took her. And you used her," echoed Marian. "For yourself." She moved away from the window and sat heavily on the gilt bamboo chair at the hideous tea table, her elbows splayed on either side of the manuscript, her head in her hands.

"You forgot what I told you," Kay said. "When we first met."

"What's that?" Marian said to the tabletop. Her temples were beginning to throb.

Kay leaned in close.

She murmured, "I'm the one holding the bat."

The problem was that Kay wasn't that smart.

Of course she was a bright girl. And cunning. Marian couldn't deny that. And she was a capable enough student, she supposed. But no one was that capable.

Marian turned it over and over again in her mind, all the long hours of her journey back to New York, and on the train alone through the sallow Connecticut marshlands as she made her desultory way home to Cambridge.

How? How could an undergraduate have really invented all that out of whole cloth? How could she have thought to come up with that story? A story good enough to fool her? All those details? All those plot points? How was it possible?

"I understand," her father had said in the restaurant car of the train as they rattled through Savannah, one long finger resting alongside his white temple. He looked sunburnt and tired around the eyes. "I wanted it to be real too."

"That's not it," Marian insisted.

"I'm sorry to be the one to tell you this, Monkey," her father said as two plates of fish were laid before them, decorated with little lemon halves tied in cheesecloth. "But that is it."

Marian poked the pale flesh of the fish with a fork, frowning.

"The truth is," John Beresford said, peering critically at his own fish, "it was too good. The foxing. The leather. A lot of the details. I see no reason why you should be remonstrating yourself. Truly. Some people are born to fool. And others . . ."

He didn't finish his thought. He didn't need to.

But Marian couldn't stop turning it over in her mind. She would be sitting, idle, gazing out the window at the passing trees and marshes and houses as they trundled up the length of the East Coast, thinking about not much of anything at all, when out of nowhere a paroxysm of rage would explode behind her eyes. At Kay, mostly. But also at herself. She loathed her complicity in her own humiliation. After the first two nights on the train Marian hung a hand towel over the mirror above the wash-stand in her sleeper car, because she didn't want to see herself anymore.

Campus was shuttered and asleep when Marian arrived home, hiber-nating under a blanket of snow, undergraduates all gone home. Marian set down her suitcase in the front hall of her apartment and ignored it for three days.

It was a restless three days. Marian prowled about her apartment like a caged animal. She lit a fire in the hearth and listened to it crackling, hated it, and then let it go out. She made tea. She thought about calling the Modigliani and making a jaunt down to the city, burying her hot angry face in the cool neck of a woman she barely knew and only half remem-bered. She decided against it. What would they talk about, anyway?

She bought an expensive cut of steak and cooked it and ate it alone.

She listened to the radio. She flipped from one program to another and got bored and snapped it off.

She didn't sleep.

Kay was cunning. But cunning wasn't the same as smart. Marian wor-ried at this idea like a stone. But more than anything else, Marian found her thoughts dwelling on Hannah. Visiting her, as though visiting an old friend. Calling on her. Restructuring her in her mind, her sunburnt face, her weedy young hair, the swagger of her cutlass at her hips. Still unable to shake the idea that something, some key component, some obvious thing, was missing.

At times, when she was alone in her apartment, and it was late at night, and Marian was lying awake in her bed glaring at the ceiling, she imagined she could hear Hannah laughing.

New Year's Eve came, and Marian spent it at the apartment of her friend in the French department, an elegant woman of a certain age who had studied at Smith and then lived in Montparnasse for ten years. She told Marian sordid stories about making love with American writers in the back of the Café de Flore and dancing drunk to jazz with absinthe on her lips and then dashing to the Bois de Boulogne in the dark in a hack-ney cab with her stockings rolled down over her knees. Marian never knew how many of these stories were true, but she sat on a settee in her friend's drawing room with a glass of pink champagne and managed to forget her anger just long enough for the clock to strike twelve.

She was on her third glass of pink champagne and her shoes were off when her friend collapsed on the sofa next to her and said, "Darling, you are boring me."

"What?" said Marian.

"All this talk of Kay. It is boring me," her friend said, matter of fact in the French way, even though Marian knew for certain her friend had been born in Minneapolis.

"But it's just not possible," Marian insisted, and her friend laid her fingertips on Marian's lips to silence her.

"Yes, yes, it's just not possible, you've said. This is very boring to me." Her friend refilled her own champagne glass, sipped, coughing a bit on the bubbles, and said, "Why don't you go there? To Beverly. Go and see for yourself. See what it is that made this Kay decide to turn pirate. If there is something there, then you will know. And if there is nothing, and she made it all up, then you know she is smarter than you thought. Either way, you can stop talking about it."

"But," Marian said.

"Stop," her friend whispered again. She leaned in close and kissed Marian softly. She was wearing rich perfume, a perfume that reminded them both of Paris and other nights and other kisses in other doorways.

Marian put her champagne glass down on the coffee table and took her friend's face lightly in her hands.

"Okay," she said.

THE BEVERLY HISTORICAL SOCIETY reopened on Monday, January 5, 1931, and Marian was there, waiting on the stoop, standing in spitting snow, when the curator unlocked the door. The curator proved to be a woman about her own age, in a practical cardigan and low-heeled shoes, who held the door for her as Marian stepped inside and unwound her muffler.

"Cold one," said the curator.

Marian stamped her feet to bring the blood back into them and said, "I'll say."

"Come on in. The register's over there." She pointed, and Marian signed her name with a flourish under *Professor*.

"Genealogist?" the curator asked brightly. Marian supposed that their primary stock-in-trade lay in genealogists. That, and local dignitaries looking for places to store their family heirlooms when their children no longer wanted them.

"No, actually," she said. Treading carefully. "I'm a professor at Radcliffe. I wanted to . . . Well, I wanted to double-check some work one of my students did for you over the summer. For an internship. Cataloguing work. Books, mostly. Was my understanding."

The curator beamed. "Oh, sure! Kay! We were so excited to see her in the papers! You all must be so proud of her down in Cambridge."

"Oh, yes," said Marian, her left temple beginning to throb.

"Wasn't it marvelous? We saw her in the *Globe*. Why, I hear she's gone off and turned Hollywood on us; is that true?" As she spoke, the curator opened a filing cabinet and walked her fingers through some hanging files. "Such a pity they didn't find anything, but then again, it always sounded a bit of a wild-goose chase, if you ask me."

I didn't, Marian thought sourly.

"But even so, we just about bust our buttons seeing all the attention she got. Why, did you even see her in the newsreels? Didn't she look so pretty? I always begged her, when she was here last summer, Kay, darling, won't you wear just a little bit of color on your face? You could be so pretty, I told her, with just a little bit of color. Not too much, of course."

Prattling, prattling, prattling. It was enough to drive Marian mad. At least now the curator had withdrawn a typewritten list and was finally handing it over.

"Thank you so much," Marian said, her voice tight. "I don't suppose I could have some of these books paged, could I?"

"Well, sure. I've got a lady coming in at eleven, but anything you need before then, just ask."

Marian settled at the reading table in a room lined with ship paintings and spread the pages out before her. It wasn't such a very long list. Maybe twenty books all told. What kind of book had Kay said it was? Some kind of yearbook? Something she was sure no one would ever want to read.

"I'll tell you," the curator continued from behind her desk. "We didn't know what an up-and-comer we had here at the hysterical society." She laughed a bit at her joke and paused, waiting for Marian to laugh too.

Instead of laughing, Marian pointed to a line on the finding aid and said, "What about this one?"

Excerpt from the 200th Anniversary Celebration Yearbook of Beverly, Massachusetts, Published by the Beverly Historical Society, 1868

Recollection of Anna Lanphear Cabot, widow, aged 86 years

When I was a young girl, at the end of the last century, I was always afraid whenever Father said it was time for us to visit Grandmother Lanphear. Not because she was ever unkind to me, exactly. I believe she was fond of me, in her way, but as was the case with many people of that generation, the expression of fondness seemed to cost them too dearly, and so it didn't often happen.

Grandmother Lanphear was bedridden for the last decade of her life, and in her final months, Father would often prevail upon me to sit and read to her. Though Grandmother had sundry grandchildren who could have done this unpleasant duty, for whatever reason, the honor always fell to me. She always demanded that I read her the newspapers, with particular attention to the comings and goings of ships out of Salem and Beverly, and what cargo they held, and never any interesting books or stories or novels. And certainly never the Bible. Grandmother Lanphear could swear like a sailor, and she would say, "I don't want to hear any of that God d—d nonsense. Not in my last days. I've had enough of that, and you can keep it." Which I always found funny, as one would think that a woman lingering at death's doorstep would be more inclined to hear the Word, and not less. But not Grandmother.

Father told me that Grandmother Lanphear had been of obscure parentage in Beverly, and that she was bound out for service in Boston when she was only a child. After a youth of unfortunate circumstances, the details of which were always rather hazy, she had returned to Beverly in her late teens, wed to a maroon mariner she had met no one quite knew where, a man few years older than her called Charles Harris. Charles Harris worked in the yards and was killed in an accident when Grandmother was still a young woman, after which time she, married Grandfather Lanphear, who was a dentist, and that's when she had Father and my aunts and uncles. They lived in a modest clapboard house on Queen's Road, later Washington Street. Grandfather Lanphear died long before I was born, but the house where Grandmother lived out her days was much the same as it had been when he was alive, with two rooms below and two above, connected by a central stair, a great fireplace in the kitchen that always smoked, and windows that were drafty.

One wintry afternoon, I came upon Grandmother feeling especially low. She had had a cough for some weeks, her color was bad, and a sour smell to her skin and breath that made me not want to linger in her room. I asked her what ailed her, and could I bring her anything that might settle her nerves. She said, "Yes. I would have a measure of rum in the silver cup in the cupboard on the wall."

I had never heard Grandmother ask for hard drink before and wasn't even sure there was any in the house. But sure enough, I found a single sterling silver cup in the wall cupboard, which was generally closed up with a key, and next to it a small, corked jug, which proved to contain some very foul-smelling rum. I poured Grandmother a measure whilst holding my nose, and she drank it down in one draft.

"Another," she said.

I was shocked, of course, but Grandmother sharply said, "Don't stand there idling, girl, but do as you're told," and so I did.

She drank down the second draft in one swallow and leaned back in her pillows with a long sigh. I asked her which newspaper she would have me read, but she didn't attend. She was staring at the ceiling.

I settled in the chair next to her bed with the newspapers and my sewing bag and waited for my allotted visiting time to pass.

"Did I ever tell you," Grandmother said after a time, "that I was once at the hanging of a notorious pirate?"

I set the *Salem Gazette* aside and said, "You were?"

"Oh, aye," she said. "One William Fly. I watched him hang from the milldam with my friends. The famous Cotton Mather presiding."

I had never heard of this supposedly notorious pirate. In her dotage Grandmother occasionally confused her dates and times, or conversed with people who weren't there. Sometimes she called me by the name of my sister or my aunt. I never bothered to contradict her, but instead let her natter on as she preferred.

"Oh, really," I said, and pulled out my needlework.

Grandmother smiled her toothless smile and said, "Really. Only man I ever saw that authority could never make sorry."

A long silence wore between us before she added, "And then I turned pirate myself, you know."

"Did you?" I said, worrying away at my sampler. I was never much of a needlewoman, and I knew Grandmother hadn't been either. The X in my alphabet was hopelessly crooked, and nothing I could do would change that.

"I did. I disguised myself as a cabin boy and went pirating. I was in the crew of Edward Low." I'd never heard of this pirate either. Grandmother was lost in dreams of some kind, and I didn't give it much thought.

Grandmother's cough returned, rattling and thick with phlegm, like a demon had taken hold of her wasted chest and refused to let her go. I got to my feet and hurried to fetch her a sip of water.

"None of that!" Grandmother shouted at me. "Rum! Give me rum!"

I was afraid of Grandmother's temper, for when I was small, she was always ready with a cuff on the ear if I disobeyed or moved too slowly or sometimes for no reason at all. I dared not contradict her. I fetched her another measure in her silver cup, and she threw it back with all the brio of a longshoreman.

"Perhaps you ought to rest," I said timidly, but Grandmother barked, "Pishposh. I've never been less tired in my life. Don't think because I'm old that my soul is tired. Just you wait. One day you'll wake up locked in a body as old as mine, and you'll see how you like it."

Those words of hers come back to me often now, as I am of an age close to what she was when we had this peculiar interview, and truly I have begun to understand how she must have felt. Grandmother was uneducated, to be sure, but she was wise. There are mornings when I awake and do not know myself in the mirror, because for a moment I have forgotten that I am grown old.

"I had no idea you'd been to sea," I said, not at all certain that what she was saying was true. As far as Father had told me, Grandmother had lived a life of drudgery, first in service and then in keeping house, and had never set foot outside of Massachusetts.

"I was," said Grandmother. "There was a mutiny, and then we put in at New York to offload some of our number and I was afraid we'd be put in prison, but no one saw us. After that we took a pink, and because I was first to spot it, I was given first choice of arms to have as my own. Oh, that was a fine day. I chose a cutlass."

I knotted my thread and started on the *Y*. "Mm-hmm," I said. I had no idea what she was talking about. As far as I knew, a pink was a flower, or a color, and she was speaking the gibberish of dreams.

"The boys always wanted to play with it when they were growing up. Running up and down the stairs with it, yelling, *Avast!* and *I'll make you walk the plank!* Oh, I used to laugh and laugh. I told them it had been my first husband's. But it was really mine. They didn't know. Your uncle has it now," Grandmother said.

"A cutlass would have been a fine thing to play with for a boy," I said. I remembered Father telling me how they had coveted it when it was discovered amongst some junk and miscellany in the attic. He told me it had belonged to Charles Harris, who had traded for it on some voyage to the West Indies in his youth. It was found in a trunk with some coconut husks and odds and ends, mementos of a life we never knew.

Grandmother laughed and said, "Except it gave your father the scar over his eye."

I was reasonably certain that Father had told me that injury came when he was serving in the militia. But no matter.

"Indeed," I agreed, pulling my thread through the frame with my head down.

"I took a man's eye out myself. When we were taking the pink." Grandmother's tone seemed to suggest she was daring me to disagree with her.

"Oh?" I said, because by then I had learned not to take her bait.

"Aye. With my rigging knife."

My needle paused. She certainly sounded sincere. But I had no way of knowing what was true and what lay only in her fevered imagination.

"Then we were hit with a great hurricane and had to rush to safe harbor. Once there, and in fear for my life, I endeavored to scuttle the pink and escape in the schooner."

Another hacking fit overtook her, and I offered her a handkerchief. She cleared her lungs and spat in it, a great glob of blood and sputum. When the worst was past Grandmother lay back in her pillows and closed her eyes with a sigh. At the time I wondered what it must feel like to have death stalking your lungs. Even now I don't know which I would like better: to know where death will come upon me or to have it lying in wait in secret.

She quieted, and I thought Grandmother had drifted off to sleep.

She added, "Without Charlie, I don't know what I would have done."

I looked up. None of us had ever known how Grandmother met her first husband. Grandmother never spoke of her life before Grandfather Lanphear. None of us knew where she had been born, and though we assumed it was Beverly, we could never be sure. Her name when bound out to service had been Masury, we knew, but that name had been chosen by her mistress, to keep the name of her birth obscure. None of us ever knew why. There were rumors that her father had been a terrible rogue, a violent criminal who fled Boston in disgrace, going off to sea to seek his fortune. Her mother had died in her infancy, and so she had been placed in one family after another before stopping in a tavern.

"Charles Harris?" I said. "He was with you?"

Grandmother waited a long time before replying, "He was a philosopher."

I didn't know what she meant. In her last months, Grandmother moved in and out of sleep as easily as she breathed, and I often wondered if she was passing her last days in a kind of dream.

"Then we came home to Beverly and set up in a house of our own," Grandmother continued, her eyes still closed. "This house," she waved a wrinkled hand weakly from atop the counterpane, to indicate the modest room where we were sitting. "I bought it with my own money."

I looked around. The house wasn't much to look at. If anything, it filled me with a mild creeping dread since I was always so afraid of Grandmother and her fearsome temper. And Father's house was much nicer. Bigger windows and more modern and better situated. Grandmother's house was mean and small and smoky and dark. When I married, I hoped my husband would build me a house like the one Father had built for Mother, with a curving stair and arched windows and airy and bright.

"When I'm gone, I'll be leaving it to your father," Grandmother told me. "With the intention that it should be passed on to you. That, and my ruby earrings. Every woman should have her own house."

I forced a smile and said, "Why, Grandmother. How kind you are." She had no ruby earrings. I'd seen her wear drops of heavy red stones, far too big to be rubies, garnets, maybe, at best. Or paste.

"Hmmph," Grandmother said. "Anyway. I thought you should know. That once upon a time, a long time ago, I went pirating."

I looked up from my sewing to see if Grandmother was going to say any more, but as I surmised, she had drifted into an uneasy slumber. Her mouth slipped open and emitted a soft, rattling snore. I gently took the silver cup out of her hand and set it aside. Father would be furious if he found out that I had given an old woman so much rum, and so I kept our secret by rinsing out the cup and hiding it back in the cupboard, locking it up as it was before.

Grandmother died a few weeks thereafter. I thought nothing more of her story until coming upon a mention of the trial of William Fly in one of the newspapers, as a recollection of the days of Boston past. I could scarcely believe such a thing had happened. To think that now the excursion steamers passing out of Boston Harbor full of merrymakers with parasols on their way to the summer resorts on Nahant go right by Nix's Mate, where the poor unfortunate man's body had hung in chains. To this day I don't know if Grandmother Lanphear's story is true. I know nothing of Edward Low, the supposed pirate with whom she cast her lot, nor do I know of any kin of Charles Harris, apart from us, or if indeed that was his real name.

As promised, Grandmother's will left her mean little house to my father, who sold it and divided the proceeds amongst the grandchildren. My eldest uncle was given her silver cup, my younger uncle had the mysterious cutlass. An old flintlock pistol was found in a drawer with a finely wrought ivory handle, which was given to my brother.

In her last years, Grandmother had labored very hard to gain her letters, having never been educated properly when she was a girl, and though reading was never easy for her, which was why I was prevailed upon to read to her in her last weeks, she was finally able to sign her own name. It was, as I gather, her proudest achievement, apart from the healthy rearing of her many children, and so her most prized possession, an otherwise undistinguished writing desk, we gave in her memory to the East India Marine Society, in commemoration of Grandmother Lanphear's long and eventful life, which extended almost from the days of witches until well past the days of Revolution. And now, in these years of the Reconstruction of our Union, it gives me great pleasure to recall my fearsome Yankee Grandmother on the occasion of Beverly's bicentennial, as I am today a grandmother myself, whose grandchildren might live to see the dawning of a new century, replete with piracies that none of us could ever imagine.

SALEM

The gears ground with a fingernail-curling whine before Marian got the gearshift under control on the Model A roadster that she had borrowed from her neighbor. Marian avoided driving whenever possible, and now was regretting not taking the train. But she couldn't wait. She couldn't take the time to look at the train schedule, to buy the ticket, to wait at North Station. The car was right there in the driveway, waiting to be driven. Marian took it.

The windshield kept the worst of the air out of her eyes, but the icy wind pouring over the doors of the car filled Marian's ears and flapped at her scarf and smarted on her cheeks. Her neighbor had offered a pair of goggles and a leather cap, like a Great War flying ace, the same color of hunter green as the body of the roadster, and now Marian was regretting not taking them. When she finally got where she was going, she would look like a seagull blown ashore after a rough storm.

She came to a snaking gravel curve leading in one direction to a narrow causeway that was awash in the tide, and to the other in a sharp rotary that tooled along the coast. She had to downshift to keep the wheels from spinning out as she peeled through the curve. Marian swore under her breath, riding the clutch. The roadster objected, and she swore some more. Away off to her right the wide blue ocean swelled into view, lapping softly around the rocky shores of Nahant.

Seeing the ocean inexplicably renewed Marian's incandescent rage. She had tried to resume her quotidian life. She pushed her anger aside. For minutes at a time, sometimes for as long as an hour even, she would forget. And then something innocuous would flick a switch in her mind and boil to life, a clear mental picture of Kay's beaming young face, lit up with flashbulbs. Her heart rate would rise, and blood would beat in a vein on her forehead and then her temples would begin to ache.

The roadster picked up speed without Marian noticing she was leaning on the gas pedal until she had to swerve to avoid a small dog with askew ears and a stump tail darting into the street and she screamed as she skidded to a stop. Breathing hard, Marian put the car in gear and continued on her way, the dog safely escaped under a garden gate.

KAY HADN'T MADE Hannah's life up at all. She'd stolen it. The yearbook from the Beverly Historical Society contained all the broad contours of the story. But even so.

A True Account of Hannah Masury's Sojourn Amongst the Pyrates, Written by Herself was written by a clever, self-promoting undergraduate with a basic knowledge of pirate history and access to the letterpress machine in Westmorly Court. It beggared the imagination. Kay had left Key West on the predawn express train a few hours after their fatal interview and changed for the Sunset Limited from Florida, rolling through sleepy Gulf Coast towns draped in Spanish moss. Then over the Mississippi River into New Orleans, across wide Texas plains dotted with cattle and spindletop oil rigs, and through the Southwestern desert until it chugged finally into Los Angeles breathing steam and leaving a scattering of newspaper clippings in its wake. Newspapers breathlessly reported on the intrepid young girl adventurer at every stop as she made her solo journey west. There were even rumors that upon arrival, she'd been offered a contract at Warner Bros.

Marian's fists tightened around the steering wheel and she became aware that her jaw was starting to ache.

The road divided into a fork, the left branch snaking into a dense wood, trees naked and brambly in the thin winter light. Marian slowed, the roadster jouncing through a muddy patch and spraying muck up the sides of the car. Her neighbor would be annoyed. Oh well. Too late now.

In the occasional moments when Marian forgot her anger long enough for it to simmer down to a rolling boil, she begrudgingly appreciated what Kay had accomplished. Kay had spun an elaborate, compelling fantasy out of what was little more than an anecdote, accidentally discovered in the driest and dullest of town chronicles. Hannah Masury had been a real person, at least. That much was true. And in her old age, Hannah Masury Harris Lanphear had told her doubtful granddaughter that she had gone pirating in her youth. All the contours of her story were there, in the recollection of Anna Lanphear. The hanging of Will Fly. The mutiny aboard the *Reporter*. The taking of the *Rose Pink*. The hurricane. The scuttling and her daring escape. Even Ned Low and Seneca, aka Charles Harris. Somehow Hannah survived a sojourn amongst the pirates with her neck intact and built a quiet life near the docks back in the small New England town where she might, or might not, have been born.

And in that town, she had built a house. A house her granddaughter had found undistinguished and drafty and embarrassing, a badge, by the nineteenth century, of relative poverty. But a house built with Hannah's own money.

How would Hannah, a teenage wife with no education and only a life in service, have had the money for a house? Marian smiled, a piratical gleam shining in her eye.

The road to Salem dipped and swerved, the trees growing around it so thickly that their branches knitted together overhead, creating the sensation of driving through a narrowing tunnel. Marian checked her watch but found in her haste to get on the road she had forgotten to wind it. The deepening darkness in the tunnel of tree branches made Marian feel as though she were traveling through time, as if she might emerge on the other side of the wood into a small colonial town of clapboard houses and horses and sheep and women with covered hair, straight out of Nathaniel Hawthorne's imagination.

Instead, after a few more twists and turns, the roadster putted out of the woods and down a genteel lane lined with naked chestnut trees, peopled by sedate Samuel McIntire houses bristling with chimneys and freshly painted shutters, with polished coupes and Tudors in the driveways. Salem in this neighborhood was a town of quiet wealth, of rambling houses with bespoke cupboards filled with China export porcelain, and stables in back that had been made over into garages. Nothing like the showy wealth that marched up Fifth Avenue in New York, marble palaces all in flight from the wrecking ball. Another quarter of the town was entirely Portuguese, a diverse and bustling Salem of recent immigrants living in older eighteenth-century houses, down close to the waterfront where the work was to be found. Marian had imbibed some of Hawthorne's mixed feelings about his home city, apparently, for though she had spent her entire adult life down in Cambridge, this was only her second or third time venturing up the North Shore to the city that had once rivaled, or even bested, Boston and New York for wealth and prestige.

Marian spotted an open meter and screeched to a stop with one tire up on the curb and tumbled out of the roadster, breathless and disheveled. She took a wrong turn down an alley and had to retrace her steps before finding herself standing before the Greek Revival edifice of East India Marine Hall, with its blank-eyed arched windows and signage reading *Asiatic Bank* and *Oriental Ins. Office*. A cold drizzle had begun to fall, plastering Marian's hair to her head and seeping down the collar of her shirt. A giant iron anchor stood sentinel outside the building, darkening in the rain.

The East India Marine Society had gone moribund a generation ago. It was originally an organization of mariners who had navigated beyond the Capes of Good Hope and Horn, all of whom pledged to bring back souvenirs of their travels to create an idiosyncratic museum of natural history: a museum of the world, as seen from on board the ships that sailed from Salem and Beverly. Throughout the nineteenth century, elderly sailors gave tours of a collection replete with ostrich eggs, stuffed penguins, bits of marble from ancient Corinth, a hornet's nest from Suriname, elephant tails and tusks, even—it was rumored—a pickled shrunken head from New Zealand concealed behind a velvet curtain. The Society, its hall, and its cabinets of maritime curiosities were eventually absorbed by the Peabody Academy of Science, which had in turn, a decade and a half ago, been rechristened the Peabody Museum.

Which was where Marian now found herself, standing on what should have been one of the busiest streets in downtown Salem but which was largely empty except for a few people hurrying by under umbrellas.

She went inside, shaking drops from her overcoat and rubbing out her hair. She proceeded down a modest hallway lined with glass vitrines full of a display of feathers, each with a small typed explanatory note card, and came upon a ticket desk with an older gentleman sitting behind it, reading the *Lynn Daily Item*.

"William Endicott, please," Marian said.

The elderly gentleman looked up. He had rheumy eyes behind half spectacles and a nose patterned in constellations of capillaries. "And who shall I say is calling?" the gentleman said. Marian noticed his cardigan sweater had been eaten through in more than one place by moths.

"Dr. Marian Beresford," she said. "Tell him we spoke on the phone."

"Ah," said the gentleman. He folded his newspaper into a methodical square and folded his spectacles into a methodical rectangle. "So we did," he said at length. He added, "Guess it started raining."

Marian was dripping into small puddles around her boots. "Oh," she said. "Yes. Yes, it did."

William Endicott got to his feet, one foot at a time, while Marian did her level best not to scream in frustration.

"This way," he said. He set off at a shuffling pace.

"Thank you," said Marian, practically dancing in her desire to hurry him along.

They went through a door and passed into a gallery with a wooden-beamed ceiling lit by a bright brass chandelier, the walls hung with every square inch covered in paintings of ships. They all looked the same to Marian—square white sails, indifferently painted water, arcane flags and pennants and burgees with meanings she didn't understand. Glass vitrines lined the center of the room, crammed with bits of nautical ephemera, and at the top of the room near the ceiling, polished wooden half hulls swelled forth in frames.

"Marine Room," said Mr. Endicott with a wave of his wrinkled hand.

They passed through another heavy door, and then they were in a gallery much like the first, with the same polished brass chandelier and gleaming wooden beams, only this time the walls were covered over every inch in framed portraits of men. Old men, young men, fair men, dark men, men with long, luscious sideburns and men with shaved heads under turbans, men with high Napoleonic navy collars and men in brocade dressing gowns. Yankee men who had been painted by itinerant artists in China, looking stiff and wrongly proportioned. Chinese men who had been painted by itinerant artists in New England, also looking stiff and wrongly proportioned.

Some of the men weren't men at all. Some of them were boys. Smooth-cheeked, ponytailed, with the self-satisfied smiles of youth not yet sunburnt or cynical. Marian stared at these boys as she passed them and wondered.

"More Marine Room," said Mr. Endicott without looking round.

They came to a door concealed in the wainscoting and he pulled out a ring of keys. Marian looked at her watch, forgetting it had stopped, a nervous habit designed to convey her wish that he would hurry. Mr. Endicott would not be hurried. He tried one key. He tried the next. He tried another. Marian wondered what would happen if she lay down on the floor and screamed at the top of her lungs. Could she scream loudly enough that all these frozen painted faces would break free from their frames and look down at her in surprise?

A click, as at last the correct key was found, and the door was opened.

"Now, lessee here," said Mr. Endicott, groping about in the dark. He found the button at long last, pressed it, and a single bulb buzzed on overhead.

Marian found herself standing in the first of a near-infinite row of metal racks with shelves, extending all the way to the ceiling. The storage room smelled musty and old, like insect wings and dried leather and dust.

"Don't come back here a lot," he said. "This way."

He shuffled down a narrow passage and Marian stuck close to his stooped sweatered back, passing racks filled with winking geodes, then racks of carved whale teeth made into household objects, like dice and pie cutters. They moved farther away from the lone lightbulb and deeper into gloom. The shapes on the racks grew vague and hard to discern through the creeping darkness.

They came to a long hallway, and Mr. Endicott stopped short. "You bring a flashlight?" he said.

"What?" said Marian, screaming in frustration inside her mind. "No. I didn't know I needed one."

"No matter." There was some rustling and groping, and then a dim yellow circle appeared on the floor, illuminating two pairs of feet, one in weathered oxfords from the turn of the century, the other Marian's, in practical winter boots wet with rain. "Come along."

The yellow circle tracked along the edge of the metal shelving. At one point it touched upon the quick brown back of a mouse, who vanished. Marian yelped and clapped a hand over her mouth. Mr. Endicott chuckled through the darkness. "Nothing to be scared of," he assured her.

Presently the yellow circle slid up the bottom shelf, which was lined with sea chests, all of them bound in hobnails and peeling leather, locks hanging open.

"What'd you say it was?" he asked.

Marian said, "A writing desk. Small."

"Oh," the venerable director said. The yellow circle slid up another shelf and settled on an untidy heap of wooden boxes, held together with brass on the corners and edges, with brass locks. They seemed to be made of pine or oak, most of them, a few with brass wires bent and poking out of alignment, some with cracks run through their faces and lids. "Know which one it is?"

"No," said Marian. "It was donated in the early nineteenth century. Or maybe 1799. By the Lanphear family."

"Lanphear," he said. "Lanphear, Lanphear. Lanphear?" The yellow circle of light winked, buzzed, flickered, and went out. The museum director muttered to himself, and Marian heard a smacking sound. The light blinked on again, aimed at a clipboard that was hanging on a nail nearby, holding a sheaf of yellowing typewritten paper. An elderly finger appeared, running down the list, reading aloud, a veritable directory of vanished families, their fortunes swallowed by time and the sea.

"Here it is," he said. "Number 101."

The light circle slid from the clipboard to the shelf crowded with nearly identical writing desks. Each one, Marian saw, had a paper circle affixed to the keyhole with a thread. The circles had numbers on them, some typed, others written in spidery script. 303. 421. 236. There didn't seem to be any rhyme or reason, with newer-seeming numbers buried beneath older ones, all of them jostled together. One by one Marian turned over the accession numbers while William Endicott held the flashlight. Her nose filled with dust, and she sneezed into her elbow.

"God bless you," said William Endicott.

112. 199. 228. Marian was beginning to despair.

"You're sure it's here?" she said.

"Where else would it be?" he answered philosophically.

Some of the desks were held in place with a crust of grime, as if they had been placed on the shelf and had never moved again. A deep sneeze rocked the hallway and the light disappeared.

"God bless *you*," said Marian.

"Thank you," said William Endicott. The light reappeared, mis-aimed at the lower shelf with the sea chests. There, sitting slightly askew atop the domed lid of a large sea chest from the nineteenth century, sat an unassuming box. It was covered in a thick layer of dust.

"Wait," said Marian. "May I see that?"

The director passed her the recalcitrant flashlight, and she brought it in closer to the box. It had a paper tag tied to the keyhole with twine, brown with age. Marian turned the tag over to face the light.

There, written in faint spider script, was the number *101*.

"That's it," said Marian, her nerves alive with excitement. "That's it! Do you mind if I take it down?" She inhaled deeply and imagined that she could smell the sharp brine of the sea.

"Be my guest," said the museum director. "Don't think it's ever been on display. Not a very fine example, as you see."

Marian already had the box in her hands. Indeed, she did see. While some of the others had fine inlaid woodwork and beautiful patterns on their lids wrought in brass, this one was plain and workmanlike, with no initials or decoration of any kind. And it was heavy.

Marian grunted as she tried to set it carefully on the floor, but it slipped from her hands and the box landed with a loud thud. And a chink.

"Careful now," the director said mildly. "It'll be fragile."

"I know, I know, I'm sorry," said Marian in a rush. "I didn't mean to. That is, it's heavier than I expected."

"Oak, probably," Mr. Endicott said from behind the glare of the flashlight.

Marian ran her hands over the lid, feeling for Hannah. She closed her eyes, hunting through her skin for a hint of the living warmth that might have once run her hands there, as if Marian could reach through time and braid their fingertips together and finally understand. Her palms came away covered in dust.

"May I open it?" she asked. She felt like a little girl, before her mother died, before her father went traveling all the time, when she awoke in her safe and private room in the townhouse in New York on a cold winter morning, happy and eager to put on her slippers and see if Santa Claus had come to fill her stocking in the night with clementines.

"Go ahead," he said. "Ought to be empty, but."

Marian brought her fingertips to the lid and carefully lifted it open.

Inside the box was a writing surface of cracked and curling leather, held in place with a little brass lip. She knew that under the writing surface there would be compartments for notepaper and pen nubs and ink, and sometimes drawers for letters, or even a lockbox for cash and

receipts. This desk was simply wrought, probably with only the stationery compartment, and no drawers. But it wasn't empty.

There, resting on the leather writing surface, lay a folded-over sash.
It was faded and discolored from so many decades pressed between
untreated leather. But Marian could tell it had at one time been blue.
Blue with gold tassels.

"Well, now," said the director. "Would you look at that."

"May I lift it out?" she said softly.

"Don't see why not," he said. "Be careful."

Marian's hands moved into the yellow circle of light and softly, carefully, using fingertips only, she lifted the rotting sash out of its resting
place. It was satin. It had at one time been very fine.

Marian laid it carefully to one side. She slid the brass nub that held
the writing surface in place to the side and with a fingernail opened the
compartment that would have held notepaper.

It was empty.

Just plain wood. Somewhat ink-stained. Nothing else. No fragments
of pencil, even. No scraps of paper. Nothing.

Hot salt water flushed Marian's cheeks, and she turned her face away,
wiping her eyes on the back of a wrist.

"Happy?" asked the museum director from behind the flashlight.

Marian couldn't answer. She moved to close the desk again. But it was
so heavy. Why was it so heavy?

"May I please see the flashlight again? Just for a second," she said.

When the light was in her hands, she aimed it into the compartment
under the writing surface. Methodically, minutely, she traced the light
along the surface of the wood.

There.

In the far corner, away from any light, was a tiny hatch mark on the
wood, as though it had been scored with a knife. Marian brought the
light closer, narrowing the circle until it grew brighter.

The hatch mark was in the shape of a floridly drawn capital X. And at
the center of the X was a notch just big enough for a fingernail.

Marian's chest flooded with light. She was afraid to laugh, because if she laughed, she knew she would sound hysterical. Marian didn't laugh. Instead, she reached into the belly of the desk, caught the hatch mark with a fingernail, and delicately pulled.

The false bottom gave way.

"Here, here," she hurriedly gave the flashlight back, and lifted the false bottom free of the desk and set it aside. The museum director aimed the yellow circle of light into the desk's notepaper compartment.

Something gleamed.

"Well, I'll be God damned," said William Endicott, and as he spoke, Marian clearly heard the sound of delighted young laughter dancing in her ears.

The desk held coins. Hundreds and hundreds of coins. Shining under a thin haze of dust.

Marian sank her fingers into the pile of gold and silver coins, stirring them, feeling their cool weight against her skin, some of them hardened together from long exposure to air and salt water. French livres, Spanish reals, Spanish doubloons. And there, as the flashlight moved slowly over the glittering hoard, Marian spied a reddish gleam, which suddenly split the light into crimson shards that made the treasure glow.

Hannah Misery. You sly pyrate.

This is all ridiculous.

Marian took up the delicate gold filigree of the ruby earring between her finger and thumb and lifted it up in the beam of the flashlight, spilling its warm red sparkles in a glittering starburst across the museum storage room.

"Masters of vessels," Marian said softly. "Carry it well to your men. Lest they should be put upon doing as she have done."

Author's Note

I can't stop thinking about pirates.

Maybe it started in graduate school when I first settled in a small town in coastal New England, and I felt like I had finally arrived back home. I had known that I loved living in coastal cities—in fact, I had only ever lived in coastal cities—but living in Marblehead, Massachusetts, put me in closer contact with weather and tide—that is, nature's time—than I had ever felt before. I stared at the sailboats moored in Marblehead Harbor with a yearning that was hard to explain, even to myself. My life on the water began in earnest.

I had spent several years crewing on racing yachts in Marblehead when my uncle informed me that it was my turn to assume stewardship of a small sailboat, a 1962 Pearson Ensign daysailer that had belonged to my grandfather. This "yacht" is worth less than the computer I am writing this on, but she is mine, and when I sail her I remember being on the water with my grandfather in Galveston Bay in Texas. My grandfather named her *If*, because he was a worrier, but a better name for a fiction writer's boat would be hard to come up with. She lives now in Salem Harbor, and on warm summer afternoons my husband and young son and I take her out and bomb around, and those moments under weigh are the only times that I am ever fully present, I think—except for when I am writing.

Salem Harbor is closer, as the Ensign sails, to the mouth of Beverly Harbor than it is to Marblehead. To understand the relation of coastal towns in New England, you need to understand that water, not land, connects them. In one of those funny twists of personal history, it so happens that for several generations, from the middle of the eighteenth to the end of the nineteenth century, my family were all mariners out of Beverly Harbor. Perhaps that's why on the day, at low tide, when we banged our keel on the *one* easily avoidable rock in the middle ground between Salem and Beverly, I imagined I heard a ghostly groan of dismay followed by laughter. *I can't believe she hit it*, one imaginary voice said to another.

I like to think the voice may have belonged to my fifth great-grandfather, Zachariah Gage Lamson. Around 1820, Lamson was presented with a coin silver coffee service by a Louisiana insurance company in thanks for his defense of their cargo against a raid by pirates. A couple of these coffee service pieces now sit, tarnished, in a corner of my dining room. My grandmother used to tell us that this ancestor had been "strung up by his thumbs by pirates," but from the available records, it seems he was actually hanged by the neck from a yardarm but then let down in time to save his life. He would finally die of fever in Grenada, broke and obscure, in 1846, but not before writing a memoir. If you are simultaneously a sailor and a historical fiction author (two pretty big *ifs*), it's a pretty exciting read. So what is it about pirates that we find so compelling?

We celebrate pirates because of their promise of liberation. The organization of a pirate ship was a radical departure from the rigid hierarchies of the land, hierarchies of race and class and sex and everything else. On the land, everyone had a place, but the sea cares little for social distinctions. The Articles, as represented here, reflect the real history of the proto-democratic self-determination of pirate crews. Just as small coastal communities developed common points of culture due to their orientation outward toward the sea, so too did the ocean itself form a littoral space, a shifting and moving country with culture and mores and rules of its own. Perhaps this is what attracts us about going out on our own account: the possibility of forging other ways of living apart from those that we are born to, or that are imposed upon us.

Pirates enthralled us even during the age of sail, when a shadowy author ostensibly named Captain Charles Johnson first published *A General History of the Pyrates* in 1724, the massive tome that gives us many of the most notorious real-life pirate stories of the 1600s and 1700s. From Johnson we learn that two now celebrated working-class women, Anne Bonny and Mary Read, disguised themselves as men and went pirating, raiding the Caribbean in terror and escaping the gallows only because they were both pregnant. Such women existed but they were the exception. More common than disguised women in pirate crews were self-liberating enslaved men who saw in piracy the possibility of self-determination and freedom denied them ashore. In this novel, these men are represented by the character of Seneca. Pirate crews typically consisted of men from all over the maritime world, of many different races, speaking many different languages, and having experienced a range of degrees of conditions of servitude or imprisonment. What they all had in common was a ruthlessness, a willingness to mutiny in violation of the law to govern themselves, even at a risk of their lives. A merry life, and a short one, as Bartholomew Roberts put it.

This novel is driven by women longing for their own kinds of freedom. Marian Beresford's life as a Radcliffe professor is certainly more cosseted than Hannah's, but she too chafes at the strictures of her world. Elements of Marian Beresford's life are drawn from history as well, most notably the existence and details of the Mad Hatter tearoom, which was one of several centers of life for queer women in New York City in the early decades of the twentieth century. At a moment in time when gender roles were rigidly enforced for both men and women, spaces like the Mad Hatter allowed expressions of both gender identities and sexualities that were a lifeline for people like Marian. Even Kay longs for freedom from the rigid expectations of her life, but she goes hunting for it in the world of fame.

However romantic our vision of a pirate's freedom, it was never far from violence. The bloodshed of this novel required no imagination (and I don't think I could have imagined some parts). The trial, hanging, and public gibbeting of William Fly in Boston in 1726 happened just as it is described here. In fact, the remarks on the scaffold are taken verbatim from the account of the trial published by Cotton Mather, who oversaw the proceedings. Edward Low was a real pirate who was based for a time in Boston. He really was married, he really did leave behind a daughter after his wife died, he really did refuse to have married men in his crew, and he really had—according to Philip Ashton—a soft spot for dogs. But Low really did slice off a man's lips and roast them and feed them back to him. Ned Low's cruelty was even more famous than his heart.

And what about Hannah? The elements of her escape and disguise owe much to histories of the few real women who took to a pirating life in the age of sail. She is a work of historical fiction, though she too is inspired in part by the life of a woman who tested herself against the sea—and pirates. Her namesake, the real Hannah Augusta Masury, was born in Beverly, Massachusetts, in 1834, to a family of mariners, in a small coastal community facing the sea. At twenty-three, she married a man named Edward who lived up the street, and when he became captain of a clipper ship, she took to the seas with him. In 1866 they sailed a load of locomotives around Cape Horn, offloading them in California before traveling to Hong Kong to pick up Chinese laborers. But as they were crossing the Pacific, Edward died. They started to run out of water, and the crew and passengers mutinied. Hannah held them off with a pistol and signaled her distress by hanging their colors upside down off the stern, finally being rescued by the Navy off the coast of San Francisco.

Hannah Augusta Masury Howe—my third great-aunt—sued for Edward's percentage ownership of the clipper's proceeds and used the money to buy a house near her in-laws in Beverly. She remarried a dentist whose last name was Lanphear, lived quietly, and died in 1910 without having had children. Not a pirate, but a woman who had been around the Horn and put down a mutiny all by herself. When I first learned about Hannah, I tracked down her address and discovered that whenever I went to Beverly for dinner, I was in the habit of parking in front of her house.

That's when I knew, when I ran my little sailboat into the rock, that it was Hannah I heard laughing.

This story is for her, and for everyone yearning to turn their back on the land and the life they have known and go out on their own account.

—Katherine Howe
Marblehead, Massachusetts
February 2023

Acknowledgments

My thanks first to my wonderful and brilliant agent, Suzanne Gluck at WME, and her right hand, Nina Iandolo, for her editorial eye and patience with my pirate phase. Thanks also to my editor, Shannon Criss, for her hard work guiding this project to publication, to Amy Einhorn and everyone at Henry Holt, especially Julia Ortiz, Kelly Too, Alyssa Weinberg, Hannah Campbell, Marian Brown, and Emily Mahar for making this fever dream of a book a reality, and to Barbara Jones for bringing me into the fold. My great thanks also to Melanie Locay and the Center for the Humanities at the New York Public Library for giving me writing space and access to primary sources that made this work of historical fiction possible. I am grateful also to the Beverly Historical Society and the Peabody Essex Museum in Salem for the work they do to preserve the maritime history and material culture of Essex County, Massachusetts, and I hope they forgive me for their brief cameos in this story.

Readers of classic pirate literature will recognize many nods to *Treasure Island* in Hannah's true account. I am grateful to Robert Louis Stevenson for writing the original pirate novel, and to my son Charles Howe for reading it with me at bedtime. Thanks to Harborlight Montessori, Annalise Wolf, Abby Peach, and Patty and Greg Kuzbida for consenting to play Admiral Benbow Inn with my favorite pirate while I wrote Hannah's story.

The wide-ranging work of Marcus Rediker on the history of pirates and piracy has long informed my thinking on this topic, as has the scholarship of Mary Beth Norton, whose work on women in the seventeenth and eighteenth centuries continues to populate my imaginative life. Dan Bouk, Ginger Myhaver, and Richard Vermillion provided invaluable support for my early drafts of this book, and I am grateful to them for their time and their friendship. Thanks to my husband, Louis Hyman, for being a willing commenter on everything I write, and for being my able helmsman. Thanks to Charles Susman and George and Kath Howe for taking me sailing first, to Jim Susman for keeping *If* afloat, and to all the friends I've made on the water since then, especially Pete, John, Boat Rob, Rob, Diane, Roscoe, the ladies of the silent *e*, Ensign Fleet 16, Margie and Bob Herrick, Bob Weiner, Alex More, and even the Band of Angels. Finally, thank you, reader, for consenting to follow me out to sea on this voyage. Here is your brim cup, my mates, and your full carouse to make a merry heart.

About the Author

KATHERINE HOWE is a *New York Times* bestselling and award-winning historian and novelist. She lives and sails in New England with her family, where she is at work on her next novel.